TOWER OF BONES AND DIMMED STARS

INK OF THE FAE 2

N. Z. NASSER

HANORA SKY PRESS

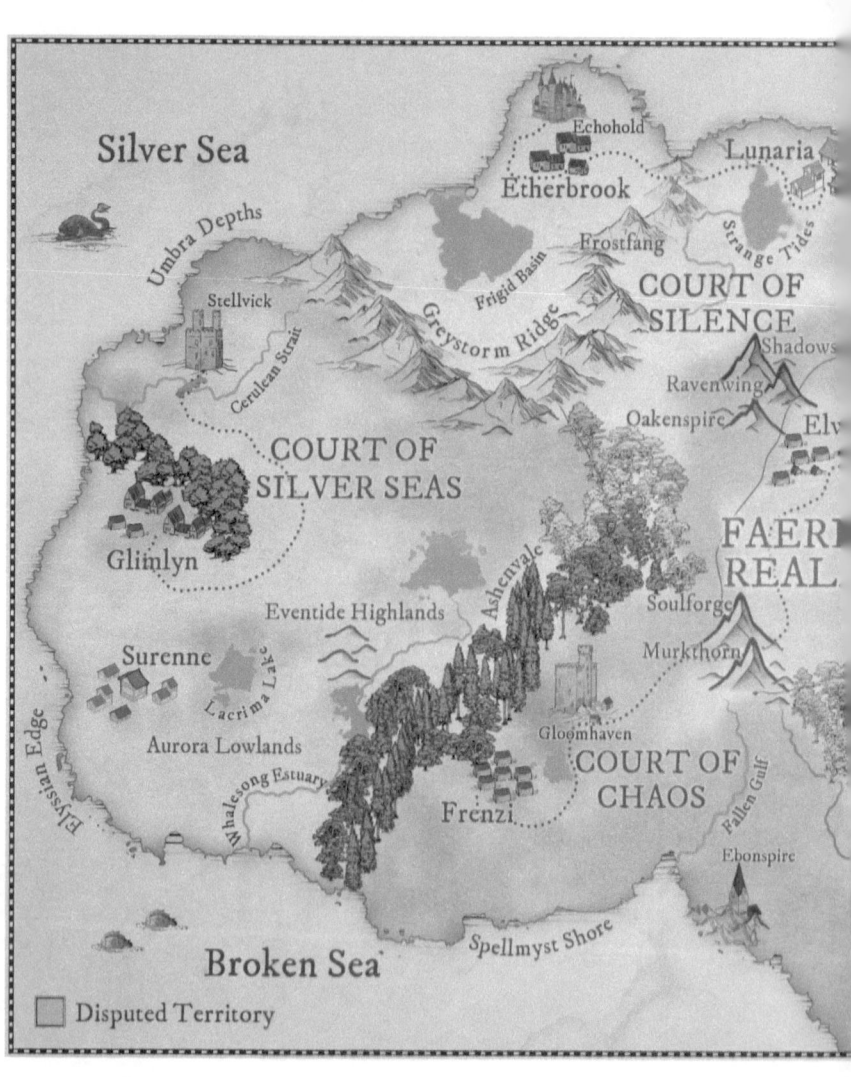

COURT OF
BONES

Marrowreach

Wyvern Reach

Dead Man's Ridge

Runeth

Pale Reach

Loch Bare

Wilvoria

Moltenkeep

Loomveil Lake

Duskmire Glen

Scattered Crags

Nightblaze Isle

Blackbrine
Ocean

COURT OF
EMBERS

The Wastelands

Scorched Plains

Merwine Hills

COURT OF
NEBULAS

Wraithwoods

Celestiva

Feylight Marshes

Shrouded Forest

Sylvanturm

MORTAL
REALM

Pinelight

COURT OF
LUMINOSITY

Serennor

Riven Cliffs

Ebonmere

Larkspur

PRONUNCIATION GUIDE

YSADORA: *EE-suh-DOR-uh*
ZEPHYR: *ZEH-feer*
KAZIMIR: *KAH-zih-meer*
LUNARYS: *LOO-nah-ris*
MAREN: *MAR-en*
FERRITH: *FEH-rith*
DANAË: *duh-NAY*
THIAGO: *tee-AH-go*
CYPRIAN: *SIP-ree-uhn*
WYLDA: *WIL-duh*
SEQUOIA: seh-*KWOY-uh*
GABOR: *GAH-bor*
LOXLEY: *LOX-lee*
ROWENA: *roh-WEE-nuh*
VEDA: *VAY-duh*
MYTHROS: *MITH-ros*
XAIRE: *ZAIR*
ELOWEN: *EL-oh-wen*
TANUHJA: TAH-noo-jah

ESOLAS: EH-soh-las
THALINDRA: *THAL-in-druh*
ARAMINTA: *ARR-uh-MIN-tuh*
LIORA: *LEE-or-uh*
CALDORON: *kahl-deh-ROHN*
RYVARIS: *ree-VAH-ris*

WHAT CAME BEFORE

In the first book of *Ink of the Fae, Garden of Ink and Ancient Stone*, Ysa follows her kidnapped father, Kazimir, into Faerie. Kazimir is the last calligrapher from a dragon-riding order.

This order was responsible for maintaining the Grimoire, which underpinned the balance of the mortal and faerie realm. When the Order of the Glyph was destroyed, the balance in Faerie was upended, and the courts began to fall. Kazimir and his lover Tanuhja, the Queen of Chaos, decided that Kazimir should hide their daughter Ysa in the mortal realm with the Binder's help.

Dark factions are at large in Faerie, and as the child of the Court of Nebulas and the Court of Chaos, it would be ruinous if Ysa fell into the wrong hands.

When Ysa arrives in Faerie, she discovers she is fae and that she has ink magic, just like her father. She meets the mercenary Zephyr, who also hails from two courts: the Court of Silence and the fallen Court of Lore. He has been tasked with bringing Ysa to his uncle Thiago, the Faerie

King of Silence, and his wife Danaë, a mortal woman turned fae. Danaë had been Kazimir's wife in the mortal realm, Ysa's stepmother, before the faerie king stole her away.

To counter the faerie king's manipulations, the Binder releases Ysa's star from the heavens, thus allowing her to set her own destiny. The Binder knows that the possibilities for Faerie will change the moment Ysa and Zephyr meet.

And they do. Ysa and Zephyr fall in love, and together with Kazimir and his dragon, they fend off the attack from the King of Silence. Zephyr, who for many years has been preoccupied with caring for the outcast fae—members of fallen courts cursed to be monsters—starts to believe a more just Faerie is possible, especially with his mate at his side.

But when Ysa touches her fallen star, the meteor, the chaos magic she has inherited from her mother ignites. Not only must she learn how to wield her magic, but the Kings and Queens of Faerie are keenly aware that whoever controls Ysa, with all her gifts, will have the ability to reimagine Faerie, its courts, and what it will be in the future.

That is where we begin *Tower of Bones and Dimmed Stars, Ink of the Fae 2*.

YSADORA

The first time I walked their crooked streets, I expected nothing. But the mortals saw you swaddled in my arms and offered us refuge. The stars felt farther away in the mortal sky, but for the first time in an age, I felt free from the binds of everything that had come before.
— Kazimir's entry to the memory stone

When we lost our mortal lives in Larkspur, we lost any sense of stability and the illusion that we belonged anywhere at all. Our village had given us roots, and without them, we were unmoored. The weight of it all didn't truly register until Zephyr accompanied us to say our goodbyes. Maren and Ferrith went their own way, while my mate returned with me to the home I'd shared with Father.

We'd been here for hours already, and still I couldn't make myself leave.

"We can stay as long as you need." Zephyr leaned against a flaking tree trunk. The dying light of dusk caught his eyes, and the flicker in them told me he'd rather not linger, in case trouble followed us here.

It felt wrong to be here without Father, wrong to walk through rooms where he had dozed with spectacles askew and a book still open on his chest. Wrong to see the bookshop hushed and hollow: no fire in the grate, no scent of parchment and pipe smoke, no voice muttering at the shelves.

Father's dragon had carried him to the Court of Bones to heal his warped body. I missed him so much that I carried his absence like a physical wound. Without him, our house was just a collection of objects: dew-dampened thatch and threadbare rugs, half-burnt logs and faded bed linens, lanterns hanging dull and empty like forgotten fireflies.

The garden smelled of summers long past and childhood dreams too fragile to survive. Maren and I trained here since we were younglings, but where there had been discipline, there was now disarray: overgrown grass where we had once sparred, sagging targets that would never again feel the bite of arrows, fraying ropes we would have long replaced.

My father's beloved bench with its hidden inkwell waited for a male who would never return. My chest grew tight at the sight of the patch of ink plants destroyed by the faerie king. Only withered stalks and smeared pigment remained.

But for Zephyr, I mustered a faint smile. "No use waiting. The horses will be champing at the bit by now." We had a practical reason for returning to the village. I looked down at my bloodied palm, where I'd made a shallow cut. The memory stone demanded a blood price to spill its secrets.

Zephyr straightened, storm-cloud eyes wary. "Be careful, Inkheart."

"Of course."

Before I could second-guess myself, I pressed my palm to the cool stone, just as Father had instructed. The moment it drank my blood, it exhaled, its power like a fishhook intent on reeling in its prey. The world did not tilt; it collapsed inwards, folding under memories that intruded on my own. My mate's terror reached me through the mate bond.

This was no gentle blending, no seamless transition.

Father's fears coiled around my own. His joys burned behind my ribs. Bitter regrets cut paths through me. A thousand carefully chosen memories layered over my own like a storm of glass shards. It was a forced intimacy. The taste of his emotions clung to my tongue. The scent of places I'd never been filled my lungs.

His memories poured like the ocean into an already full vessel, pressing against my skull: his recollections of my childhood, his calligrapher's mastery of ink magic, the chime of singing bowls at the Order of the Glyph, the scrape of his quill against parchment, the fierce longing for his dragon, and the sigh in his bones when he chose silence over honesty to keep me safe.

I trembled, my knees buckling, his choices reverberating like an aftershock in my body.

A hand tugged at my palm to release the stone, and it was Zephyr, wrenching me from the web of memories. His voice was insistent, his breath warm against my cheek, first out loud and then in my head. "That's enough, Ysa." *Inkheart, come back to me.*

I wrenched my hand away. The knowledge was muddled and twisted inside me, like an unspooled thread tangling in my head. My limbs were heavy, my pulse sluggish. The wind stirred, and I heard Father's voice and recalled past drills with Maren: echoes from another life.

"There was so much."

"I know." He looked as though he wanted to break the damn thing apart. "Breathe. Deeper. That's it."

I concentrated on my breathing until the memories siphoned away like a star going cold. My thoughts dulled, edges softening until I was neither here nor there, like frost creeping across glass, shutting down the parts of me. As though the meteor's magic would smother me entirely, pulling me into a vast oblivion where I wouldn't have to feel, to think, to remember.

The mate bond tugged. But he was there. "Inkheart?"

I refocused on the present, clawing my way back to Zephyr as if he were a tether. The fading light played over the sweep of his cheekbones and the slight curl of his dark hair. He was like a blade sheathed in velvet, all restrained strength and quiet control, and I wished I knew what was playing in his mind. I wished I could read him like he could read me.

"I'm okay." The twist of his lips told me he didn't believe me. "Just let me come back into myself."

But it was impossible to be the same person again. We had outwitted the Faerie King of Silence, and I was so grateful that Father was safe. But neither my newfound magic nor the memories enshrined in the stone in our garden could repair the hollow inside me.

I had walked these village streets barefoot as a child, traced my name in the dust on the windowsills, laughed beneath crooked eaves, and spent endless hours splashing in its streams. It seemed foolish to tell Zephyr that nostalgia twisted my belly into knots. That, despite all my good fortune, despite finding him, part of me yearned for simpler days: for the quiet sorting of books in the bookshop, for swims in the creek, and the sound of Father's grizzled snoring in his armchair before I urged him to bed.

It wasn't only me. Maren missed her mother's flour-dusted face and the cinnamon scent of the bakery more than anything, and Ferrith missed brawls over lost wagers and the rare occasions he and his father sat together in companionable silence.

"Will you tell me what you saw?" Zephyr asked, and I wondered how much had leaked through the bond.

"Yes. Just not now, okay?" I drew in a steadying breath. "Let's find the others."

He nodded and stooped to kiss the corner of my mouth, drawing back when I wanted him to deepen it. Then he pulled up the hood of his cloak. "We won't have to hide what's between us at Ebonspire."

He was right. The villagers were already suspicious of our return, and adding a beau to my arm would only hasten the rumours whispered in doorways, at the market, and in the tavern. Though men sometimes left our village —venturing further afield for trade, soldiering, women, or ale—women never did. Women were bound to the land, to hearth, and duty. But Maren and I had vanished. No letters. No goodbyes. No explanations.

Once, the villagers might have overlooked strangeness,

but the chaos with the Binder at Bloomtide, crop failures, and drifts of strange weather due to the unravelling of the Grimoire heightened misgivings.

The villagers were right to mistrust us: we had changed in ways that could never be reversed.

I looked up at my mate. Wylda had glamoured away our most obvious physical changes—our pointed ears and too bright eyes—but it was still a risk to spend too much time in Larkspur, especially for him. "Wait for us at the edge of the forest."

"Not a chance," he shot back. "Consider me your shadow."

I darted a look at the house and thought of the books housed within. "All those books…"

Zephyr tipped up my chin and brushed his thumb over the line of my jaw. "The Court of Lore libraries are yours."

Then he let go and stalked forwards, his cloak rippling over long grass. Beneath it were two sharpened daggers, strapped to his outer thighs, easy enough to draw if needed. The light around him bent, blurring his edges until he disappeared into the dusk. His footsteps made no sound against the earth. My heart tightened as I followed him.

There was nothing left for me here now.

My childhood home was just another forgotten corner of the realms, left to decay.

I walked, seemingly alone through Larkspur, experiencing the aching pain of knowing that my beloved Larkspur could never truly be mine again. The briefest caress of Zephyr's shadows—at my cheek, at the back of my hand—punctuated my thoughts.

The village stood as it always had. The scent of sun-warmed earth and wildflowers carried on the breeze, and its people moved through their daily lives. The cruellest part was knowing that it wasn't the village that had changed. I had.

Without the suppressing effects of Lunarys's binding potion, the mortal world was thick with iron and the plodding weight of time. The air was thinner, the pulse of humans too slow for my fae instincts, and our footfalls on old paths seemed remote.

Once, I had been part of Larkspur's rhythm; now I was an outsider looking in.

The tavern. Ferrith and Maren are bound to be there, I said through the bond, knowing that Ferrith would be drawn like a homing pigeon to the ale he sorely missed, and Maren would accompany him to stop him from getting into any trouble.

Zephyr sighed. *I am not carrying a drunk through the Shrouded Forest.*

My stomach knotted. Ferrith was mortal. I couldn't imagine him leaving Larkspur, nor could I imagine us going without him. I rounded a corner, moving quickly over the cobblestones to the tavern. True to form, Ferrith was being swarmed by villagers, who longed to hear the stories of his exploits with the king's army.

I peered through a milky pane as they brought him sloshing tankards of ale. Maren feigned interest, though her gaze flicked to the door every few seconds. When she caught sight of me, she jostled Ferrith out of the door, to a din of complaints from fellow drinkers, and tugged him around the tavern to where we stood under the slate-grey sky.

7

Ferrith huffed in exasperation. "You could have let me finish. I was just getting to the good part."

Maren rose on her toes and brushed a soft kiss against his cheek, and warmth spread across his face, bright and unmistakable. "You think I didn't notice the thousand embellishments, you big oaf?"

"People like a good yarn."

"Well, I don't want to share you all night, not when…" She turned to me as Zephyr unravelled from the darkness like a spectre made flesh. "Is it time to go already?"

Dim lantern light flickered over the hard lines of Zephyr's jaw. "I'm afraid so. It's not safe here."

Ferrith wiped the last traces of ale from his mouth. "I'm coming with you."

"Ferrith—" I started.

Resolve replaced his usual easy grin. "I know I'm not magical, but I'm not sitting here while you two run off into Faerie."

Cautious hope flickered across Maren's face. "I was afraid you'd say that."

He grinned. "Then you should've left while I was still on my third tankard."

Zephyr crossed his arms, studying him. "It's not just a drunken whim, mortal?"

Ferrith shook his head. "I may be a little intoxicated, but Ysa, Maren, and I are family."

I exchanged glances with Maren. We could have tried to convince him to remain in the village with his infirm father, but Ferrith's restless spirit wouldn't have allowed it. Our separation from him during our early days in Faerie meant we couldn't fathom being apart. "What do you think?"

"I think my selfish heart can't endure more loss," replied Maren.

Ferrith swept her up in his arms. "Atta, girl." Then it was my turn.

"Put down my mate," said Zephyr, as solemn as moonlight over a battlefield. Then he gave a slight bow, and his eyes caught mine. "I formally invite the three of you to make Ebonspire your home. To join your family with mine."

"Thank you," said Maren, although I knew it was the Court of Nebulas she yearned for.

Thank you, I echoed through the bond, as Ferrith reached out to shake Zephyr's hand.

It was instinct to crave comfort and pleasure when in peril, but choosing each other in this moment required vulnerability. Zephyr loved me, and I loved him. That much was not in question, although I didn't understand the mate bond. I didn't understand how to behave, or whether we were at war with Faerie, or seeking a new sense of normal.

I craved closeness, yet feared it. Sometimes, I feared my yearning for Zephyr would eclipse the whole sun, that it would wrench my focus away from our survival.

Hours later, we arrived on horseback at the gatehouse where I'd once been a prisoner, although Ebonspire had long since accepted me as one of its own and I had the unlocking rune to prove it. The night air was thick with quiet tension as we dismounted, and our boots sank into the earth.

No torches burned in sconces, no merry greeting. Only the jagged edges and spires of the gatehouse, sharp against the stars, half-veiled in Zephyr's shadows. Beyond it, the Broken Sea was restless and silver beneath the moon, and the wind carried the scent of salt and storm.

We're home, Zephyr said through the bond, one hand on Mythros's reins.

I nodded. It didn't feel like home yet. But I hoped one day it would.

But Ebonspire, like Larkspur, was no longer safe. Not since the faerie king had discovered it. Not since he and his consort had wanted to control me, and Zephyr had sided with me against them.

Zephyr didn't know what came next any more than I did. Not in Faerie and not with us.

How could there be room for the fragile shoots of love when faced with cold, hard facts?

Father, Maren, and I were fae. Magic and dragons existed. Faerie was unravelling, and our enemies coveted my volatile magic. My village had been nothing but an interlude in the vast span of a fae life. At the precise moment when we needed stability, the protection of Larkspur and Ebonspire had dissolved like mist at dawn.

Home should have meant safety, but neither of us knew how to survive what would come next.

2

YSADORA

Inkweed: slender, dark green stalks and broad black leaves. Favoured for its smooth flow and unfading quality. Resonates with the intentions of the writer, making it dangerous in the hands of those with ill intent.
– A Compendium of Faerie Flora and Terrain

Our romance was a dance of careful courtesy punctuated by fiery passion. Zephyr pressed kisses across my flushed skin when the moon rose, and the tenderness lasted until the early hours of the morning before his emotions shuttered.

Sometimes, he laid gifts outside my door sent by my estranged mother, the Queen of Chaos—carved combs adorned with pearls, vials of rosewater and myrrh, soft silks in plum tones—instinctively understanding that bringing them into our bed chamber would taint our sanctuary. Her knowledge of our whereabouts was just another reminder of our precarious situation.

Most days, I woke in a bed that Zephyr had deserted, and when I reached for him through the bond, the star that represented him in my mind was smothered by shadow as if he shielded his preoccupations from me. Sometimes harrowing images slipped through the bond: feral beasts pacing, a predator's throaty snarl when woken from slumber, the drag of sinewy bodies, the burn of bargains made with abandon.

That morning, I pretended not to notice him leaving. I wanted to ask him where he was going, wanted to ask him to stay. But too often, he brushed off my questions or his face tightened into a mask of neutrality. So, I squeezed my eyes shut as he dressed and evened out my breathing, letting the words die in my throat.

Eventually, I went into another day that unravelled like a lit fuse.

I arrived for training dressed in a sleeveless tunic in deep blue—having tired of ink splatters on the cuffs of my clothing —and soft-soled boots. The mercenaries were helping me to discover how the meteor had reshaped my magic.

Maren and Ferrith had their own training schedules, much to Ferrith's disgruntlement, who disliked interaction with the mercenaries. My only weapons were a dagger strapped to my thigh and Father's quill, its nib rich with the emerald ink from an inkweed. Father's siphoned memories taught me which inks were suited to training.

Today, Cyprian lounged in the stairwell, waiting to escort me outside, his jaw tinged blue from a knock he'd taken sparring yesterday. Zephyr had adjusted the rules that governed comings and goings: exiting Ebonspire alone was strictly forbidden, in case an ambush waited.

His shrouding of the gatehouse had kept its secrets safe for decades. But now the Court of Silence and the Court of Chaos knew of Ebonspire's existence, as did the Circle of Emberlight, putting us in danger.

Cyprian pushed off the wall. "Recovered from yesterday?"

"Just about. Is it just you and me today?" I asked, yearning for Zephyr.

He placed his rune against the door. "Don't worry. He's already out there."

"That is what I'm worried about. One rule for him, another for the rest of us."

"He takes risks you wouldn't imagine. For us. He's always been that way."

"I didn't mean to sound ungrateful."

He gave a half-smile. "I know you didn't."

I'd grown accustomed to the easy familiarity of Zephyr's chosen family: the casual barbs and laughter, the way words could be thrown like daggers and caught just as effortlessly. The mercenaries didn't tiptoe around bruised feelings. Not usually. But standing here, the shift was a tangible thing. Cyprian's tone conveyed a protectiveness for Zephyr, one that indicated he thought I was a risk.

Magic eased the heavy door open. I took a deep breath and followed Cyprian outside to the rugged training ground. The early summer heat was thick but not yet oppressive, and the scent of warmed stone and tang of sweat lingered in the air. The grass was a patchwork of green and gold, trampled down by heavy boots and Mythros's hooves.

Behind us, the black stone of Ebonspire caught the sunlight at odd angles, shifting between light and shadows cast by the male who had once been a faerie prince, and who had reclaimed the seat of his fallen court. By my mate.

I felt him before I could see him.

The mate bond stirred like a whisper against my ribs, a thread pulling taut just before Zephyr stepped from folds of darkness. His shadows clung to him for a breath. Then the world shifted, as if reality bent to acknowledge his presence.

I swept my eyes over him, checking for injuries, for any hint of where he had been and what he had been doing: tending to the monsters in the belly of Ebonspire, perhaps, although there was nothing to suggest he had been doing manual labour.

His dark leather vest and trousers hugged the lines of his body. Scars and runes traced the bronze skin of his arms, a history written in silver-black lines. The mate bond was guarded and quiet, stripped of emotions and words. A single dagger was strapped to his thigh, not for show but from habit. These days, he was always on alert.

Ocean-deep eyes found mine, holding me in place as surely as a hand at my throat. Zephyr's lips quirked at one corner, like he was reliving what we had done between the sheets. Heat flooded my face. For a moment, everything faded: my awareness that we weren't alone, the gusting wind, the churn of my thoughts. He was familiar and yet utterly devastating: a storm I'd learned to navigate but could never outrun.

Then Zephyr palmed his dagger, and the world rushed back in, loud and waiting.

Cyprian snorted. "You saw each other mere hours ago. Can you hold off on the longing looks?"

Zephyr's jaw ticked as he dragged his gaze from mine. "Maybe if you focused on training instead of running your mouth, brother, you wouldn't fight like a drunken faun."

"You call that training? It felt more like you pummelling out your frustrations."

Good, I thought. At least I wasn't the only one wound tightly, caught between the strain of worries neither of us voiced. If Zephyr's usual controlled strikes had turned reckless, then I wasn't alone in feeling the weight of everything pressing down on us. Somehow, it made it better that I wasn't fretting alone.

I let out an uneasy breath. "So what have you two planned for me today?"

The mercenaries had tried to coax out controlled bursts of my magic in a warded space, attempting to map its patterns. But the power inside me was unyielding and unfamiliar. It had been a week since I'd touched the meteor. Sometimes my magic responded as I willed it to, but more often it reacted illogically.

We'd tested it against curses and elemental spells, but my magic either devoured or repelled them. The mercenaries watched for how the magic affected my body: did it make me stronger or faster? Was I more resistant to iron or more vulnerable to cold?

The more I tried to control it, the more unpredictable it became. There was talk of a seelie noble at another court, who might have been able to decipher what was happening to me, but Zephyr baulked at me being a curiosity on someone's shelf. As did I.

The males exchanged glances. I wasn't sure I was going to like what came next.

"Something new." Zephyr's steely expression made my stomach lurch. "It's dangerous. That's why the others aren't here."

Normally, the rest of the group milled about, placing bets or engaging in their own sparring matches.

Cyprian rolled the stiffness from his shoulders. "The theory is that your magic only responds to real threats, rather than feigned ones."

"It's going to be okay," said Zephyr, but the mate bond remained silent, like it didn't exist at all.

My breath quickened, then Cyprian struck, faster than I expected, plucking a sword out of a pocket of time. I barely managed to dodge, and when I tried to summon my ink, it was sluggish. I spun, reaching for my magic again, but Zephyr was already there. He disappeared and reappeared behind me in a pool of shadows. His dagger lashed out. I barely threw up a shield in time, jagged ink snapping up between us. But his blade cut through it like it was nothing. And then Cyprian pressed the attack. Their movements were effortless, synchronised.

A bolt of panic shot through me. I wanted to cry out that it wasn't fair, that we'd never practised like this.

I'd faced them both individually, time and time again, but never like this. Never without Zephyr's gruff care, his silent reassurance grounding me. Never with Cyprian actually trying to harm me.

My pulse pounded in my ears. Ink curled at my

fingertips, and in the other hand, I grasped my dagger, but it wasn't enough. They were faster. Stronger. Steel nicked my arm, pain flaring white-hot. I flinched, and one moment of hesitation was all it took for Zephyr to take advantage. His shadows surged forward, swallowing the space between us, thick and suffocating. They wrapped around my limbs, dragging me down as Cyprian's blade came towards me.

Something inside me snapped. Ink exploded outwards in a violent rush, twisting through the air like a living force. It hummed beneath my skin, skittering in time with my heartbeat. It didn't just lash out; it gushed.

I saw the flash of a memory that wasn't my own: memories I fought to keep chained in my mind in case they pulled me under. My father stood amidst the ruins of the Order of the Glyph, his ink a vast, shifting sea that swallowed his attackers whole.

The ink curled along his arms, turning his home into a dark flood. In another blink, instinct guided me to use my magic in new ways. It was no longer confined to one direction, no longer fixed in the direction of my attention.

I cast it, and it flared in all directions, spiralling outwards in a vast radius, covering the ground, the air, the very space around me. It formed sigils I didn't recognise but somehow understood: ancestral glyphs, protection, counterforce.

The moment my ink touched Zephyr's shadows, they shuddered, unravelling at the seams. My magic didn't just push them back, it twisted them violently, breaking them apart into streaks of black mist.

Zephyr stumbled, his grip severed. Cyprian's blade

halted mid-strike, caught in the ink barrier that had risen around me, a barrier I hadn't even meant to form. He yanked at it, but the ink wouldn't let the sword go. I stood there, my breath ragged, ink coiling wildly around me. It had never reacted on its own. Never reached beyond my sight, my knowledge.

The mate bond remained silent for one heartbeat longer, then it thrummed back to life in a rush of recognition, triumph, and a sharp wariness. "Well, Inkheart," drawled Zephyr. "That was terrifyingly new."

Cyprian relinquished his grip and slowly backed away. He left his sword dangling from the dark matter and forced a smile onto his face. "She's as strong as either of us. You fit in well with our band of misfits, Ysa." His hazel eyes told a different story.

The battlefield knowledge that had not been mine moments ago echoed in my mind, raw and staggering. My father's ink had swallowed dozens of fae warriors. Mine had ripped apart my mate's shadows and halted steel in midair.

I hadn't formed a conscious intention, and it had acted for me all the same. It hadn't been logic that triggered my magic. Not strategy or focus. It was fear. It was pain. I swallowed hard, my upper arm beaded with crimson.

"I hurt you," said Zephyr. "For that, I am sorry. Wylda can tend to that before we go any further."

A tight, nauseous coil twisted in my gut. The two of them had agreed to push past my control without involving me in the decision. I'd put them in harm's way. "Don't ask me to do that again. I don't want to risk your safety."

Zephyr stepped closer, his eyes soft, voice low. "Fae

mend fast, even without healers. You'll be okay. Don't overreact."

My hand shot out, palm flat against the heat of his chest. His heartbeat was steady beneath my palm, but mine was wild, erratic. "Overreact?"

"Uh, oh," said Cyprian.

Zephyr's mouth pulled down at one corner. "I phrased that poorly. I meant that taking risks is part of survival in Faerie."

My chin lifted. "What *I* meant is—and I really need you to hear me—no more risks."

Something flickered in his eyes—frustration, or maybe something darker—and I realised he didn't like being told *no*. He searched my face, waiting for me to change my mind, but I held my ground. Then, he let out a slow breath. "You're scared."

The ink slowly settled, some melting back into the quill like the tide retreating, the rest pearling in the dirt and staining the grass. How long had it been since Zephyr had been scared of anything? "What if I am?"

"Fine. We'll stop." There was something in the way he said it, something quiet and edged.

Cyprian gave a slow shake of his head. "We can't give up. We have to know what we're dealing with."

"Forcing it won't help." Zephyr scanned my arm and turned on his heel towards Ebonspire's looming silhouette. "Come, I don't like to see you bleed."

The space between us felt colder, emptier, but at least it was mine.

"He's all in his head." Cyprian fell into step beside me. "You did well."

19

My wound stung as I wiped my trembling hands on my tunic.

My magic was quiet now. *Obedient.* But I wasn't naïve enough to think this was over.

3

YSADORA

Those fae males with their impossible grace and muscles meant for myth. Next to them, I am clumsy, dull-edged, forgettable.
I watch them and wonder if I was ever built for the same world.
– Ferrith's diary

Hazy light streamed through latticed windows in the infirmary. I sat in a wicker chair beside two bed palettes layered with pelts. Notes of honeysuckle and bitter yarrow reached my nose, and beneath it, the metallic sharpness of my fae blood. Wylda knelt beside me, assessing the torn flesh on my upper arm.

She let out a low whistle, made all the more effective by the slight gap between her front teeth. "Zeph did this?"

I winced at her touch. "Maybe. It happened so fast."

"I bet he's kicking himself."

"I'm not ready, Wylda. A few weeks ago, you were teaching me rudimentary ink extraction skills."

"Nonsense. Cyprian said they didn't hold back, and you wiped the floor with them. You're progressing so fast that Zephyr Ashmoor unleashed his warrior self on you. If that's not a compliment…"

"I'd prefer a more traditional gesture. A flattering remark, maybe a toffee."

"I'll be sure to let him know." Wylda yanked open a narrow oak drawer with its crooked, burnished handle. Inside, dried herbs lay tied with twine or left loose to curl in on themselves. Plucking a sprig of deep green leaves, she snapped the stem with a twist. The scent of sun-warmed bark and the loamy depth of the forest floor filled the room. "This will sting."

She didn't wait for permission.

Biting heat flared over the wound before the pain dulled. Beneath her breath, Wylda murmured an old fae incantation, soft as wild grass, then pressed the herb directly to my skin. She watched with quiet satisfaction as the wound knitted itself together, then brushed the crumbled remnants of the herb from my arm.

"There. It'll hold. Try not to go tearing yourself open again before sunset, hmm?"

I huffed a laugh, my brain skittering over the immediate dangers: my volatile magic, Thiago's uncloaking of Ebonspire, Tanuhja's determination to reconcile with me. "No promises. Trouble seems to be a constant companion since I arrived in Faerie."

She closed the drawer and turned back to me. "Tell me about it. How are you holding up?"

I didn't like the way Father's memories surfaced

without warning, turning my reflexes into his. I wanted him as my teacher, not the crude memory transference he'd fashioned. He neither received nor returned my letters, although my ink magic reached Elowen just fine, and her messages emerged from folds of air into my hands. Zephyr assured me that no harm could come to Father with Caldoron at his side, but I still worried.

"I miss Father."

"Of course you do. Family separation is kind of a theme around here, you know. I wish I could have healed Kazimir here. He's in capable hands at The Court of Bones." She tilted her head as though she could see through my carefully held composure. "May I give you some advice?"

I gave a wry smile. Wylda was, by her nature, open and welcoming. In fact, she'd welcomed me into the group quicker than anyone apart from Zephyr. "Please. Go ahead."

She paused. "A long time ago, I decided to follow Sequoia into this life."

"You're from the Court of Wild Ferns."

She nodded. "Our father was a Winged Guardian, entrusted with protecting the forest canopy, and our mother was a botanomancer." Her brown eyes became watery. "When our court fell, they stayed in the ruins. They chose honour over survival."

"But you and Sequoia left."

"I followed my sister. But I know our parents still had much to teach us."

"Oh, Wylda. I can't imagine being pulled in two directions like that. Are they still alive?"

"It's okay. I've made peace with it. The reason I

23

brought it up was to show you that every kindness has a cost in Faerie. Every betrayal has a reason. Morality here isn't a sturdy oak. It's ivy, creeping where it pleases, choking one thing and sheltering another. You have to forget fairy tales and learn to live in the tangle. That means maybe forgiving those you didn't intend to forgive."

I looked her in the eye. "You mean Tanuhja."

"It makes sense, doesn't it? That she'd have something to teach you as well as Kazimir. You could even ask her how she created the cursed fae. If we knew, maybe we could reverse the curse."

I couldn't fathom seeing my mother, couldn't envisage her telling me anything but a lie, so I diverted attention away from myself. "Zephyr's estranged from his father, too."

Wylda nodded. "He calcified after Rowena and Veda died. Orin isn't brave or bold like Zephyr, and Zephyr blamed him for not saving them."

"I feel like I'm on the periphery, looking in." I hoped she'd draw me deeper into her confidence. Wylda was looser-lipped and gentler than her sister, who oscillated between brooding silence and a lack of sugar-coating.

"I'm not even sure Zephyr realised how deeply he'd be able to feel again until you. But he'll figure it out. He always does."

I traced a constellation on the chair. I didn't tell Wylda how I sometimes hid underneath my ink cloak outside the war room to glean information. Or that Maren and Ferrith fretted until my return, despite the crude invisibility afforded by my magic. I didn't tell her that I pressed myself into alcoves when the mercenaries passed, and feared that Zephyr would sense me if I lingered.

"Just talk to each other, okay?" She smoothed the creases from her trousers. "Now, please, let's get breakfast. Before your mate stalks in here to ask what I've done with you."

Wylda's tone brooked no argument, so I nodded. "You do know it's Loxley's turn to cook? Maybe we should take our chances with an empty stomach." As newcomers, we shared most chores, with the exception of tending to cursed fae in the dungeons.

"Foraging is the safer choice. His cooking could be classed as a weapon."

We made our way to the breakfast chamber. Returning indoors should have been an escape from the pressures of the training ground, but coexisting with our kin was tricky. It was as if even the slightest misstep might set off a small explosion.

At one arched window, Zephyr was embroiled in hushed conversation with Cyprian and Loxley, likely discussing a looming mission. He inclined his head when our eyes met, and a band of shadow brushed my wounded arm, probing to check I'd been healed.

He turned back to his conversation. When I found the bond between us rigid rather than porous, my doubts swirled. Perhaps the likeness of me that his seer sister had painted long ago on the walls of the bath chamber had an unfair hold on him. Perhaps the mate bond made him a prisoner, and he would never have chosen me for himself without it.

He stayed in the fortress of his mind, as though it was best to shoulder his worries alone or share them with his fellow mercenaries, never with me.

"Leave them to it, and come and sit with us." Wylda

slid into a seat at the table next to her sister. "Did you see that, Sese? Zeph actually checked my work."

"The mate bond does odd things to a male." Sequoia stabbed her fork into a rock-hard pastry crust and picked it up with her fingers instead when the fork failed to pierce it.

Wylda eyed her plate. "I still haven't worked out whether Loxley's poor attempts at cooking are a ploy to be dropped from the rota or if he has a troll's idea of fine dining."

Sequoia's eyes narrowed on my arm. "Lover's tiff?"

"Just complications."

"Some things never change. All I wanted was to fuck and eat together, but Zephyr's always scheming."

Wylda's gaze snapped to her sister. "Behave."

Sequoia huffed. "I was just trying to distract myself from how every meal feels strange with Gabor gone."

I placed a slice of charred moss bread on my plate. Maren, Ferrith, and I weren't the only ones who were coming to terms with a new equilibrium. Gabor had infiltrated Zephyr's tight-knit circle as my mother's spy, but for countless years, he had been their friend, a brother, and the group's cook. He had risen with the sun without the slightest rancour to bake malted bread and prepare stews and meats for the mercenaries to devour in between their training rituals and missions. His loss created a chasm.

I zoned out from the clanking of earthenware and Wylda and Sequoia's low-level sisterly chatter. Half-formed thoughts collided and split like waves against jagged rocks. Gabor had tempted my meagre appetite with his sumptuous cooking, but his lies had primed me to think that the faerie queen of the Court of Chaos was a heroine, when my biological mother had long since been corrupted into something else. By healing me when I faced certain death, Gabor had robbed me of the catharsis of calling him a true villain.

Easy, Inkheart, came my mate's velvet tones in my head in response to the rising tide of my emotions, and I wondered if he had learned to read the details of my mind and not just the broad strokes of my passions.

I shivered at the memory of his naked body curled around mine last night before he extricated himself as the grey light around Ebonspire turned golden. His soft sigh caressed our mate bond.

Come and sit with me, I asked him.

But he didn't come to my side, even though Loxley and Cyprian had since joined the breakfast table. Instead, he stayed by the arched window, facing the ink-soaked training ground. I didn't want to process what had happened out there. Not here, where my fears could spill out onto everyone else.

"Morning," said Ferrith in passing, tugging me from my brooding mood.

Maren sank onto a stool, reached for a starfruit. "Not a word."

I grinned, noticing how her green eyes tracked his progress across the room. I was glad she and Ferrith had found their way to each other, even as I felt a pang of regret that the dynamics of our trio had shifted. "You look like you didn't sleep at all."

"Well, there are strange noises and bumps in the night in this blasted place."

I hid my smile. "It's going well, I take it?"

"Ferrith's prone to wandering around the gatehouse when I'd much rather he was warming my bed." She laughed and tucked a lock of russet hair behind a pointed ear. "But better than you and Zephyr, judging by how you look about as joyous as a fawn caught in a snare."

"You know you don't always have to be forthright with your opinions?"

She took a bite of the fruit. "Has that big brute opened up to you yet?"

I glanced at Zephyr. "I'd much rather talk about you two. It's not a sin to be happy, Maren."

She waggled her eyebrows. "Tell me you're at least drinking the fertility-blocking tea."

"It tastes like piss-soaked bark. Are you?" I shoved her none-too-gently, and we burst into laughter.

The light in her face dimmed just as surely as it appeared.

I leaned my head on her shoulder. "What's wrong?"

"Ferrith will get old. And I won't. Not like he will."

I squeezed her hand. "Don't think about that now."

She glanced up. "He's coming back."

Ferrith brought Maren a mug of tea with a rueful look and took the only empty spot at the head of the table. I could have offered to swap seats, but I wanted him to make friends with the others. In Larkspur, Ferrith put everyone else at ease with camaraderie and rounds of ale that he summoned forth, though rarely spared coin for. But in Faerie, he tended to sit stiff and morose, hovering at the edges of the group, unless accompanied by me or Maren.

He would thaw, eventually. Ferrith Namara couldn't help but make friends.

Although Loxley didn't seem in the mood for building bridges today.

He dragged his sleeve across his mouth. "That seat's taken."

Ferrith's brows knitted as the breakfast chamber grew quiet. "No, it isn't."

"Go somewhere else, mortal." Intervening wouldn't do Ferrith any favours, especially with someone like Lox, who had more hard edges than soft ones.

Ferrith steeled himself. "Don't be a jerk, and next time, take a bath after you've tended to the monsters. You smell like arse."

"Are you deaf? That. Seat. Is. Taken," repeated Lox darkly. It wasn't the first time he had dug his heels in, nor would it be the last. For someone who could change the will of others, he was a stubborn mule.

Then suddenly, I understood. Lox only cared about that seat because it had been the one Gabor had always filled. The two males had often clashed, but that didn't matter. None of Gabor's sins mattered as much as the manner of his death and how he had chosen us in the end—*this* family.

"Just let me eat in peace, man," Ferrith said quietly. "The Larkspur tavern, the king's regiment, this gods-forsaken hideaway…wherever I go, it's the same story. Always one cock trying to out-piss another."

"You think me a man?" Loxley sprang up and shoved Ferrith, spoiling for a fight when magic would have turned matters his way in a moment.

"He finds *man* more offensive than *cock*?" asked Maren.

Ferrith's cornflower blue eyes widened as Lox balled his fists. "You can't be serious."

29

I glanced at Zephyr, who still faced the training ground, though shadows writhed at his feet.

"By the embers, stop it. Or I swear, I'll–" Maren's voice was lost in the kerfuffle.

Inside me, power stirred, dark and restless, like shifting galaxies.

But Ferrith had never been someone to back down from a fight. He was sunshine, yes, but he, too, was stubborn. It was why he had never accepted his little sister's death all those orbits ago and what made him a good soldier and an even better friend. Though he possessed none of Loxley's wildness, though his muscles were honed rather than bulging, he would be a skilled and resilient opponent, for a few minutes at least. But a mortal couldn't ever overcome a fae, certainly not one with nearly a century of battle training under his belt or without a sizeable weapon to even the odds.

Galaxies whirled in my mind, constellations unravelling and reforming with every breath. Over the past week, since the meteor's touch, Zephyr had at times sensed my struggles and had used our bond to anchor me, but for the second time that morning, he maintained his distance both physically and mentally. I was so scared, so scared that my magic would be *disobedient* again. I pushed it down and willed it to sleep.

Ferrith and Loxley couldn't come to blows. I worried that our fragile togetherness would crack like glass under pressure. That our new grouping wouldn't weather a rupture. I had forged bonds with the mercenaries during our time together, but they had no particular love for Maren and Ferrith, no understanding of the deep ties between us and how I would forsake others for them.

Sequoia's fuchsia lips curved against night-dark skin. "Let them get it out of their system."

"No broken bones," pleaded Wylda. "I won't lose another patient to distant healers."

It was Father she meant. Father and I had only ever had each other. And now, he didn't have me.

The meteor's magic inside me wouldn't stay quiet. It was a tempest of shadows laced with starlight, a force both terrible and beautiful. I wrestled with it, beads of perspiration pooling on my brow, as the scent of sloshed tea and crushed pastries mingled with the tang of adrenaline.

Maren scrambled out of her chair, but Cyprian raised his arm to halt her, his eyes on Zephyr at the window. I reached for the mate bond, but it was brittle and dark, and I couldn't get through. I wondered why they were waiting, wondered if they wanted Loxley to hurt Ferrith even though Zephyr had chosen to save the three of us over Gabor, whom he had loved.

Even though Zephyr loved me.

Ferrith's boots skidded on the polished wooden floor as he skirted the breakfast table for more space. Loxley loomed over him, fists flexing, then one hand flashed out, but Ferrith ducked, and the fae's nails gouged deep furrows into the table.

A butter dish clattered to the ground, shattering there. Loxley flashed me an odd glance, then struck again. Ferrith deflected with a silver serving tray, and Loxley's snarl of frustration ripped through the room as he vaulted over an upended stool. Ferrith drew his dagger, and surprise flashed across Loxley's rugged face.

He hadn't accounted for the dagger that Ferrith had

worn without fail since arriving in Faerie, given to him by the king.

In Loxley's brief moment of imbalance, Ferrith pressed the dagger against the fae's bearded throat. Both froze, breathing erratically, surrounded by the wreckage of what had been the calm breakfast chamber.

I didn't know how I reached them, didn't know how one minute I sat unblinking at the table, the next winched between them. The meteor's magic whispered to me in unspoken tongues, a vortex of infinite possibilities and the quiet promise of destruction.

My body, no longer fully mine, moved without thought. My fingers clenched my quill, its nib slick with ink, and magic surged through me in a blinding rush. The air around us rippled and fractured.

Ferrith reached for me, and Loxley recoiled, horror coating their expressions as reality distorted and inky folds appeared in the breakfast chamber. They scrambled to escape, but the magic—my magic—snatched them, two silhouettes yanked in opposite directions, going stars-knows-where.

A fractured void loomed on one side; on the other, a starlit moonscape. The sheer vastness of it stole my breath, and I barely registered the shouts to stop, *for the lore and the dragons and all that shines in the night sky, stop.* Zephyr's voice was in my mind, pleading *Inkheart, Inkheart,* but his echo reached me as though from the furthest reaches of a great chasm.

I couldn't stop.

I could only endure it, and let it crash over me like a storm.

The two silhouettes were dragged into the inky folds.

They scrambled, feet trying to gain purchase, slipping against the cold floor. Desperate cries and lunges from others, and my mind so murky, unable to reason, as if the dust from the cosmos was blinding me and I was not a thinking being, simply a reactive one.

Violet fire flamed in Maren's hands, and part of me wanted her to do it. Wanted her magic to collide with mine.

Then suddenly, Cyprian was there, his eyes turning from hazel to gold against his midnight skin as he stretched time's fabric. He tugged it back just three or four seconds, and somehow the light drew back and shadows flooded forth.

I shivered as they pooled around me, absorbing my magic. I recognised the essence of those shadows. They knew me. Sometimes they teased me with a caress or a flutter. Today, they soothed me, quelling the rage of the meteor. Zephyr's strong arms followed the path of his shadows, holding me until the meteor's magic released its grip. Until all that was left of me was a quaking husk.

Leaving only deathly quiet. A quiet that spoke volumes.

Horror burrowed into my bones, and my pulse was a drumbeat in my ears as I braced myself.

I'd killed Ferrith and Loxley.

I'd killed them. Torn them apart or flung them into the cosmos to drift or burn.

What have I done? The words circled in my mind, each syllable a spike driven into my soul.

Faerie had demanded such feats from me: acts of cunning, cruelty, and strength. It tested me at every turn, taking away my allies, stripping away hesitation, forcing me to abandon my old comforts, reshaping me into something sharper and wilder.

It didn't care for my exhaustion or uncertainty. It didn't care that I missed Father and my village. It pushed and pulled, demanding I rise, survive, and prove myself worthy of walking its treacherous paths.

Shadows crept into the edges of my vision, curling like ink in water, blurring the world into something shapeless and uncertain. My breath came fast and shallow. I couldn't tell where Zephyr's magic ended and mine began.

This time, Faerie had broken something in me. It had pushed too far, demanded too much.

For all of the monsters in Ebonspire's cellars, Faerie had made *me* the monster lurking in the dark.

4

YSADORA

Ebonspire is a gothic gatehouse in the Court of Lore, seat of a gentle faerie queen, where art is both archive and diplomacy. Its walls hold more than stone: stages layered like petals host memory plays, prophetic reenactments, and a warren of libraries. Here, actors, scholars, and artists trade riddles, poems, and miniature portraits instead of greetings.
– A Tapestry of Courts and Crowns

The silence rolled over me like a dense fog over the moor. It curdled inside me, making me fear the worst, making me a pariah. Then, there were shuddering exhales and splutters of disbelief, before voices crowded in on me. Zephyr ground out an order for Ferrith to drop the dagger. It clattered to the floor.

"You carry a weapon into the breakfast chamber?" A question wrapped in civility.

Ferrith spluttered, "The rest of you are walking armouries, and I can't carry a dagger?"

"You turn it against one of my own?" Zephyr's quietly damning voice brushed the crown of my head.

Sequoia shrugged. "He tried a tray first."

I expected death. Twisted bones and slack limbs. Oozing blood and lifeless eyes. The wails of my best friend and the horror of my mate. But their bickering unspooled the tight ball of my fear. When I forced myself to look, there were no crumpled bodies, only Ferrith and Loxley, dazed but breathing.

The realisation seeped into me: they were alive.

I inched out of the circle of Zephyr's arms without glancing at the judgement I knew would line his face.

"If you want us dead, Ysa, you'll have to try harder than that," said Loxley.

"It was hardly her fault." Wylda narrowed her brown eyes at him and Zephyr.

"I pray you're not standing close to her next time," said Loxley.

Ferrith's gaze snapped to mine, eyes glazed with fear. "What was that?"

A ball of hurt expanded in my chest, but I didn't speak up. How could I answer him when I didn't understand myself? He understood Faerie even less than I did: what it cost and what it took. I didn't try to explain how trying to control the meteor's magic was like catching smoke or that it sickened me every time it stirred inside me.

I didn't tell them that there was nothing enshrined in Father's memory stone in Larkspur to help me navigate my growing magic. How the Binder had not answered my desperate calls. How even attempts by the Circle of Emberlight to scry my fate using cracked mirrors and bowls of blackened moon water hadn't revealed any answers.

Most of all, I didn't tell them how I worried that the meteor's magic resisted being known like a living thing that refused to be caged.

It's okay, Ysa. Zephyr's shadows hovered a hair's breadth away, in case I might still be a threat.

Maren moved to Ferrith's side, her face tight. "You could have killed them."

"I'm so sorry," I whispered as shadows gathered at the small of my back, warm and firm as a steadying palm.

"Don't apologise," said Sequoia. "We learned to control our magic as younglings, and yet you expect to manage overnight?"

Cyprian wiped the sweat from his brow, and I realised by the small patch of white in his hair that pitting his time magic against me had cost him. "At the moment, it's controlling her. But we made progress this morning."

The note of quiet satisfaction in his voice made me jerk my head between the males who had congregated at the window: Cyprian's brow was lined with relief; Loxley studied me with the same detached amusement he wore when he was playing chess; my mate's expression was carefully neutral, but something in his storm-dark gaze niggled at me.

He was pleased. He was actually pleased.

Heat prickled at the back of my neck. I replayed the events in my mind: the trio of mercenaries deep in conversation at the window, Loxley picking a fight with

Ferrith at the table and his furtive glance at me mid-fight, the way Zephyr hadn't stepped in to demand civility until my magic had woken.

Realisation struck like flint against stone. My fist curled around my quill. He had intended Father and me to have the choice to hide in the mortal realm with the help of the invisibility granted by the whisper rings, but I had told him I was done running away. Only, he'd clearly decided that avoiding the exploration of my magic *was* running away. They had tricked me. Again.

"You set me up." My voice wavered, but my rage was unmistakable. "You promised not to do that again."

Zephyr met my gaze, unflinching. "No, I didn't. I offered a break, not to stop pushing."

Words were my area of expertise. I had been brought up in a bookshop. I hated his clever fae ways of building loopholes that I didn't see quickly enough, how I could take cheap words as a promise. I had drawn a line, and he had ridden roughshod over it. Damn him, he didn't even look guilty.

"You needed proof," he said simply.

My pulse pounded. "Proof of what?"

"That you don't need time to think. That when the need arises, your magic answers." Zephyr's brow furrowed, like this was a puzzle rather than my life. "It's not fear that fuels you. It's instinct. Maybe something to do with protection. It's more defensive than attacking, I think. Now we know that your magic goes beyond what the calligraphers in the Order of the Glyph could do. You opened pathways to the damn stars, Inkheart."

I wanted to fling ink at him, wanted to rip the triumph off his face. But Zephyr was right: it had worked. I had been scared, but my magic had been like a separate being, sure-footed and calculating. It had reacted in defence of Ferrith, unfurling like instinct, quick as breath. Despite the leap in understanding, I couldn't shake the feeling that my mate had changed. He was putting me above everyone else, even the mercenary family he had chosen.

Zephyr had disassociated from the harm I could have done, from what I had become. The Binder had unshackled my destiny, and with that came the crushing pressure to make the right choices. I was agonisingly aware of the horror I could have inflicted on my friends.

"You overbearing, arrogant arse."

He blinked. "Excuse me?"

I glared at him. "You heard me."

Somewhere, Loxley guffawed.

"She's not wrong," said Sequoia. "Her Father is dragon leagues away, her village is pretty much off limits for her, and instead of easing her in, you're prodding and poking her like—"

Zephyr's eyebrows shot up. "Like what, exactly?"

"Magic of this nature can't be forced. That's all I'm saying." Sequoia crossed her arms over her chest.

"I'm well aware of what my mate needs." Eyes as cold as glacial waters met Sequoia's, as if their former romance had never happened. "But do give us the benefit of your wisdom."

"Lay off, Zeph," warned Wylda. "You're like a dog in heat."

In that moment, our mate bond was a thorn I wanted to dig out of myself. The endless schemes of Faerie didn't allow me to catch my breath. "Stop it. Stop the fighting. What if I can't be who you want me to be? What if we can't save the monsters and mend Faerie?" *What if we can't save Elowen? What if I can't even save myself?*

Concern darted across the hard lines of Zephyr's face, but I turned on my heel. My magic writhed beneath my skin, ink seeping from my quill into the air around me. I didn't need to reach for it—it was already there, listening. Good.

Zephyr's shadows stirred, reacting instinctively to my rising power. A warning. A challenge.

He reached out through the bond. *Please. If you'll just listen.*

Get out of my head. How dare he lock me out when I needed him? How dare he use the bond only on his terms? I left them all where they stood. Their voices rang out behind me as I fled, each word stoking my anger and confirming that they didn't give a damn about my goals or desires.

"What if we're not around to stop her next time?" asked Cyprian.

Zephyr's shadows swallowed the light. "Who said she needs to be stopped?"

"Stop brooding and talk to her, or I swear it, I will bind you together with my vines until you do," said Wylda.

"Hers is the kind of power that topples empires," said Cyprian.

Loxley's tone was dry. "She's certainly a weapon."

Then I was out of hearing range. I went to the one place I knew Zephyr wouldn't follow: the Forgotten Garden, on an outcrop of Ebonspire, facing the crashing ocean. The garden, where he had been trapped while his mother and sister had fought a battle that ended their lives. The garden that housed their memorial statues, but which he couldn't bear to face.

I went there, with Father's quill in my cramping fingers.

Only when I reached the garden did I realise that neither Maren nor Ferrith had followed me there.

5

KAZIMIR

The Court of Bones is a sanctuary of reverence,
where druids, bone-shamans, and artisans shape
the dead into relics of memory. Its members
practice bonecraft, healing, and grave-
whispering, honouring the balance between decay
and creation. They draw power not from fear, but
from fidelity to the fallen.
- A Tapestry of Courts and Crowns

As his brothers' corpses lay in the ruins of The Order of the Glyph and Faerie discarded her kingdoms like fallen petals, a mewling baby emerged pink and slick from between Tanuhja's pale thighs. That tiny mewling baby had given Kazimir a reason to live. He knew, in that precise instant, that he would stand naked in a dragon's flame or dance with a redcap in its blood-soaked lair to secure his youngling's happiness.

It was Ysadora's happiness that mattered to him above all else.

Certainly, safety had played a role in his choices. No soul could be happy if life and limb were at risk, or freedom and self-determination. He and his daughter could not have stayed in Faerie when all other calligraphers had perished.

But happiness—not mere safety—was what made the long centuries worthwhile. With the death of the brotherhood, his priorities shifted singularly to Ysa, despite the agonising severing from Caldoron.

His stomach churned, recalling the tether between dragon and rider, stretching as taut as a wire with every step he took. His body rebelled at the distance. Since the *Kindling*, every fibre of Kazimir had been trained never to stray far from his dragon—two minds in tandem, bound by trust and bloodshed.

It was a sacred tenet of the brotherhood: dragons and their riders didn't part easily.

Caldoron didn't articulate his question, but it hung between them all the same: *why?*

Dragons did not understand separation without purpose.

Kazimir focused on the youngling coddled against his chest, on the cold stone beneath his boots that contrasted so starkly with the heat of dragonfire he missed. For endless orbits, Kazimir's body held the phantom sway of their flight, as if the wind still tugged against him. A pathetic mimic of Caldoron's soaring might; one that deservedly made him sick to his stomach.

How odd then, to be back in Faerie. Books and ink brought Kazimir contentment, but it was his two true loves that made his long life fruitful: Ysa and Caldoron. This time, Kazimir rested more easily knowing that there was one other who put Ysa's well-being before their own. Not Tanuhja. The separation of their family had leached the softness from her soul.

He blamed himself for that. Had he stayed, perhaps he could have anchored the softness he had experienced.

It was Zephyr Ashmoor, prince of the fallen Court of Lore, who had become Ysa's protector. Once, Kazimir had thought that his fierce protection of Ysa was her birthright: a father's primal duty. But he had only to watch Zephyr's lingering gaze on Ysa—softening when he thought no one was looking—or note the instinctive way his shadows always drifted closer to her—even when there was no danger—to know he had been replaced. And strangely, Kazimir didn't resent it.

Instead, it filled him with a peculiar kind of peace, even as it stung.

Once, the brotherhood might have ordered him to sever a bond between individuals as powerful as this.

Twice burned by love, Kazimir wondered how much sweeter the centuries might have been with a love of his own. For all his disappointments, he wished fervently that it would be possible for Ysa and Zephyr to reach their potential together.

The Binder certainly seemed to think theirs was a match that held vast and world-altering possibilities. But then, she was a starry-eyed romantic at heart for all her cryptic prophecies and crude calculations.

At Ebonspire, Kazimir refused a chamber, resting

instead against the dragon's flank as he had done every night since they had been reunited. The soft hush of Faerie enveloped him. The sky was unfamiliar here compared to his own court: a little wilder, a little stranger.

Caldoron's exhales clouded the night air with faint plumes of heat, momentarily misting the stars. He had forgotten how still Faerie could be at night, as though if he reached out, he could stir the stars with his fingertips. He breathed in the night—the scent of rain-soaked moss, the delicate spice of unfamiliar blossom—and took in the glow of the stables.

As he drifted off to sleep to the occasional crackle of embers stirring in Caldoron's throat, he wondered why the dragon didn't curl as close as before, why he hadn't made a protective canopy of bronze scales and membrane over Kazimir as he once had. Why he didn't sense bone-deep contentment from the dragon at his return. In that fraction of a second before sleep claimed him, he remembered his old master telling him that dragons were slow to forgive.

THE NEXT MORNING, Kazimir met the shadow prince while Caldoron hunted for his breakfast. The two males stood alone under the eaves of a starfruit tree to discuss Ysa's fate. It seemed to Kazimir a cruel parallel to a time when he and the Faerie King of Silence had discussed Danaë. That female, too, had surpassed him.

"Liora warns us that The Court of Bones is a fickle ally." Zephyr's eyes were a storm-touched sea. "You must find a way to shore up the alliance while you are there."

Kazimir didn't bristle at the implicit suggestion of who

was in command. His days of might had long passed. "I will."

"Be careful. There are spies and informants everywhere." Zephyr pulled a dagger from a pocket of shadows. "This is yours, I believe. We found it in the ruins of the Order of the Glyph."

Kazimir knew the mercenaries hunted artefacts as well as monsters. Even so, emotion thickened his voice. "You were there."

Zephyr shrugged. "A long time ago. There's not much left."

The calligrapher took the dagger slowly, fingers brushing the hilt like it might vanish again. "I didn't think I'd see this again."

The weapon was elegant, its blade gold like the nib of his crimson quill and blessed by dragon fire. The hilt was wrapped in deep brown leather, worn smooth by time and use. A single gemstone, dark as dried blood, was set into the pommel. It was a relic, a piece of history that carried weight. Memory. Blood.

Without ceremony, he handed it back to the fallen prince. "Give it to Ysadora. May it bring terror to her enemies."

A glimmer of respect lit Zephyr's eyes. "Are you certain?"

"I am." Kazimir's broken body and spirit could not compete with what this male could offer his daughter. He had protected Ysa from even his own kin. *Fatebreaker*, the Binder had called him. This male, not Kazimir, stood at the crossroads between Ysa's sorrow and hope. "You'll ensure she never stands alone, no matter what the cost?"

The shadow prince grasped his forearm in the way of

old faerie lords. It was a pledge more honourable than a bargain, because it did not require clever tongues or twisted loopholes or bargains branded on the body. Such pledges were not bought, but given freely. "You have my word, calligrapher. One more thing…"

"Yes?"

"What are the origins of the compass Ysa discovered amongst your belongings in Larkspur?"

"The Binder left that in my bookshop a long time ago." Kazimir's eyes sparked. "But Lunarys isn't one for trinkets. Why would she need trinkets when she hangs the very stars that line the night sky?"

Zephyr gave a curt nod. "I wish you well, calligrapher. I will ensure Ysa does not stand alone."

Only then had Kazimir allowed Caldoron to carry him away to The Court of Bones for healing, although the dragon seemed not to hear his first command and complied only after a second, more forceful order. Only then had he allowed the last of Wylda's pain-numbing herbs to ebb so that he experienced the new reality of his tortured body.

Eternal stars, what agony! To think that a voice that had brought him such pleasure had been the breaking of him. A woman he had shared a bed with, a life with, in Larkspur. A woman whom he had chosen to mother Ysa in Tanuhja's absence. Danaë had broken his bones as simply as if she were snapping a loose thread in one of her elegant gowns. She believed he had deserved it; she believed Thiago was the better male.

Kazimir feared it was true. He feared his honour had died with the brotherhood.

But cowardice was not an option while his great loves still needed him.

As his dragon bore him upwards, Kazimir clamped his thighs against the ridge of Caldoron's spine, his legs trembling with the strain. His muscles protested, begging for respite. Sweat pooled on his forehead, but he held fast to bronze scales until Caldoron mercifully levelled out in the cool blue sky. Until Ysadora and the stern shadow prince became specks beneath him.

Then, carefully, fearfully, he readjusted. Finding a secure perch was difficult in his fragile state. Danaë's cycle of torture and healing had caused misalignment. Kazimir's bones pulled and strained at odd angles, and his body felt alien, as though harbouring a deep, internal dissonance: twisted vertebrae and ribs that lurked underneath his skin in jagged, imperfect shapes. His arms —a dragon rider's arms, once strong and capable—now seemed hollow in some places, heavier in others.

His body was no longer the reliable fortress it had been; it had become a twisted map of war.

Gold eyes slitted as Caldoron's head swung towards him. *Perhaps you need a harness, after all.*

There had been a time when the dragon had instinctively shielded him with his wings or tail or the angle of his body in flight. Kazimir's goggles rattled against the rushing wind. *Perhaps you could have taken that angle less steeply, old friend.*

He took a deep breath. Somehow, the muscle memory of flight returned. His knees locked with old precision, his arms tucked low along the dragon's spine, recalling the techniques of a younger, undamaged man.

Kazimir sought out the imperfections in Caldoron's

scales, scars from battles they had fought together, and when he hooked his fingers into them, it was like finding his place in the grooves of a beloved instrument. Like coming home.

The dragon's voice rumbled through him like a landslide. *I will not cheapen my legendary manoeuvres, calligrapher. Even for you.*

Nor would I wish you to. They both knew that it was Kazimir's ailing body and lack of balance that was the real problem. *Although it would be quite the stain on your character if I ended as a splatter on the landscape.*

Caldoron snorted a ring of smoke. *You'd fall for miles. It's your dignity which would be impeded, not mine.*

Kazimir let out a soft, disbelieving breath. He had missed this: the way they traded barbs and half-insults, despite weariness. The dragon's presence in his mind was as he remembered: vast and primal, a voice of wind and stone, of fire and sky.

Their bond—the one he'd thought long severed—had slipped back into place with a seamlessness that stunned him. The warmth of it was so familiar, so heartbreakingly right, that Kazimir couldn't help the tears that trailed his face, though he'd be damned if he'd let the dragon see them.

Caldoron filled the quiet spaces in him that Kazimir had grown used to leaving empty. He hadn't realised how fractured he had been until it was mended. His physical ailments paled in comparison to that brokenness. The bond with his dragon was as essential to him as breath. Although their bond, once warm and constant, seemed cooler and more distant.

The dragon's wings carried them higher, and Kazimir

49

let his eyes close for a fleeting moment. Countless times, Caldoron had been his lifeline through the harshest of terrains, and this time was no different. Despite the dull ache of his broken flesh, there was relief in the sensation of flight.

The rhythmic beat of the dragon's wings soothed the erratic rhythm of Kazimir's breathing. Caldoron's movements were rougher than he remembered, forcing him to adjust repeatedly. Even so, the howling rush of the air filled Kazimir's ears, drowning out the crackling and creaking of his bones.

Caldoron's ancient strength anchored him, the steady pulse of the dragon's consciousness interwoven with his own, a brother-in-arms. His solitary years felt small and pitiful in comparison. Exhaling slowly, he turned his gaze to the horizon, where the sun's light streaked along the clouds in flaxen ribbons.

Enough admiring me. We have necessities to discuss before we reach the lonesome court, said Caldoron.

Kazimir raised a bushy brow. *Your vanity is as vast as your wingspan.*

The dragon rumbled with amusement. *And yet, both serve me well.*

The Court of Bones was renowned for its mastery of earth-based crafts. It was a court of artisans, jewellers, sculptors, and weapon forgers, who used bone, clay, stone, and metal. A court of druids attuned to the natural rhythms of life and death, and bone shamans, keepers of hidden tombs and burial grounds. A court of bone healers and bone breakers.

Its queen, Thalindra Nightmourne, was rumoured to possess soul-binding magic and a necrotic touch. Her suspicions of outsiders were complicated further by her court's proximity to Nightblaze Isle, where the dragons had fled.

Sweat pooled down Kazimir's back. *Will the queen honour the pact she made to heal me?*

Caldoron released scalding smoke. *If she values her life.*

Kazimir gave thanks for his borrowed riding gear. *And if she turns our sanctuary into a snare?*

You fret, calligrapher. Fatherhood has softened your instincts. Mild disdain laced the dragon's voice. *Your ailments are the perfect ruse to visit this court. I seem to remember that secrecy was never a problem for you.*

Dragonkind is also secretive. Kazimir leaned with the dragon's drift, grimacing as pain jolted through his spine. Even as his strength waned, his instincts kept him glued to the beast.

I do not complain, calligrapher. A secret kept is power hoarded, like embers in my chest, said Caldoron. *It merely surprises me that you have not once mentioned your sister.*

Kazimir's breath misted in the cold air, and his ribs tightened at the thought of his sister. *She did not fly in the formation that came to our rescue when the white dragon attacked.*

I was there. I am aware. The dragon snorted. *And I did not need rescuing.*

I beg to differ, my friend. Despite the evidence of his own eyes, it was hard to believe that female riders existed.

The brotherhood had trained initiates for five orbits before they had even attempted to bond a dragon. He wondered if Araminta still lived. She had been older and fiercer than he, with a passion for adventure rather than books, better-suited in many ways to dragon-riding than him.

Araminta's grievance against the brotherhood—and by extension, him—had been so strong that he imagined she had lived just to spite him. To show she could ride, when females had only ever been dragon attendants: cleaning, grooming, applying salves to minor injuries, or preparing for the sacred ritual. It was painful to accept that Araminta had, in all likelihood, never achieved her dream.

He shut down the old grief and turned his thoughts back to his daughter. *The memory stone might not be enough to guide Ysa. But I will correspond with her.*

Each wingbeat cut through the air like the measured rhythm of a drum. *You've worked in solitude for too long, calligrapher. There are others who must also play their part in preparing her. The shadow prince, for one.*

Yes, for my sins, I trust him. Kazimir didn't like to leave things to chance. *But will you pave the way for Ysa with the riot?*

Caldoron's thoughts brushed against his. *I will go to Nightblaze Isle and tell them what has passed, but I will not interfere in the Kindling. No dragon will tolerate a rider unworthy of their wings. The old truths remain.*

A trapdoor of memories opened in Kazimir's mind of his own *Kindling. A rider must have three things. A spirit unshackled by pride. A spine that will not bend. A heart willing to burn.*

He laid his forehead against the dragon's warm, smooth scales as the world blurred around them. He didn't even know if Ysadora wished to ride, hadn't dared even to mention it, but surviving in Faerie was about building alliances, and there could be no greater ally than a bonded dragon.

Kazimir wished it so much for her that bile rose in his mouth. Ysa had the requisite backbone: the stubborn will that neither frailty nor fae magic could snuff out. The same will that drove her to brave the Shrouded Forest after he had strictly forbidden it. The same tenacity that meant she met the faerie king's wrath with her own steel.

And yet, Kazimir knew the dragons. He knew their cunning, cruelty, and capacity for indifference. They were not sentimental creatures. They would neither be moved by bloodline nor nobility of purpose. Instead, they would weigh her strength, cunning, and resourcefulness against ancient wisdom and primordial fire.

He sighed. Perhaps his past errors with Araminta had come back to haunt him.

Would Ysa embrace the idea of dragon-riding? Had he provided her with enough tools to succeed?

He prayed to every forgotten god that he had.

Beneath them, Faerie was a blur of green and stone, the horizon endless and wild. Kazimir pressed his torso flat against the dragon's back, minimising the space between them. His cheek pressed against the heated scales, his breath shallow as he tried to move with the dragon's rhythm instead of against it.

For a moment, Kazimir felt that nothing could touch them, that rider and beast could soar above the rot and ruin of the world, where no monarchs or courts could claim them. But when the meteor fell, the Binder severed the threads that once bound Ysa's future to a fixed path. She deviated from a secure path to a potentially deadly one. Worse, the meteor had imbued her with unfathomable magic.

It wasn't just power that lived inside his daughter now; it was raw, chaotic energy. Ink magic was deliberate and controlled, passed down through centuries of scholars. Meteor magic was wild and unpredictable, an external force thrust upon the world. Tanuhja, too, had been powerful, with flares of emotion that Kazimir had tempered.

Their daughter's destiny was unmoored, but Kazimir could still play his part.

I must warn you. The Court of Bones has changed somewhat since your last visit. Caldoron's claws flexed rhythmically against the wind. *The fall of courts tipped the fragile balance here.*

Left unsaid was how Kazimir might have prevented the unravelling of Faerie if he had attempted to maintain the Grimoire after the Order of the Glyph had perished. If he hadn't abandoned the realm for Ysa.

The dragon carried them closer, and a shiver of apprehension skirted up Kazimir's unevenly stacked spine. He remembered the Court of Bones as one of life and death in harmony: reverent bone sculptures, carved to honour the fallen; the scent of dry bark mingling with the sweetness of night-blooming flowers; mournful soldiers made of bone patrolling the boundaries of the court.

Caldoron banked sharply, the stretch of his wings blotting out the sun. *We are almost upon them.*

Understood. Kazimir's boots scrambled for purchase in a narrow crevice between Caldoron's lower scales, calf muscles trembling with effort as the dragon tilted into a descent towards the pre-agreed grove. His knuckles whitened on Caldoron's scales at the grim tableau coming into sharp focus beneath them.

This was not the court he had known. This was a place hollowed out, its beauty consumed by desolation. The once-vibrant grove had withered into a skeletal wasteland, stripped of life. The trees were nothing but bleached husks, their limbs brittle and broken, roots shrivelled into dust-choked ground.

Once, graceful remembrance sculptures jutted from the ground like cruel effigies: spines and femurs fashioned into gnarled spires, skulls and ribcages flayed open like grotesque flowers, their surfaces etched with glowing runes.

A pungent scent of decay pervaded the air. It seeped into his nose and throat, and Kazimir gagged, slipping for a panicked moment. But instead of taking mercy on him, Caldoron made a lurching movement away from the court.

Kazimir held on with dogged determination, tasting blood where he bit the inside of his cheek. The entire grove felt wrong: leached of warmth, of colour, of anything living. The dragon's scales rippled beneath his palms, as if he, too, found the scene distasteful.

They had come seeking aid, but this court reeked of ruin.

Kazimir sighed. *We have no choice but to land, old friend.*

Then may your gamble pay off, calligrapher. Caldoron fanned his wings wide, and the downdraft stirred the branches, sending a brittle rain of dead twigs swirling into the stagnant air.

Kazimir gritted his teeth against the pain of Caldoron's jarring landing. The sheer weight of the dragon splintered the ground, and a cloud of bone-dust and ash billowed outwards.

The cold drag of magic pulled at Kazimir's skin. *Do you feel that?*

Barrier magic, said the dragon. *It will be impossible to communicate with Ysadora.*

When the dust and ash cleared, it revealed the pale, thin Queen of the Court of Bones standing at the heart of the grove. She twisted her hands, and from the hidden corners of the grove, bone soldiers moved to flank her.

They arrived at her side, hollow-eyed, bones chafing and rattling in the wind. But after they took up formation, a funeral stillness befell them, as if the laws of flesh and breath no longer bound them.

These weren't reanimated skeletons. They were jigsaws of ivory, reforged with cruel magic and bands of blackened metal: fractured jaws fused open in revolting grins, horn-like protrusions curling from temples, vertebrae poking out like malformed spikes, tibias stretched into jagged stilts, giving them an almost insect-like gait. Runes carved deep into their bones glowed with death magic. These soldiers were wrathful, not mournful.

I could sneeze, and half of them would crumble. Should I test the theory? asked the dragon.

Absolutely not. Kazimir's stomach knotted. In the Court of Nebulas, dust meant rebirth: the remnants of stars forging new life. Here, the dust of splintered bone was nothing but death lingering too long.

Caldoron offered him a dispassionate stare, and for a moment, the calligrapher questioned whom the cool look was for. *I wonder if they scream when they have no lungs.*

Kazimir dragged his eyes back to the queen. He

bowed, unable to shake the feeling that healing would come with its own price. "Queen Thalindra, you have my gratitude."

She wore a grey silk gown and a circlet of antlers bleached white over auburn tresses. Aristocratic features graced her face: a high forehead, a narrow nose, a smooth jawline, and surprisingly full lips. It was impossible to tell from her face whether she was kind or not.

The queen considered the dragon with narrowed eyes, then slid her silver gaze over him as if she had already mapped every fracture, misalignment, and stiffened movement. "Welcome, calligrapher. We will see you made whole again."

At her nod, the bone soldiers advanced towards Caldoron.

Kazimir wondered—too late—whether unnatural bones could burn.

6

YSADORA

*Starbinder: deep indigo leaves dotted with white
flowers. The flowers open only at night and glow
like miniature constellations. Ink from the sap
may be used for prophetic writings or sending
hidden messages, depending
on the phase of the moon.
- A Compendium of Faerie Flora and Terrain*

My heart was hammering by the time I reached the Forgotten Garden. I found a wedge of sunshine to sit in and avoided the haughty stone gaze of Rowena Ashmoor's statue. In the distance, Mythros's hooves hit the hard earth in a gallop. Breathing in the scent of clematis and salty air, I retrieved a vial of veilstem ink from my pocket and lifted my quill.

Ink shimmered in the air. *Can you talk?*

Despite the distance, danger, and rocky beginning, Elowen and I had forged a deep bond. Our bargain had been set: twelve moons for us to rescue her from the Court of Silence in exchange for her secrecy about how we had stolen the whisper rings. The silver ouroboros circling my ankle was a stark reminder of the promise I had made, although securing her freedom would be nigh on impossible.

We couldn't fathom a way to do it that would allow us to keep our heads.

Elowen's psychic abilities couldn't cross the realms, but my ink magic could. Once a day, I snuck away to the Forgotten Garden to write to her. With Maren and Ferrith wrapped up in each other and Zephyr often absent, I was grateful for the distraction.

We took precautions, taking note of the times she was likely to be alone. Veilstem or starbinder ink provided invisibility against prying eyes if used correctly. If Elowen didn't dawdle, residual magic allowed me to tug a message back from her, like plucking a silken thread from the fabric of the universe.

It didn't always go according to plan.

During my first attempts, the words flickered in the air like a candle, pulled apart by the breeze. A slight hiccup in my breathing pattern, and they splattered across my hands, my sleeves or face, smudging across my cheek like an impatient hand had brushed it there.

More than once, the ink refused to hold Elowen's response, leaving a ghostly smudge where her words should have been. Some days, her words arrived distorted, curling into meaningless symbols before dissolving. There were near misses when the wraith attendants, the faerie king, or Danaë suddenly appeared or hovered too close as if they suspected.

A single mistake could mean discovery, but neither of us could bear to stop, least of all Elowen.

Her parents continued to subject her to the mouth binding, silencing her with magic so cruel that even her breath carried no sound. She ached to be heard, and with each message, she cast off her shackles.

Her words, sent in sharp strokes, were defiant. She was our spy at the Court of Silence, but even when she had little news to share, she wrote anyway—half-thoughts, fierce emotions, dreams she couldn't voice out loud.

About how Xaire was the golden child, but she couldn't resent him, not when they loved each other so fiercely. About how she hated her mother's snow leopards because she suspected Danaë preferred them to her. How Zephyr had always been kind but distant. About how she yearned to leave, but how she feared she might never fit in elsewhere. As if proof of her own mind was something she needed to see formed in ink to believe in its existence.

I wondered how often she wanted to scream. If she feared that one day she'd forget the sound of her voice. If she regretted the information she fed me about the Court of Silence. If it made her feel dirty or more whole, after all they had done to her.

So, I never missed a day. Even when the exhaustion from training weighed down my limbs or when I longed for Zephyr's touch, I carved out time to write to her in the knowledge that she was waiting.

Soon, we had practised enough to send and receive missives in moments. Our words flitted between realms like whispered rebellions, ink fading and reappearing like starlight blinking through a storm. For all the ways Faerie had stripped me of certainty, this was a lifeline I held close: no matter how far we strayed, neither Elowen nor I would ever truly be alone.

I tried again, imagining Elowen in dark halls, ensuring no one watched, wondering whether to hide or to use her whisper ring for adding security, although in a home such as Echohold, with Thiago the spymaster as a father, magic use was a risk, and secrets always found their way into the open.

Are you there?

A long minute passed before the ink bled into existence. *Let me retire to my chambers.* Five minutes stretched before she wrote again. *By the breathless dawn, what's wrong?*

Relief settled into my bones. *I just needed to hear from you.*

Liar. Your emotions colour your magic. I nearly had ink splattered across my face again.

I huffed out a silent laugh. *Zephyr tricked me into using more magic than I wanted.*

Her reply came almost instantly, sharp and certain. *That's what he does—trickery, shadows, and an unreasonable amount of brooding. You'll get used to it. Just remember, the mate bond does not take away your free will.*

Don't worry. I'll stand my ground. I tried to locate the star at the edge of my awareness that represented Zephyr, but the bond was still mired in silence. If he could live without it, perhaps I could, too.

I wish I were there to see the fireworks. Elowen's words bloomed in fluid tendrils before sharpening into consonants and vowels. *At court, Zephyr had half the females in a storm of irritation and the other half trying to claw his shirt off. Clearly, he's still impossible. You have my sympathy.*

I grinned, in spite of myself. *I bet he didn't even realise the effect he had on them.*

Oh, he realised. I think he almost pitied them. Wisps of blue ink unfurled in the air. *There's a reason my cousin rarely attaches himself to anyone for long. Lovers—let alone mates—complicate things, and Zephyr doesn't like complications he can't control. How did you leave things?*

I replenished my supply of ink from the vial. *He said: please, let's talk. I ran.*

That male never says please to anyone. A pause. *So that begs the question…what made you run?*

How could this magic be so innocuous when my meteor-infused magic was so monstrous? *I almost killed Ferrith and Loxley.*

Maybe they deserved it, came the retort. *If you're going to feel guilty every time you almost maim someone, you're going to have a very tedious existence.*

The knot in my stomach loosened a little. *Do you ever fear your own magic?*

I coaxed a splutter of ink through the universe, malformed and meaningless. I understood her well enough to know I had rubbed against a wall of vulnerability and that patience was required. After a few moments, I felt the tug again that told me she had decided to share.

I revel in it. Elowen wrote, *Xaire's magic manifested as a youngling, but mine took its sweet time. Now I find it advantageous only to share its full extent with very few people. Be careful who you choose to trust, sister.*

She didn't ask me about what new magic I had discovered. Either she didn't believe that she had earned my trust, or her family had so damaged her that she was accustomed to unequal relationships. It made me sad that, in Elowen's place, Maren would have demanded I spill the beans.

I hadn't told anyone, not even Zephyr, that Elowen's psychic communication stretched beyond Xaire. It wasn't my secret to tell. *Enough about me. How is everything your end?*

The ink was blotchy, as if her quill had been pressed with an unsteady hand. *My parents have been treating me poorly, but that is not unusual...*

My chest constricted. Sometimes I could read her pauses as well as my own. *Danaë is not torturing you?*

When her words finally appeared, they were smaller, tighter. *No, she would never do that. Not to her children.*

A rush of quiet fury stirred in me. She had no qualms about hurting my father. *What aren't you telling me?*

Blots of ink preceded her answer. *They sense the quiet shifts in my rage. That makes them uneasy. The leopards circle me as though I am a threat. Father no longer binds my mouth every suppertime, but I guard my silence all the same.*

I drew a sharp breath. *One day, when you are ready, I'll help you make them regret every stolen word.*

The ink was smoother this time, loving almost. *I will hold you to that promise, sister.*

Stars, if they found out—if they noticed how she had begun to hope for something beyond their grasp—I wasn't sure what they would do. *How did Danaë become fae? Was it a spell, a bargain, a sacrifice, a curse? How did her voice become her sword?*

A tug, and her response spooled out. *Father set her change in motion. At first, his gifts of the snow leopards and whisper ring were deemed enough protection, in addition to guards. But Faerie is treacherous, and fae are cunning. A kelpie pair lured Mother into the mist-choked Frigid Basin shortly after Xaire and I were born. Then faerie revellers under a blood moon gave the snow leopards a sleeping draught and dragged Mother to a masquerade deep beneath a hill. Father hacked them to pieces.* There was a pause as if she replenished her ink. *He realised Mother needed to be stronger. As Spymaster, he trades secrets to achieve his aims.*

My grip tightened around the quill. *What did he trade?*

That I do not know. He and Mother travelled to the Wraithwoods, and when they returned, we were forbidden from her chamber for a month while healers attended her. Xaire said she had bitten out her own tongue. When we saw her again, she had lost her mortal softness and stopped ageing. Maybe she ate a certain fruit or danced under a specific moon. I don't know. After Wraithwoods, her voice didn't just captivate. It could cause devastation. She can hold crowds in her thrall. She makes her enemies double over in pain and bleed from every orifice. She breaks bones and charms storms. My father considers her his greatest success.

I exhaled slowly, wondering how Elowen's life might have been different if Danaë had stayed soft and mortal. Would her mother have sung to her at night, voice low and warm, like she had with me? Would Echohold have smelled of honeyed tea and wildflowers instead of cold steel and warding salts?

Maybe Elowen would have known gentler things: what it meant to fall asleep in someone's arms, to cry without shame, to grow up without the weight of legacy clawing at her spine. Maybe she wouldn't carry herself like someone always waiting for a knife in the dark. The mortal version of her mother would have made Elowen happier, but this one had made her a survivor.

I frowned. *Will Xaire stay quiet about our alliance?*

The words, when they arrived, were smudged as if streaks of tears had run through them. *Xaire is practical. He won't risk alienating me unless he's certain it will benefit him. But we can't rely on his silence.*

Her response wasn't exactly reassuring, and I didn't like to leave her with such heavy thoughts. *My family web is as knotted as yours. Tanuhja keeps sending me gifts. As if gold and silks can mend the past, and she can tempt me to step back into her orbit.*

You have my condolences. Gold and silks? She could at least throw in a kingdom or a curse-breaking blade. To possess a wit so sharp and to be gagged by her own court—her own family—was an unforgivable crime.

With each passing day, it became harder to leave her there. *Elowen, you do understand? We can't just spirit you away. We have to concoct a plan, a bargain, a way to shield the gatehouse again.* But my friends and family couldn't even eat a meal together without chaos unfolding, let alone formulate a plan.

A splurge of ink formed into letters. *Refuge is found in people, not places.*

You have my word, we'll come for you as soon as we can.

I waited, but she didn't respond, and my stomach tightened, imagining her trying to give shape to her disappointment. I sensed the edges of her resolve fraying. I wasn't sure if her brittle heart could endure in that hollow palace, where love was wielded like a weapon.

Twelve moons—a full cycle of the seasons—had seemed ample time when I made the bargain.

Now, it felt like a countdown.

7

ZEPHYR

Border merchants dwell where courts meet and collide, their tents, caravans, and stalls a mosaic of cultures and magics. They are the lifeblood of Faerie's margins, trading secrets as well as spices and wares, their loyalties as fluid as the shifting borders they inhabit.
— A Tapestry of Courts and Crowns

H e pushed hard, leaning into Mythros's wild flight, without a single thought to his safety, Ysa's wounded expression emblazoned on his psyche. Zephyr had brushed off Cyprian when he'd wanted to follow. He didn't give a damn about the rules he'd so carefully set: the ones meant to keep them all safe, to keep *her* safe—no solo excursions, especially beyond the warded perimeter.

He just needed to think.

Mythros sensed his turmoil and moved like a creature

possessed, muscles rippling, unbothered by the narrow paths or the sharp turns. The wind tore through Zephyr's hair, and the jagged rocks below blurred into a treacherous smear. He welcomed the speed, the sheer force of movement to drown out the doubts and the ache.

To care for a mate was like carrying a blade pressed to his ribs, sharp and ever-present. Yet, somehow, he wanted it there. The depth of feeling unsettled him. There was something terrifying in how natural it felt. How instinctive. As if some ancient part of him, long dormant, had been waiting for her. His magic recognised her. His soul knew her. His body couldn't get enough of her. His regard for her well-being had entwined with his own so seamlessly that he could no longer tell where he ended and she began. Ysa was a part of him now, as much as the shadows that curled at his command.

He was no stranger to war, to strategy, to control.

But this was the first tussle he had no idea how to survive.

For over a century, his choices had been his alone, the risks his to take. It scared him that he had known Ysa for mere weeks, yet had developed such a need for her. He'd protected his heart since his mother and sister had been killed.

Yes, he had mercenaries, Mythros, and even the monsters. He had bled for them, fought beside them, and worked himself to the bone to make a better life for them. He'd lay down his life for any one of them without hesitation. But they gave him space when he needed it; none demanded entry past the walls he'd carefully constructed.

Ysa was different. The mate bond wasn't something he

could keep at a safe distance. The calligrapher's daughter was all-consuming. She had been from the first moment he had crouched in the grass at her feet at Bloomtide.

When she was happy, the bond was a thing of quiet beauty, gold spilling across dark waters. It cooled him when his temper flared, soothed him when exhaustion dragged at his bones. It did not demand. It did not take. It simply flowed.

But when rage or sorrow filled her, the river of the bond wound around his ribs like a constricting tide. Or worse, an icy tide, like the meteor's coldness had enveloped her. She swept him into her storm and drowned out reason. That terrified him more than any battlefield because he needed to think and plan to keep his loved ones safe.

Above all, how else could he keep *her* safe?

Zephyr had already lost so much. Sometimes, he woke up sweating after reliving how his uncle had burrowed his dagger into Ysa's stomach.

Shuddering, he closed his eyes, lashes sweeping against wind-chilled skin, sensing how Mythros's muscles coiled and released like a bowstring loosed again and again. He didn't hesitate when they curved dangerously close to the edge of the cliffs, and he barely needed the reins at all. A memory snuck up on him: Veda laughing, brushing a hand over his unruly hair with choice wisdom he wasn't ready to hear.

"The mate bond will unravel you, little brother. It will be a storm inside your ribs. You won't be able to break it. And you won't want to."

He'd stuck out his tongue. "I'll swap the mate bond for a warhorse."

Veda's eyes had been alight with knowing. "You'll have one of those, too."

He opened his eyes to the present, though his heart was still stuck in the past. Back then, he had been wild and untamed, too smart-mouthed for his own good. To think of how he had wasted the opportunity to pry her with questions. Now Veda was gone.

What he wouldn't give to tell her she was right. Nothing had prepared him for the truth of it—his magic rose and thrummed at the mere thought of Ysa, his instincts sharpened, the bond hummed in his marrow and made a home beneath his skin.

The first time he touched Ysadora—truly touched her —was like grasping the hilt of a blade forged just for him: familiar, fated, and dangerous all at once. Her warmth seeped into his skin, into his bones, into the spaces he hadn't even realised were cold.

The curve of her waist beneath his hands, the way her breath hitched when he got too close, set something primal alight in his chest. When she moved, his instincts followed, drawn like the tide to the pull of the moon. She pressed against him, sometimes unthinkingly, without meaning to, and it wrecked him all the same. A single glance, a single touch, and he was ready to carry her to bed.

By the lore, his sister had been right. He was unravelling.

Mythros whinnied, and Zephyr spied the stall in the distance. He'd seen it before, had half-hoped it would be there today. It stood at the edge of the road, cobbled together from driftwood and weathered canvas, strung with faded ribbons. It bore the look of something that had stood here for a century but could vanish overnight without a trace.

Zephyr eased Mythros to a halt and swung down from the saddle. Unfastening the water skin from his saddlebag, he tugged the cork free with his teeth. With a practised hand, he tipped a stream of water into his cupped palm and offered it to Mythros.

The horse drank eagerly, dark eyes half-lidded in pleasure. A few stray drops clung to his velvet muzzle. Zephyr wiped them away with a rough swipe of his thumb before giving the horse a firm pat.

"Stay here, old friend." He strode towards the stall, dust coating his boots.

Beyond the stall, the land stretched in wild, rolling meadows, broken only by a distant scattering of mossy ruins, remnants of a time when this place had been more than a lonely crossroads. Serennor sat farther down the road, a small cluster of thatched roofs and crooked chimneys, smoke curling lazily into the mid-morning air. He scowled at the merchant, an old fae with sharp features half-hidden by the deep hood of his cloak.

The merchant gave him a once-over and smirked. "Rough ride? Or just a rough morning?"

Zephyr arched an eyebrow. "Neither is your business, friend." He added the last word as an afterthought, in case the wiry old fae cursed the item he'd procure for his mate.

Long fingers tapped idly against the counter as he considered the wares: small jars of honeyed nuts, dried lavender, thick squares of golden toffee, lucky charms, flint buttons, and tiny carved animals that carried the scent of wild magic. He almost bought the miniature dragon, but on second thought, pointed at the jar she'd choose.

"A fine pick." Sly eyes studied him. "Perhaps the dragon, too?"

He shook his head. He had to tread carefully. Ysa wasn't ready for any of this.

Zephyr had known she was powerful from their first encounter, even before she realised she was fae, before her dormant magic had unfurled. It was in the way she held herself, refusing to bow, even when it would have been easier. But the meteor had rewritten something fundamental inside her. Her magic rippled in the air like heat off stone, poured from her in barely controlled bursts. It thrummed in the mate bond like a second heartbeat.

Ysa had been remade by something far older than either of them.

He had seen power corrupt, twist, and consume. But even as his mate stood on the precipice of something vast and unknowable, he had faith in her. He was proud of her. How could he not be? She was magnificent.

The sight of her in the breakfast chamber, having created those voids from nothing, made him want to shout to the world: she is *mine*. She learned quickly and adapted faster. He couldn't predict what she would become, but that didn't worry him.

Still, there was something about this power that set his instincts on edge.

In the darkest part of the night, after they had sated each other, he wondered if Ysa would become something greater and choose to leave him. He wouldn't keep her from her destiny, even if part of him wanted to. The calligrapher's daughter wasn't his to control or shape.

Moreover, he had learned that power did not change hands without cost. The others worried about Thiago and

Tanuhja hunting Ysadora. But Zephyr knew that power like Ysa's called to the ancient things that slumbered beneath root and rot, that whispered from tangled brambles and hollowed-out trees. Magic like hers was a beacon flaring in the dark. Power did not go unanswered in Faerie.

They would come. Forgotten gods and hungry fae, the ones who prowled the edges of legend, would wake from their long rest. Creatures that fed on power, that bartered in soul-deep oaths and promises laced with venom, would scent her strength on the wind.

Not all at once, nor in the ways he could predict without Veda. Some would send gifts wrapped in sweet words and silk-threaded lies. Others would watch from shadows even crueller than his own, waiting for the perfect moment to strike.

Zephyr knew this because he had seen it before. Wasn't that why his own family had been killed? A queen who altered small details in history and erased or enhanced memories. A daughter who painted foretellings. A young son who drew out the truth and commanded shadows. Just like then, history would repeat itself: he and Ebonspire would fail to keep his loved ones safe. His fists flexed.

It was why he was pushing his mate so hard. It was why he was making arrangements for them all to leave Ebonspire, despite all it meant to him. Despite his concerns about how the monsters would fare. Better to adapt than for any of them to fall prey to Faerie's machinations.

He heaved a sigh. First, he had to get into his mate's good books again. "No. Just the toffee."

A slow smile twisted the merchant's lips. "A rare treat for a warrior. Sweet tooth?"

"It's not for me." He had no idea if Ysa would even accept the damn gift. She had been furious with him when he left. Rightly so. But he found himself here anyway, rolling his shoulders to ease the tension as he dug in his coin pouch. He placed a silver coin on the counter. "Keep the change."

The merchant grabbed Zephyr's wrist before he retracted it, and Zephyr bared his teeth as the old male pushed up the sleeve of his tunic to reveal the thin grey lines of bargains etched onto his bicep: eight in total. "I'd rather have one of these."

By the time Zephyr finished executing his plans, there would be many more bargain lines on his skin. He had been surprised by which courtiers were willing to bargain. It was almost as if allegiances were shifting, unseen.

He turned his attention back to the merchant. "No."

The merchant shrugged and released him, before tucking away the coin quicker than a kelpie dragging a fool beneath the waves. He took his sweet time working the twine and gauze free from the jar with spindly fingers. Eyeing the toffee, he licked his lips. "I hope she's worth the trouble."

"She is." Behind him, Mythros stamped with impatience.

"The crossroads weren't always so empty. The roads whisper warnings to those who listen. A storm is coming…bigger than tempests, bigger than kings. Even the crows have fled."

Zephyr's expression darkened, and his shadows readied, just in case an ambush awaited. Stupid, really, for him to be out here with only daggers strapped to his thighs. Thiago could emerge from a portal and make him disappear from where he stood, and then where would Ysa and his family of mercenaries be?

His mood grew grimmer still. Although if he had anything to do with it, it would be *him* making Thiago's life more difficult. "Are you selling or not?"

A chuckle, low and knowing. "Patience, warrior. Even the stars take their time to shine." He made a show of smoothing out crisp parchment, then laid out five pieces of toffee, and another after a pause. Eventually, he tied the bundle up and slid it across the counter. "May your gift be well received."

Zephyr nodded, slid the toffee into his pocket and turned back towards Mythros. The stallion was irked to have been kept waiting for so long, with not even a pitted date or velvet fig for his trouble.

Zephyr swung into the saddle and reached for the bond, sensing the change in the river that ran between him and Ysa. She was no longer furious: the churning current told him she was anxious. He kicked himself for keeping so much from her. For causing her pain when he'd intended to protect her.

With a click of his tongue, he urged Mythros forward, leaving the crossroads behind.

"Mind your step, warrior," the merchant called after him. "The road ahead is paved with bargains and bones. Try not to add yours to the pile."

Zephyr didn't look back as he picked up speed and rode for Ebonspire and his mate.

8

YSADORA

Thiago sends no flowers or gems to Larkspur, just a whisperwind, his voice laced with hush. He says nothing of love, and yet I feel it in the way the air stirs like breath against my throat. The whisperwind said: "Do you still dream of being heard?" I do not answer, but I keep it sealed in a bottle of riverglass, and each night I unstopper it.
– Danaë's annotations in her Faerie books

The mate bond flared like the first light after an eclipse: brilliant and impossible to ignore. It was like a bridge rebuilt in an instant, as if Zephyr had restored it with nothing more than a flick of his will.

Beneath it all was a quiet thought that wasn't mine. *You need me.*

I swallowed hard. Need was dangerous. Need was surrender. I could try to shut him out, but his presence seeped into me like ink into parchment, an inevitability I could not erase. In all honesty, I didn't want to fight it. I didn't want to lock him out and sit in the cold silence that would follow. My fear of vulnerability warned of all the ways our relationship could break me, but something ancient whispered back: this was not a trap, it was not a cage.

It was a choice, and stars help me, I wanted to choose Zephyr.

The thought travelled through the bond again, insistent. *You can deny it all you want, but you need me.*

This time, I didn't argue. *I need to see you.*

Good, came the thought through the bond, laced almost with tenderness.

Resolve straightened my spine. I would tell Zephyr and the others that tricking me was unacceptable. *All of you.*

I sensed the wicked quirk of his lips. *That can be arranged.*

Heat warmed my cheeks as I corrected him. *All of the group.*

It's a little early in our relationship for that. I'm not sure I'll ever be ready to share.

If only the bond were a slingshot instead. *To talk. We need to set things right as a group.*

His voice tingled down my spine. *Meet me alone first. I'm in the stables rubbing down Mythros. I have a gift for you.*

My sigh was threaded with the faintest bite. *Now I'm allowed to exit the gatehouse alone?*

His voice rumbled, low and sure. *Only this time. There are fewer ears here. Nothing can happen to you with me at your side.*

I didn't know whether to kiss or kill him, but a smile played on my lips as I made my way outside. It didn't unnerve me to visit the stables, despite how the Faerie King of Silence had breached Ebonspire's wards to infiltrate them mere weeks ago, because it was true: I had utter faith that Zephyr would keep me safe.

My mate sent his shadows to escort me. The warmth of the afternoon did little to dispel their presence. They moved with the confidence of creatures that belonged to neither light nor dark, only to him. One looped around my wrist in a fleeting touch, urging me forward, and I fought against gauche shyness at the thought of seeing him.

We were so new, the need between us so strong. We hadn't yet established patterns between us. I didn't know how to fight with Zephyr or how to make up, who would sour and who would cajole. I didn't know whether our mate bond meant that fights were meaningless, whether he would disregard my feelings because we were irrevocably entwined. I didn't know if that made us less or more.

When I entered the stables, Zephyr was smoothing out a wool blanket across a stack of hay bales, his broad frame half-lit by the slanting sun. He placed a small package on the blanket and turned, stormy eyes lingering on me just long enough to make my breath hitch. He noted the ink stains on my hands and the droop of my shoulders, and I returned his scrutiny just as boldly.

The scent of the road clung to him: dusty earth, salt air, a hint of male musk post-exertion. A lock of wind-tousled hair lay against his forehead. There was a looseness to his stance, the kind that came after hard riding, but the edge to him told me that the ride hadn't soothed the bitter sting of our argument despite his confident invitation.

I lifted my chin. "Did you need the scent of hay and leather to cool your temper while we talked?"

"I'm trying to make amends." He extended his palm towards me, fingers curled. "Come here."

Not a command. An offering. When I didn't move, one dark brow arched.

He brushed against the bond with a featherlight touch. "Or do you need more convincing?"

My pulse stuttered in my throat. "I can't think when I am near you."

Zephyr let out a low laugh. "Welcome to my hell."

I walked into Mythros's stall to keep a fraction of space between us, in case my composure unravelled completely. The stallion let out a soft nicker and nuzzled the palm I offered him, his warm breath brushing my fingers.

"Seriously? You're my damn warhorse," Zephyr muttered under his breath, but I knew he liked the rapport between us by the softness of his gaze.

I offered another affectionate scratch along Mythros's inky coat and said to Zephyr, "You make everything impossible."

He leaned against the stall, arms folded. "Do I?"

It wasn't true, of course. I was capable of so much more than I'd ever thought possible since I'd met him. "You didn't just ignore my wishes. You crushed them underfoot like wilted petals."

His mouth pressed into a line. "That's fair. I've been a fool."

"Do you regret having us in your home?"

Zephyr blinked in disbelief. "Of course not. You and your kin belong with me."

"I don't want to be someone you trick, even if it's with good intentions."

"Understood." One corner of his mouth lifted. "Anything else, while you're in such a forthright mood?"

"Yes, now you mention it. Where do you go before I wake?" I skimmed light fingers over Mythros.

He sighed. "I've been scouring old ballads for mentions of meteor-touched fae, and—"

"You didn't think, having grown up in a book shop, that I could help with that?"

The stallion skittered backwards at my injured tone.

"You've been adjusting to losing your home, to your magic, to *me*."

Father had made the same mistake. I wondered if it was me. If I were weak. "What did you find?"

You're not weak. I've never considered you weak, Zephyr assured me through the bond. "I found nothing to set our minds at ease."

My mind whispered insidious possibilities. Fear curled cold in my stomach, remembering what it felt like to create that void, remembering the wild, merciless thrust of power. "What if I can't tame my magic? What if it tames me instead?"

"You won't lose yourself. Not while I breathe. Ysadora—" He rarely used my full name. "Come sit with me on the blanket."

When my mate held out his hand, I took it, and his thumb drew lazy circles on my palm. Straw crunched beneath his boots as he stepped onto the hay bales, thighs flexing. His hands found my waist, and he scooped me up onto the blanket in one smooth motion. The warmth of our bodies sang through the bond, and he stepped carefully away. When he sat and stretched out his legs, I followed suit, though I tucked my legs to my chest.

"What do you need from me?" Zephyr asked.

I didn't need blind loyalty or duty. When the storm broke over us—and it would—I needed to know that he wouldn't lock me away in a cocoon of shadows or put his body between me and the fight as if I were something fragile to be preserved. I needed someone who would let me walk into the storm with him.

I tightened my arms around my knees. "I want to be the one you discuss your plans with. To be your equal and stand beside you as we build the world we want."

I didn't know if he could do it. Even amongst the mercenaries, he'd carried his burdens alone. I searched his face for resistance, for some flicker of the arrogance that came so easily to him, for the ironclad will he wielded so easily in battle and strategy alike, but there was none—just quiet consideration.

A muscle ticked in his jaw as he turned my words over in that sharp mind of his, testing their strength against his instincts. "Is that all, or do you have other demands, Inkheart?"

My pulse accelerated as he shifted to face me. "I need you to never shut me out of the bond. Swear it."

Zephyr exhaled, his voice rough at the edges. "I swear it."

He did something to the bond then, like the loosening of a fist that had been clenched too tightly—then—stars. The bond yawned open, raw and unrestrained. For the first time, I truly felt him—not just the faint echoes I'd grown used to, but the full weight of his psyche.

I gasped, my breath stolen by the sheer force of his emotions crashing into me: his exhaustion, his determination, his fierce love for his kin, his sense of duty to the monsters, the aching grief for his mother and sister, the sharp edge of fear that had nothing to do with our enemies but everything to do with *me*, his need to build a better world, and his scheming about how to achieve it.

Most of all: a love for me as enduring as the mountains, woven into the core of him. Skies, the depth of his desire. His every thought, every instinct, every carefully guarded emotion had me at its centre. My whole body thrummed from the connection between us.

His jaw was tight, his breathing uneven. "I didn't want to overwhelm you."

The tension between us coiled tighter, electric and inevitable. Then my mate tugged me towards him, the sheer mass of his body dwarfing mine. His hands slid to my waist, and he claimed my mouth. His mouth moved over mine, sucking, nipping.

Heat pooled low in my stomach as his hands splayed against my back. Then he moaned my name and tangled his hand in my hair, tilting my head to deepen the kiss. I gasped softly, and he swallowed the sound. My hands smoothed over the planes of his body, the way his heartbeat drummed against my palm. When I reached lower, to the hip bones beneath his waistband, and my fingers ghosted over where he strained against his breeches, he emitted a guttural sound.

"Witch." He pulled me flush against him as if he could

fuse us into one. "Eyes like rain-washed sapphires, hair like spilt ink, skin like warm silk…"

My eyes fluttered open. "You missed your calling as a bard."

He laughed then, his teeth nipping at the column of my throat in punishment for my teasing.

I didn't want my clothes on, didn't want any barrier between us. Zephyr watched me undress, taking in the pink of my newly healed wound, the lines and circles of my runes, the ink smudges on my hands, sweeping his gaze over me as though he was committing every inch of me to memory.

I heard the rustle of his belt, and he removed his clothes, moving with quiet confidence while I waited with breathless need. He pulled his tunic over his head, each ridge of his abdomen cast in the slanting barn light, his burnished bronze skin marked with scars.

The breadth of his shoulders, the cut of his hip bones, the smattering of hair on his muscled thighs—he was exquisite. There was no hesitation in his movements. Only the haughty certainty of a male who knew what he wanted, and knew that I wanted him just as much.

"Hurry." I cupped my breasts as he muttered a curse.

He threw the last garment aside and guided me down onto the blanket. The haystack beneath us shifted as his hard warmth settled over me. His scent—wild moss and leather—wrapped around me as his lips found the curve of my jaw, then the hollow at my collarbone, and the valley between my breasts, his touch both reverent and possessive.

Stars, his mouth, his teeth, his kneading hands. I returned every kiss, every stroke, pausing over half a dozen marked lines I'd never noticed before on his right bicep. All logical thought fled as he roamed lower, and I bucked into his hand when he brushed me with his knuckles, roughly, then dipped a single teasing finger into my core.

"Hold still." Shadows looped around my wrists.

"You wretch," I whispered, writhing as he withdrew his hand and raked his gaze over me.

"Do you like that?" he murmured as he caught my lips with his.

"Stars, yes."

His forehead pressed against mine for the barest moment before his fingers entered me again and he claimed my mouth again, hotter, wilder. He knew exactly where to work me, exactly where I needed attention. My pleasure ramped up, and I barely held on.

The bond was open, and with it, there were no more secrets, no more barriers. Every breath, every lick, every caress of his shadows sent a fresh wave of heat through me, amplified by our connection. His desire surged through the bond, crashing into mine, feeding it, deepening it until I could no longer tell where he ended and I began.

I arched against him, and he released his shadow bonds from my wrists as he bent his dark head to take my rosy peaks in his mouth. My hands threaded his hair as he lapped each breast in turn, flicking his tongue across the bud, swirling until I bit down on my palm, until my hands clawed against the hay, against his back, and my legs hooked around his waist.

I felt everything: his hunger, his need, the way he was holding himself back for my pleasure.

"Your wetness," he groaned, "is taunting me."

I got onto my knees then and took him in my mouth. He shuddered when my tongue worshipped the salty taste of him, tangling his hands in the lengths of my hair. I cupped him and stroked him. When his moans faded into concentrated stillness, I tipped him back onto the hay bales and lowered myself onto him with a thin gasp, not caring if we spooked the horses, not caring if the whole realm heard as my hips moved against his. The friction took my breath away. He filled me so deeply, the bond between us hummed with such life that the universe—so frighteningly large since the meteor's touch—narrowed to us.

He cupped my face in his palm. "Look at me, Ysa."

Our eyes locked. "It's more than I can take."

His breath was ragged, and his plea reached me. *Ride with me, Inkheart.* He rolled me onto my back and thrust deeper, hard, harder still, until my fingers dug into his shoulders, desperate, seeking something to anchor myself against the storm of sensation. He was right there with me, his shadows grounding me even as his own control frayed.

"Together," he said. "Good girl."

He was breathtaking, the golden light through the roof slats illuminating his gleaming masculinity. I shattered in his arms, pleasure streaking through me like lightning, bright and blinding. He was beside me in a way that went beyond touch, beyond flesh. It wasn't just desire. It was devotion.

Afterwards, we were deliciously sated. We watched the sunlight bleed through the roof as we caught our breath. The sting of the day started to fade, if not the worry.

Zephyr pulled me against his chest and dusted a kiss on my brow. "Speak your thoughts."

"Elowen thinks her parents are suspicious of her."

He stilled. "I remember how that feels. I'll ask Father to look out for her."

"You'd do that? Mend things with your father?"

When he spoke, his voice was steady, as if old wounds could be set aside just like that. "For you, anything."

"How will you get a message to him under Thiago's nose? With my ink magic?"

"No, my love. I'll find a willing servant to carry a whisper wind, echo stone or moth courier to him. In Faerie, anything is possible, especially when I can be certain the other party won't betray us."

He said it as though it were simple, as though there were no risk, as though the act of slipping a message through the shifting veils of power in Faerie was as easy as passing a note between courtiers at a mortal banquet.

But I knew better from the texts he brought me still. The whisper wind would have to be caught at just the right moment, prepared with utmost care so no other could steal its message before it reached its intended recipient.

An echo stone could carry the words safely, locked within the crystal depths until the one it was meant for touched it—but stones could be lost, intercepted, cracked open by those with enough power.

And moth couriers, if chosen well from the swarm, could find a person across impossible distances, slipping through veils and unseen paths. But they had to know the scent of the recipient to stand a chance of success.

"Are you sure your father won't betray us?"

"It would be my first ask since leaving the Court of Silence. I think he will listen. If not for me, then the love he bore my mother." He said it so casually, but the star that represented him in my mind dimmed, as if under a cloud of sorrow.

I laced my fingers with his. "And if he doesn't agree?"

His gaze settled on me, dark and steady. "Then I will have misjudged how to use the last of my father's goodwill. And I will find another way. For you and my cousin, it is not too much trouble. Speaking of which, I almost forgot…" He reached across and handed me a package with an almost boyish smile. "A peace offering."

I accepted it with a shy smile and smoothed out the crinkles of the paper. The scent of caramel sweetness seeped into my nose as I unwrapped it to reveal glossy pieces of toffee, dusted with sugar. I placed a piece in my mouth and closed my eyes as it melted, a thousand times tastier than the mortal toffee. "You know the way to my heart."

A lone dimple studded his left cheek. "I'm learning."

"Thank you." Somehow it seemed right to voice my fear out loud. "Zephyr, what if my magic makes me a monster?"

"If the world calls you a monster, I'll teach it to fear you on your terms. I would love you even then."

I thought of the monsters in the belly of Ebonspire—creatures, feared and forsaken, with jagged wings and hollowed-out eyes, with talons sharp enough to carve through bone and voices that had long since forgotten softness—and I believed him.

He never flinched from the dark, never loved in halves or with conditions. Zephyr had the capacity to love broken things. They had a home at Ebonspire and a place at his side. He did not see ruin and recoil—he saw what could be remade, what could still be whole, even in its brokenness.

But if I did something unforgivable, would he still look at me the way he did now? Would he still reach for me, still call me his? Could I still love myself?

His gaze darkened, and I wondered how much of my thinking he discerned from the bond. I was so peaceful in his arms that I didn't want to ruin it. The steady rise and fall of his chest was a lullaby against my cheek. The troubles waiting beyond his embrace felt like they belonged to someone else. He stroked my hair as I nibbled on the toffee, and after some time, I traced the new lines of scars on his bicep with a quizzical look.

"Care to tell me where you got these?"

There was the smallest pause in his breathing. "Your power calls to all the power hungry in Faerie. I think the time will come when we have to leave Ebonspire. I've been arranging sanctuary for the monsters in case that happens."

My brow furrowed. "You've been making bargains to keep the monsters safe."

He gave a bitter laugh. "It turns out many across Faerie are in need of my skills."

"You think we'll have to leave." We'd only just made Ebonspire our new home. It wasn't exactly a surprise, but stars, this gatehouse meant so much to us all, but especially him. "Zephyr…"

"No, don't look at me like that." He ran a possessive hand over my naked body and squeezed my bottom. "I'll do all it takes to keep our kin safe. Look, there's stuff you need to know. I'm due to meet the others in the war room. After you've made yourself decent, meet us up there."

Did he sense through the mate bond that I knew *exactly* where the war room was? I kissed him. "No walls between us."

"No walls between us," he repeated, eyes darkening with desire again. "And Inkheart? Maren and Ferrith may come."

"Can we distract ourselves from our troubles first?"

He smiled and bent his mouth to mine. The warmth of his kiss melded with the toffee sweetness lingering on my tongue.

9

YSADORA

You must not waver, even when doubt creeps in.
Every truth we've omitted is a thread in the veil
that keeps Ysa hidden.
Let them call it betrayal. We will call it love.
– Cairn's note to Maren, delivered in the hollow
of the old ash tree in Larkspur

Maren scrambled out of bed at my knock, one foot tangled in the sheets as she reached for her tunic. Sunlight spilt through the closed curtains, and Ferrith lay back, eyes half-lidded, still catching his breath. The scent of musk and lingering pleasure was thick in the air. Though glad Zephyr had gone ahead to the war room, sensing my need to make amends privately, I couldn't wait to paint this scene for him.

Relief flooded through me. "*This* is what you've been doing? I thought you were angry at me."

Her cheeks flushed. "I was angry. I feel better now that I've checked Ferrith is okay."

I met their eyes, heart heavy. "I'm sorry about earlier."

Ferrith sat up. "We know. It's okay."

Maren tied her hair back. "With books, you're ravenous to learn. Why not with magic, Ysa?"

"Books don't rewrite who I am."

Maren sighed. "It's the world we live in now. Get dressed, Ferrith, before those dawn-rising mercenaries decide we're good for nothing."

"Yes, matron. Although it's too late for that."

She threw his breeches at him, and he ducked just in time, the fabric sailing past him. Then she turned to me with a grin and plucked hay from my hair. "You made up with Zephyr, then."

I blushed. "He's invited us to the war room. All three of us."

Frowning, Ferrith tugged on his shoes. "Why would they invite me? Unlike you two, I'm unclaimed by court or craft. The whisper ring is the only thing that gives me an edge.

"Who cares what they think?" said Maren. "We need you."

I hooked my arm through his, and there was a little resistance, as though he hadn't quite forgiven me for what happened at breakfast. "Come on, or they'll start without us."

We made our way along the hallway and up the winding stairs. I couldn't help thinking that Elowen would find it as hard to fit in as Ferrith. Sometimes, I caught myself still thinking in mortal terms: assuming whispers wouldn't be heard, that shadows offered true concealment, that strength was measured in muscle alone.

But Faerie played by different rules. I had seen it in the way Zephyr's cunning was more effective than his brute strength, how Cyprian's time magic allowed him to read a room before a single word was spoken, in the unnatural stillness of Sequoia before she struck.

This invitation to the war room was crucial to us working as a family. When we arrived at the top of the stairwell, I used ink magic to hear through the runed war room walls, hoping to ease my nerves. Drawing out my quill and ink pot, I pressed my hand to the wall. The ink swirled into a transcription of the discussion inside, the war room's secrets bleeding into the air in black loops.

We stared at the words forming.

In Rowena's day, the price of entry here was information. By its tone, that was Loxley.

Ysa's price of entry is being Zephyr's mate. I was almost sure that was Cyprian.

And the queen Veda painted. Much more likely to be Wylda than Sequoia.

No. It's surviving what none of you could. My heart skipped at Zephyr's conviction.

Ferrith winced. "They don't sound in a conciliatory mood."

I knocked against doors carved with snarling beasts and curling thorns. "Please let's try and get along." The engravings twisted into ever more gruesome shapes with every errant sunbeam, and then the door folded inwards.

Cyprian beckoned us in with a flourish. "We wondered where you were. Welcome to the war room."

We eased past him into the war room, which had

existed since Zephyr's mother's reign. Its former grandeur had dulled into something more lived in. Narrow window slits let in meagre light, casting long shadows over the mercenaries inside. Wax dripped from iron sconces, pooling like melted bones onto the cold flagstones. The air carried the scent of the mineral damp of stone and dried ink that called to my magic. Shelves of ledgers and scrolls lined crooked shelves. No weapons cluttered this space; those belonged in the armoury. An oval darkwood table dominated the room, scarred with knife marks, burn stains and the ghost of maps pressed too long into the grain.

Zephyr stood with his arms braced against the table, studying a rough sketch of unfamiliar terrain. Whatever had driven them to gather was no idle conversation. At our entrance, he straightened, made to roll the map up and on second thoughts left it open, as if remembering our pledge.

He beckoned me to his side. *There you are.*

Sequoia, sitting at the table, playing with a knife from her belt, didn't bother with a greeting. Her boot was propped on the edge of a chair, and she kicked it out for Cyprian when he returned to the table.

Loxley leaned back against a bookshelf, tracing the rim of a silver goblet. "Make yourselves at home."

A mercenary learning manners. Wonders never cease, I said through the bond.

I had a word with him. A smile ghosted over Zephyr's lips. *And please, don't tar me with the same brush as the loose cannon.*

You're far too calculated to be a loose cannon. I pinned Loxley and Cyprian with a stare, and the meteor's magic hummed beneath my skin. "What happened today is the last time any of you trick me. We're on the same team, or you're not in mine."

"Just trying to flush out your magic." Loxley shrugged in Ferrith's direction. "That wasn't personal. Like swatting a fly."

Ferrith squirmed. "It felt bloody personal." He and Maren stood on the outskirts of our circle, beneath a faded banner of blue damask embroidered with two interlocked keys of the Rune of Unveiling, as if not quite sure of their place here.

"We need everyone pulling in the same direction," Zephyr said without heat, but the attention in the room coalesced to a point. "Let's get back to business. We have known for some time now that there are those in Faerie who covet Ysa's gift for calligraphy and chaos. With those gifts, Ysa can rewrite the Grimoire or tear it up in its entirety and reimagine Faerie."

I bit my lip. "I'm putting you in harm's way from external threats just by being here. Not to mention my lack of control."

Cyprian folded his arms across his chest. "We're not afraid *of* you, Ysa. We're afraid *for* you."

Zephyr's teeth glinted. "My contacts tell me that failure hasn't deterred my uncle. He's regrouping and will strike again."

"You should have killed him when you had the chance," growled Loxley.

"You know as well as I do that even our combined power doesn't rival a faerie king's. This time, he'll be even more determined. As Spymaster, he has likely stitched together scraps of information and new loyalties. Whatever gives the edge."

In another life, maybe my stepmother would have sided with me, rather than against me. Maybe her place at the faerie king's side would have made her a valuable ally, rather than a dangerous rival. "Thiago is dangerous, but we have someone on the inside," I ventured. "I've been exchanging letters with Elowen."

Sequoia stuck the point of her knife in the table. "The Faerie King of Silence's daughter is your spy?"

I nodded. Spy. Friend. Sister. I'd work on them accepting her later.

Cyprian frowned at Zephyr. "You tried to help her when you were at that damned court, and she said no. Why now?"

"Because of me." At their blank stares, I pulled up the fabric of my trouser leg to expose one ankle. "Elowen asked for refuge. I struck a bargain." All eyes traced the ouroboros branded there.

My mate sighed. *I must teach you about not rushing into bargains.*

"Well, I'll be damned," said Loxley. "That wakes the wyrm beneath the roots."

Sequoia smirked at him. "I'd say Ysa well and truly meets the entry requirements to the war room, wouldn't you?"

"My cousin has endured endless cruelties." Zephyr flexed his neck. "We're working on bringing her here."

"A sound plan," said Loxley. "That pair treat the snow leopards with more courtesy than their daughter."

Cyprian stared at Zephyr as if he'd grown another head. "I admire you for your need to save everyone in Faerie, but this is a step too far. We barely escaped Thiago last time around. If we force him to endure a further grievance such as conspiring *to steal away his daughter*, he'll portal an army to forlorn corners of Faerie to put his boot to our collective arses."

Maren lifted a hand into the air to display her whisper ring. "Or if he finds out who stole from his vault."

Ferrith sank his head into his hands, and the second whisper ring glinted on his finger. It had been an easy decision for him to wear one, given he was the only mortal amongst us, the only one of us without magic. "Just catch me up here. The gaunt older guy with the shadow magic? Fuck. Maybe I want to go back to Larkspur. Hell, it might be safer reclaiming my spot in King Azeem's army." He risked a glance at Maren, who shook her head. "Thought as much."

Sequoia snorted, clearly enjoying Maren's power over him.

Loxley's expression was grim. "Calm yourself, mortal, before you soil yourself."

Cyprian pressed again. "Thiago was restrained by his lingering affection for you, Zeph. We won't be so lucky next time."

"Do not mistake affection for ambition, or love for need," said Zephyr, quietly.

Maren sighed. "Remind me again why we sent Kazimir and Caldoron away?"

Ferrith shook his head, as if he still hadn't accepted Father's fae name, let alone his dragon.

"His body was broken. Not even Wylda could fix him." Sequoia's wings gave an agitated flick. "Where is my sister? Planting those seedlings shouldn't be taking so long."

Zephyr's gaze snapped to hers. "No one ventures out alone."

"Do you want to buddy up with her for hours while she's fussing over bedding? She spent forty-five minutes debating the merits of moss mulch versus leaf litter. I almost lost my mind."

"She has a point," said Cyprian. "I'd rather face a wyvern. At least they don't lecture you about root systems."

Zephyr rubbed a tired hand across his temple. The weight of decisions—the choices, the consequences—was etched into the lines of his body, an exhaustion deeper than mere fatigue. "As we were saying, Kazimir was in no fit state to remain here, and his presence at the Court of Bones secures a key ally. To keep this family together, we are going to need allies very soon, in addition to power. But this is about more than our freedom and self-determination; it's about a fairer Faerie. My plan is three-fold: stabilising Ysa's magic, securing more allies, and finding a cure for the cursed fae."

"And rescuing Elowen," I added helpfully.

"And rescuing Elowen," my mate repeated.

Loxley took another swig from his goblet. "I hate to say it, brother, but finding a cure is even more of a pipedream than rescuing Elowen. For all our efforts, cursed fae don't tend to recover. They rot or rupture. If a cure existed, someone would've sold it for a mountain of coin by now. This is something older and crueller than a spell. Maybe that's why Gabor's sacrifice broke its hold."

Sequoia carved off the tip of one braid with her knife. "If we had an inkling of how Tanuhja engineered it, we'd stand a chance." Her eyes flicked to me as though my mother's actions were mine to remedy. "But we're past guesses in the dark."

Zephyr's jaw ticked. He had nursed hopes that Gabor's return to his normal self in his last moments held some clue, but without death magic, there was no way to test the theory, and he wouldn't sacrifice one monster to save the others. To Zephyr, each life was precious.

When his eyes found mine, they were clear, though his star spun out of rhythm in the mate bond. "All three parts of my plan require us to leave Ebonspire before others come for us. We've been preparing for this."

Maren balled her fists. "This doesn't feel right. It's too abrupt."

Zephyr had a faraway gaze that swept across the war room, focusing not on us, but perhaps on a distant memory. "We've all gotten so comfortable in our lives at Ebonspire—"

"Funny you say that, because this gothic castle has monsters in its basement. Not exactly cosy." Ferrith's blue eyes were intent, snagging on the maps laid across the table. "What preparations have been made? Where will we go?"

My mate hesitated, but he had agreed to trust me, trust those in my inner circle, even if they weren't in his. "We've been moving the monsters, calling in debts, making bargains—" He indicated the grey lines on his bicep. "—in exchange for accommodating them in small groups."

Loxley grunted. "By *we*, you mean *you*. Zeph won't let us share the burden."

Cyprian gave him a knowing glance. "After this morning's mission, nineteen cursed fae remain at Ebonspire."

"Tomorrow, the last of them will be cared for, and then we leave Ebonspire, grouped into mission teams. I will not risk any of you falling into the wrong hands." Zephyr's knuckles were bone white against the table. "But neither will I force this decision onto you. We are a family, and families decide together." He held each of us in his steady gaze, but when his eyes met mine, his mask slipped—just for a breath—and I felt the intensity of his need for me, his certainty that this was the only way. "Make your cases before I call a vote on whether we should leave Ebonspire to fulfil the four points of our plan."

Cyprian folded his arms. "You're not making this easy on us. Claiming Thiago's daughter as one of ours puts us in danger, but I suppose it's no more danger than we already face. We have no choice but to leave. Thiago knows our whereabouts. Losing his battle to control Zephyr wounded his pride. He won't rest until he controls Ysa."

Sequoia's clear brown eyes glinted. "What information did our enemy's daughter feed you, Ysa?"

If I didn't know better, I'd think she was impressed. "Xaire is resentful of the pressure his father places him under. Danaë is ashamed she couldn't get a handle on me, and Thiago plots to become the High King of Faerie. He has built a greenhouse to cultivate the ink plants he stole. And the bloodheart tree is shedding."

Maren and Ferrith exchanged a perplexed look.

"The bloodheart tree only sheds when there is an imminent power change at the Court of Silence. The return of a long-banished monarch, the rise of a new ruler, or a violent surge of magic. It marks the changing of hands, the ascension or destruction of power, and it never lies," explained Zephyr, his eyes narrowing to slits. "It hasn't shed in centuries. Which means we're either on the brink of a shift or it's already begun. Last time, an entire bloodline was wiped from existence."

"Good fortune is with us." A cruel smile played on Sequoia's lips. "Let them fall."

"That would include me," said Zephyr, drily.

"You know as well as I do that you are more Ashmoor than Hendrick. How many endless orbits did your father and Thiago demand that you take their name before they gave up?"

I tried not to mind that she knew little facts about his life that were still alien to me.

"But where? Where will we go?" asked Ferrith.

Loxley refilled his goblet. "A moving object is safer than a still target."

"Will anyone else speak?" Zephyr's throat worked as he swallowed. His gaze swept around the war room, lingering on the Court of Lore banner. "Then we vote. Tomorrow, we leave Ebonspire. Are you with me?"

Maren gawped. "Whole hierarchies are in place to decide such things at the great courts."

Zephyr's storm-cloud gaze was steady. "I know. But we're building something different."

Cyprian's *yes* came first, clipped and authoritative, like a sword striking true. Loxley muttered his like a curse, thumping Zephyr on the back. Maren's voice was clear and defiant, and Ferrith's was hesitant, like his fate had been hemmed in. When my turn came, the bond vibrated faintly with tension.

"Yes," I said, and the smallest breath escaped Zephyr, as though he'd let go of something heavy.

Sequoia stood with a jerking motion. "Where *is* Wylda? There can be no vote without her." She had barely finished speaking when the sconces flanking the war room sputtered out all at once.

Cyprian charged for the window, just as warding runes along the gatehouse flickered, dimming for a fraction of a heartbeat before pulsing back to life. It was subtle, almost imperceptible, but magic didn't stutter without cause. He flung open the window, and the scent of charred iron wafted on the breeze, the unmistakable stench of broken wards. Turning, he met Zephyr's eyes in horror.

Sequoia didn't wait for a command. She sprinted for the window, already palming her knives. Her boots skidded against the stone before she leapt over the sill, her wings snapping open mid-air, Wylda's name on her lips. Her flight was fast and furious, her braided hair an arrow behind her.

I spun around to Zephyr. Shadows had burst from him in a violent, writhing mass, unfurling in jagged tendrils that clawed at the walls and slithered over the stone. His power, usually so measured, thrashed and snarled with unchecked fury.

I had never seen him so angry, so devastatingly lethal. The sharp planes of his face hardened into ruthlessness, and the bond between us shook with his rage, flaring too bright, too hot, clutching at my ribs with a fierce, splintering pressure.

His voice was as cold as tempered steel. "Arm yourselves. We're under attack."

Anyone standing in his path would be reduced to ruin.

10

ZEPHYR

Scorched Ember Wolf: burned hide, smoke pouring from mouth, poker-hot claws. Once Ylva Ashrest of the Court of Languish, twin sister of Caelus, gifted at walking unseen and creating illusory visions.
– The Secrets of Faerie's Veiled Beasts by Zephyr Ashmoor

A surge of rage rose in Zephyr, quickly tempered by a cold, calculated focus. The violation of the sanctuary he'd rebuilt inflamed him, but not as much as the danger it brought to those he loved. He never thought anyone would get this close again. Not after his mother and Veda. Not even after Gabor.

He'd spent his every waking moment preparing Ysa. When she slept, he'd researched, planned, moved the hulking, moaning beasts to their new homes or executed some godsforsaken mission for fae he wouldn't even drink mead with. He thought he'd done enough. That he was a hair's breadth from pulling it off.

The attack shattered his illusions. This was personal: a breach not just of stone walls, but of his ability to keep everyone safe. If anything happened to them, he'd never forgive himself.

Shadow walking had its limits when he carried others with him, and he'd never ask Ysa to abandon her friends. They were made of the same steel that way.

"Ink cloak, whisper rings, now. Arm yourselves, but stay hidden. There's a false wall behind the spear rack in the armoury. If we fall, then get to Mythros." His words were clipped, directed at Ysa and her friends. He was used to giving orders.

The mate bond hummed with calm compliance, but something sharp simmered underneath. He was already turning to Loxley and Cyprian, handing out weapons from behind the false bookshelf in the war room. His mother had intended this place to be one of strategy, but only a fool would have gathered royalty, diplomats and commanders in this room without access to weapons.

"I've sent out shadow scouts. It's not Thiago," Zephyr bit out.

Cyprian palmed the sword, testing its weight. "Another court?"

Behind him, Ysa took her pick from the weapons stash. He tried to focus. "Likely. If Ebonspire falls, we get everyone to safety and reconvene in the Wastelands. No one would think we'd venture there." He turned to Loxley, stomach roiling with what he was about to do. "Release the monsters. We have to give them a chance to survive this."

Loxley gave a grim nod. "Are you sure?"

Zephyr's jaw clenched. He hadn't spent enough time with them. Not to collect their full histories. There was never enough time for that, and he sometimes exhausted himself in his attempts. "It'll thwart my uncle's attempts to create a dark army. They'll cause mayhem. Just take care to avoid their bites."

"I can work with mayhem." Loxley raced for the stairwell, axe in hand.

Zephyr had to trust that Sequoia would secure Wylda's safety. The thought scraped like gravel in his chest. Every heartbeat now was a choice. "Cyp, I'll take the west side of the building. You circle north and deal with what you find. Don't wait, don't warn. Fast and clean. Keep the focus off the others. If it looks messy, fall back. I'm not losing you."

Cyprian gripped his arm, then turned on his heel. Fear burned hot in Zephyr's gut, but his friend—his brother—was cautious. He wouldn't allow himself to get caught in a trap.

Zephyr's body sharpened into a weapon. It was always like this for him in the heat of battle: his mind shifted to counter the immediate threat, blotting out the storm of his emotions. Blotting out even *her*, the one he breathed for, because until Ysa gained more control of her magic, he was the most powerful of them.

If he failed to function, they were all dead.

His shadows were already doing death's work. Within these walls, they were unstoppable. The narrow corridors seemed to drink in his darkness. One by one, the invaders fell, bodies crumpling to the ground without a sound.

There were no weapons, no blood, not even screams: just the soft, unsettling rustle of shadows wrapped around necks, snuffing out lives with methodical, almost detached care.

The Court of Silence had provided him with a taste of shadow magic, but Ebonspire had given Zephyr the means to become a master. Here, the shadows did not merely obey him. They were a manifestation of his sense of belonging, forged over orbits spent living within its walls, breathing its air, and feeling its heartbeat beneath his feet.

After all, Ebonspire was his, and it always would be. It had cradled his family during their brightest and darkest hours. This ground, soaked by his mother and sister's blood, was sacred to him. The shadows whispered to him, moving in silent waves, aware of every crevice, every corner, every breath the invaders took.

He checked the mate bond once, making sure Ysa and her friends were following orders, and relief filled him that they were almost at the armoury. Then he sheathed two long swords across his back—he already had his thigh dagger—and melted into the darkness, moving across his beloved Ebonspire like a predator stalking its prey.

The attackers came in flashes of blinding light, not far from one of the oldest stages of the Court of Lore: figures so radiant that he could barely distinguish their forms. They moved like lightning, almost impossible to track.

Dropping into a crouch, he pulled his shadows around him, senses honing in on the vibrations in the air. A flash of brilliant light cut through the corridor, and Zephyr's instincts kicked in. He shadow-stepped, disappearing from sight just as a sword of pure light slashed through the space where he had been.

Recognition crawled across his skin: their attackers hailed from the Court of Luminosity.

That explained why his shadow scouts hadn't returned. His breath was steady as he materialised in an alcove beside the male. He had been in that court as a child and snuck into it many orbits later to steal an artefact, back when he had hated himself and was reckless with his own skin.

But this wasn't a game. Without the calligraphers maintaining the Grimoire, even seelie courts behaved in unexpected ways. All that passed through his mind as he sliced a dagger across the attacker's throat.

Onwards, through the gatehouse. The world became quiet, each heartbeat measured, each move calculated. Zephyr could hear the soft footfalls of his enemies as they split and scattered throughout the gatehouse.

He slipped from shadow to shadow, towards the flashes of light, tripping up his next opponent with a dark tendril, not even looking down as he took his head from his shoulders. He couldn't afford to show mercy. Not when his people and his home were under threat.

Somewhere, trees heaved and fell, and he knew that Sequoia was rising to the challenge; he recognised the signs of her rage.

On and on, through the gatehouse, completing the work his shadows had begun. His shadows gouged the next attacker's chest, and for a moment, his palm caressed the shocked male's one, just long enough for him to use the gift from his mother's lineage. He roared at the memory he pulled: Wylda, stripped naked and bruised like fruit, her rune used to unlock the gatehouse.

By the ancients, he willed Sequoia to have freed her. To

have drained every drop of the invaders' blood for that cruelty. The need for vengeance settled into his bones with a cold, devastating clarity that burned from the inside out. His family had stood beside him when he was nothing but shadow and scars. They'd been brutalised on his soil. All of it became a crescendo of rage that tightened his instincts and steeled his steps.

He needed to finish this.

His roar had called his enemies to him, and he welcomed their advance as rage poured from him. He blended into the shadows—where there was light, there was always shadow—cracking an invader's skull against the wall and pressing on as the male slumped to the ground.

More light warriors appeared before him. This one was different, more dangerous. His form split into three bright copies, each brandishing a weapon of pure light. A perfect illusion that it took him a moment to decipher. The sting of a burn hit his upper arm as he shadow-stepped, leaving behind nothing but a faint ripple in the air. Grinning sadistically, he smothered the duplicates in inky shadows and felled the male with a diagonal slash of his sword.

By now, he was almost outside. The slithers and growls of released monsters met his ears. He had tended to them for so long he could picture who roamed Ebonspire's training ground, and the thought of it made his knuckles whiten against the hilt of his sword.

Zephyr almost missed the rustle of a cloak, turning at the last moment to witness an inkstream tightening around his attacker like thread around a bobbin. A light sword clattered to the ground, extinguishing on impact.

His mate gave him a small smile as she shrugged off her ink cloak.

Her dark hair was mussed, her violet eyes shining with triumph. *You're welcome*, she said through the bond.

His heartbeat ratcheted up at the sight of her. Had his focus masked the bond, or was she an even quicker learner than he gave her credit for? *I told you to hide with Maren and Ferrith.* He didn't know whether to throttle her or kiss her.

You would have lost a limb if I had. Ysa glared at his arm. *You didn't train me for nothing. And you don't get to choose what I survive.*

Zephyr sighed. He'd always liked stubborn women. *Stay behind me. I swear it, Inkheart.*

She stalked past him, forcing him to follow. In one hand, she held her quill, in the other a dagger. He was reminded of her father's weapon and prayed to the ancients that he'd have a chance to give it to her. If Cyprian had made good progress, the gatehouse itself was by now clear of invaders. That left the grounds.

The air still shimmered with residual magic, the kind that prickled at his skin and made the shadows restless at his heels. His instincts whispered of a trap not yet sprung. He thought of Cyprian, Loxley and the monsters, Sequoia's desperate chase after Wylda. He needed to know they were still whole. Though cautious, Ysa's instincts weren't yet as honed as his.

He caught her wrist before she stepped outside and pulled her flush against him. *Wait.*

The light that spilt over the threshold wasn't sunlight. It was too cold. Too clean. Zephyr's every breath was tight with tension, every footstep angled to silence. One arm wrapped around Ysa's waist, while the other stayed free, fingers curled around the hilt of his sword. She met his eyes, steady and knowing, the quill tucked in the channel of her breasts and the dagger ready in her hand.

Then he stepped sideways into the dark, the liminal space where light bent and sound dissolved, where nothing was solid and she was the only warmth in the weightless dark. Ysa's heartbeat thrummed against his ribs. He looped around the training ground, and the world beyond passed in sound and motion: the clash of steel, the hiss of magic, a distant roar that might have been monster or Loxley's fury.

Zephy didn't linger. He gathered intel like a wolf scenting blood on the wind. Light warriors felled by Wylda and Sequoia, vines sprouting from still glowing orifices and bark tightened around necks. A small group of still-standing attackers moved like fractured sunbeams.

Monsters scattered, one slithering towards the cliffs, two more lumbering in the direction of the Wraithwoods. Loxley shaped the intent of a bear-like beast, its vicious growl turning into a protective roar.

A once-dark grove glowed with false dawn. Sequoia— who had always been as broken as him—seethed and spat her rage as she knelt in the dirt next to Wylda. A faerie king's cloak covered Wylda's nakedness.

Zephyr drank in the monochrome images, and each one stoked his resolve.

When they emerged, it was on a knoll beneath a broken arch where Kazimir's dragon had liked to sleep. Zephyr's grip loosened, but he didn't release Ysa yet. Not while the light still moved like a hunter across his lands. Not while vengeance still simmered beneath his skin. *I needed to see.*

Ysa's violet eyes were wide with dread, as if she had—

in the span of his shadow-step—realised this wasn't a game. *Next time, warn me before you carry me off like stolen treasure.* Her ink cloak had evaporated somewhere along the way.

You are stolen treasure. They've come to take you back. The need to help Loxley clawed at him, but he needed to protect his mate.

Ysa stepped out of his arms and glared in the direction of the enemy, not a hundred metres away. *It's the Court of Luminosity.*

So she had kept her eyes open this time. Later, Zephyr would deliberate over whether their bond meant she had weathered the shadow-step better than others he had travelled with, male or female. *Yes. Pull up your ink cloak.*

She ignored him. *I can't be effective with the cloak and channelling. We help Lox. Then we go for the faerie king as a team.*

He didn't argue. Ysa's clarity cut through the chaos like glass through silk. He rolled his shoulders, shadows coiling along his back like restless serpents, and gave her one of his swords. It was heavier than her frame could manage for long, but he didn't intend to draw this out. *Fine. We stay together and move fast.*

Her expression softened. *You've already seen me die once, Zeph. I'm not planning to make it a habit.* She grasped the sword, swung it once, twice, and checked that the crimson quill nestled in the valley between her breasts was still there.

Gods, he loved her. The mate bond felt like a silken waterfall that he wanted to immerse himself in. *Just don't get ahead of me when we face the faerie king.* Neither of them wore armour, dammit—he wished she'd at least taken some from the armoury—but they were quieter and faster for it.

He took her hand, and they slipped through the fractured light like a whisper, their steps aimed towards the flare of Loxley's steel: wild, bright, just a touch desperate. Then they stepped into the fray. They moved together, not because they were of one mind, but because they trusted each other more than the chaos around them.

Ysa's mouth curved into something sharper than a smile. *Don't slow me down.*

She took off, and the bond between them hummed—taut and focused—as they darted towards Loxley and the light. Towards war and vengeance. She didn't falter even at the bodies Wylda had felled with thorny vines speared through one male's abdomen and another corkscrewed in a copse of trees.

A bolt of radiance cracked the air. His shadows sprang up around them to absorb the hit. Across the training ground, Loxley shouted, calling a monster by its fae name, Ylva, as it lunged in his defence. The monster, a golden wolf, dragged its victim across the soil, and there was no humanity, no mercy, as flesh was torn from bone.

They pressed on towards Lox. Zephyr fought harder now, with his mate a hair's breadth away. The battle whirred: shadow claws and bright steel, broken necks and arteries fountaining with blood. He couldn't let the light blind him or tear him apart, couldn't afford to let the strongest ones get to Ysa.

He cursed as he fought. As light danced around him like a living thing, teasing and blurring the air. These males were more skilled than the ones he had encountered inside, a further clue that their faerie king was near.

Zephyr struck, raking across one warrior's form, but the sword of light slashed through the air, barely missing him as he ducked. He wrapped shadows around the warrior's feet and jerked, but the light bent, reshaped itself, shifting into shields that blocked him.

His failure only made him more furious, more determined. Surging forward, he grabbed the attacker's sword arm, twisting and using the warrior's own momentum to slam him into a broken arch that had once supported a trellis of moonflowers. It collapsed, burying the invader beneath it. Ebonspire protected its own.

He glanced back at Ysa. Her sword was slick with gore. Both blood and ink soaked the soul. The bond snapped between them, full of rage and satisfaction. He wished he had witnessed the flow of her violence.

Loxley thundered towards them, now riding the wolfish beast he had called Ylva. It came to Zephyr then that the wolf hailed from the fallen Court of Languish, just as Cyprian did. She had been a clever choice for Loxley's magic, with a burned ember hide and poker-hot claws that melded with the light, and smoke pouring from her mouth on occasion to obscure her attacks. Loxley rode her hard, and they worked in perfect harmony to axe an invader behind the knees.

Then Lox leapt to the ground, leaving the ember wolf skulking at some distance behind him. He approached them at a thundering run. "About time you showed up. Isn't Ysa supposed to be hiding?"

"Long story." Zephyr raked his gaze across the field.

"Not that long," said Ysa, catching her breath. "I saved him."

"That sounds like a good yarn." Loxley rolled his neck

with a crack. "But first, we have to deal with that one. Looks like this one's been buffing his armour to a shine instead of training."

Their final obstacle before the faerie king had the sun-kissed skin of his court and was heavier in the torso than the legs. Zephyr noted the weight distribution immediately. If he could get low, he could use that to his advantage.

The male didn't seem dismayed by the death of his colleagues, but Zephyr knew well how high emotions dulled instincts. It was the male's calm in the face of three opponents that irked him. He had the quiet confidence of someone who'd climbed to just beneath a faerie king's notice and survived.

That made him dangerous.

The male eyed Ysa as though she were a rare jewel wrapped in silk that he couldn't wait to place at his faerie king's feet. His gaze lingered on her ink-stained fingers, her lips, her waist.

Zephyr felt the chill of it like a blade against his own throat.

"He's mine." Shadows already curled at his boots. He itched to help Cyprian get Wylda and Sequoia off their knees.

"I was hoping you'd say that, outcast." The warrior smiled and lunged.

Light poured from his skin and armour, the kind that made Zephyr crave the dim comfort of drinking dens and the cool wash of a faerie stream. The burning energy made his shadows curl back like smoke in a windstorm.

The male swung arcs of radiant steel that forced Zephyr to dodge rather than parry. Every time he summoned a cloak of shadow, it thinned. The light unmade his magic, layer by layer. Still, he pressed in, baiting the warrior, trying to tire him out, conscious, ever-conscious of his mate's rising emotions, her concern. It fuelled him that she cared as much as it distracted him. But the warrior's movements were too finessed. Mercenaries knew how to fight dirty, to fight with bare knuckles and the odds stacked against them.

Zephyr dropped low, aiming a sweep at the male's legs. "Got you."

The warrior staggered a step, amber eyes narrowing. "Not bad."

"Keep talking like that, and I might think we are destined to be friends."

But the light flared. A pulse blasted from the male's chest like a beacon, sending Zephyr skidding backwards into the dust. His shadows scattered, ragged and limp as torn cobwebs. He braced himself, sprang up and shouted a warning as Loxley flashed in his peripheral vision.

"Let's see what shines when I crack you open, pretty boy." Loxley charged, axe cleaving through the air.

Unlike other fae folk at the Court of Madness, Lox had always been one for fair play in single combat. His influencing powers gave him such a strong advantage that accumulating other advantages made his victories less satisfying. Instead of maintaining a height advantage, he had dismounted again from the ember wolf. The fool.

There was no finesse in his swing, just brute force. His axe was met with a shield of solid light that flared so brightly it left afterimages dancing behind their eyes. Loxley fell back, momentarily blinded. A punch across the jaw sent him tumbling. It was almost insulting in its casualness. As if he wasn't even worth a swing of the sword.

"Is that the best you've got?" Loxley spat blood. "I expected you to hit harder than my mother's ghost."

Zephyr moved then. He didn't announce his displeasure, nor did he posture. One moment, he was shadow, the next his sword was aimed in a low arc at the back of the light warrior's knee.

The light warrior turned just in time, parrying with a blaze of light. "Admit it. You're outmatched."

Loxley came in again from the side. They moved together now, a rhythm forged in war. Loxley struck with bone-splintering strength, and Zephyr was a whisper of precision in between. They almost had him. But their enemy released a burst of light so intense it knocked the air from their lungs.

Loxley dropped to one knee. Zephyr staggered back, shadows flickering like dying moths. They'd brawled in drinking dens, trained against each other, pitted their strength and skills against spies, monsters, and corrupted fae. Against the Faerie King of Silence. But this warrior didn't tire. Like he was charged by the sun.

Either way, Zephyr was out of ideas.

Metres away, the ember wolf tried her luck. She surged in a blur of smoke, fangs bared, poker-hot claws ready. A bellow filled the air as she tore into the light warrior's side and scored skin. Thank the ancients!

But he grabbed her by her scruff. One open palm glowed like the sun. The ember wolf yelped as the force burned through her hide, and Zephyr's shadows couldn't reach her. The light warrior dropped her body unceremoniously to the ground.

The ember wolf, that had been Ylva Ashrest—who Cyprian had taken to a dance long ago—didn't rise.

Zephyr's chest cracked open at the sight of her twitching body before she grew still. He helped Loxley up, and their eyes met. No shame, no retreat. Just the quiet realisation that strength and shadow would not be enough. "He's got orders not to kill us."

Loxley's breath was ragged. "Huh?"

"He hasn't turned those palms on us."

"Fuck, you're right."

"Which means this is a show of power, that's all."

Zephyr frowned as the current of the mate bond quickened and Ysa's resolve surged like the pull of undertow, urging him to brace. He spun to her. She looked nothing like the girl he had met at Bloomtide, more like a myth unspooling into form.

The wind tangled in her inky hair, and for a moment, even his shadows seemed to lean towards her. Her violet eyes were still and deep, as if some vast sea stirred behind them. He sensed the void curling behind her ribs through the river of the bond. The darkening within her threatened to turn it into a riptide.

Holy hell. "Ysa—"

Her hands shook. No sword in sight, quill tucked still between her breasts. "I didn't want this," she said softly. Power collected around her like a shiver just before the world broke.

His mate had stopped asking for permission and, for an instant, Zephyr was proud. Maybe he could have stopped her. But these males had invaded their home. Threatened his people.

She tore the air. A slit of darkness widened to a chasm

behind the light warrior, a hole in the world that devoured light, wind, and breath. He lifted his blade, and the void closed around it, sucking in one half, shattering the other into prismatic pieces.

The warrior looked on in stunned disbelief. "That sword was sung into being by the Dawnmother herself. Nothing in Faerie should have touched it, let alone unmade it." He took a slow step backwards, gaze fixed on the calligrapher's daughter as if she were a riddle. The light flared in his palms and then flickered, unstable.

It was over, Zephyr thought. They could subdue the male now.

But the bond pulsed, and his mate whispered. "I still have more."

Loxley planted his axe into the ground, and Zephyr threw himself around his friend, anchoring them with shadow. Not a moment too soon. The void opened again, a gaping maw within Ebonspire, and there was his mate, channelling with such ease that it took his breath away.

The light warrior's body arced back, every muscle straining against the pull. Light crackled in vain around him. But not even the sun outruns a black hole.

With a curse of fury, the warrior vanished into it.

Zephyr flashed a sharp grin. So, they weren't supposed to be friends after all.

He stared at his mate, the taste of starlight on his tongue: dry, fine particles, like powdered silver. Her palms were scorched with magic, but she retracted the darkness in a controlled manner. It folded in on itself, but a palpable sense of unspent power hung in the air, like a door shutting but never fully locking. He had never seen her so clearly. She was magnificent. No longer subdued, no longer small; this was her, as she was meant to be.

It was time to end this and save their own.

He wrapped soothing shadows around her palms. "Are you ready?"

The calligrapher's daughter nodded and went to retrieve her sword.

11

YSADORA

Bloodheart tree: dark crimson bark, long blade-
like green leaves, edged in red and iron-scented.
Native to the Court of Silence, it is privy to the
secrets of the court and said to shed its leaves
only at the death or rise of a ruler.
– A Compendium of Faerie Flora and Terrain

My meteor magic didn't terrify me when it was directed at those who meant us harm. Its weight was the same, but my spine straightened beneath it. It felt like justice, rather than a curse. Like maybe I wasn't monstrous after all. Zephyr stared at me in awe, as if I had exerted control over my magic. But I hadn't.

I was fury and fracture, barely stitched together.

Something dark and old still crackled in my veins, and somewhere, the void whispered, but there was no time to pick apart what had happened, to consider the moral rights and wrongs of sending that male into the darkness.

Not when our friends needed us.

The grove at the edge of the training ground glowed with too-bright light: brightness created by the Faerie King of Luminosity. When Zephyr and Cyprian had rebuilt Ebonspire, they had chosen the grove to be a space for duelling and had embedded a wide ring of dark stone into the earth at its centre.

It was where blades clashed in shade when the sun scorched the upper field—a much cherished spot, now a stage for cruelty. Zephyr and Loxley bristled with rage and an eagerness to engage, despite the minor injuries they nursed.

Loxley swung his axe over his shoulder. "Let's hope Cyp hasn't got himself caught like a rat in a sack."

"You're my failsafe. Stay far enough away that Esolas won't sense you, and listen out for my signal." Their signal whistles blended in with birds and beasts. "And check on the ember wolf."

"I don't like it. I'll flay him if he—"

"I know. This place does not yield, and neither do we." Zephyr grasped his arm. "Stay alive, brother."

We walked towards the grove, and I darted my mate a glance. "Shouldn't we shadow step?"

He shook his head, as if he had abandoned strategy for directness. "He already knows we are coming."

"You're not asking me to stay back."

"I'm learning you can handle yourself."

We slipped through the trees that had been moved like a jigsaw, some cracked and splintered, boughs reaching unnaturally, and I recognised Sequoia's magic. Then the light changed, and my eyes narrowed to slits against its onslaught.

I flinched, as much from the sight before us as from the emotions pummelling through the bond. Fresh runes had been carved into the dirt of the duelling ring. Our three friends knelt within, bound like bait in a trap. A long silver cloak, clearly made for royalty, covered Wylda's nudity. She was dirt-streaked and cowed like a wilted sapling, crushed green shoots sprouting from her palms, whereas Sequoia held herself with the proud stillness of a redwood.

I averted my gaze from the shame in Cyprian's eyes and noticed a new patch of grey coils on his head, as if he had exhausted his time magic in futile attempts to thwart our foe.

The faerie king's voice met us like the hush before sunrise over a still field. "The shadow prince and the calligrapher's daughter. I am pleased to see you, although disappointed that you emptied the cellars of their beasts. There are those who wish to use those creatures for their own ends."

I tugged my attention away from our friends and studied the faerie king. He stood alone—as if he didn't require the protection of royal guards—with our friends at his feet. Daring us to come closer. His skin gleamed like hammered gold, and his eyes held the brightness of a noonday sun: blinding if met too long. His armour was etched with tiny suns, and a disc of burning stone orbited his staff at its highest point.

Zephyr inclined his head, acknowledging the faerie king's rank. But his voice was edged with the kind of iron politeness that cuts deeper than fury. "Welcome to

Ebonspire, Esolas. You must be exhausted from bringing war to my doorstep."

A sparse eyebrow rose. "The Court of Lore fell long ago. You hold no dominion here."

Shadows coiled like smoke at Zephyr's heels in the harsh light. "History has a way of waking when you least expect it."

The faerie king's focus was wholly directed at Zephyr as if this wasn't about me, after all. "I didn't believe it when I learned you had been here all this time. Then a merchant on the edge of Serennor told me a warrior had come riding out of the mists to buy a gift for his love. My light sentinels had trouble finding you."

Zephyr was icy calm. "You'd be surprised how easy it is to fool a court that thinks itself invincible."

"Guard your tone, shadow prince." Tiny motes of light hovered like fireflies around him. "I came here to talk."

"Then it would have been wiser to send courtiers instead of warriors. Now let my people go."

"I would love nothing more than to be merciful, but mercy has to be earned. And your violent reprisals were unfortunate."

"I'd wager you *wanted* to get rid of your most powerful lieutenant and his devotees."

Grudging respect flickered over Esolas's face. "My sister warned me about your cleverness."

"I remember the Dawnmother. She is not easy to forget."

"Aurielle believes that light should never be blinding, prideful, or cruel. For her sake, I'll deal fairly with you."

"I remember her phrase well. What was it? *Darkness is the canvas on which light can be understood.*" Pure contempt dripped from my mate's every pore. "Is that what drove you into my uncle's shadow?"

"The Spymaster is not the only one concerned about developments in Faerie. He believes it is time for a high king."

There it was: the confirmation that Esolas had been sent by Thiago.

"A high king?" echoed Zephyr, as if the words tasted foreign in his mouth. His eyes flicked momentarily to Cyprian in disbelief. "That's madness. The crown was buried after the Sundering. No one's worn it in a millennium."

Esolas gave a mirthless chuckle. "Indeed, Faerie fractured for a reason."

Zephyr's eyes narrowed. "Yet still you agreed. He holds your leash."

The air around the faerie king's staff hazed with heat. "Careful, little shadow, tug too hard and you might find that the leash loops around your own neck. You should know better than anyone how refusing the Spymaster is unwise."

"What are the terms of your arrangement?" The bond was a dark, churning current, as if he already knew the answer.

"Thiago offered me a place at his right hand." Esolas pointed a long, jewel-ringed finger at me. "In exchange for her."

Zephyr didn't so much as blink, but the bond tightened, his fury wrapped in silk. His instinct was to shield me, to speak for me, but he didn't. He simply moved closer. The air thickened, as if the land itself took offence. After everything, there were those in Faerie who still thought they could barter me, hide me, dose, and silence me.

Inside me, the void whispered. "Be careful, Majesty. You're not the first to mistake me for something pliable."

Zephyr's mouth curved into a slow, wolfish smile. "You think to trade power for her? You underestimate us both."

"And you presume to think that the two of you can rival a faerie king." Esolas tightened our friends' bonds without even turning, and there must have been heat in those bonds because Wylda let out a whimper and sweat beaded on their skin.

My magic howled in my veins, pushing towards the surface like a creature unchained.

It wanted release. It wanted retribution.

The faerie king's voice turned curious. "Tell me, calligrapher's daughter, does your magic flinch every time you do?"

My boots didn't budge from the cracked earth. *He wants a demonstration,* I said to my mate. *I think I'll oblige.*

The darkness in me wasn't playful, or scholarly, or a connective link like my ink magic. This part of me broke things, and sometimes that was necessary. The air around me folded inwards like a held breath. A sphere of darkness flowered out from my chest, and the faerie king's unnatural light flickered like a flame struggling to survive a gust of wind.

Esolas's face tightened as my magic brushed up against the edge of the warded circle, swallowing light greedily, stretching his own shadow against his will. The stillness was broken only by the soft echo of my voice, cool and confident. "You were saying?"

Approval gleamed in Zephyr's eyes, dark and hungry. The kind of look that promised both trouble and reverence. *I don't know whether to bow down to you or bed you.* "As you can see, Ysadora is nobody's toy."

"Not even yours?" Esolas clenched the sundial with barely restrained tension.

Zephyr's brow lifted, his voice dry. "Not even mine."

I lifted my chin, thinking of the adoptive mother who had once rocked me. "Did Danaë sanction this attack?"

The faerie king tracked my every movement with the sharp focus of someone recalibrating a threat. "She stands in the Spymaster's way of a full assault, but he tires of waiting. He has called a meeting of the remaining faerie kings and queens in a fortnight. He means to convince us that he is too powerful to oppose. My task is to retrieve you before then."

Shadows curled around Zephyr's boots and fists. "Then you will return in pieces or full of regrets. Tell me, Esolas, what good does it do your court to serve as a tyrant's right hand?"

"Better to serve a tyrant than be punished by one. I am under no illusions that the Spymaster has personal regard for me or my particular skill set. Ours would be a strategic alliance, given the geography of Faerie." Amber eyes met mine. "Come with me, Ysadora Silberquill, and the rest may go."

You will not answer that. "What does my uncle have on you?"

Esolas looked away, but not fast enough. Guilt is quick. Guilt is loud.

"Tell me, and maybe I can make this right."

"You are Silence, just like him."

"I am Lore, more than I ever was Silence. If you can't trust me, then trust my mother. And trust Wylda and Sequoia, who hail from the Court of Wild Ferns, once allied with the Court of Luminosity. And Cyprian, who hails from the Court of Languish, with its shared reverence for light. Trust us, because my uncle is as loyal as a smiling bog sprite, mud-slick and ready to drown you." The choice wasn't cruel. It was clean.

"You ask too much."

"The bloodheart tree sheds. I presume you know what this means?"

The silence was sharp and acidic. "That there may be a chance to turn the tables on the Spymaster after all." Esolas considered for a moment. "I cannot return to him empty-handed. But Thiago does trade. Bring me something of consequence that I may give to him, and I offer you a reprieve. I will leave today with a bargain to mark our promise. As long as the calligrapher's daughter attends the appointed meeting in a fortnight."

"Your bargain is with me," I said.

"No, it's with me." *Let this one be mine to bear.* Zephyr's shadows writhed, and my magic rose in response.

"I accept Ysadora's bargain." Esolas's smile danced like sunlight on a blade. "What do you offer as the trade?"

Perhaps when this is over, we should both be less careless with bargains. "How can we be sure that Thiago hasn't extended the same offer to other rulers of Faerie?"

"You can't." Esolas gave an elegant shrug. "Power draws hunger, and you've made yourself a feast."

He's right, growled Zephyr through the bond. *But I know what we must trade.*

So it was agreed. Loxley returned with the shadow

rings from Ferrith and Maren. Zephyr scowled as Esolas branded my skin with sunlit chains that wrapped around my left wrist like a bracelet. The bargain's warmth crept up my forearm, blooming through muscle and sinew until it reached my heart, alive and Faerie-deep.

Faerie dealt in flesh and freedom, and bargains mapped out on fae bodies. They rooted themselves in meat and bone: thin, sunlit lines curling around a wrist, or looping around an ankle, or dark lines laddering my mate's bicep.

Bargains that threaded along collarbones. Spiderwebs over the heart. Ribcages traced with oaths. Shoulders marked by debts. Spines wrapped in allegiance and treachery. Every curl, every burn, every whispering scar mapped who fae loved and who they hated.

I had made my choices, with or without the Binder's guidance.

Then it was over, and the faerie king placed the whisper rings in a tiny compartment beneath the gold bracer on his forearm and retrieved his cloak from Wylda with an apologetic glance. She wrapped her bruised body in a protective embrace of leaves and vines.

"I regret the harm caused today. I offer you release with an open hand, not a clenched fist," the faerie king said.

Zephyr's smile in no way indicated friendship. He dipped his chin in measured acknowledgement. "I ask that you withhold from making an immediate report to my uncle."

"You have until dawn. May the sun be kind enough for you to unseat Thiago before he is crowned as High King. I would sooner see you tear down his crown than see the realms rot beneath it."

Esolas's bright eyes flicked to me, and the air around him wavered like heat in a forge. Then he dissolved his wards, freeing our kin. With a final glance, he stepped sideways and vanished, leaving only the faint scent of ozone and sun-warmed trees. Ebonspire was ours again, though it didn't feel as safe, and we had lost more than the monsters in the newly empty dungeons.

Wylda's voice was hoarse. "You bought our freedom, but at what cost to yourself, Ysa?" Her knees buckled when she tried to stand, and Cyprian and Sequoia caught her.

I had dared to walk into the grove with stars in my blood and shadows at my back.

I had dared to bargain with creatures born of spite, whose promises glittered like the sun but cut like blades.

I wasn't sure if we'd walked away the victors.

12

YSADORA

The Court of Luminosity shines beneath an endless amber sky, where light is both weapon and shield. Guided by luminous sibling monarchs, here, light reveals truth, blinds enemies, and shrinks shadow. Its people forge sunlight into radiant weapons and armour, heal with the warmth of the sun, and are masters of illusions.
– A Tapestry of Courts and Crowns

Zephyr's jaw worked as he took in the damage to Ebonspire. A fine trail of what looked like iron filings led from the outer boundaries to the gatehouse, barely visible now the breeze had scattered it. It smudged against his fingertips when he crouched to touch it, warm and oily: the telltale residue of fae wards being forcibly broken. His expression was unreadable save for the flicker of protectiveness in his stance, but the bond was raw and open—a tight knot of helplessness lodged in my chest.

I wanted to comfort him, but my touch felt too small against the vastness of this blow.

"Go to him," rasped Wylda, slack now the danger had passed. Her braids were dishevelled, cuts crusted with blood.

I shook my head. "Not yet."

Sequoia murmured in approval, as if she understood his need to bleed alone. Her hollow-eyed silence was more disconcerting than her rage. Zephyr and Cyprian both wandered as though they were in a graveyard. The eastern spire leaned now, a subtle shift in its proud spine, as if a great weight had heaved against its base.

Fleeing monsters had carved deep gouges in the earth. Scorched ground steamed in patches, where light magic had flared. Verdant trees had splintered outwards and hung half-burnt and brittle. Cyp stared at a broken pillar, now cracked through the middle like chalk.

Zephyr's shadows drew close around him like a cloak. "We'll rebuild."

Loxley beckoned. "I need you both." The ember wolf lay crumpled beside him, now little more than a broken heap of fur, sides barely rising. Her poker-hot claws guttered like dying coals. "It's Ylva. She can't be saved."

The three males took up vigil beside Ylva, and Cyprian sang a lament that fell like a mist over us. Like Gabor, the ember wolf became herself once more in the moments before her passing, revealing a female with tangled silver hair and charred skin. In a last surge of will, Ylva summoned an illusion of golden plains and two children dancing past.

Zephyr laid a hand on her brow to absorb her memories. Then the illusion stuttered, and Ylva's body was still. Cyprian scooped her into his arms and memory walked with Loxley to the place of rest she had shown him through her restored magic.

They had given her a beautiful death, although bitterness tinged the mate bond.

I went to Zephyr, heart lurching. "She changed back before death, just like Gabor did."

His gaze was soft, full of grief still. "But we are no closer to knowing whether the curse is broken by death or sacrifice. Either way, the outcast fae are scattered across Faerie once more. And death is not the release I want for them."

He was so tired. We all needed to rest.

Then Cyprian and Loxley were there once more, bringing the scent of heather with them. The remnants of ritual clung to them: ash smeared on their cheeks, clothes scuffed from kneeling on bark. Loxley's swagger was tempered to a grounded heaviness. He was never one to please others for the sake of it, but he was always there when they needed him.

Zephyr ushered Wylda inside, stormy eyes darting to the spire. "Time for us to take care of you."

We headed inside, where light magic lingered in the air like static. Zephyr's shadows pulsed against it, testing its edges with quiet defiance. Shattered glass crunched underfoot, and once-hidden sigils etched into the stone pulsed faintly, like a faltering heartbeat.

There were no corpses. Esolas had taken his fallen warriors with him, leaving behind only the aftermath:

gloopy residue, scorched walls, half-melted weapons, the stink of burned air and extinguished life.

Maren found us in the infirmary, her face livid after I had locked her and Ferrith behind the false wall in the armoury. Her eyes fell on Wylda. "By the molten core of Faerie, what happened?"

"I went against the rules," said Wylda. "I stayed out alone."

Guilt bloomed bitter in her, as if she could have prevented Esolas and his warriors from infiltrating our wards and walls. I understood. I cursed myself for not using my void magic sooner. For how the ember wolf might have lived if I had intervened earlier.

"Do you think it would have been any different had you been stronger, faster, shrewder?" snapped Sequoia, whose knowledge of herbs didn't match hers.

Once, Gabor could have healed her, but he was gone.

And Sequoia wasn't done, "You fool yourself, sister. There were too many to drive back alone. You did more than enough. You sent choking vines and spore clouds. Your spears pierced organs and pinned our foe to the ground. Your blight roots sprang up from the ground, turning into caskets around our enemies. Your dandelions pushed out from eye sockets, and your bluebells choked airways. By my count, you killed eight of them, made three more hallucinate."

We didn't give voice to the rest. They had held her down, and they stripped her, crowing at her humiliation and their cleverness when they found the unlocking rune: the mark of the place that had become our sanctuary, and hers before that.

"My magic brought death instead of growth," said Wylda, "and it still wasn't enough."

It didn't help that the Courts of Wild Ferns and the Court of Luminosity had a natural affinity. Plants rise towards light, bend to its will, unfurl in its warmth. That old understanding shrivelled during the attack. It counted for nothing in a Faerie remade.

Zephyr stooped before Wylda. "It's not your fault. You heard Esolas. He'd been weighing up my uncle's information. The merchant at Serennor gave away our position. My choices, not yours."

"Stop it, all of you," said Cyprian. "Do you think it doesn't scald me that I can only go back a meagre handful of seconds, and I'm often too late? For you, for Ylva, for my own damned court? We were not the architects of this aggression."

Wylda's dull skin and the emptiness in her eyes said it all. The self-disgust she felt was too much, the energy she'd poured out too vast to be swayed by words.

We sent the males away, and Sequoia, Maren and I tended to her. Wylda's magicked clothing dissolved like sugar, revealing bruised, dirty skin. The infirmary filled with the quiet murmur of our efforts: damp muslins being wrung out after cleansing her skin and lemony balm being applied to burns and green shoots that hadn't fully retracted. With each expression of care, the worn-out exhaustion in Wylda's face faded a little more. Then we tucked her into one of the infirmary bed palettes, pulling the pelt over her to stop her quivering, though it was summer.

"When you are broken, so am I." Sequoia stroked her hair back from her face. "Rest."

Wylda drifted into a much-needed sleep. For the first time since the battle, the air felt still and calm. Even though we were bruised inside and out, we had found a sense of belonging with one another. Maybe broken things didn't have to stay broken; maybe they could be remade into something stronger.

I almost believed it.

13

KAZIMIR

Rider: Braf Falkonisk, The Order of the Glyph
Dragon: Drakmire (Nebulite)
Skills: high-speed dives, breaking through enemy
ranks, seasoned tactician in dragon formations
Known alliances: Tanuhja Gris
Whereabouts: Presumed dead
- The Dragons and Riders of the Nebula Court

The bone soldiers tightened their ring around the calligrapher and the dragon, their joints twitching and clicking with death magic. Some dragged rusted blades; others clenched claws that radiated sickly green. To Caldoron, whose senses were attuned to the wild balance of flame and flight, the very ground at the Court of Bones felt wrong.

But Kazimir was in enough pain that the thought of turning to the skies again was more terrifying than taking a chance on the strange queen before them.

Caldoron recoiled mid-step, nostrils flaring. *That scent. Like nature corrupted.*

Kazimir almost gagged on the putrid stink of dark magic and sweet decay. *I must ask you to show restraint, old friend.*

Unease rippled through the dragon's powerful frame. *You have always asked too much of me.*

It would be difficult to find healing and an alliance if Caldoron reacted. After all, a dragon's reactions were almost never tempered. Millennia of dominance had left them with little need for restraint, and even less interest in diplomacy. They were creatures of instinct, responding with fire, fury, and unwavering conviction when provoked. One wrong move, one flash of betrayal, and the sky would burn before any of them could draw a second breath. Wasn't that why Ysa and the shadow prince had agreed with Liora's suggestion for him to come here?

Although Kazimir couldn't understand why the joy of his reunion with Caldoron was hampered by a resistance and unreliability that hadn't existed between dragon and rider since *Kindling*, there had been moments during their flight to the Court of Bones where he imagined that Caldoron had actually wanted him to fall.

He shook his head. Clearly, his physical ailments and exhaustion had stripped him of logical thought. He tried to ignore the clacking, gurning bone soldiers and turned his attention to the faerie queen. She toyed with a length of chain made from finger bones—long enough, perhaps, to ensnare a dragon—winding it idly around her pale wrist.

Thalindra's silver gaze gleamed with old magic. "I pray your dragon isn't going to cause trouble, calligrapher. Liora Bramick has vouched for you, but I will not hesitate to strike if the beast decides to make ashes from our sacred bones."

Caldoron released a jet of searing smoke. *I have never burned a queen alive. I should like to try.*

Tempting, I know. Diplomacy first. Incineration later, said Kazimir.

For a heartbeat, the calligrapher pitied the queen. Non-dragon-riding fae always assumed the dragons belonged to the riders. A laughable arrogance. As though fire and sky could be owned. There was nothing further from the truth. The bond was a dance, not a leash.

Caldoron's wings shifted restlessly, his slitted orbs never still, assessing the bone soldiers, the queen, the skies. *Do their bones count as sticks? Perhaps I should start fetching sticks and licking faces.*

Kazimir's stomach churned at the thought that the dragon might abandon him, as Kazimir had abandoned him once. *Only if you wish your dignity to combust spontaneously.*

He could barely hold himself up anymore. He regretted not asking Liora for more information on the nature of the Circle of Emberlight's alliance with this strange queen.

Thalindra spoke directly to the dragon, her circlet of antlers clouded with sulphur and brimstone from a puff of his breath. She gestured to a carved perch above the citadel. "You may wait there while we fix your master, dragon. But take note. If you kill, the calligrapher dies. If you refrain from unleashing fire, he lives."

Caldoron's tail swung towards her. *It is dangerous for a stranger to ask a dragon to withhold flame. The longer I wait, the hotter the inferno burns beneath my scales.*

"Isn't he clumsy?" The faerie queen did not cede

ground. Her stance remained regal, but the bone soldiers surged forward with renewed menace, their spears jabbing in a sharp rhythm, their bones humming with necrotic power.

"Since he was a hatchling," agreed Kazimir, although the archives at the Order of the Glyph had recorded that even as a hatchling, Caldoron had moved with lethal grace. Hulking though he was, even amongst his kind, he had the precision of a hawk in freefall. *Do not give her cause for enmity, old friend. We may need this alliance yet.*

Caldoron's bronze scales vibrated with a warning growl. *She has earned my stillness. But for how long and at what cost, I cannot say. There is a foul smell here, calligrapher. It seeps into my nostrils with every breath. It evokes buried memories of dragonkind.*

It seemed to Kazimir that only his borrowed riding clothes now held him together: thin seams pressing against broken ribs and crooked limbs, and his poor agonising spine, like the fabric alone remembered how to stand tall when he no longer could.

His mind frayed at the edges, and he would have begged for rest and nourishment, had his pride not stood in the way. This was why he had run from Faerie with his precious load. This was why Larkspur, for all its mortal drudgery and meagre comforts, had been a home to him and Ysa.

What he wouldn't give for a rest in his armchair and a body that could put one foot in front of the other without gnawing pain. His daughter, a breath away.

"Feed the dragon if he hungers. Otherwise, leave him to his vigil," said Thalindra to her bone soldiers.

They did not respond. Kazimir didn't know if they even could, fleshless, malformed horrors that they were.

You will come back to me, calligrapher, said Caldoron. *Our story is not yet over.*

Kazimir did not even turn his head. *I mean to, my friend.*

For his rider, the dragon curbed his instincts. He did not strike. Instead, Caldoron coiled like a waiting storm, while two bone soldiers shepherded the calligrapher away under the weight of his slitted gaze. When Kazimir had hobbled some fifty metres away, the dragon's shadow passed over him, wings outspread like a bad omen, before he soared to the citadel perch.

The calligrapher's body failed with every jolt of movement, pain ghosting through him. The queen stalked ahead, taking long, elegant strides. Though Kazimir's vision flickered at the edges, he caught glimpses of the Court of Bones around him.

Artisans sat hunched over slabs of ivory and stone in a vaulted hall. A jeweller pressed slivers of topaz into the eye sockets of a wolf's skull. A sculptor mixed black clay with a smooth tibia. Further on, druids walked barefoot across mosaic floors, robes inked with tree rings and root patterns. Some knelt around a skeletal elm, its branches lit with soft blue flames.

There were bone shamans, tattooed and blindfolded, their fingers stained with burial clay. There were tomb guardians bearing urns. One whispered a blessing in a tongue Kazimir couldn't decipher. A tongue that made him fearful.

By the time they reached their destination, below the catacombs, hidden in the marrow of the Court of Bones, white spots swarmed his vision. The corridor narrowed, sloping downwards into a pearly gloom. The bone soldiers dropped behind, and the faerie queen removed her circlet of antlers.

Thalindra's voice was like gauze, barely there. "This is our sanctum. The attendants will remould you now."

Kazimir's pulse dragged as heavy slabs yawned open to reveal a sanctum carved from smooth stone, slick with the scent of old marrow and magic. A trio of dark-skinned females stood waiting for him, naked save for their bone masks: the first wore the polished skull of a mountain lion; the second the elongated cranium of a comet fiend dragon, its hollow eyes inked black; the third wore the helm of a war-elephant, the trunk shortened and shaped into a horn.

He shuddered at the sight of them. They undressed him from his riding leather, and he was relieved that they did not flinch at the sight of his twisted limbs. When they turned, he noticed runes had been carved into the curve of their ribs and the slope of their spines. He did not know if they were bone healers or bone breakers. He did not know whether his healing was guaranteed or whether he was at risk of death. The attendants did not console or explain.

The attendants led him into the belly of the sanctum, where broken things were unmade and rebuilt. Kazimir took in the chamber only in broad strokes, his feet dragging soundlessly across the floor.

A pool of bone milk dominated the chamber, like a quiet moon in a stone sky. Everything was pale: pale walls, pale light, pale steam rising from the pool in curling wisps that smelled faintly of salt and bone dust.

Runed bone rods surrounded the pool, each engraved with glyphs and vibrating with recalibration magic. They tilted to minute degrees, synchronised. Skeletal motifs wove through the architecture: arches like vertebrae, sconces held by bony hands, mosaics of anatomy in mother-of-pearl. There was no blood here, no gore. But Kazimir wasn't reassured.

Not a sound could be heard: neither the rustle of the queen's robes, the drip of liquid, nor the faintest breath. Though Kazimir had valued the silence all his life—in the halls of the Order of the Glyph, when he laid Ysa in her crib as a youngling, and in the quiet of his Larkspur bookshop—he found *this* silence anything but comforting.

Still, Caldoron was near, so he wasn't entirely alone.

That was something, at least. That was everything.

"Will it hurt?" he asked, and something gonged in his brain, as if he were being punished for disturbing the quiet.

The queen held up her index finger to her mouth and then gave a cursory nod to the masked attendants.

The attendants could have invited him with careful nudges to enter the pool of bone-milk; instead, they pushed him. As the bone-milk pool demanded surrender rather than caution. As if he were in a mortal church being baptised.

Kazimir spluttered for a moment, going under before resurfacing. The gong in his head warned him to compose himself. The pool was warm, with the consistency of melted ivory, thickening and swirling to accept him. Making him float. Making him weightless.

He sighed with relief, leaning back, splaying his fingers, feeling the creak in his bones ease. The surface shimmered like quiet thought, as if it had a memory of structure and form, and what bones should be.

Then they entered the pool with him and stood waist-deep around him. Kazimir lay submerged within it, his body stripped of all armour and dignity, suspended in the cradle of the bone-milk. With every slow rotation around him, the attendants measured, mapped and judged the fractured geometry of his body.

His breath, though shallow, fogged the surface when he exhaled. He wanted to be whole again, but it was a selfish desire: Ysa didn't need him as she once had. Held within a ritual-induced trance, he was caught between pain and memory. Although it wasn't quite physical pain. The pool seemed to keep pain in stasis—like a wound suspended in running water, never healing, never bleeding out. He was aware that he was small and inconsequential, and he was at the mercy of the fates.

Something inside him sagged, gave way, like a structure left standing too long on hollow foundations. He didn't slip beneath the surface, but the bone milk pulled him lower, and he swayed—just enough for the world to tilt at the edges.

And then came their hands. Not cruel, not violent. Just industrious, focused on the sacred labour of restoration. They moved with the quiet focus of those who had done this a thousand times before. Soon, he didn't know anymore if there were six hands on his body or sixty.

The queen watched while they worked, sitting prim and poised to one side with her circlet of antlers on her lap.

Kazimir's head lolled back. High above, barely visible through a narrow skylight, Caldoron's silhouette lingered on the citadel. Cool, silty pressure slid along his spine and limbs. His left arm clicked back into place in his shoulder socket, with the careful coaxing of hands that knew bone like a sculptor knew marble.

His ribs shifted. Cartilage refound its path, and muscles unknotted like soft rope soaking in water. The sensation was uncanny, pain muted. The bone milk grew more viscous where it touched his wounds.

Along his back, he felt the slow recalibration of his spine, a deep, internal shifting, like ancient stone settling into alignment. His hips and pelvis followed, drawn back into their proper tilt, legs eased into evenness beneath him. Tendons uncoiled. The attendants undid the damage Danaë, in her wrath, had inflicted on him, and he almost wept in gratitude.

When the sanctum's work was done, he climbed the steps from the pool, and he thought he heard Caldoron roar. He was wrung out, balanced, spent, and emerged from the bone milk with the slow grace of a statue come to life.

He did not resist as the attendants rubbed him down with cloths that smelled faintly of sage and mineral salts. Their touch was impersonal but not unkind. The masks made their intent unreadable. They moved like shades, their black skin dotted with the pearlescent crumbs of the bone milk residue.

They wrapped him in a black silk robe to preserve what little dignity remained, and his limbs jerked slightly, as if remembering pain. The robe was a mark: not of luxury, but of completion. The attendants gave no signal of satisfaction or approval. They simply stepped back in silence and left him standing there, alone and clothed in black silk, in a sanctum that still smelled faintly of death and rebirth.

Kazimir wanted his riding leathers. He wanted the dragon at his side.

He realised then that his morbid thoughts in the pool had been premature. He wanted so much to see Ysa again. With this new chance, he was no longer too proud to admit it: his daughter might not need him, but a father needed his child.

He was nothing without the two greatest loves of his long life.

"Thank you," said Kazimir to Thalindra, and this time, there was no gong in his head when he spoke.

"Fixing you is one thing, calligrapher. Trusting you is quite another."

14

ZEPHYR

Moaning Briar Stag: scythe antlers, gargantuan body, sleep-inducing moans. Once Alaric Thuin of the Court of Wild Ferns, mate of Eldarin, gifted in calming animals.
- The Secrets of Faerie's Veiled Beasts by Zephyr Ashmoor

Zephyr's mother had raised him to believe that lore magic wasn't just power. It was a sacred duty. To remember was to honour; whereas to forget was to fail. Every pain, every joy, deserved a witness. He had always treasured this part of himself: the gentler side of him that spoke to his mother's influence and balanced out his father's silence and shadows. It felt right, noble even.

After his mother and Veda had died, he had been voiceless in the halls of silence. It seemed vital to him that the fae outcasts from the fallen courts didn't vanish without anyone caring. So he became their cenotaph, their archivist, their chronicler.

His brothers helped him in this sacred duty. Loxley's influencing magic and Cyprian's time magic made it possible to absorb the stories of even the most cursed amongst those fae. They allowed Zephyr to get close to nightmarish creatures: ravenous wryms, swamp creatures, hounds with bodies hewn from wax, and stags with scythes for antlers.

It was the least he could do given his failure at returning them to their true forms.

Before the fall of the Order of the Glyph and the unravelling of the Grimoire, Zephyr's lore magic had been a source of connection and even flirtation. He'd been beloved at Lore festivals for offering retellings of past joys in exchange for a silver coin or a kiss from some fancy.

He sat at the feet of elders, trading stories and dreams for a sweet apple or candied acorn. His first sexual experience had been with a young actress at court, who bared her breasts to him in the orange blossom gardens after he offered to retell a cherished memory for her. It was consensual, intimate, electric. How innocent he had been. How full of the joy of life and magic and possibilities. How sharp his memories of that version of himself were.

Back then, he had taken a strong mind for granted.

He was no longer that male. The more Zephyr used his lore magic, the more he struggled under the weight of it. The memories from the fae outcasts didn't provide balance. There was no space for pleasure or hope, with all that had been stolen from them.

The histories he absorbed from them were swamped with trauma, thick with horror. They didn't settle quietly or with ease. They festered like smoke in sealed lungs. They churned like a storm-swollen river.

There was no time to sift or process or give each memory its proper weight. Flickers of memory caught Zephyr unaware. A mother wrenched from her child. A spell that stole a fae's glittering wings. Sleep offered no reprieve. His dreams were cluttered with the broken and silenced. Their lives haunted him. Without the anchor of Ysa, he would have sunk beneath it all. He was becoming a vault for the wronged.

It was too much, and it wasn't what *she* needed from him. Ysa needed him whole.

But Zephyr didn't stop. To stop would mean to forget.

His mother wouldn't want that, and so he couldn't want that.

It had brought him comfort to restore Ebonspire, not just for himself, but for his mother. It pained him to abandon it, but the gatehouse could not protect them, and he kicked himself for not working harder, for not anticipating Esolas's attack.

He toiled in the war room alone for some time, poring over maps, although even the best cartographers couldn't keep pace with how Faerie reshaped itself with every turning moon and whisper of ambition.

His orders had been clear: two hours of recuperation for those who required it. Not him, of course. He despised leaders who rested when their people were in need. Even so, he ached for his mate and cursed himself for promising to keep the bond open.

He only had to close his eyes to know that Ysa was resting as he demanded, and he pictured her waiting for him on their bed palette, bare legs strewn across the pale linen. Heaving a sigh, he tended to his next task, slotting daggers into a travel chest that had once belonged to his maternal grandfather.

The methodical movements opened the trap door to a flood of Ylva Ashrest's memories: her pain, her fear, her final breaths. He tasted smoke on his tongue, gagging on it like she had, endured the burn of claws in his own skin, mourned the loss of illusions, though that magic had never been his. Feet scuffled across the floor, and his vision swam, caught between what was real and what was not.

"He was trying to break into the artefacts room." Lox dragged Ferrith by the scruff of his neck.

Zephyr's mind caught up. Ferrith's eyes were too blue, too wild, like a youngling caught tampering with elder runes. He'd never been entirely sure of this mortal's intentions, even though Ysa vouched for him.

For her sake, he gave Ferrith the benefit of the doubt, and Maren was loyal to the bone. She had protected and trained Ysa at great risk to herself and never made the easy choice to save her own skin.

Ferrith was prone to good cheer but also bursts of spontaneity that weren't always well thought out, like when he had insisted on coming to Faerie without once thinking that his human frailty might put Ysa and Maren in more danger just by virtue of his presence.

Ferrith's lips moved with excuses. "I was lost...I was helping Ysa."

Zephyr's brows drew together at the mention of his mate, because he knew it wasn't true—the bond told him that Ysa slept.

Lox's freckled skin was flushed not with mischief, but with anger. Lox hadn't trusted Gabor. Not fully. And here he was again, calling out one of their kin. Zephyr should have been grateful. Instead, he was ashamed. Betrayal wasn't new, but it always found fresh angles to cut from. Heat spiked in him, and he breathed hard through his nose, trying to cool it, contain it.

His orders had been for those without need of rest to split the necessary tasks between them: repairing Ebonspire's wards, preparing clothing, medicine and food supplies for travel, selecting weapons and ink, and tacking the horses. Why then, when half of their kin were resting and half tending to chores, had Ferrith Namara tried to access the artefacts room?

For Ysa, he kept his anger in check. "Was your intention to steal?"

Ferrith swallowed hard. "Of course not."

The Rune of Unveiling burned on Zephyr's hip, as it always did when confronted by a liar.

Shadows flickered at the edges of the war room, drawn by the sharp flare of his temper. They curled along the walls, restless, hungry. Zephyr didn't push them back. "You lie."

"Fuck, I was hoping I was wrong." Lox shoved Ferrith into a chair. "I kind of like the arsehole."

Zephyr snorted. "Could have fooled me."

Watery blue eyes flicked between them, then to the door. "I didn't touch anything."

"Don't bother. No one's coming." Loxley took up position behind the chair, and even though he didn't lay a finger on him, the effect was like a looming storm. "I don't want to use my magic on you. Just tell us what we need to hear."

A nerve ticked in Zephyr's jaw. "He can be gentle, but

he won't be if you lie again. Why did you insist on coming to Faerie, Ferrith? Why didn't you stay in Larkspur with your father?"

"Because Ysa and Maren are my oldest friends, and Maren loves me back at last."

This time, the Rune of Unveiling warmed Zephyr's hip, rather than searing it. He crouched in front of Ysa's friend, his tone kinder this time. "You speak the truth in that, at least. But it doesn't absolve you. Nor does it explain your actions. Tell us of your own accord. It'll be easier that way." Easier than explaining to Ysa why he allowed Lox to interfere with her friend's mind.

Ferrith looked away. "I made an oath."

"A mortal one." For Zephyr, mortal oaths were things of breath and belief, proclaimed with no real meaning, anchored to no real punishment. They could be rationalised, forgotten, rewritten. When Zephyr gave his word, magic wrapped around his ribcage like threads spun from iron. Punishment was written into his very veins. What did this mortal risk with a broken oath?

Loxley caught his mood and stepped forward, as if he'd known it would come to this. He placed one hand on either side of Ferrith's head, large palms spanning from temple to jaw, fingers lightly resting there.

Zephyr had witnessed this countless times, on monsters and fae, but never on a mortal. This crossed a line in more ways than one. Strategically, he had no other choice. If this man had broken their trust, he couldn't stay amongst them.

Trust was everything: more important than steel or shadows, spells and bargains, more important even than ancient wards. When glamours distorted perception and magic made every enemy unpredictable, trust and connection were the only compass.

He stared at the man he had provided refuge for, shadows begging to be released. This man had sat around his fire, eaten his food, fucked his lover under Ebonspire spires. Zephyr had long since stopped believing in perfect loyalty, but he needed to know that when he handed Ferrith a weapon, he wouldn't strike one of their own in the back.

"Don't. Please." Ferrith blanched. "Ysa will hate you for this."

Zephyr's gut churned. It was true. She would. He feared her judgment. He feared the loss of her love and respect even more. His logic, however, was sound. The danger Ferrith posed justified the need for swift action, but the question remained: would his mate see it that way? Would she see the leader in him or the monster Faerie had taught him to be?

She had begun to accept, even enjoy their bond. What if his decision now resulted in her viewing the bond as a tether to someone she loathed? His lips twisted in a bitter smile. He could no longer breathe without her.

As a male who valued connection above almost all else, he wouldn't survive if she spurned him.

He wouldn't blame her, either.

In some other life, he would have joined her beneath the sheets, matched his breath to hers, or woken her to taste her rosebud lips and sink into her velvet folds. But destiny had mapped out a thorny path for him, over and over. *Fatebreaker*, the Binder had called him. As if he had control.

Still, protecting her came first. "Do it."

Lox leaned forward with a grimace, his auburn beard slightly brushing the crown of Ferrith's head. Then he forged a connection. Ferrith's expression shifted: first came defiance, then confusion, and finally a flicker of pain. A sheen of sweat broke out on his brow, and Zephyr stepped forward, a protective instinct twitching.

Loxley shot him a sharp look. "You know we have no choice."

Zephyr stilled, and then the mortal's intentions buckled. "Ferrith?"

His blue eyes were accusing. "All my life, I've heard stories of *the days of plenty*, and then King Azeem trusted me enough to tell me that our lack of abundance is because of the unravelling of the Grimoire. He asked me to bring him back something that can turn the tide."

Loxley cursed long enough to turn a maiden's ears crimson.

So the mortal king had plans for Faerie. That didn't bode well for any of them.

Ferrith was trembling, now. "I didn't believe that any of the old tales told in the tavern were true, not even when my sister vanished. Who knows what's real or not in this gods-cursed place? In Larkspur, I understood the meaning and order of things. There were rules about how to climb, fall, and belong. I knew the rhythm of market days, which captain of the king's guard would take a bribe, who I could best in a brawl and who to avoid. Because it was all in plain sight."

Loxley snorted, unimpressed. "Clearly, brawling with me was going to end in disaster."

Ferrith's gaze was flat. "It's all a joke to you."

"Maybe I wear the world lightly because otherwise I'd

be crushed beneath it. We gave you hospitality, man, without any requests in return other than loyalty. Not fealty. Loyalty. Do you know how rare that is in Faerie?" replied Loxley.

"Hospitality? I walk into a quiet room, the next minute, a fae male is broiling for a fight or war is being waged. Not to mention your *talents*. Talents I'm supposed to believe are gifts when you can play with my mind, and Ysa can throw me into a void."

"You could have stayed in your home," said Zephyr quietly.

Ferrith's breathing was thin. "My sister died in this blasted realm."

Zephyr knew the deep guilt of losing a sibling. He would drag himself to the gates of the underworld if he could bring Veda back. But he couldn't give an inch. "So you betrayed us."

"I promised to bring King Azeem Faerie secrets." Ferrith's voice faltered. "But I started thinking that I could find a way to be what Maren and Ysa need. Until the ambush today. I'm a soldier. And yet I'm helpless against your kind, male or female. How am I supposed to help Maren and Ysa?"

Zephyr quirked a brow. "*I'm* helping them. This family is helping them."

"You gave away the whisper rings, as though I don't matter at all."

"If that's what you think, then you don't deserve your place amongst us," said Zephyr.

Ferrith's anger flared greater than his fear. "What should I think?"

Loxley gave a sly grin. "Rather than waiting for the

Spymaster to discover the theft, we proved that we bested him. In the direct gaze of the allies he wishes to secure."

Zephyr's shadows crept closer, and Ferrith recoiled. "We don't owe you an explanation. But you should know that there are no laws in this—what did you call it?—*gods-cursed* realm that determines what to do with traitors. Your fate is in our hands. Tell me, plainly. What does the mortal king want from Faerie?"

Ferrith turned pale beneath his tan. "He'll exploit internal rivalries, work out who is vulnerable to betrayal or bargains so that he can neutralise threats spilling into the mortal realm. He wants a return to *the days of plenty*. To make it so that the fields are full of corn again, and the cattle are fat, and that men and women read and write, and learn, and the unnatural storms ebb, and nature regains its balance. He pledged to protect us."

Loxley's brow creased. "Us? You mean the mortals? But the females you love are fae."

A heavy silence fell, then Ferrith said, "I chose the world I knew. You think that makes me the villain?"

"I think," said Zephyr coldly, "that when fear governs choices, someone else always pays the price. I'll explain to Ysa. You wake the others, Lox." The taste of the ember wolf's smoke still filled Zephyr's mouth, but he ignored it.

All he could think of was the pain he was about to cause his mate.

15

YSADORA

Vixora's laughter was the sun.
I carry her memory like a wound that never
heals. I loathe Faerie
for taking her from me.
– Ferrith's diary

T he longer I was separated from Father, the more I appreciated the peaceful childhood he had provided for me. How easy it was to take contentment for granted when it flowed naturally. I made my way to the Forgotten Garden, despite Zephyr's orders to rest, intent on keeping my promise to write to Elowen. But despite my tugs of ink magic, she didn't respond.

Eventually, I returned to the bed chamber I shared with Zephyr, but my heart tapped a wary rhythm beneath my ribs. I lay in the dimness, aware of every creak of Ebonspire's bones. Though Zephyr was not beside me, I felt his unrest as if it were my own, and something else roiled through our connection, although I hadn't learned to read him accurately yet.

At least he hadn't shut me out this time.

Eventually, sleep claimed me. I wandered through a nursery adrift in time, where lullabies played backwards and toys wept in corners. Beyond the window, the landscape shifted with dream-logic: mountains melted into oceans, stars blinked in and out, and forests grew and burned in seconds.

When I turned around, a cradle swung gently, suspended from nothing, lined in black silk. A familiar figure stood beside it, humming a melody that drew me closer. Her void-dark hair spilt over her shoulders, and her violet eyes shimmered with sorrow and the terrible stillness of a female who had waited lifetimes to be seen.

I peered into the cradle. It was empty, but I had a sense that all was not lost. Not yet.

You never accept my gifts, she said. *There's still time.*

Then she turned and walked from the nursery, and her crown slipped from her head. It fell at my feet like a serpent curling into sleep. In my dream, I knew that the serpent would always be there until I was ready to uncoil the truth hidden beneath its scales.

I woke to Zephyr stroking back my hair from my damp brow, disoriented and holding onto the wisps of the dream.

His serious expression shook me from my stupor.

"Did I sleep too long?"

He pushed away from the bed and paced the chamber. "I have something to tell you."

I sat up, heart thudding, my dream secondary to what had befallen him. "Is it Elowen?"

He shook his head. His brief report about Ferrith hit like a slap.

I stared at him. "You let Loxley do that to him? How could you?"

"This isn't the mortal realm, Inkheart. The truth matters more than Ferrith's comfort." His tone hardened. "He admitted it, Ysa."

My heart lurched. I wanted to find something to absolve my friend, but the admission of guilt had come from Ferrith's own lips. Could human mercy survive in a realm like this? "Does Maren know?"

"She will by now." The bond pulsed not with malice, but weariness. "Come. I'll take you to him."

We didn't talk, although Zephyr glanced at me more than once, like he might speak. In the end, he remained silent, and our boots echoed in sync. His jaw was tight, and my spine was stiff, the kind of body language that didn't invite conversation. The quiet made it easier for me to focus on the bond and discern his sadness: it matched my own and told me he hadn't wanted this any more than I did.

Ferrith was my oldest friend. His betrayal hurt, but I understood his fear. He was sunshine and frivolity and had always stood in our corner, but Vixora's death was a festering wound. To him—even more than me—Faerie must have felt like a fever dream he couldn't wake from, with its impossible dragons and twisting magic, and centuries-old fae who viewed mortals as mere sparks: bright, brief, and already burning out.

I dragged in a breath, thinking of the decaying white dragon Gabor had forced Ferrith to ride, how he had seen me run through by the Faerie King of Silence, how the woman he had known as my mother in Larkspur was now capable of singing songs that flayed skin from bone. How I had almost sent him into the void.

I hated that his allegiance was to a king who never had any answers, who only ever started wars to distract from his inadequacies. Still, it was no wonder Ferrith clung to something that felt solid: the mortal king's command, old prejudices, and familiar fears.

We gathered inside the war room, the mercenaries standing in a tense semicircle a few feet apart from Maren and me, although Wylda rested in her chamber, still. There was no satisfaction in Zephyr's face, only fatigue and a flicker of guilt that he quickly buried under cool detachment. Maren was barely leashed. She wrapped her arms around her midriff like she was bandaging herself together.

My stomach sank at the sight of Ferrith. He sat miserably in his chair. He seemed like a stranger wearing my friend's face, and in a way, he was. The small part of me that wanted to console him was dwarfed by cutting disappointment. Elowen would have given everything for the sanctuary Ferrith had received. His usual charm had bled out of him entirely.

No one moved to defend him. Our silence was judgment; the mercenaries' stillness was a collective restraint. We gave Maren the floor. No one interrupted.

She stood a few feet from him. Her shoulders were trembling with the effort of holding back tears or perhaps something hotter. "Is it true?"

Ferrith stood, as if he longed to find himself at her side again. "Maren…"

"No, don't you come closer." The gold-green flecks in

her eyes flashed, and violet sparked in her hands. I took a step towards her, but she gave me a warning glance as she smothered them with effort. "Vixora died, and it hurts, but *we're* alive, Ferrith."

His eyes were rimmed with red. "I was trying to protect you."

Maren balled her fists. "Protect us? Kazimir trusted me to look after Ysa, and whatever your intentions, you were working against us. And you know as much yourself, because you've never kept secrets from us, Ferrith Namara. Not once in your life. I hate that you did this. But I hate what you've done to our friendship even more. Our love. You've poisoned it."

I bit my lip. It wasn't for me to intervene. Not yet. Not when this was still between the two of them.

"You were a fool for pledging yourself to the king and his fruitless, posturing wars. Now this."

Ferrith winced. "It was just easier for you both to ignore my doubts."

My throat stung with unshed tears. Even now, some part of Ferrith still believed he had done the right thing. I didn't know if that made it better or worse. "Why didn't you come to us?"

His gaze flicked away, as if he couldn't stand to look me in the eyes.

"I'd rather we'd parted ways in Larkspur than this," said Maren. "I wish I'd never let you into my bed."

Ferrith stretched out a hand, as if she might take it, even now, even after everything. "You don't mean that. Don't you get it? Larkspur isn't home without you two."

"Why can't you think before you act? You have no idea

what's at stake." Then, softer, broken and raw. "I loved you."

Ferrith's breath shuddered out of him. "I'm sorry, Maren. Let me prove myself. Please."

"You broke my belief in you." With every ounce of dignity she had left, she turned to me and the mercenaries. "Send him away if you must, but don't hurt him."

She walked away to pace in tight lines, her eyes flashing death to anyone who neared her. I knew as soon as we were alone, she'd crumple into my arms.

Zephyr's jaw was tense. "We leave at first light, and we can't take him with us. He's your friend, Ysa. It's your call what happens to him."

Sorrow curled along the threads of the bond: a quiet ache beneath my sternum that was not my own. There was something else beneath the surface, too, a vast spiralling that didn't feel like him.

I met Zephyr's eyes. "No harm was done."

"Only because Lox found him. What should we do with him?"

Blistering stars, how could I decide? The question hung between us like a drawn blade.

A shadow caressed my cheek. "It's an impossible decision, but we need a way forward."

Ferrith pleaded. "Ysa, I can't go back to Larkspur. Not now. Let me make it up to you."

I thought about all the times he had been there for us, and how I would still trust him to defend our lives with his own, because friendship like ours didn't evaporate overnight. It weathered grief and disappointments. It lasted a lifetime. I thought about how he was good and kind, and how fear made new shapes of us. I thought about how all the best decisions I had ever made hadn't been about weighing facts or listing choices. They had been about following my intuition.

Had that been why the Binder had wrenched me free from fate and let my star fall? Her wish for me as a mewling babe had been for courage, discernment, and love. She had warned me to choose carefully who belonged in my inner circle.

Drawing a deep breath, I met Zephyr's clouded sapphire gaze. "I have an idea."

16

ZEPHYR

*Faerie objects are rarely obedient. The compass
was never meant to point north. It latches onto
yearning, not destination. Trickery dulls it. Force
breaks it. Malice confuses it. Only longing can
guide it true, but the heart has many longings,
and therefore, even when it is working,
it can lead you astray.
 - Kazimir's entry to the memory stone*

Ysa's plan was so impossible that Zephyr wanted to beg her to change her mind. During their last clash with the Spymaster, the Circle of Emberlight's intervention had been crucial, but restricting his meeting to Faerie rulers disqualified the Circle of Emberlight from getting involved. Gathering allies of equal standing to Thiago was the only path to success, and Ysadora knew where to begin.

Strategically, her outsider thinking gave them an advantage. She wasn't shackled by centuries of history and established tactics. She didn't bow to custom. What was more, if Faerie intended to turn his mate into a pawn, Zephyr intended to prove what a humiliating error that would be. He would burn their assumptions to ash, or she would. Who could control his mate when she could summon a void? His lips curved into a wicked smile just at the thought of it.

So, here he was with Cyprian in the dining hall, taking the watch together. The wards had been repaired and strengthened, of course, but these last hours amounted to a goodbye of sorts. Zephyr couldn't be sure that Esolas would keep his promise.

Shadows at his feet ribboned left and right, over the ceiling and sinking through the floor, probing for breaches. The dining hall was lit only by the low glow of coals banked in the hearth. There was no laughter at Loxley's antics this time, no hearty enjoyment of Gabor's feasts, nor the clatter of wine goblets; just the soft glug of water from a skin passed between him and his oldest friend.

Zephyr sat with his elbows on the table, fingers threaded together as though in prayer, though no god had ever heeded his pleas. "My fucking uncle. I can feel his shadows reaching for me already."

He shuddered, remembering the frost-laced cliffs of Echohold when Thiago had dragged him to live with his father after his mother's death. He'd been too alive for that court, too full of grief they didn't want to name.

The chill of that place had reached deeper than bone. There, brokenness was seen as something to exploit or erase. In time, Zephyr had learned to don the mask of a courtier for political necessity. For survival. He'd become a stranger to his own self, nearly erasing the youngling who ran wild through Ebonspire. But this time, it was worse.

Returning to the Court of Silence for the meeting of Faerie rulers meant delivering Ysa to his uncle.

Cyprian read the darting shadows across Zephyr's face. "You're not going back as a youngling or the Spymaster's protégé. You're going back as a prince of the Court of Lore. *The Fatebreaker*. A ruthless bastard who's got nothing left to prove."

"What if all I am is a liability to Ysa?"

"Sounds like you need me to knock some sense into you again."

Zephyr huffed a sound that might have been a laugh if it hadn't sounded so much like pain. "I promised her I'd send a moth courier to my father asking him to look out for Elowen." His cousin had maintained silence since the attack, and it made Ysa uneasy about her well-being. He shoved down a prickle of anxiety from his days at that court.

Cyprian edged forward, the newly grey locks of hair on his head shining in the hearth light. "Did Orin respond?"

Zephyr scowled. "He can't even look after himself."

"Are you sure you gave the moth courier the right scent?"

"I found a horse-shaped flint Father gave me in a trinket box. It still smells of his pipe smoke. I hated that Mother pined for him." He shrugged, embarrassed almost. "Maybe she kept mementoes for reasons like this… No doubt he'll still find a way to let me down."

"Maybe. But he sure as hell taught you what it means to show up for your chosen kin." A pause. "In your place,

Thiago would have harnessed a monster army. Lox could have shaped their intent, just for a short while."

The knuckles around Zephyr's waterskin were white. "You say that even after Ylva?"

"A warrior's death is a good death."

He hated pulling rank, but this was one thing he couldn't shift on. "I can't use them. I wouldn't."

"You had no problem asking Lox to break Ferrith."

"He made his choices. The outcast fae are innocent."

They sat with that for a while, then Cyprian said, "I hate seeing Wylda hurt. We built a good thing here. It's a shame it's over."

Zephyr ran an absent hand over the bargain lines on his arm, all the minor alliances he'd made in the hopes of building a net big enough to catch them if they fell. But the games in Faerie were spiralling out of even his control. "Yes, we did."

"So why in all the realms are you going to Tanuhja?" Cyprian held his gaze.

He didn't need to say Gabor's name for Zephyr to know he was thinking it. Gabor, whose betrayal still stung like blood kissed with salt, festering in the gut of every interaction. Gabor, whom Tanuhja had made a spy, then a monster.

"Wylda convinced Ysa to embrace both sides of herself, Nebula and Chaos. She dreams of her mother sometimes. A curse, a gift, I don't know. Just be grateful I'm not dragging you with me."

"I'd follow you to hell, brother. Still, it might be best to talk Ysa out of it."

"What makes you think I can talk Ysa out of anything?"

Cyprian quirked a brow. "You underestimate your influence on her."

Zephyr shrugged. "Perhaps, but what better ally than the mother who yearns for her?"

"The Chaos Queen who made the very monsters we have spent years battling."

Zephyr wished for something damn stronger to drink than water. He had wrestled with whether Tanuhja's decision to turn Faerie's gaze away from Ysadora in the mortal lands by corrupting the outcast fae was forgivable. It wasn't.

She had robbed Ysa of her fae nature—her strength and skills, thereby putting her at more risk—*and* made innocents suffer. Still, there were strategic reasons for agreeing to this mission. "Maybe she can unmake them."

Cyprian grunted and leaned back in his chair.

"Spit it out, brother." Zephyr wasn't a fool. He knew the dynamics at Ebonspire had shifted in more ways than one. Bringing two families together did that, but so did finding his mate. Cyprian had always been the one each of them confided in, and who, in turn, told Zephyr matters the others shied away from. "What are the rest thinking?"

"You squeeze me like a maiden wrings out a cloth at the river."

"And you enjoy our shared confidences."

Cyprian wheeled up his middle finger and arced his cocky brow.

Zephyr wanted to bottle moments like this. The brotherhood between them, especially knowing they would have to part from each other for a time. "Well, go on."

"I am well and truly wrung…" He heaved a sigh. "Lox

spoke truly. There's not a risk he wouldn't take. Sese only agreed because she's mad as hell and wants to take on the whole realm after what happened to Wylda."

"You'll have to stop her from doing anything reckless."

"Telling that female anything is like dangling my manhood over dragonfire to see if it sizzles."

Zephyr gave a weak grin. "Don't I know it."

He lapsed into silence. They were only hours from leaving his beloved Ebonspire. After the Court of Silence, Ebonspire had restored him. Zephyr hadn't yet decided which was more painful: to be wrenched away from his home as a youngling or to be forced to walk away as a grown male.

Every time he turned from Ebonspire, a part of him stayed behind. As if the gatehouse itself stitched together the broken pieces of him, memories too fragile to survive the Faerie wilds. The stone remembered: his childhood laughter in hollow stairwells, the swell of his mother's goodwill, the scrape of Veda's paint brushes against its walls, the once-vibrant presence of Court of Lore fae lingering in the hush between candle flickers.

Zephyr needed it more than ever.

He could feel himself fraying since he'd absorbed the ember wolf's story, his mind blurring into patterns that weren't his. Without Ebonspire as his anchor, he feared he'd be dangerously unmoored. The stories clawed at his mind like roots in dark soil. His mother had told him long ago that stories were meant to be told once and released, unless they evolved.

But the cursed fae stories festered in his mind. They whispered at the corners of his thoughts. Faces he didn't know lurched out of his subconscious. He saw reflections that didn't move with him. They wanted acknowledgement, justice, and retribution.

They crawled under his skin. The clawing talons of the hollowsight gargoyle while he ate his supper. The burning hide of the scorched ember wolf while he washed himself. The clicking lattice of the bone feline in his dreams.

He caught himself listing them as he went about his day: which ones killed fastest, which had children, which had almost lost every kernel of themselves. He kept his troubles tucked close, not wanting to worry Ysa or his kin. Not even Cyprian.

Not when there were battles to come.

"Stop brooding. Leaving this place is hard. You know I get it."

"There's nothing to get." No, he would not speak this pain aloud and burden his friend.

"You're as stubborn as ever. If it were me, I know I'd be taking solace where I could find it." Cyprian met his gaze for a heartbeat. "In the name of the slumbering skies, go to her."

Zephyr gave a tight nod. He stood, shadows shifting with him, and though he tried to keep his tone light, the words fell flat. "You always did enjoy pushing me towards trouble." He paused and dug into his pocket. "I want you to take this on your mission."

Cyprian stared at the item Zephyr placed in front of him. "Ysa's compass."

Zephyr nodded. "It's tricky magic, Cyp. Kazimir hinted that the Binder left it in the bookshop aeons ago. It's crafted to search for something unfamiliar. Be careful how you use it."

"Do you think it's true...about what might be buried in the Silver Sea?"

Neither of them dared to speak it aloud, as if both were fearful that the damn thing was cursed. Zephyr shrugged. "I don't know. I only remember Thiago mentioning it once, when he still trusted me."

"Why are you giving the compass to us? Why shouldn't you and Ysa take it? Why not Lox?"

"Because Wylda needs a win." He clapped Cyprian on the shoulder, then strode away from the dining hall without looking back.

17

ZEPHYR

Anger and distance may cloud your path with
your father, but in time, even broken ties can
mend.
There is good in Orin, waiting beneath the weight
of past mistakes.
- Rowena Ashmoor's letter to her son Zephyr

When Zephyr reached the chamber he shared with Ysa, he couldn't bring himself to disturb her sleep, restless as his mind was. Instead, he leaned against the hallway outside. His shadows continued probing outwards, returning to him in an endless pattern of absorption and reengagement. In a way, this reminded him of all the grunt work he'd done for his uncle.

Back then, he'd blunted his emotions. Now they stormed through him.

Just after the clock struck midnight, Ysa padded out of their chamber, as though somehow the bond told her he was close, even though she hadn't learned to read it as well as he had yet. She jolted at the sight of him. Her gaze swept over him, taking in the dark crescents under his eyes, the churn of shadows, how he carried blades even at this late hour.

He offered her a small, weary smile. "Couldn't sleep?"

"Not after Ferrith. And Elowen's still silent." The glow of the moon at the window painted her face in silver. She pulled long tresses over one shoulder. "I could ask the same of you."

He should have told her to leave him be, to rest before dawn broke, but he needed her. As if by instinct, his hands found her waist, and he pulled her close. At that moment, he would have given anything for the distraction of her body.

She leaned into his touch, but she scowled. "You think they might come for me before first light."

He wanted to kiss away her frown lines. "It's possible. I'm not taking any chances."

He traced a slow circle with his gaze, measuring the dark beyond, then his lips brushed hers, and his hands grazed her breasts. He was satisfied only when he found the quill beneath her tunic and the ink pot in her pocket. The quill pressed lightly against her chest, a quiet reminder of what might be required of her if their enemies struck. His mate had made ink and feather as sharp as any blade.

"That's my girl."

Something trickled through the bond, a sweet melancholy that had no edge of fear. As though all those years sneaking down to her cellar to read faerie tales in Larkspur had given her a whimsy that had not yet been met.

He, too, wanted her to enjoy the wonders of Faerie without looking over her shoulder. He wanted the calligrapher to teach her the intricacies of ink magic and dragon-riding. He wanted to take her for picnics under flowering canopies and make her call out his name when he ravished her next to blossoms that only opened by starlight.

He wanted to ride with her on Mythros through the endless wilds, their laughter snatched by the peaks, their paths unguarded and wide. He wanted to lie in a meadow with her and bear witness to only clouds.

Not skeletal wings. Not circling vultures of war.

Then Ysa arched a brow. "You're checking I'm armed?"

"I'm checking that you understand the demands of Faerie."

"I always carry the quill now." She gave him a wry smile. "Just like you always count exits."

Zephyr's mouth twitched. "I like a quick learner."

Then he dipped his head again. This time, his kiss was slow and consuming, drawing her into a quiet storm. His shadows still pulsed around them, slipping over her calves as they left and returned. They kissed in that half-lit corridor, two hearts in an uneasy rhythm. He poured himself into the kiss, needing to wash away their disquiet, even if just for a moment. But she pulled away with a quizzical look, as if the silence had pulled things to the surface.

She tilted her head, observing him. "The bond feels different."

He cocked an eyebrow in question, praying that she didn't sense the discordant notes within him. "Different, how?"

She bit her lip. "Like it's saturated with parts that don't feel like you. Like a constellation rewritten by a stranger's hand." Confusion marred her face. "I don't know."

But Zephyr knew. He sensed the rage that was less controlled than his own and the ache of regrets that weren't his. The pieces of the outcast fae no longer fitted neatly together like a jigsaw. His lore magic was taxing. It cost him to keep functioning.

He sighed. He'd promised to trust Ysa, to include her. "The stories are rarely quiet anymore."

"Which stories?" But then surprise flitted across her delicate features, as through the bond, she sensed how the stories bled into his bloodstream, the jaggedness of the outcast fae's pain wearing against his sense of self. How the sharp and dark stories he'd absorbed had no exit, only walls to rattle around in.

Her fingers curled against his shirt. "Stars, Zephyr, you can't hold all that."

He gave a small, dry laugh, but it didn't touch his eyes. "They must be louder than I thought."

His shadows still looped, and she looked at them aghast, as if she wanted to shout at them to stop. As if she wanted the world to slow on its axis just so she could fix him, and he loved her for it. Loved her so much that he wondered if she'd be happier without him.

But he also knew that no one, no one else would spend themselves down to the last drop of crimson, the last crack of bone, to protect her. So he pushed down his feelings of unworthiness and explained, "I thought I could manage. But they're bleeding into who I am."

Ysa cupped his face and turned it so they stared into each other's irises: his storm-grey eyes locked on her violet ones. In that moment, Zephyr felt closer to her than anyone across his existence in all the realms.

To his undying shame, she didn't protect herself from the rogue elements of other fae lives that polluted their mate bond. She poured comfort into the bond instead. Love that didn't ask him to be whole, only to let her help. Love so generous it made him want to fall to his knees. But her offering vanished too quickly, swallowed by whatever rose inside him.

Still, she didn't give up, slowly rebuilding his faith in himself through her persistence, even when he looked away.

"When I touched Father's memory stone, I thought I'd drown in it. One male. That was enough to break me for days."

His gaze snapped to hers. Wordlessly. Reverently.

"So I learned to sift. The memories come, but I choose what to hold and what to let go." Her hand drifted downwards to his clavicle and came to a stop between his pectoral muscles. "Maybe Father founded the bookshop to teach me how to sift through what was important. The point is, you don't have to absorb every sorrow like a sponge, Zephyr."

"That's easy to say when your court didn't build its magic on memory," he murmured.

"Maybe you don't have to hold on so tightly to them."

"There's no one else left to carry them." But her prompting made him realise that maybe he was a historian who had wandered too deep into the archives. He wished his mother were alive so he could ask her if it had happened before.

Ysa's rosebud lips pursed. Lips that drove him to insanity. "If you can't let them go, I can help you write down the stories so that others can bear witness. Or we can anchor you to your own stories. How does that sound?"

Zephyr hesitated. It sounded impossible, but he trusted her instincts more than his own. His silence wasn't agreement, but neither was it resistance. Just exhaustion. He gave the slightest nod and laced his fingers with hers.

"I know where to begin."

He led her through the halls of Ebonspire. Her face softened, anticipating that he wanted them to visit the Forgotten Garden, but he hadn't entered that place, not since the day his mother and sister died, and they trapped him there for safekeeping despite his pleas to join the battle.

Maybe he should have had the courage to enter; maybe he wouldn't ever have another chance, but still, he avoided that aching pain. Instead, he veered off into a dark hallway without sconces that now knew no other footfalls, except his.

Ysa's twilight eyes widened as they neared the archway wreathed in silver thistle and old magic, and Zephyr's tight chest eased slightly as he witnessed her wonder.

"I've never noticed this part before."

"There have always been locked doors and shadowed corners here."

He enjoyed showing her the hidden alcoves packed

with books, spiral staircases that led to engraved doorways where the great dramatists of lore had once lived, the now dilapidated stages with a touch of velvet-curtained grandeur still.

Ysa nodded. "I like how the gatehouse unfolds its mysteries to me slowly. As if it knows that my mind has had to encompass almost too much and is taking care of me."

She talked of Ebonspire as if it were a person, and it pleased him more than he could say. So few understood that the castle was more than bricks and mortar. Sometimes Zephyr even thought it sensed his moods.

His voice was gruff when he replied, "But now our pace is dictated by outside forces." He opened the door and rubbed a calloused thumb over her palm before letting go.

Ysa crossed the threshold, her expression gentle. "This place holds the same sadness as the Forgotten Garden."

His voice was quiet, as though he might wake ghosts. "It was once a private family space away from court business. After my mother and Veda died, an aide suggested turning it into a Room of Remembrance to help me grieve." He hadn't appreciated it at the time, but that aide, long dead now, had been right. "It's not much, but it's what I have left of them…"

"It's wonderful."

"I know we've barely begun. I know I've already put so much on your shoulders…"

He had wanted her to see it before they left, in case he didn't get another chance to share it with her. In case the coming battles destroyed this piece of him, too.

She pressed her palm against his chest, as if that might

calm the rush of his sadness. It bloomed instead, and he cursed himself for his softness.

"Sharing your story isn't burdening me. It's giving me a piece of your heart."

Then she turned away to examine the room and took careful steps as if it might actually be his heart she trod on. She lingered over small details. The space was carved from smooth grey stone veined with silver, and he couldn't remember the last time a servant might have polished it.

Rugs layered the floor that he had splayed on as a youngling, kicking his feet up while his shadows unravelled the yarn. He could almost hear Veda scolding him. The air was warm and thick with lavender, as though someone had just left.

A hearth burned low, but there was no wood there, no cinder glow or flickering flame that indicated a real fire. Latticed windows looked out over the spires, and oil paintings lined the walls, many unfinished or half-faded, dreamlike in tone.

"Veda's visions?" asked Ysa.

"Yes." Zephyr swallowed hard, the apple bobbing in his throat. How he wished they had met. He would have given anything to show this room to her when it was full of life. Now it was a shrine to the dead.

She stared at the singular flame in the hearth, steady and purple in colour, as if recalling something, and he realised with a start that he had sanctioned Gabor to teach her about this spell. Even then, he had somehow known that she'd be his.

"It's cast by a spell that feeds on nostalgia. Every decade or so, it needs to be replenished."

"Oh, of course," she said, as if the lesson had come back to her.

Zephyr motioned to a stool by the window. "Veda used to sit right there and paint the storm before it came." A wave of melancholy washed over him. He didn't know whether it was his or hers.

"Did she ever see her own end?"

He took in the dust and hush. "My sister saw many endings. But she didn't predict what silence would follow, or maybe they would have let me die with them."

"Don't say that."

"Forgive me." He shuddered. The stories inside him clawed to get out. "I don't want to forget them. Any of them."

Her gaze swept over relics of lives once lived: his life, before it all changed and Faerie began shedding its skin, changing, as it often did over the millennia. There was a low table scattered with dried, yellowed petals in a pattern reminiscent of ritual, a chessboard abandoned mid-game, a woman's cloak draped over a chair.

"I'll help you remember. Show me."

Zephyr led her through the room with care but didn't dither. The stories he offered were clipped and clinical because he couldn't bear to dip deep into the waters of memory. Now and then, emotion broke through, revealing the layers beneath his restraint: wistful smiles at a charm bracelet his sister had worn, a silver locket engraved with his mother's crest, a rune she had carved to stop him fidgeting on the day he'd broken her favourite clay pot, a music box that still held the scent of honeysuckle, a paint palette Veda had bought him when all he had been interested in was horseplay, and a faded portrait of

Rowena and Veda laughing by a tree that still stood in the grounds.

At that, the bond vibrated with pain, and clouded eyes gauged his reaction.

He was ashamed at the flare of emotion, but Ysa didn't seem to judge him.

"You look so much like your mother," she said.

She always knew the right thing to say. He reached for her then, wrapping his arms around her as if she were the final scrap of driftwood in a black, swallowing sea, and exhaled.

Somehow, the bond had steadied, like a pendulum coming to rest. Where it had once jittered with fractured impressions and too many voices, now it moved with a familiar rhythm, matching his heartbeat. He was so damn grateful.

Her eyes snagged on a wall that bore a half-finished mural. A darkened figure blighted its centre, the paint smudged as if Veda hadn't settled on its identity. A frown knotted Ysa's brow as if she recognised the landscape with its vast frozen wasteland and forbidding castle, even before she recognised the woman. The woman stood in the distance, two snow leopards curled at her feet. They were rendered with painstaking care, down to the shimmer of frost on their fur.

"That's the Court of Silence." He could see from her expression where her thoughts had drifted. "You know, Elowen's silence doesn't mean she's not okay. She's clever. Maybe she doesn't want to raise further suspicions. Maybe she's being watched too closely to communicate with you."

"But she begged for a lifeline beyond the walls of silence."

"Survival comes before desire there." He kissed the top of Ysa's head, then approached the painting. "Veda painted it the year before they died. She used to say art could warn us where words failed. But I never understood this one. I thought the smudge was Thiago. Or even our father. But now I'm not so sure." His jaw flexed. "Perhaps it was never meant to be finished."

Ysa didn't reply, but maybe she sensed the churn that took hold in him again, because she retrieved a stack of parchment from the table and readied her quill and ink pot. Then, she sat at the low table and invited him to tell her the stories of the outcast fae. He joined her, boots unlaced, legs outstretched.

At first, his Inkheart wrote carefully, as she might have in the calligrapher's bookshop, recapturing the flow of the letters, the curves, lines and dots. His chest tightened, imagining her in the calligrapher's bookshop, learning to shape her letters, oblivious about who she was and all she would be to him.

But then, as his stories deepened, as they grew more plentiful, as she traced connections between monsters who had been corrupted from the same court, her magic flowed. It was a thing of beauty, as though the muse herself had found her.

Her ink captured tone, emotion, even scent from Zephyr's memories, crafting entries that seemed alive. The stories were no longer trapped in him. They breathed. Stories of siblings and lovers, mothers and their daughters, fathers and their sons, and loners who preferred the company of the stars to community, and those who spent all their life tending to the land, and so many who wished for more when their fae bodies became corrupted.

When they had finished, Ysadora Silberquill took another page and titled the manuscript *The Secrets of Faerie's Veiled Beasts* by Zephyr Ashmoor. She handed it to him, and an endearing shyness came over her, as if she were unaware of the gift she had given him, how light his mind was in that precise moment. How she was new to Faerie but had changed it and him in ways that should have been impossible. He feared he had exhausted her.

He brushed a lock of hair behind her ear. "Thank you."

"None needed." She shimmied over to him and leaned against his chest. "Zeph? Do you think my father is well?"

He sighed. Kazimir still hadn't responded to her ink missives, almost as if Faerie itself had not yet chosen a side in this game they played.

"Yes. I do. The dragon will keep him safe. Kazimir will find a way to form an alliance with Thalindra, I'm sure of it."

"Okay."

"I gave Cyprian the compass. Is that okay with you?"

"He's your favourite," she murmured.

"Nonsense. You are."

Ysa smiled, then her body sagged against his as if the weight of the day had finally caught up with her.

As the slow tide of sleep washed over her in the Room of Remembrance and his shadows resumed their patrols, Zephyr held Ysa like she was the last sacred thing in a realm that had lost its gods.

As she slept, he wove idle patterns in her hair. He had lived over a century without his mate, after Veda's promise that she would one day come. How lonely he had been after Mother and Veda had died, how doubting before Cyprian had joined him. Against all odds, he had a family of his own once more.

As his beloved Ebonspire creaked around him, one thought consumed him: that he was the luckiest male in all the realms. He would give every drop of himself to build the Faerie of his dreams. But when all was said and done —bargains struck, fae blood spilt, and dragons darkened the skies—all he needed was Ysa, because she was his home.

18

KAZIMIR

Species: Sunflare Drake
Appearance: golden or red scales, lithe body, bat-
like wings, sharpest claws of the Nebula dragons
Characteristics: playful, short-tempered,
affectionate
Abilities: fire-breathing, bursts of light to
disorient foes, precision and agility
- The Dragons and Riders of the Nebula Court

The queen placed the circlet of antlers on her auburn tresses once more. Her silver gaze was shrewd. "Come."

Kazimir was relieved when sound found his ears as they walked out of the sanctum and through the citadel. He tried to get his bearings and absorb details about the practices of this court. He caught the march of tomb guardians, the crunching of bone, the hint of a weapons forge in the distance with rising smoke.

You are well? asked Caldoron, some distance away.

I believe so, Kazimir replied.

Though he was still testing out his frame, he was pleased beyond measure that his gait was straight, though he was still shaky on his feet.

Thalindra was austere in her grey gown, and he was self-conscious in his black robe and still-damp skin. It struck him as a gift of hospitality when she led him to a balcony, where his laundered riding clothes waited alongside a platter of food, its offerings curiously vibrant against the stark surroundings.

Kazimir changed behind an ivory screen, and she watched Caldoron from the balcony until he emerged. The dragon's bronze scales rippled as he shifted his weight from claw to claw. He dwarfed his perch. Though clearly restless, he remained obedient for now.

She beckoned him to a small table. "Sit, calligrapher. Let us see whether your presence is a wound or a salve."

Thalindra sipped from a chalice as Kazimir poured water down his parched throat and took small bites of fruit and bread. No clever strategies came to his mind in his depleted state, and his eyes drifted over white blooms potted in skulls, sculptures—quite beautiful if he didn't dwell on whose bones had been twisted so—and elegant maids dressed in bone filament dresses.

He hadn't yet seen any ink plants, though he wondered if his magic would return to him as quickly as his strength seemed to. He wondered, too, whether the queen would lift the wards long enough for him to send Ysa a message about his rejuvenated health. Perhaps he would even soon have news of an alliance.

"I understand it was your mortal wife who left your body in such ruin," said the faerie queen.

Humiliation was now a frequent companion. He felt almost ludicrous in the riding leathers, like he was better suited to a mortal life of dusty books and an old man's cardigans. Part of him loved that segment of his life. It had been a beautiful life, with Ysa and his songstress wife. But nothing ever stayed the same.

"Danaë is mortal no more."

"I should like to meet her. Her melodies wrought havoc with your body. She's quite the artist."

Kazimir wondered whether Thalindra liked ruins because ruined people could never pretend or because she liked breaking things.

"She resides at the Court of Silence as Thiago's consort."

"Perhaps she finds herself at the wrong court. Many in Faerie have not found their place since the Order of the Glyph fell."

The silence stretched between them, and Kazimir grappled with how to build a bridge between this strange queen and himself that would be to Ysa's advantage.

"How did you and the Circle of Emberlight come to be allies?"

Thalindra surveyed him with unnerving calm. "They came to me burning with pride," she said at last. "Desperate to prove they could ride the dragons and rule the skies, although not one of them has been able to cement her place on the throne of the Court of Nebulas." She paused as if she might share a secret, then her voice rolled on, as smooth as the lacquered vertebrae strung as a necklace around her throat. "They didn't want to be merely the daughters, sisters, and wives of silence in a sky their fathers, brothers, and husbands forbade them."

Araminta flashed into his mind. Kazimir forced his sister out, together with his regrets. This wasn't the time for sentimentality.

"They came to you to consolidate their power."

The faerie queen plucked a petal from a skull-bloom beside her and let it flutter from the balcony, watching it drift ever downwards towards chanting bone shamans.

Her lips curled into something that was not quite a smile. "I do not like outsiders. Did Liora tell you that?"

"She said you tolerate them the way a vulture tolerates a guest near its carrion."

"How is that?"

"Briefly, and only if they don't touch anything."

Thalindra's not-quite-smile deepened, though it didn't reach her eyes. "I always liked her way with words."

Kazimir tried to appear only mildly interested. "But then, why did you seek allies at all?"

"You must understand, calligrapher, nature abhors a vacuum. Even bones require an ecosystem. Scattered in the dust, they are nothing. But bound within a body, supported by sinew, nourished by blood—they endure. I did not want to get involved in the games of Faerie, but this court, like others, was not immune to the Grimoire's collapse."

"So you began to trade with the Circle of Emberlight." What had she traded?

His mouth was dry in anticipation. If he found out what they needed, perhaps he would be able to navigate an alliance. Not food. There seemed to be no lack there. Not clothing. Their robes were made of unusual fibres but of high standard. Not weapons either, judging by the bone-forged, rune-etched ones they wielded.

"Yes, we did." Thalindra sipped deeply from her chalice, then set it down. "Faerie is life. It is flow. Even a court such as mine. Bones are for the living and the dead." She brushed the edge of the table almost tenderly. "The living wear them, shape them, test their strength against the world. And when the life has gone out, the bones remain as a testament, as tools, as warnings. But when the calligraphers stopped doing their work..." she spat the words. "When *you* ran from Faerie, my death magic wasn't enough to stem the flow of magic from this place. I was unable to keep the balance. What is broken in Faerie must be fed."

What is broken in Faerie must be fed. He stared at her, revulsion tightening his spine. Caldoron had warned him that nature had been corrupted here. Kazimir understood her need to keep her home. However much others disparaged him for leaving Faerie, he had fought hard to protect the Order of the Glyph. He would have given his life for it. He had worked just as hard to create their home in Larkspur.

For all the centuries of change he had endured, he was fearful of the changes that the Court of Nebulas had experienced. Maren's glimpses of it and Liora's stories had made his gut clench. However, he would never have stooped to unnatural ways to save his home, as he suspected this faerie queen had. Some paths should never be taken. He had loved Tanuhja until she had made such choices.

"What did you do?" he asked the faerie queen, quietly.

She lifted her chin. "You find the changes here unsavoury. You come here as a diplomat, do you not? My bone shamans have told me how your daughter's star fell and that her decisions shape this realm. I have received the invitation from the King of Silence to visit Echohold to determine all our futures."

Though the calligrapher flinched at the news, Zephyr had been clear: his uncle's rise would not be clean. Unless he found a way to play his part, Ysa would just be another piece on the board to be placed, sacrificed, or claimed.

"You come here to ask for my aid, my friendship, and yet you flare your nostrils and curl your toes at the choices I have made to keep this court intact. Well, calligrapher, I will take no lectures from you. My court and those within it matter more than your discomfort."

"What did you trade with the Circle of Emberlight?" Kazimir asked again.

She threw another petal from the balcony, and Kazimir blinked, transported to the night the Order of the Glyph fell, and then back again, into his body, Thalindra's words spiking dread in him. "I provide the Circle of Emberlight access to the sanctum when their bodies break. In return, Liora offered me something that anchors our existence— stabilising wards, structures, and my death magic— purifying the necrotic energy to ensure we don't decay into oblivion. Her offering acts as a preservative in the presence of so much death. It's how this court remains a functioning ecosystem, not just a crypt. Plants still grow, creatures still move, and decay is not a collapse without conclusion."

Kazimir's skin crawled, as if the magic of this place

settled in his marrow by virtue of breathing its air, being healed in its sanctum. The food laid out before them now made his stomach turn. "What currency keeps the balance from tipping? What did Liora offer you that you so gladly accepted?"

"A small amount of something only dragonkind can give." This time, Thalindra's smile was genuine, and it revealed that she did not understand dragons or their wrath, and that maybe Liora Bramick didn't either. How could an order of females so quickly replace what it had taken their male counterparts centuries to learn? "Dragon bone dust."

Kazimir went still. Not the stillness of calm, but the brittle quiet of incandescent rage. The dust of dragon bones carried the memory of immense, enduring life. Dragon bones still hummed with the echo of life force long after death.

His bond with Caldoron buzzed like a live wire through his ribs, burning with rage, betrayal, and mourning. Kazimir didn't try to soothe it. He shared it. He let it rise. The bronze dragon launched from his high perch atop the citadel with a thunderous snap. Great wings spread across the sky, metal-bright membranes that caught what little light pierced this damned court's dim sky. The dragon's descent was furious: less flight than plunge.

The calligrapher was taken back again to the night that haunted him more than any other. More than the night Lunarys had dusted and he had feared that Ysa and Maren would be imprisoned by Thiago too. More than even the night that Danaë had tortured him. That night lived in him, coiled behind his ribs like a shard of metal too deep to remove. It was one memory he hadn't put into the ancient stone.

It hadn't just been calligraphers who had died when the Order of the Glyph fell.

It had been dragons.

Kazimir had watched dragons fall from the sky like stars being snuffed out, their wings torn, their roars breaking like thunder across a darkened horizon. Dragons that died in the wild glory of battle, except that death was never glorious.

It was wretched and agonising, and for dragons, it was slow. A dragon didn't die cleanly. Their bones groaned apart. Magic burned out of them in waves: violent, bright, then dimming like the last embers of a fire choked by ash.

He shuddered as he remembered. A last blaze before silence. Wings that twitched against scorched ground. Eyes, once full of stars, bleak with pain and confusion, long before the last breath. There was nothing noble in it. Nothing poetic in the way fire seared flesh or blood thickened to black tar. So many of them died alone.

His chest tightened. Some chose to fall. From Caldoron's back, he had witnessed a ruby-scaled, long-necked riderless Sunflare Drake veer away from the fight, climb high into the sky, wings shivering with strain. It locked eyes with him across the chaos, but the ink stores were entirely depleted by then for Kazimir to intervene. He wept as the Sunflare Drake folded its wings, turning inwards with a haunting kind of peace, deliberately—no enemy at its tail, no cry, neither protecting its rider nor in a blaze of unity—spiralled to the ground like a dying comet.

That dragon wasn't the only one that chose death. Why choose to fall? Why abandon their riders?

He didn't understand it then; he didn't understand it now.

Kazimir turned to the faerie queen, and the pulse in his throat thudded like a war drum.

His voice was low and dangerous, as if speaking the words too loudly might ignite something he couldn't contain. "Dragon bone dust."

His eyes flicked to the citadel, to the place his dragon had perched just moments before, now empty.

They disturbed dragon remains. Sulphuric smoke filled the air. Caldoron's roar reached deep into bone and marrow. *Not remnants from a battlefield. They desecrated the pyre that my kind built in memory of our fallen. They ground our bones. Refined them. They bottled and bartered our remains to feed the hunger of a decaying court. And I sat like a tame beast while you healed.*

Kazimir stood as screams rang out across the Court of Bones, fists curling. *We will right this heinous wrong.*

Be ready, said Caldoron. *Let us hope your healed body can sustain what comes next.*

Thalindra rose from her seat and took a single step back, silver eyes narrowed, her voice silken. "You would abandon diplomacy, calligrapher?"

He glimpsed the dragon, and his heart sang. Wind shrieked around Caldoron's form as he sliced through the air, his talons curled with violent purpose. Sparks flew from his nostrils, flecks of molten gold flaring across his scales as if his rage had seared through from within.

The very stones of the balcony trembled at his approach. Thalindra's maids scattered like windblown leaves, their composure gone. Somewhere, Kazimir heard the clack and clatter of bone soldiers surging forward to protect their queen.

Kazimir didn't answer. He was already moving, body coiled with instinct before his mind weighed the precise calculations of an old dragon rider to make this leap, if his health had recovered enough in the pale sanctuary to attempt such a thing.

He vaulted the balcony rail without hesitation, the fall brief and brutal. He found that his body felt like his own again, and the healing had knitted him together piece by piece. His breath came easier. The ache in his spine had softened to memory. Muscles moved without hesitation.

Caldoron swept beneath him in perfect rhythm, and Kazimir landed hard on the dragon's shoulders, his knees locking into the familiar grooves of scale and spine.

The world snapped into focus.

Beneath him, Caldoron opened his vast jaws with a hiss that sang of ancient fury. A familiar glow built in the dragon's throat, golden-white and rising, illuminating the bone-lined parapets like a false dawn.

The calligrapher knew he wouldn't blame the dragon for taking revenge.

But as flames licked at the dragon's teeth and his breath scorched the air, he also knew with grim certainty that any hopes of an alliance—crucial to Ysa's freedom and survival—had crumbled.

19

YSADORA

They sang of her with silver tongues
the queen of dusk-stitched skies
But chaos cloaked in kindness comes
with softest voice and lies
She wept for child and lover both,
yet loosed the beasts she blamed
And in her gaze the world dissolved
too wild, too far, too shamed
Her voice was hush, her will was storm,
a lullaby mid-war
With violet gaze and hair like night
her daughter's face she wore.
Her crown was forged of iron bloom,
with violet flame it burned
A queen of love and ruin both
too far to be returned.

– An old faerie ballad

Our departure from Ebonspire was a quiet, weighty cut.

There was the soft rustle of cloaks, the snap of fastened buckles, the grunt of the males heaving shut a battered trunk. We took only essentials. Wylda, now healed, gathered the last of the salves with Sequoia and added them to the pile in the stables. Maren prepared packs of food and filled waterskins. I busied myself with inks. Cyprian hid the trunks in pockets of time, and we prepared saddlebags to carry the rest. Loxley readied the horses.

Zephyr moved through the bustle like a thread of dark silk, checking packs, lending his strength to one job then another, a shadowy fortitude beneath the churn.

Ours was a love that flared bright in battle and burned steady in quiet, stolen hours. The hours in the Room of Remembrance, when Zephyr had stripped away all artifice, brought calm to my soul, like a pond after a storm, as though we'd affirmed to each other that we'd choose each other, again and again, even in the darkest corridors of our past.

But our growing personal happiness was about to be upended.

Earlier, Maren had sobbed, muffling her cries on my shoulder. Now she packed in tight silence, her usual chatter stilled. Ferrith, freed from his place in the dungeons, gave everyone except her a wide berth. Love didn't vanish neatly. It lingered like sap on the skin: sweet, stubborn, and impossible to scrub off. That was as true for her as for him.

The radiant chain coiling around my wrist was a reminder of the bargain I'd struck with Esolas to attend the meeting of the rulers. For Thiago, I was a tool to reimagine Faerie. But Thiago had underestimated not only me, but also my mate.

Zephyr's resolve to shift the scales was a dark, seething thing. The mercenaries whispered of how his magic had been powerful enough to cloak the Binder in death from those who wished to control Faerie. How he could cloak me in the same way during the journey. How, for the first time, he was a match for his uncle. How he had never been willing to inflict pain on his uncle before, but I had changed that.

It was true. Zephyr's mind had sharpened into a weapon of strategy, fed by the release of the monsters, the loss of Ebonspire, and the threat to those he loved most. He'd find a way not only to bring Thiago to heel, but to quiet every other greedy ruler circling like vultures around me.

I believed it. Still, fear pooled in my gut like stagnant water.

Our plan was three-fold: to strengthen our alliances across Faerie, hone my magic, and maximise time for both by preventing my capture before the meeting commenced.

Only then would we stand a good chance of overcoming Thiago. Whether he would be High King would be determined by a simple vote cast by the remaining rulers of Faerie.

Seven courts remained: Silence, Luminosity, Nebulas, Embers, Chaos, Bones, and Silver Seas.

The Court of Silence was ruled by Thiago, and the Court of Luminosity's allegiance was muddy. The Court of

Nebulas was governed by the Circle of Emberlight in the absence of a true ruler, and they could not vote. And, according to Zephyr, the Court of Embers had not once allied with another court in Faerie history.

That left the Court of Chaos, the Court of Bones, and the Court of Silver Seas as the king makers. And that was where we decided to focus our efforts.

Zephyr, Loxley and I would seek an alliance with my mother, the Chaos Queen, in addition to a cure for the outcast fae.

Father already sought allies at the Court of Bones.

Cyprian, Wylda, and Sequoia would form a delegation to the Court of Silver Seas, where whispers claimed the High King's crown had been buried in the deepest ocean trench after the Sundering.

The last part of the plan was the simplest—but perhaps the most difficult for me—because it involved parting from Maren and Ferrith. What cleverer way to split the attention of would-be attackers than for our group to go in different directions?

Maren and Ferrith would venture past the Wraithwoods—with strict warnings to stay clear of entering them—to the Court of Nebulas, where Maren would brief the Circle of Emberlight.

Smoke and mirrors. Bargains and sacrifice. Zephyr had told me that's what it took to win battles in Faerie.

"The journey is too dangerous for Maren. I'll go alone," begged Ferrith, as though running the gauntlet and returning with his head held high could mend our friendship.

He'd heard the stories of the ever-shifting maze of trees in the Wraithwoods that trapped wanderers until madness took root and ghosts that wailed with the echoes of their final thoughts. And the bone feline, with sockets like starless voids.

I'd told them all of Elowen's belief that Danaë had gained immortality after an ordeal in those woods. An ordeal that had made her bite off her tongue. The stories played into the cautionary tales whispered in Larkspur to keep children close to hearth and home. They prised open the wounds of losing Vixora.

Ferrith wasn't a child anymore; the warnings rang louder, more viscerally as a grown man who knew enough about Faerie to understand that shadows did, sometimes, have claws. That woods sometimes breathed at the edge of paths. That scraps of lore and half-lost ballads often had their basis in truth.

It struck me as twice as courageous that, with all Ferrith's beliefs and loss, all his weaknesses as a mortal in Faerie, he was willing to undertake a journey to spare Maren the pain of it.

Not that she agreed.

Maren spun around, and her horse threw its head in agitation. "Will you just stop it? Will you stop spouting nonsense?"

"Let me make this right," Ferrith shot back. "Unless you don't trust me?"

She threw her hands up. "Blistering stars, of course, I don't trust you. Likely you'll go running to King Azeem."

The air went out of him. "Is that what you truly think?"

"You don't get to play the martyr," Zephyr cut in. "This isn't about redemption. It's strategy."

"You've lost your chance to have a say," I said quietly.

"If our friendship means anything to you, you keep Maren safe."

I didn't mean it to come out like that. I needed them both to survive.

"You really think so little of me." Even now, he was more lost lamb than wolf.

"I don't know what to think. But the two of you, with your scent, give us the best chance of fooling our enemies."

He looked at Maren and me in disgust. "That's how it is then. And you call *this* a family." A shadow passed over his face as though he prepared to sacrifice himself if it came to it.

I wished that he had stayed neatly in my past without his newer, more complex colours. I wished he hadn't tainted how I felt about our friendship and that he had remained safely in Larkspur.

But it was the smartest strategy to send Maren and Ferrith to the Court of Nebulas, glamoured to be our doppelgängers.

Wylda beckoned Maren and Ferrith to a corner of the stables. Her fungal magic, linked to hallucinations, made her particularly skilled at glamours. To fae senses, the human world dulled distinctions. Maren, Ferrith, and I had lived so long in Larkspur that we had absorbed the same scent-markers over time: damp timber walls, the oily undertone of lamp smoke, frayed wool, stews brewed too long, baths in the creek, and soap sold by sweet, mad Annie.

Individually, we carried threads of self: ink and old paper on me, cinnamon and sourdough on Maren, and ale and rye fields on Ferrith. But our scents tangled, layered atop one another like overlapping brushstrokes. To distant hunters, we'd harmonise into one composite fragrance: mortal.

The lines of Maren's round face became heart-shaped, her rusty hair dulling and lengthening into inky waves, her amber eyes became amethyst, their expression equal parts warning and wonder. She had known me her whole life and mimicked my bearing with ease, turning her vivaciousness into stillness.

Ferrith's glamour didn't take so well because glamours didn't sit neatly on those unsure of themselves. Wylda's magic stretched his frame just a touch and honed his muscles. His boyish charm sharpened into Zephyr's measured elegance. His rumpled shirt became Zephyr's high-collared garb. Cornflower blue eyes darkened to the colour of stormy skies. Light drained from his golden curls, and they unfurled into raven-dark waves. But his movements seemed too twitchy to be my mate's.

Fae glamours could mimic appearance, but not always essence. The lightness of footsteps, the rhythm of breathing, even a slight tilt of the head could puncture the illusion. Still, we gambled on the haste of our enemies. The clock was ticking not just for us, but for them.

Most wouldn't stop to breathe us in. They'd glimpse the silhouette of a male with dark hair and a female with violet eyes, and that would give us time to get to the Court of Chaos. Ferrith would never let anything happen to Maren, and she was formidable in her own right. At least, that's how I quashed my misgivings.

Perspiration shone on Wylda's brow as she assessed her work with a grim nod. "No glamour is perfect. But they will hold at a distance. Until someone looks too closely or the magic frays... I give it two days."

Loxley's grin was feral. "The corrupted fae or the real monsters still in their fae skin will have caught them by then."

Ferrith's temper snapped. "Better to face the monsters out there than the ones playing king in here."

Before Lox could bite back, Maren stepped between them, eyes glittering like twin suns. "Mockery doesn't make your warnings any more useful."

"She's right." Zephyr's voice was as cold as a northern gale. "Enough, both of you."

Loxley backed off with a shrug and sauntered towards Sequoia, but the spark of challenge remained in his gaze. All was far from forgiven, and only Zephyr's leadership stood between Ferrith and them using him for sport.

Then Zephyr came towards me. Sadness pooled in the bond, like a river struggling beneath winter ice.

I tried to distract him. *Remind me what it feels like to be alone again.*

Interest piqued in his gaze. *Warm. Breathless. Probably illegal in three courts.*

My mind flashed to our tangled bodies on the hay bales, the toffee kisses and riding him until we both climaxed. *Tell me more.*

The way you're looking at me is how wars start. A shadow caressed my cheek and dipped lower. *Now I'm furious we're not alone.*

"Zeph, Mythros isn't keen on this saddle," called out Loxley. "And he looks murderous that I have the gall to do this job."

My mate groaned. *Let's fake our deaths and retire to the Feylight Marshes.*

I sighed. *Could you abandon your dreams of a fairer realm?*

If our kin were safe. For you…yes, I could. A caress shivered through the bond before he turned on his heel.

When the hour of our departure arrived, some of my mate's shadows peeled away to cloak the gatehouse once more. Because Zephyr Ashmoor would always leave a part of himself at Ebonspire.

"Secure your allies," commanded Zephyr. "We gather in a fortnight at the meeting of the rulers. Do not risk yourselves. If all hell breaks loose, remember the safe havens we have in place. Keep moving. Ysa must resist ink messages, and you must not risk making contact unless you can be certain you won't be intercepted. Bide your time until we meet again."

We mounted the horses. I rode with Zephyr, and our group parted ways: the mercenaries vigilant and unmoored, Ferrith tense and regretful, and Maren equal parts fierce and vulnerable, and it seemed even Mythros dragged his hooves.

All I could think of was whether we would ever find our way back to each other again. There was no fanfare, no banner hailing from the Court of Lore, although for Zephyr, we all would have stood under it. There was no quiet blessing for the sanctuary we loved, except in our minds. Soon, the spires existed only in my memory.

Only when we were some distance away did I remember Elowen and how Ebonspire had been a beacon of safety for her, now cruelly out of reach.

20

ELOWEN

Glass remembers what younglings forget—
That love without reverence turns quickly to debt.
– Danaë's song lyrics

Come snow or shadow, throughout her bitterly lonely life, Elowen was forced to sit at the needle-thin table to eat supper with her family. Sometimes, she sat in her stillness, picking at her food, and imagined their heads sliced off by invisible wire just for the thrill of it: her father in the middle of another insufferable decree, her mother's poise broken at last, her uncle slumping into longed-for oblivion.

She'd twiddle her whisper ring and do it herself, the ghoulish snow leopards first of course, for practical and emotional reasons, given that she suspected her mother loved them more than her children.

Xaire, however, elicited no such thought-violence. For

all his vanity and arrogance, she was devoted to her twin, although sometimes she suspected his affection did not quite rise to the level of hers.

Still, in a court as cold as Silence, even a crumb of warmth felt like a five-course feast.

Once, she could have gone days without affection. It had taken a lifetime's work to harden herself into something sleek and untouchable, all glass edges and frozen marrow. She wore her detachment like a fine cloak, and in some ways, her cousin Zephyr had been a sort of role model. Affection was not offered at the Court of Silence, so Elowen taught herself not to need it.

But something had shifted in her, subtly at first, and the blame lay at Ysa's feet.

Ysa was her mother's other child, the one Danaë had cared for in the mortal world but left when power beckoned. A deep, entirely unpredictable, connection had developed between the two women in the course of their message-writing.

But now that the practice was too dangerous to continue, the absence of affection was louder than ever. Elowen longed for a hand to brush hers, not in command, but in comfort. For someone to glance at her not with scrutiny, but with softness. She longed for Ysa's friendship and sisterhood. She felt its lack like a phantom limb: no longer there, but always missed.

All those thoughts reeled through Elowen's mind while she kept her face blank.

Any vulnerability shown here would have lasting consequences for the unfortunate person who showed it.

The table was long enough for three dozen courtiers,

yet only five ever dined, each spaced out as though they feared contagion. Tonight, her father's shadows licked at the walls, shifting as if in response to breath or betrayal.

The obsidian table reflected the glimmer of candles, and the despicable snow leopards prowled in a slow circle at the backs of chairs. Plush rugs swallowed the footfalls of grey servants bringing platters to the table: glazed pheasant on pearled ice, bloodless roots carved into lilies, and violet grapes on silvered vines.

Elowen didn't know the servants' names, and she wouldn't have said thank you even if she had been able to speak. Her mother frowned upon improper relations with the staff. A mere hello as a youngling had resulted in one of her father's spiders whipping her shins.

Instead, Elowen listened to her family talk around her, feigning civility and cool menace, while her mouth stayed magically muzzled until mealtime. They thought muzzling her reinforced their power, but there was a strange power, too, in imagining how one day she would set the table ablaze.

When her father's magic released her binding at last, she waited with folded hands in her lap, allowing the rest of the table to take first pickings of their food. It was her silent rebellion for the humiliation, an act of control not to give them the satisfaction of knowing she was hungry and at the mercy of their whims.

Her father swirled his wine glass, anger evident from the way he clutched his stem. He was often angry. She had gleaned her father's rage earlier that day from elsewhere in the castle, though not the reason for it. It would have shocked her more to see him relaxed. She didn't think she had ever seen him bubble with laughter; she doubted it had even happened in his youth.

Her mother's mouth thinned into a line. "Is something wrong, my beloved?"

Danaë's golden eyes darted to the stem. She had commissioned a thousand replicas from the court's glass smiths for precisely this reason. But there were similarities between her parents, too. Sometimes, when in a fury, her mother went down to the cavernous cellars to sing and shatter them one by one.

"Esolas returned the whisper rings." Threats as sharp as icicles formed in the pause between breaths. "But not the girl."

Elowen did not move, though her heart jolted into a frantic rhythm. He was talking about Ysadora. He had to be. So that was why earlier that day servants had hidden in the walls, their terrified breaths echoing through stone; why the temperature had dropped across Echohold and why her father's shadows had thrashed along ceiling beams like serpents; why her uncle had arrived at dinner with a bloodied cheek and hair pulled from his scalp.

Her father had asked the King of Luminosity to bring Ysa to him.

Elowen's hunger pangs evaporated, leaving a roiling angst. If her father got his hands on Ysa, he would do unthinkable things, and Ysa wasn't as unbreakable as her. She hadn't known the cold kind of anger Thiago was capable of.

Thank the frost veil, she had Zephyr to protect her.

How galling it must have been for the illustrious *Spymaster* to discover the two whisper rings had been stolen from under his nose. But then, Zephyr had practised thievery with his mercenaries for decades and had been quick-fingered even as a youngling.

Zephyr had once stolen one of her father's spell maps from under a spider's belt. He hadn't even used his shadows: just charm and audacity. He'd winked at Elowen afterwards, ink on his fingers, before disappearing into shadow.

That had been the first time she realised her cousin would be dangerous, that he was more than the desolate thing that had arrived from the Court of Lore.

There had been a time Thiago himself had benefited from Zephyr's guile, before uncle and nephew had become estranged. But now, her cousin had taken Ysa from under her father's nose and lived to see the dawn.

Even before this latest sign of their deteriorated relations, Elowen had found a portrait of Zephyr, once hung in her father's office, slashed across the face and burning in a rubbish heap in the gardens. She dreaded to think what her father planned to do with them now. Or what revenge he had planned for the King of Luminosity.

Because, regardless of what minor prize Esolas returned, her father was not a man who could turn the other cheek when thwarted. His ambition determined every choice.

Her mother's porcelain voice was full of soft, performative calm to keep his wrath from erupting again. "It's good the whisper rings have been returned to us, beloved."

"Good?" asked her father coldly. "Zephyr makes me look a fool before the court. Before the kings and queens of Faerie."

At the mention of his son, Orin muttered like a male hoping to dissolve into shadow.

Her mother's golden eyes flickered, and Elowen wondered how often in the privacy of their bedchamber they had discussed Ysa, whether her mother would choose power over the safety of the child she had raised before her life in Faerie.

"Perhaps the calligrapher's daughter can be convinced." The othering of Ysadora, the reluctance to name her or claim her as someone other than a stranger, marked out her mother's cowardice and caution.

Throughout the exchange, Elowen feigned disinterest, her expression schooled to impassivity. Her father never told her his plans, but she very much wanted to glean information for Ysa. Her uncle was even further out in the cold, although there had been a time when he and her father had been close. Before Orin fell in love with Rowena Ashmoor.

Across the table, Xaire said nothing. Elowen had seen him hedge his bets a hundred times: the way he retreated, playing the careful heir when their father was in one of his moods or embroiled in another scheme.

"The question is, wife, if we are to boil down the matter, was a faerie king...*unable* to persuade Ysadora Silberquill to come to this court..." Pale grey eyes glinted in his ashen white face, blue veins running beneath, as he sipped his wine. "Or was he *unwilling*?"

Her mother was as beautiful as ever tonight, blonde hair smoothed into a chignon at her nape and her gown a delicate rose that made her seem more innocent than her dark heart. After all, what mother would inflict silence on her daughter when most mothers tucked their daughter's truths into their hearts like love notes?

Instead, Elowen had learned to fold her thoughts inwards, to bury them beneath layers of frost and poise. There were no soft confidences in the Court of Silence, no shared giggles over pastries or whispered warnings about cruel faerie lords and their hungers. Her mother's version of love was an absence of inconvenient emotion.

Her mother finished chewing the single grape in her mouth and dabbed her mouth with a damask napkin. "Thiago, you cannot mean to harm a faerie king of this realm."

Her father's smile curved like a sickle. "I've done worse." And yet it wasn't Esolas that Elowen worried for, it was Ysa. Her father wanted Ysa as a means to reshape Faerie, especially now that she had denied him.

"We must tread carefully. You are not High King yet, beloved."

Elowen froze. Her father meant to be High King. He meant to exert even greater control over them all. If he were High King, there was no place in Faerie she could hide that he wouldn't reach her. She had to warn Ysa. Waiting until tomorrow wouldn't do. Perhaps after supper, she could use her whisper ring.

Her father's gaze snapped to Xaire. "Well? Have you nothing to say? You're meant to be my second."

Except they all knew that Zephyr had been his favourite. He had preferred his nephew over his son, and certainly over his daughter. His mastery over Zephyr had been a way to humiliate and assert his dominance over Orin, and show the court that the throne was always meant to be his.

But it pleased Elowen that the bloodheart tree was shedding. From its twisted branches, crimson leaves curled and dropped like embers, slick with a dew that gleamed too red to be morning-born.

Elowen had been born a princess of the court, with all the privileges that entailed, but she—more than Xaire or even Zephyr—had been subjected to such harms that she couldn't help relish the possibility that her father might be toppled from his throne.

A lock of dark hair fell into her twin's brown eyes, the colour their mother's had been before Wraithwoods had made her fae. Xaire's jaw worked, a subtle clench and release. "I thought that's what you offered Esolas."

That earned him a glance sharp enough to wound from their mother, though no words followed.

The snow leopards seemed to smile, relishing the scent of fear.

Elowen swallowed a whimper, afraid for her twin. The binding spell had been removed for the meal, but no one expected her to speak, least of all Xaire. The mood had been strained between them since she had turned her magic on him under the bloodheart tree, allowing Gabor to escape with Ysa. He hadn't forgiven her yet.

Still, she worried for him. She caught every tightening of muscle in her father, every place where pride cracked and control thinned. Her father thought them all beasts to be controlled with reins. To provoke him was to risk too much.

But to her relief, Xaire didn't seem to be the target that suppertime. Her father took a long, swirling sip of wine, his pale grey eyes hooded, and gnawing quiet followed: a silence meant to fray nerves, not soothe them.

Then he turned his attention to Orin. "What shall we
do with that son of yours, brother?" The question was
asked only to goad, not to consult. It was a blade wrapped
in silk, meant to cut deep without the mess.

Orin's knife scraped the plate, drawing a shrill note.
"Whatever you deem appropriate, my king. You've always
had the better judgment in such delicate matters." He had
always been too soft for this court: more moss than stone.

In happier times, Orin had been plumper, although
even in misery, his genes were not as predisposed to
gauntness as her father's. Almost as though her father's
mean streak meant that his body didn't waste energy on
softness.

Pity curled in Elowen's gut, but she couldn't bear to
look at him. The way he shrank in on himself, the way his
voice folded like damp paper. What good was family if it
folded when pressed? Orin should have spirited Zephyr
away from the Court of Silence when he had a chance. He
should have tried everything to save his relationship with
Rowena and his children. But he hadn't.

Now he was stuck here like the rest of them. Only
Elowen's trust that Ysa would make good on their bargain
gave her the strength to bide her time and sit there with a
straight spine.

Her father set down his glass with a distinct clink, like
the sounding of a gavel. The glint in his eyes told her he
was enjoying himself. "As King, I can exile Zephyr from
this court. As High King, I can strip him of his name."

Orin flinched. He straightened his posture, but only a
little. "Why not silence him, like you do all things you
don't understand?"

Her father laughed softly, a sound with no mirth.

"There it is. The spine of a wyrm, writhing for attention. I understand more than you think, Orin. Including the depths of your cowardice."

Her mother fixed her gaze on her cut of glazed pheasant, her fork carving without appetite. "Remind me, Thiago, why do we allow him at the table?"

"What interests me more is why there is a spark of colour in our daughter's cheeks."

Her mother hesitated. "I've said it before. You do look different, child. Yet whatever you and Xaire have been arguing about is unresolved. So what is going on in your pretty head?"

Elowen tensed, but she refused to speak.

"Still bitter, then," said her mother mildly. "Or perhaps still too fragile."

The snow leopards behind her blinked lazily, their eyes catching the candlelight like coins beneath water.

"You're not fragile, are you, Elowen?" Her father's shadows thickened around the room as if listening. "Your steps have been lighter around these halls of late. Answer your mother. Or is that too much to ask?"

Xaire coughed into his hand. *They're baiting you.*

Elowen folded her hands in her lap, glad beyond measure that Xaire's anger had thawed enough to speak to her. *Baiting me is nothing new.* But it *did* feel new for them both to attack her in front of Orin. Her father never broke with the pretence of an idealised family in front of his brother. It was at that moment that Elowen realised she was the prey that evening.

Still, she did not cower; she was utterly and completely done with cowering.

Her father's fingers drummed the table once, twice,

then stilled. His voice was low and venom-smooth. She recognised his coiled fury, pressed into every mannerism like a dam bracing before the flood.

"Care to explain this?" He plucked a vial from the shadows and flung it down the table like filth. It skidded to a stop near her table setting, jostling a slice of frozen pear on the platter in front of her.

Across the table, her mother's breath fogged her wine glass as she stared, unblinking, at her daughter. "Elowen, surely you've not been scheming behind our backs?"

One leopard's lips curled back in a soundless snarl. Its eyes burned with a predator's fury, the same fury simmering beneath her mother's crystalline composure. For one out-of-body moment, Elowen wondered where the other leopard was and whether she'd been foolish not to take a single bite of food.

Then she pinged back into herself, looked at Ysadora's captured ink, and realised that for all her attempts at subterfuge, she didn't have the skill of her father and his spiders. That she had been found out as easily as a youngling playing hide and seek in the marshes.

Her father knew she had been communicating with the enemy.

"Elowen is loyal to a fault," said Xaire, but Elowen knew that even loyalty had its limits.

Uncle Orin stirred opposite her, his wine untouched. "This is not the time for such discussions, my king."

"This is exactly the time." Her father watched her with the purview of a man who had built a monument from stone and silence and didn't yet realise the foundation already cracked. "*My* daughter is more loyal than *your* son. Let Elowen prove she's not just a cage of unspoken things. Let her prove that she is useful beyond her telepathic bond with her twin."

Elowen vowed that she would save the knowledge of the full force of her magic until the time when she could hurt him most.

Her mother lifted her wine glass in quiet ceremony, as if to sip away the rising tension.

Beneath the table now, the leopards rumbled a warning low in their throats.

Tell them of what you spoke with the calligrapher's daughter that night. Tell them all you know, said Xaire. *Save yourself.*

Elowen met her brother's brown eyes, and it surprised her to see compassion there. *I won't betray her.*

Xaire hardened. *They will find the mark of your bargain with her. They will hurt you.*

Did he mean their parents or their father's spiders? She didn't even know if it mattered, now that she was resolved to take her path. She was nothing, if not consequential. She didn't move, didn't blink. Her throat was dry, but her spine did not waver, even as her father's shadows gathered at his heels and knuckles.

She had seen him act this way with many others, and it was simply her turn.

"You do not deserve the protection of this family. You do not deserve a whisper ring." Her father's shadows burst forth, first like dense fog, then like sinew, rushing across the needle-thin table before she could react, pinning her wrists to its edge.

Elowen's chair skidded back as she strained against these new bindings, but the pressure was bruising. Still, she did not make a sound. When she saw how it angered him, how the veins bulged in his forehead beneath the black cap of his hair, she doubled down.

Beneath the table, one snow leopard bit her ankle, and she sucked in her breath as the other joined in. Not deep bites, but possessive ones: a warning not to run; a warning to submit. She tried to focus on the vial of Ysa's ink droplets, on how each passing moment was one closer to being saved from her family and this court.

"Silence is not merely the absence of sound. It is discipline. Obedience." Her father's blade glinted red in the low light.

The entire room tilted. The servants faded into the thick-carpeted shadows behind the curtains. Her mother set down her wine glass, and the crimson liquid continued to swirl from the motion. Orin made a noise—half breath, half protest—or maybe it was Xaire. With her heart thudding painfully in her chest, Elowen couldn't be sure.

One shadow pulled forward her left hand by the wrist, shooting past her empty plate, grazing her elbow. The Faerie King of Silence, who was her father in name and biology only, lifted his blade and struck the table still laid with their supper.

"Leave her alone." Xaire lunged—too slow.

Elowen's brother's shadows flickered like startled birds bursting from a tree. They were no match for a centuries-old faerie king in his own court. They were raw and untrained, brittle things born of fear and love, not fury or dominion. Their father didn't spare them a glance. His shadows swallowed Xaire's in one breathless instant.

The air snapped like a cracked whip, and Elowen imagined in that flash what she would do if she had shadows at her heels. If she had been born the strongest of them.

Then their father's blade came down on her hand and sliced off the finger that bore her whisper ring, just beneath the knuckle. It was the finger mortals deemed sacred; the finger lovers swore vows upon.

The ring clattered once, then twice, before the folds of the heavy rug swallowed it, and the severed finger followed, smearing wine-dark blood across the floor.

And Elowen screamed, her poise snapping at last. The sound tore through the Court of Silence like a heresy, sharp and searing: an almost human noise in an inhuman place.

She'd never known such physical pain. She choked on it, eyes wide and gleaming, chest heaving. A cold sweat slicked her spine, and her heart thundered out of rhythm. She jerked back as the shadows released her, blood spurting and staining the fine linens.

But her father only raised his hand with terrifying calm. A sinuous shadow coiled from his wrist and slithered between them. It found her mouth like it had done so many times before—wrapping tightly, binding her scream mid-breath. Her vision turned grainy at the edges, and the taste of copper flooded her tongue where the bond had sealed too tightly.

I'm sorry. I'm so sorry. Xaire knelt beside her, his languid grace replaced by quivering hands as he reached for the napkin. "Call a healer. Mother, we can't leave her like this."

No summons ensued.

A single tear slid down Elowen's cheek. She wished bitterly that she could summon it back. There was no dignity left in her silence now. Her breath came in ragged, broken gusts through her nose.

Her father returned to his seat like the matter was settled, dabbing the blood off his cuffs with distaste.

"Your sister has shamed this table, Xaire, and risked family war for sentiment," said her mother, each syllable knifing the air with perfect, chilling control.

Her wine glass shattered in her hand, spilling pearls of crimson onto her rose gown. She had always sided with Thiago over her children, but Elowen had never quite been able to put her finger on whether her loyalty stemmed from wifely duty, indebtedness, or self-preservation.

"You gave Ysadora hope, Elowen. What will she think now? That you might take her side when this court demands her submission?"

"You will tell us all you gleaned during your illicit communications," said the faerie king. "Or you will know solitude."

Although Elowen in many ways looked like her mother, she had inherited her father's toughness.

Put your stubbornness aside, said her twin.

I'd rather be chained in body than in mind.

"She has nothing to say," said Xaire quietly. *You should have begged the calligrapher's daughter to take you that night.*

Her father smiled: a terrible thing. "Then solitude awaits. Until my spiders come to take her secrets."

Xaire's face turned ashen. "No, Father. You've done enough."

Elowen clutched her finger—blood spreading warmth across her chest—and her mind lurched back to when she had been sixteen. She had been too foolish to realise that in this court, guarding her temper was better than the temporary bliss of letting her emotions be known.

Sharp remarks disrespecting her father at tithe had earned her two weeks in a dark room on a bare pallet, with only insects for company, even Xaire gone. She had minded that much more than the lack of creature comforts.

"Children...always so ungrateful," said her mother, and Elowen wondered whether it was Ysa she was thinking of.

"Defend her, Xaire, and you'll share her punishment. Unless you've something to confess about your own involvement?" said their father.

Elowen's eyes drifted to her twin, and she gave him permission to fail her because it was less painful than his choosing to do so. *It's okay. I've always been alone. Even though we were born from one womb.*

Xaire's brown eyes filled with sadness, then he glanced away. "I didn't know," he said softly.

She didn't hate him for it. She maybe even loved him for not giving their father the secrets he craved.

Opposite her, Orin shrank deeper into his high-backed chair, his face pale as first snow.

Ask Mother and Father what part of my imprisonment pleased them most, said Elowen to her twin.

Xaire flinched, then translated without embellishment. One by one, the candles flicked out as if her father wanted them all to experience the darkness that would presently be hers. Orin buried his face in his hands. And dizzy spots danced in Elowen's eyes, her butchered finger on the supper table, as she watched her world fracture with icy grace. It would be impossible to reach Ysa now, either to deliver a warning or to receive the warmth of her friendship.

A frown furrowed between her mother's smooth brows. "You brought this on yourself, Elowen. In time, you will understand."

Then the shadows took Elowen as she grasped her dripping finger wrapped in a table napkin, wondering how often Ysa thought of her, wondering if the promise of a new family was real. She was not sorry. Not yet.

But she knew now how far her family would go to keep her caged.

A short walk away, the bloodheart tree continued to rain its foliage.

21

YSADORA

The River Sisters are chimeric oracles who dwell in rivers touched by chaos and may appear anywhere where river meets root. With opal eyes and mouths spilling prophecy, they guide chosen souls, offering power but never penance. Not averse to politics, they are known, at times, to do the Queen of Chaos's bidding.
- A Tapestry of Courts and Crowns

We rode for an hour on a path along the banks of the Fallen Gulf, which wound like a silver vein through Faerie. Zephyr set Mythros's pace to a steady trot, his hands loose on the reins, and Loxley rode his pale mare beside us.

Though my mate's body curled around mine—his warmth a buffer against the morning chill—the mist seeped under my cloak. Zephyr and Loxley traded stories from their past—tales of impossible odds, narrow escapes, strange contracts in forgotten places—in an attempt either to distract themselves or to distract me.

But I had my own distractions. Faerie passed around us in a blur of beauty and rot. I couldn't look away. Water foamed and frothed below us, crashing against rocks like the grinding of old bones. The river smelled of iron and forgotten magic, and the bitter perfume of unfamiliar blooms reached us from the riverbanks.

To our right, the lands swelled into foothills ahead of the Murkthorn and Soulforge mountains. They stood like serrated teeth against the sky, streaked with shimmering minerals. Trees grew in strange, slanted formations, some stripped bare as if scoured by winds, others cloaked in thick moss.

Patchy rain fell in hues of indigo, the like of which I'd never seen before. Whereas once I had longed for the strangeness of other worlds, now I longed for normality.

Approaching the Court of Chaos from the mountains was a precaution. The high pass would provide an advantage if things soured: a place from which to observe or to flee. We knew all too well how thin the thread of allegiance could be.

It wouldn't do to veer too close to settlements. Chaos fae were only loosely governed and notoriously territorial. Unlike other courts, their concept of hospitality shifted with mood and moonlight. One wrong glance risked inhabiting a role in a ritual or farce—or worse, a curse. To draw attention was to invite trouble, entertainment, or experimentation. Strangers rarely left as they arrived.

"Ysa?" murmured Zephyr into my ear.

I squeezed his thigh, and stars, he almost purred. "I'm fine."

Father would be horrified with our plan. Tanuhja had sought reconciliation with me since the moment Father had carried me away, pink and swaddled, into the mortal realm. Her manipulations and distortions of morality were so vast that I didn't even know whether we could be allies.

But Elowen had warned me about the impossibilities of applying human morality to fae lives, and I had already been forced to make choices I'd have once shied away from. I'd chosen silence over honesty, manipulation over confrontation, and I'd not protected Ferrith from mind wrangling I wasn't sure he deserved.

I blinked away Ferrith's face from my mind's eye and tuned into the tail end of a conversation about a mercenary exploit. "You stole gold from the goblin king and hid in a cave?"

Warmth flooded the bond, as if Zephyr was pleased that I wanted to know more of his past. And I did. I wanted to know everything, the small details that made him, as well as the large ones that unravelled him.

"As much gold as we could fill our pockets with. It was three days before the goblins gave up the search. Lox fell asleep midwatch."

"I almost started a fight with the goblins to alleviate my boredom." Loxley now knew how essential it was to recount the stories of Zephyr's past. His mare grew ever more skittish in the Chaos lands. "Then Cyprian tried to teach us a ridiculous sword dance and pulled a muscle in his back."

"Lox flirted with a wizard on the way home and was hexed with his personal raincloud."

They were both laughing now, Zephyr's shoulders shaking slightly, the sound low and unguarded. It wasn't a sound I often heard from him. I liked the way it loosened his taut edges. He needed levity to balance out the weight of all he carried, an anchor for his own life.

But when a long, low moan drifted from the direction of the mountains, his arms tightened around me. Mythros twitched beneath us.

The fine hairs along my arms lifted. "The outcast fae?"

"Perhaps. Or something worse." He patted the stallion's inky flank. "Easy, Mythros."

By now, each hoofbeat jarred my already tired frame, and a dull ache bloomed in my lower back.

"If we're going to rest, it should probably be here," said Loxley. "Before we get any closer."

Zephyr nodded, and we dismounted. He and Loxley watered the horses and conferred in low voices over a map. I drifted closer to the riverbank, the soft squelch of moss beneath my boots swallowed by the hush of flowing water. The air was dense with magic and tinted violet.

Then, from the froth and unnatural churn, faces began to rise.

They surfaced with movements synchronised enough to sharpen my unease into dread. There were five of them, eyes like split opals, irises drifting like clouds. Their hair trailed like reeds, and their skin had the iridescent sheen of oil. I readied my quill and took a step back, wild magic stirring in my cells. Only a fool turned their back on threats in Faerie.

Their voices slithered out, eyes lit with eerie recognition. "Blood of Tanuhja."

One tilted her head. "Creation and destruction dance in your veins, little Inkblood."

The smallest pointed. "Made of nebulas and chaos."

Another smiled with too many teeth. "The soil remembers your mother's warped pain."

"You are the daughter of ruin and promise," said the fifth. "Take what is owed. Take it."

They gave no command, no rite or ritual, yet I instinctively knew what to do. Kneeling at the river's edge, I pressed my palm into the damp soil where river, rock, and rich earth met in a tangle of roots.

It seemed a simple thing to draw ink from Faerie itself. A tug of my will and ink coiled around my fingers: thick, glistening, and as warm as blood, as though the earth itself bled secrets for those bold enough to ask.

It came willingly, a relic of birthright, curling in the air like steam from a sleeping beast. Not just ink. Magic. Memory. Meaning. Words unfurled before me, bright with the copper hue of riverbed iron.

A jolt flared in the bond. "Ysa!" Zephyr raced towards me, Mythros whinnying a warning nearby. He was already drawing both swords from across his back, shadows at his heels like serpents ready to strike.

The river sisters didn't flinch. They made no move to advance, no ripple of aggression. Instead, they turned their clouded gazes to my mate as though he were a storm briefly passing through their dream.

Zephyr shook me. "Ysa?'

"Should I stop?" The magic, my magic, had such a hold on me, I didn't think I even could.

Worry washed through the bond. "Nothing good becomes of those who plunder Faerie."

Water curled lovingly towards me as if the river sisters beckoned me in. "You are safe with us, Inkblood."

"*The Fatebreaker* burns too hot to understand," said the young one.

"But even he cannot sever what the land remembers. Just like the other male."

I wrenched my focus to him for a moment. "I need to finish this."

Zephyr didn't lower his swords, but his breath slowed when he noticed that I wasn't afraid. The darkness gathered around him was sleek and watchful. Though the bond was tight with warning, he let me work.

Had Father ever experienced such visceral communion with the land?

My mind offered me a memory siphoned from the ancient stone. On the day that the Order of the Glyph fell, the calligraphers' magic remained strong for only as long as their ink stores lasted. When their sacred reservoirs ran dry, their strength faltered.

Magic that had once shaped borders, bound demons, and held oaths like chains seeped away with the final drop. Then only the dragons had stood between them and death.

But why had the dragons abandoned them?

My quill moulded the ink into spirals and slashes in the air that shifted in hue from burnt copper to bruised violet. But each time I pulled from the land, my heartbeat stuttered, as if Faerie itself paused to tally the debt.

Zephyr faded to the periphery of my vision, and I was no longer aware of where the river sisters were or if they wanted to drown me in the depths of the Fallen Gulf. The world around me dimmed for a blink, colours leeching from the edges.

I wrote to Tanuhja to tell her we were coming, addressing her not as my mother, but as a faerie queen of the realm. My fingers trembled with my task, though I told myself that the chill morning air was at fault.

I told myself that it was the river fae I was afraid of and not my mother. But there was no disguising the heartbeat threaded through the lines. No hiding the daughter from the queen. Emotions bled into the ink: wary anticipation, the heavy drag of old longings for maternal love, and sharp judgment for all Tanuhja had done.

She would decipher it all: the pause before her name, the deliberate neutrality of my phrasing, the restraint it took not to accuse or beg. The strokes grew steadier only when I allowed myself to frame the visit as one of necessity, not sentiment. My message was a courtesy, not a plea.

Queen of Chaos,
My mate and I ride for your court, together with a companion.
The time has come to test whether blood outweighs old silence.
You will find us at your gate before the moon wanes.
The calligrapher's daughter.

When I had finished, the message floated between the trees and morning mist for a breath, then was carried through the veil towards the Queen of Chaos. Hadn't I told her we would meet only on my terms?

When I was done, the river fae looked on in satisfaction, chattering together as if congratulating themselves on a job well done. One grabbed my boot, and

I would have slipped in the mud, had Zephyr not caught my forearm and slashed at her.

The river sisters hissed in ire or perhaps hissed a goodbye. Then they bobbed down into the river, their dark hair splaying out on the froth, disappearing a moment later. They did not surface again.

Zephyr didn't speak at first. He stared at the spot where the river sisters had vanished and at my stained fingers.

His brows furrowed. "You pulled ink straight from the land. Not cultivating plants. No long drawn-out processes of moon cycles or distilling sap. No glyphs to refine it." Shrewdness glinted in his eyes. He wasn't looking at me as his mate, but as a strategist, murmuring almost to himself. "The Order of the Glyph couldn't even do that. The Circle of Emberlight have dragons, but not calligraphy."

The thrum of ink magic still echoed in me, and I felt diffused and directionless, as if joy was out of reach. But the warmth of Zephyr's body grounded me, as did Mythros's stamping higher up the riverbank.

I frowned, casting my gaze to the stallion's left and right. "Zeph? Where's Loxley?"

The bond fluttered and twisted. Metal rasped softly as he crossed his blades and slid them back into the sheaths strapped over his shoulders, a motion so fluid it was almost meditative.

"I don't want you to get upset."

"Why would I get upset?" I asked, quietly.

Eyes like the stormy sea met mine. "I've sent Loxley after Maren and Ferrith."

My friends had ridden north-east from Ebonspire, but

Lox was a quicker rider, even with the detour. "He's going to cut them off in the Wraithwoods."

My hands fisted. "But you agreed to my plan. You agreed to give Ferrith a chance."

Zephyr ran a hand over his face. "We have to be sure he won't betray us again."

My breath hitched. "You sent Loxley to be judge and executioner."

He stalked closer until his scent filled my nose: lashing wind and mossy ferns and the soap he washed his hair with. "No, I didn't. I sent him to watch from afar and to intervene only if he has to, as much for their protection as for ours. He'll protect them from monsters or my uncle's spiders or from Ferrith himself." His voice dropped, rough with guilt. "I let you decide Ferrith's fate as I promised, but then I did what I always do, Inkheart. I made a backup plan. I made the hard call."

Pulling from the earth had hollowed me in places I hadn't been hollow before. I blinked, trying to focus. "Did it ever cross your mind that Ferrith needed compassion? That Maren might be the one to pull him back from the edge?"

Zephyr's expression darkened like a storm front rolling in. "If Ferrith decides to betray us, Loxley is the *only* one of us who doesn't have to resort to killing to prevent it."

It crushed me that he'd put my kin at risk when he'd fought for so long to protect his own. "You'd have Loxley mess with Ferrith's mind again? His *mortal* mind?"

Zephyr's jaw worked. "Loxley is ruthless, not cruel. He has clear instructions."

"Well, that solves everything," I shot back. "Loxley bends intent like a butcher choosing which bone to snap.

Cyprian would at least have handled it with caution. Wylda would have listened. You chose steel and suspicion."

"I chose certainty. I won't gamble on Ferrith's guilt or innocence. Not with the stakes this high."

My chest felt tight, as if the bond itself recoiled. "If anything happens to them because of your choice, I won't forgive you, Zephyr. Not in this life or the next."

"I know." For the first time, he looked afraid.

ZEPHYR

*Chorus Maw: yellow-sinewed, many-mouthed,
fermenting creature that jerks and floats at high
speed and emits a harmonic ringing that unsettles
the mind. History unknown.*
– The Secrets of Faerie's Veiled Beasts
by Zephyr Ashmoor

The silence between them was unbearable.

Zephyr sat behind Ysa on the saddle, his arms not quite touching her sides, the sharpness of her last words tucked under his ribs. Her spine was straight as a blade, and he missed the feel of her body against his.

She hadn't looked back at him once since they mounted. Her chin was tilted at a proud angle that indicated she didn't want to speak, but Zephyr could sense the pressure of unspoken words caught behind her teeth, the disappointment that roiled in her like the sea.

Mythros moved beneath them, tossing his mane as if scolding him for his missteps with Ysa. Meanwhile, the stallion picked his way deftly through the warped terrain. Every few paces, this Court of Chaos shifted: colours too bright or too dark, trees bending in directions no wind had commanded, the ground glinting with glassy water though it was dry, the sky swirling in unnatural shades.

Cobblestone bled into sand, chunked into thick grass, then snapped to blackened stone. Laughter and growls echoed often, making him reach for his weapon, but they didn't belong to anyone or anything he could see. Worst of all, the trees leaned close, branches whispering that he would *leave her, fail her, lose her*.

Despair needled through him. If Ysa was so incensed that he had sent Loxley after Maren and Ferrith, how would she react when he revealed the depths of his animosity for Tanuhja? For now, it was trapped like heat behind frosted glass.

The Faerie Queen of Chaos had invited her daughter to visit her in more ways than one—attempted coercion, gifts, even dreams—but she remained dangerous and unpredictable. Zephyr was uncertain about the welcome they would receive. The calligrapher, who must have loved Tanuhja once, considered her irredeemable. Zephyr agreed with him.

But could Tanuhja's longing for her daughter mean she was capable of great acts of love as well as heinous crimes? Perhaps she could give Ysa the tools to harness her wild, unpredictable chaos magic.

Perhaps she could even restore the outcast fae. Narrating the book of *Veiled Beasts* to Ysa had shown him that he was starting to struggle to tell the stories of the cursed fae with a clear beginning, middle, and end.

He misplaced details. He'd forgotten which court the monster hailed from. Who had loved them. What magic had been their gift. Sometimes, it seemed he was trapped in a dark forest, running endlessly in someone else's nightmare. There wasn't time to ask Ysa to pause their quest. Instead, he tried to clamp down on the echoes in his mind.

He sat taller in the saddle. If the Queen of Chaos harmed a hair on his mate's head or sided against them, Zephyr considered this his best chance of killing her. And he would take it. Ancients, damn him, he would kill her fast and without hesitation, and he might even enjoy it.

But the cost would be Ysa's trust.

His mouth twisted. He was keenly aware of his tight grip on the reins, not because Mythros needed guidance, but to do something with his hands other than beg Ysa to forgive him. Yet, here he was considering escalating the stakes between them.

He was a fool for his mate. That much was obvious now—obvious in the way he recalculated the battlefield, drew new lines in the sand, adjusted his plans the moment her name left someone's lips with ill intent.

Even as he plotted three moves ahead, she was the variable he never factored correctly. With her in the equation, his war maps bled into love letters. The moment she was threatened, all logic bowed to instinct.

Wanting her hadn't made him reckless. She'd made him more precise. But being near her made him forget caution about his own safety, when caution was all he had ever learnt at the Court of Silence. It didn't matter how sharp Ysa's words were. His heart still tilted towards her, like a compass needle doomed to spin towards a broken north.

He didn't blame her; he didn't even blame himself. Some things were inevitable. How Veda would have danced with delight to have seen it. But Veda was dead, and he and Ysa would die, too, if he didn't get a grip on himself.

Ysa's safety was more important even than their love.

"Zeph?" Ysa finally looked over her shoulder, twilight eyes moon-wide, as if she'd felt his love through the mate bond.

He wrapped his arms around her just as a pulse rolled under Mythros's hooves. The stallion stopped short and snorted a warning. Tensing, Zephyr scanned the terrain.

A creature crawled around the bend behind them: low to the ground, patched together from yellowed muscle and sinew and too many mouths, a pair of uncoordinated eyes blinking across its torso.

It shouldn't have moved the way it did: jerking, floating, then crawling across the shifting ground. Ysa recoiled as it noticed them and burst forward.

In the blink of an eye, Zephyr weighed his options. He couldn't tell if this was an old creature of chaos or a new one made by Tanuhja: an outcast fae forsaken by all, who deserved to be more than collateral.

But he no longer had the means to protect the lost. It could have slithered away, but instead had set its sights on them. Fleeing across this terrain could be a deadly choice. There was nothing he could do but deal with the threat. He vaulted from the saddle before the stallion could rear.

There was even no time to remove his cloak. "Stay on Mythros. Keep moving."

Ysa made a noise of protest. *Why are you so reckless with your own life?*

You're welcome. Shadows already peeled off him, forcing the creature to veer away from the horse. From her.

I know how to kill. Ysa had spun Mythros around and stayed mounted, quill raised in case he needed her.

And I know how to bleed. Let's not test who's better at it today, he replied.

He circled wide to draw the creature's focus. It snarled, whipping around, clearly territorial or hungry or both. Zephyr's form blurred into darkness as he ran forward, cloak flying out behind him, and he palmed his dagger from his thigh.

Zephyr ignored how the ground changed and focused only on the task at hand. Dropping into a crouch, he drove his blade through one of the creature's eyes. Its many mouths released a harmonic ringing that made his skull buzz.

Then it lunged. It stank of rotting corpses and wyrms and fermentation.

Zephyr didn't falter. He'd been in this scenario time and again as the prince of a fallen court and in mercenary life. What made it different this time was his fear for Ysa. He was terrified that she would be hurt and he would be left alone in a world that no longer made sense without her.

Try not to get killed, she said helpfully.

You'd miss me? He hadn't even broken a sweat.

Hardly, she retorted.

But he could sense her worry through the bond, so he

sped up his attack. With Cyprian and Loxley, hunting monsters had become a sport. He'd enjoyed the thrill of the chase, enjoyed the banter with his brothers, enjoyed wrangling the monsters down to the Ebonspire dungeons.

But this was different. There was no camaraderie here, no sense of purpose. Just the ache of tension across his shoulders and the sharp edge of Ysa's fear echoing down the bond. The creature hadn't chosen to live like this, but it lunged at them with such unrelenting malice that he couldn't afford mercy.

Zephyr let the creature pass through him, his body shrouded in shadow. Reappearing over it, he drove his sword into its back. His shadows erupted, pulling it apart from the inside. Its skull-rattling harmonic buzz dimmed into a mournful ebb, like light slipping beneath the horizon. The last few vibrations teased the edge of Zephyr's hearing. His shadows fell away, and silence settled again, but it was heavier now.

This kind of killing struck him as unjust.

The creature had barely stood a chance, and he had killed it anyway.

Ysa sensed it, too. She didn't speak through the bond again, but comfort poured into it, like she had attempted once or twice before, and this time it didn't slide off his guarded mind like rain on stone.

This time, it seeped into the part of Zephyr that hated what Faerie had become and what it asked of him. Her comfort warmed the shadow in his chest that whispered *monster* when he moved too quickly, quietly, ruthlessly.

He willed the creature to evaporate or seep into the chaotic earth like it had never been real to begin with. There could be repercussions for killing one of Tanuhja's subjects. But even that would be preferable to killing one of the outcast fae.

But its slack, putrid body remained at his feet. It stung that he hadn't paused to absorb the creature's history. He'd been fixated on his mate's safety above all else, and he would do it again, but wondered if that made him more like his uncle than he cared to admit and less like his mother. Now its story, whatever it had been, was lost.

Only once the creature had stilled did he wipe his blades on new grass, then looked back at Ysa. "Are you all right?"

She nodded, her eyes transfixed on the dull lump at his feet. "Are you?"

Her fury had dimmed, and a thread of his tension loosened further as she slid off Mythros, patted the stallion's flank and turned to face him.

His heart thrummed beneath his ribs. "About before…"

"Yes?" she prompted.

"I stand by my decision to send Lox after Maren and Ferrith, but I should have told you."

"Next time, tell me the plan or don't expect me to follow it."

"I don't need obedience from you, Inkheart. I need you alive."

Ysa mulled that over. She blew out a breath. "I don't like arguing with you."

He didn't look away, just drank in the sight of her dishevelled dark hair and her fierce violet eyes. One day, he'd teach her how good it could feel to make up after an argument: how they could start with heated words and end up with hands tangling in hair and mouths hot against each other. He'd teach her how tension made desire sharper, and forgiveness could be coaxed out of curses with kisses. He closed his eyes for a moment. Today was not that day.

Instead, he delved beneath his cloak and drew out her father's dagger. "Your father wanted you to have it. It's blessed by dragon fire. Caldoron's, to be exact."

She accepted it as if it were an offering, smoothing reverent fingers over its leather hilt and the dull gold blade, thumbing its crimson gemstone. "It belongs with the quill."

Zephyr nodded. "Maybe that's why he wanted you to have it. It's a piece of history, Inkheart."

She tucked it into her belt like it had always belonged there, her face set with new steel.

"You're not the same woman I met at Bloomtide."

"No. I'm not. Come on. We shouldn't linger."

Zephyr had no idea how much further they had to journey, no idea if he could make the necessary choices for their survival when his brain was addled simply by standing close to her. It took him a millisecond more than it should have to notice the pressure of something ancient curling around them.

The chaos was not loud, but absolute: the air thickened, birds stopped singing, insects fell silent, and the trees did not sway. Darkness rippled around him, his shadows pulled to one point. His hand went to his weapon as he closed the space between them.

"She's here," said Ysa simply.

Zephyr didn't have to ask who. He had seen the faerie queen's likeness in the great libraries of the Court of Lore and described in the old ballads of Faerie, but nothing prepared him for her resemblance to Ysa in the flesh.

The Faerie Queen of Chaos emerged from the colourless seam between what was real and what was imagined. Her twisted metal crown was as Ysa had described in her dream, made from blackened vines of forged iron, winding as if alive, and stamped with a sapphire.

Her presence was soft and terrible, like a lullaby in a battlefield. Her hair, long and dark, was worn in loose waves: Ysa's preferred style. Her violet eyes, so like her daughter's, shone. But whereas Ysa's eyes burned with clarity and rebellion, Tanuhja's seemed a trapdoor into memory or madness.

Whereas Ysa moved like a blade, her mother stood like an altar.

And Zephyr thought to himself, if Ysadora was the storm rising, Tanuhja was the storm that tears open the world.

Mythros let out a low, uneasy groan. He did not like the queen's scent. He didn't trust her. In that they did not differ.

What kind of mother left her child with the pain of unanswered longing? He'd been marked by maternal loss too, but never like this. Had his mother lived, she would have brought down all the realms, rather than let him drown in silence.

"My darling," breathed Tanuhja. Her smile was soft and almost triumphant. "Let me learn the shape of you."

His mate's breath hitched as she studied Tanuhja in return. "You're twenty-four orbits too late for first impressions."

Through the bond, Zephyr felt her sense of self fracture and rearrange. His chest burned, and he realised Ysa's emotions surged through him: a yearning so deep that it nearly buckled his knees, like the ache of a child waiting at a window too long.

It wasn't rational. It was instinctual, full of forgotten lullabies and imagined embraces. He instinctively stepped even closer to his mate's side, so his arm brushed hers.

Tanuhja pulled her gaze from her daughter with great reluctance, and she assessed him as though she were reading a prophecy written in smoke. "Tell me, *Fatebreaker*, do you serve my daughter or yourself? I couldn't quite bring myself to believe Gabor's assurances of your devotion."

Zephyr gave her a cold smile, his fists curling at the mention of the friend she had manipulated for her own ends, the spy she had embedded in his family. "What makes you think our goals aren't aligned?"

Her answer settled over him like a curse. "Then you are more dangerous than I feared and more foolish than I hoped. Although I am grateful for the part you played in controlling the diversion I created to keep attention away from Ysadora in the mortal realm."

Diversion. She sickened him. Zephyr didn't want her gratitude. It landed like venom in his veins. She had warped the outcast fae's suffering into a weapon, turning exile into damnation. Not one of them should have been remade into horror to serve a queen's purpose. Grief burned through him, curdling into the need for violence.

Don't do anything reckless, said Ysa through the bond. *Please.*

Shadows seeped from his clenched fists before he forced them still. *I make no promises if she touches you.*

He wouldn't strike prematurely. Violence now would only blind Ysa to the truth she needed to see for herself. At this precise moment, they needed Tanuhja's cooperation. So Zephyr stayed silent, because anything he said might damn them all.

But in the quiet marrow of his soul, he made an oath: the Queen of Chaos would one day pay in blood for all she had done.

23

YSADORA

In the Court of Chaos, the faerie queen sits before a worn chessboard, its black and crimson pieces holding the fate of a rival or pawn, moved at her whim in a game without end.
– A Tapestry of Courts and Crowns

The Faerie Queen of Chaos studied me like a priestess studies an omen.

She wore a dress coat over trousers, both the colour of a bruise. I wanted to look away, but I couldn't. I'd seen my reflection in many places since my mortal glamour had been stripped away, but never so fully as in her.

We had the same dark, loose waves. The same haunting violet eyes. But in my biological mother, every trait was stranger, like a dream remembered wrong. She was beautiful in the way a collapsing star is: magnetic and ruinous. She was a maker of monsters and dread, and had abandoned me before I'd even known my own name.

I wondered what she wanted with me, even as I weighed up how to get what I wanted from her.

It seemed a cruel joke now that I had thought Danaë to be my mother.

Tanuhja glided towards me, and as she did, the leaves beneath her feet did not crunch; they rearranged themselves into fractal patterns. A flower bloomed and wilted beside her boot. Her voice was made of cobwebs and spun glass, just as I remembered from my dreams.

"I wondered if you'd have Kazimir's eyes or mine."

My throat tightened. I didn't want to be frightened of my mother, but I was.

Shadows crept around my mate like quiet wolves. He didn't show her the sliver of respect he had given Esolas. "Move carefully, Tanuhja. I may stand in your court, but I will not hesitate to defend her."

"Calm yourself, fallen prince. I assure you, you would know if I meant her harm." Tanuhja's smile turned feral, and as it did, the wind reversed direction mid-breath and the ground shifted beneath us, cobbled with phantom reflections: paths that didn't exist, doors that had never been built. "Tell me, Ysadora—" she said my name like she had whispered it into the world's bones and waited centuries to hear the echo back, "—is Zephyr Ashmoor your tether or your leash?"

A slow burn of protective anger simmered in the bond, and I allowed it to feed me. "He's *mine*. Not yours to define."

"How wonderful. You've grown sharp, daughter of mine, despite Kazimir's attempts to make you soft." Her face tightened. "But why is it that you do not seem pleased to see me, despite coming of your own accord? Despite my patience and gifts."

I huffed out a breath. "What did you expect I'd feel?" Did she expect joy or gratitude? Danaë had chosen dreams of Faerie over me, as though I'd been nothing more than a chapter that had reached its natural end; Tanuhja hadn't even fought for a beginning. Abandonment felt the same, whether it came with a calm goodbye or a cradle left cold.

"I expected hope or anger. I would take any emotion, as long as it means I matter to you."

Look to the Rune of Unveiling, said Zephyr. *She speaks the truth.*

He was right. The rune warmed my wrist rather than searing it. But I wasn't pacified. "You've done unforgivable things without ever making amends. I came because I need your alliance, that is all. It doesn't mean I owe you the feelings you imagined I'd have or that I know how to be your daughter."

"You were a swaddled cry in my arms. I wrapped you in spells and silk, and I wanted a future with you. I longed to hear your footsteps echo through my halls." Her violet eyes caught the chaos that swirled in the air. "Do not mistake my silence for apathy. I looked for you in every mirror, every dream, every flicker of stray magic. I waited with the ache of a mother whose child never nursed at my breasts, who could never say your name out loud. Don't you want to hear my story?"

Part of me really did. But I couldn't admit how much.

The bond was quiet, and I understood that Zephyr didn't expect me to pretend for the sake of an alliance, but the words

I chose were clipped and didn't entirely reflect the heat in my chest. "Should I sit cross-legged and soak up every word? I've imagined your story a thousand ways. Doting mother. Prisoner of fate. Villain. Yours would just be another version."

A beat passed. "Do you blame Kazimir for his part? Or that harlot Danaë for leaving you?"

"You can't guilt her into loving you," said Zephyr flatly.

The faerie queen smiled at me, a terrible and tender thing, and there was grim resolve in her. "He is afraid I'll take you from him. But no matter. I will take you both home, and the stallion, too, to spare him from the ragged, ruined things in this court. I was expecting another travelling companion."

"He did not come, after all," said Ysa.

Tanuhja smiled with delight. "Good."

Then she lifted her hand, and the ground beneath us cracked like paper, curling at the edges. Reality frayed, and my stomach plummeted. Trees folded inwards, and the sky creased as unholy chaos magic wrapped around us.

Mythros whinnied, and Zephyr grabbed my hand. Then the air vibrated like a struck bell, and the world spiralled, colours melting together. We were standing but also falling, walking but also galloping. Dark threads appeared beneath Mythros's hooves.

We passed through a valley choked with the roots of dreaming trees, through gorges lined with teeth, through clouds that bled forgotten prayers. I was glad for the meagre meal we had last eaten, glad that Loxley wasn't caught up in this madness, glad mostly for the mate bond and Zephyr's repeated refrains of *hold on, breathe with me, I am here.*

At last, we arrived atop a ridge in a courtyard hung with constellations that didn't exist. My limbs were sluggish, my heartbeat erratic, but beneath our boots, the ground was solid.

The breath I dragged in tasted of ash and sweetness. *I left my stomach somewhere in the sky.*

Zephyr's tawny skin had paled. *I'll take shadow corridors over chaos currents any day. Do you trust her?*

Not one bit, I replied.

Remember that with every step, he said.

In front of us, Tanuhja's castle glittered like a wound against the sky, carved from petrified twilight. The wind tugged at me with a possessiveness that made me think it wanted to know me. Zephyr's thumb kneaded my palm, and his storm-cloud gaze raked the strange landscape.

The castle was a monument not to power, but isolation. Nothing grew near the foundation. No torches lit the gates. No birds circled overhead, but the cursed white dragon that had brought Gabor on his final journey to us wheeled through the air above the castle.

Its tattered wings might have gleamed like pearl, had he not been a corruption of nature. Instead, its scales flaked like old paint, falling in flurries of powder as its skeletal shadow fell over us. Mythros stood rigid with his ears pinned flat, his midnight coat sweat-drenched, tail swishing in uneven jerks until Zephyr's calloused palm touched his flank.

Tanuhja's violet eyes met mine. "Welcome home, daughter. Welcome to Gloomhaven."

A strange grief curled in my gut. "We won't be staying long."

I didn't belong here. But I might have, once.

"We'll see," replied my mother.

I steeled myself as a statue flanking the castle gates stepped down from its pedestal, its joints grinding, brought into half-life by chaos and illusion magic. It resembled a knight, its visor up, its face blank but aware. One hand was cracked through the wrist, and when it reached the stallion, it extended a grey palm in invitation. Mythros's nostrils flared.

Zephyr frowned. "I'll tend to my horse myself."

"Of course," said Tanuhja, pleased.

Another statue, missing part of its jaw, wordlessly opened the gates. There was no fanfare for the returning queen, let alone warmth. In Larkspur, the villagers celebrated every homecoming with gusto, whereas here the welcome was calcified by a lonely queen who'd long forgotten how to live joyfully.

It was clear that Tanuhja expected me to follow her without my mate.

Zephyr hesitated only a breath before passing the reins to the waiting statue, stopping only to murmur in Mythros's ear. Then we trailed the faerie queen into her castle over night-dark floors.

Statues lined our path at intervals, still, silent, neither awake nor asleep, simply waiting for their queen's commands. Music box fragments slipped through the cracks in the petrified stone. Rooms bled into one another like liquid dreams. The cloying scent of jasmine filled my nose and throat, though there were no bouquets to be seen. Corridors stretched beyond sight, lined with doors that led nowhere. No two footsteps traced the same path twice, hallways unravelling and reconstituting themselves.

Zephyr was grim-faced beside me, trying and failing to map a return route. His agitation poured into the bond, and I was under no illusions about the depth of his hatred for my mother, though he tried to hide it.

There was no warmth here. No people or even paintings, no soft furnishings or rugs underfoot, only distorted flickers of half-formed illusions that writhed at the edge of my perception and vanished when I looked directly at them.

Every window framed a scene that was never fixed, each blink a riot of possibility: a storm-tossed sea raged beneath a blood-red sky; a horned dragon atop a tower of bones; a withered courtyard filled with black flowers.

I wasn't sure if the windows presented what was, or what could have been, or what would eventually come to pass. Chaos was the only constant: a ceaseless flux.

Tanuhja's dress coat dragged across the floor. She neither looked at us nor slowed her stride.

At times, she made brief remarks. "The east tower holds the dream archives. The library weaves its own stories at night." She scoffed. "Kazimir and I had a love of stories in common. The walls shift depending on my mood."

She led us into a hall dominated by a dusty throne hewn from a single piece of black stone, accented with webs of silver. It rippled as if it existed simultaneously in multiple places. The room twisted subtly, columns bending slightly when I looked away.

A staircase unspooled like a ribbon before vanishing again. A chess set sat on a small trunk; its pieces were worn by time and use. Though chess was a social game, I couldn't help feeling that Tanuhja played alone.

When I looked closer at the chess pieces, I realised that the knight was Zephyr, the rook was my father, and the pawns were dragons. The queen had clearly been carved in Tanuhja's own image.

Then the silver-veined doors closed behind us.

She's locked us in like prey, I said.

Then let her know we bite, replied Zephyr.

Tanuhja stood near the throne, but she didn't ascend it. She wore not the queen's mask, but a mother's, eyes ringed with sleepless centuries. "I spent centuries sculpting dreams just to see your face again. Now I need what's real."

"*I* need strategy, not sentiment," I countered.

"Then ask, daughter."

"The Spymaster has called a meeting of Faerie rulers and seeks to be High King."

Her eyes sparked. "I have my invitation."

"So you know why I ask for your alliance and your aid in understanding my chaos magic."

"We will talk, but first you promised to listen," said Tanuhja, as if after all these orbits of patience, she was done with waiting.

She didn't have Danaë's guile or finesse. Her truth didn't come in honeyed riddles, but in jagged declarations and open wounds. Her longing wasn't quiet. It filled the throne room and pressed against my ribs.

And despite all my misgivings, I listened, because I needed to hear as much as she needed to speak. Everything faded into the periphery: the throne, the statues, even Zephyr, until it was only my mother and me, and the words she chose to heal the wounds between us.

"I didn't want to let you go. Ironically, my mourning meant that Faerie factions believed our ruse that you had not survived birth. So you lived your life in Larkspur as the unravelling of the Grimoire sent Faerie into disarray. The kings and queens didn't heed my warnings to stabilise the realms. So I corrupted outcasts into monsters to keep eyes away from Larkspur. Nightmares made flesh, to keep you safe."

Anger bled into the bond, and Zephyr's shadows stirred.

My voice was flat. "You used their pain to build a moat around me."

"Yes, I did." Her lip curled. "But the Spymaster fell in love with Kazimir's mortal wife, and the chaos I had sown was not enough to protect your identity. Then you followed your Father into Faerie, and the Binder reneged on her promise to protect you. You. A youngling who had never had a chance to discover her roots and abilities. I was both morbidly frightened for you and hungry for reconciliation." The queen's eyes darted towards Zephyr. "It was clever of you to kill the Binder, fallen prince. Her temporary demise at your hands meant I couldn't track her. The games of Faerie have not been so easily played since then. Particularly after Gabor's death. But I am here to guide you now, Ysadora. What the river sisters taught you is just the beginning. *This* is just the beginning. My throne is yours, and I will be your blade."

Her words landed like a thunderclap inside me. A lifetime of being untethered, unwanted, and now suddenly I was meant to rule? My pulse skittered. "You would give me your throne?"

My mother removed her crown. "Thiago and Danaë mean to be High King and Queen, but there are other schemes that have been kept a secret even from the Spymaster. Do not be afraid. I have arranged for the Court of Chaos to remain isolated from what follows. My throne is your safety."

Dread pulsed through me. *She means to keep us.*

Zephyr's voice was like flint. *Let her try.*

A strangeness spiked in the mate bond, but my gaze was locked on Tanuhja. Perhaps she loved me in her warped way, but how comfortable would she be if my choices did not mirror her own? Did her love come with the condition of obedience?

It wasn't destruction and isolation I craved; it was creation and community.

Faerie didn't need more kings and queens. It needed Zephyr's ideals brought to life. It needed hands that could cradle what was broken without twisting it into something monstrous. It needed someone who had known grief and still chosen kindness. It needed a heart that bent towards mending, not mastery.

It needed the kind of leader who could hold silence, sorrow, and love all in the same breath. Someone who didn't dream of thrones, but of gardens grown in old ruins. It needed a spine that didn't need a crown to stand straight.

But when I turned to my mate, he was no longer beside me.

Only the imprint of his presence lingered, and the bond between us was stretched thin and silent as a held breath.

Where Zephyr had been, there was a yawning patch of shadow, rippling like disturbed water.

Nothing would have caused him to forsake me without a word. Nothing would have made him leave me in this potential trap of his own accord. I cursed myself for pulling from the earth as the river sisters had taught me to do, because my senses were still dull, and I might have realised sooner that he'd gone.

A crack split through my hard-fought calm. I'd seen Zephyr hurt and bleeding, but he always managed to survive. Now my doubts surged: was he a match for this faerie queen?

I reached for my quill and hissed. "What have you done? Where is my mate?"

There, in my mother's court, the throne room trembled in response.

24

YSADORA

I gave my heart freely once, but now I question if romantic love is but a fleeting dream beside the eternal flame of a mother's devotion.
She is all that remains.
– Tanuhja's letter to her former lover, Kazimir

"You don't need him, Ysadora. Maternal love outshines romantic love."

The Chaos Queen's words didn't give me pause, not when, over and over, maternal love had let me down. Father had saved me. Maren had saved me. Zephyr had saved me. Danaë and Tanuhja had forsaken me.

My magic was never as instinctive as when Zephyr was at risk.

I was the calligrapher's daughter. My father had shaped language into law, and I would carve new laws into the bones of the Court of Chaos to free my mate. But I didn't know what power demanded here. Wasn't that why Wylda had urged me to come? To learn from Tanuhja?

At the Court of Nebulas, ink and dragons were a conduit to power. At the Court of Silence, sacrifice and secrets were currency. But here, at the Court of Chaos, magic had no clear price. Memory lingered thick in the air, not linear or logical, but lived and relived, distorted and reshaped.

I would offer it all to protect Zephyr.

"Do you love me?" I asked the faerie queen.

"With all that I am," she said.

The Rune of Unveiling burned in recognition of the truth on my hip. "Then bring him back."

Tanuhja sighed. "No."

"Bring him back to me, and I'll give you Father's memories."

"Why would I want Kazimir's memories?" The faerie queen's violet gaze glittered with conviction. "Lovers are fickle, even mates. They come with fire in their loins and promises on their tongues, but they leave. They forget. They betray. I've watched a thousand hearts crack for the sake of a kiss, a promise, fleeting warmth in the bed chamber. But a mother's love can't be undone." She held the crown she had offered me, still. "Romantic love asks you to give until you are depleted. It craves. It clings. It abandons. My love doesn't falter with time or tide. It's a constant that even Faerie can't take from you. Let me shelter you from the pain of heartbreak, Ysadora."

Panic rose in me. I stalked the hall, looking for seams: hairline cracks in the dream-woven walls, any ripple in the air or dip in the floor that might betray where Zephyr had been dragged. But there was nothing. Even the yawning patch of shadow had gone.

The walls shifted again, making the throne room a hexagon rather than a square, and then suddenly a pentagon, with a higher ceiling and a floor that changed in pattern. Nebula magic whispered beneath my skin, ink trying to draft its logic onto a space where logic had no foothold. The void whispered in me, too, eager to be unspooled, but I didn't know how to command chaos magic with the finesse that would find my mate without harming him.

I didn't know how to do anything other than rip open a void that could swallow us all.

"Zephyr," I called once, sharply, and there was no answer of *Inkheart*, no clue as to his whereabouts in that damned castle.

Tanuhja watched me, curiously but not unkindly, head tilted like I was a painting she hadn't quite finished. "Kazimir's court reshapes reality through creation. This court reshapes reality through deconstruction. Both courts are agents of change."

Was she trying to be helpful? Was she really trying to make this a teaching moment? I listened, searching all the while.

"The nebulas become the stars, spreading light and knowledge. Chaos becomes the rift, tearing open the fabric of reality. That's why the factions want to control you, Ysadora. That's why you are so powerful. You are two sides of the same coin."

"Where is Zephyr?" I wouldn't let anything happen to him. I coiled a thick rope of ink around her, there where she stood, and pulled it tight, but she slipped the bindings with laughable ease. "What good is your love for me, if you cause me pain?"

"Your anger doesn't scare me. There's nothing you can do or say that I haven't already lived in the dreamscape."

For the briefest moment, the high windows wept stars instead of endless night, and the hall fragmented into a dozen versions of Tanuhja: some wailing, some wretched, some cruel, others hollow-eyed and rotted through with regret.

Chaos thrummed in my bones, and I knew she wasn't lying. My mother had suffered in silence and sleep. She had endured my rage in dreams where I screamed, where I fled, where I turned my back on her again and again. She had lived every abandonment, every failure, every imagined reunion, over and over until the grief became gospel.

Yet here she stood, trying to orchestrate a version of me who would stay.

Maybe there was bravery in that. But there was also bravery in fighting for family I had chosen for myself: Zephyr and the mercenaries, Maren and Ferrith, and Elowen. My quill etched lines through the air that shimmered blacker than shadow. Words didn't form; concepts did. Loyalty to my mate. Balance. Awakening. The world around me shifted, not rewritten, but rephrased.

And still it didn't work.

"You're trying to find him the way Kazimir would. Order and precision. Ink and line. You need to lose control."

My voice was as taut as a drawn bow, "First, you take him, then you try to help me."

She was as calm as a blade resting on silk. "Let this be a life lesson I teach you, from mother to daughter. We are so alike."

Anger burned my throat. "I am nothing like you."

Tanuhja blinked, and the room shifted around her. "Then you will fail."

I reached for the threads around me, for the weave of this place, but they slid away like oil. Unwritten. Untamed.

"Let go of the order in your mind, Ysadora. Tear the page. Smear the ink. Wail the things you're afraid to say."

I shook my head. "It's not safe."

"Exactly," said the faerie queen. "Chaos rises not from serenity but internal rupture."

I thought of Zephyr facing demons of his own, fighting to get back to me, and I let myself break. Just a little.

I recalled our Larkspur garden in the snow the night of Bloomtide, when I had found Father's crushed spectacles in the snow and been so fearful that I would never see him again, that I had been abandoned once more.

Grief surfaced in me like ink spilt across a page no longer willing to be neat. The marble beneath me shivered, remembering that it used to be sand. The room rippled again, but this time it was me. The bond flickered, faint as breath.

But it wasn't enough. I couldn't see my mate, couldn't reach him.

"That's it, Ysadora. Just like that. You're so close." There was sorrow on Tanuhja's face. "You need more power. More grief. You need to let it hurt and then choose what comes afterwards."

My gaze clashed with hers. "Show me where to break next."

"Only you know how to prise open your wounds."

My heart pounded. All this time, I'd kept the dam of my emotions from breaking out of diplomacy and a sense of shame. Making little emotional cuts showed more grace than revealing pain in all its ugliness.

Elowen had once taken aim at my naïvety when she told me that fae and mortal morality were not the same. I hoped that the pain I was about to inflict did not stain my soul, but if it did, it was worth the price I would pay to find Zephyr.

"You want me to break something?" My voice rang out like a spell already cast. "I'll start with the lie you keep calling love. Don't pretend you were patient all this time. You hid. You abandoned me before I even had the chance to disappoint you. Now you dress it up in thrones and maternal instinct, like it makes you less of a coward. What is love without risk? What is a home wrapped in solitude?"

Tanuhja's stillness was not serenity. It was brittle glass pretending to be stone.

Gloomhaven flickered around us, but I wasn't sure if I had caused the disruption or her. But the dam had broken. The pain caught like a hook under my breastbone, and this time I did not temper my venom.

I did not hold back. "You say you dreamed of seeing my face again. But you never earned it. You never fed me, never held me, never allowed me to make my own choices. You're neither my mother nor my blade. You're a queen who watched from afar, convinced that distance was devotion. Now you offer crowns and chaos like they're gifts to add to the trinkets and silks and shadowed dreams."

Tanuhja's fingers curled, and the air crackled with her pain and mine.

"Do you feel it now?" I asked, every syllable acid. "That ache in your chest? That's not love. That's the slow, suffocating truth that you weren't enough. Not to fight for me. Not to protect me. Not to deserve me."

Something cracked—deep in the bones of Gloomhaven —and it wasn't me. Chaos responded to pain like a harp string, trembling towards resonance. The room shook. Something ruptured. And in that rupture, I sensed where Zephyr was hidden.

I didn't erase Tanuhja's magic. I responded to it. Where it surged, I softened. Where it was sealed, I fractured it. Columns melted into liquid lines. The ground bubbled and warped. The sharp sting of triumph burned in my chest, guilt braided with relief. I was powerful, terrible, and hollow all at once. I wanted to wound Tanuhja, but hurting her didn't heal me or make me feel better.

Until the room dissolved like watercolour under a sudden rain shower to reveal Zephyr.

He breathed, thank the stars. To me, it was like Polaris had been hidden in the sky and had emerged again.

The faerie queen's pause was long and breathless. "Bravo, Ysadora. Now you, too, have learned that feeling or inflicting pain fuels chaos." I didn't know whether she referred to the monsters she had created or what I'd done to her. "Once chaos knows your voice, it will never forget. Don't you feel stronger?"

I didn't answer. Zephyr lay curled in a crater, eyes pinched shut. His shadows gathered tight around him like loyal hounds bristling at unseen threats. The residue of a terrible nightmare seeped through the bond: a deep weight of dread and the racing pulse of a heart that thought it might not survive.

My mother's devotion turned monstrous when she thought it served me.

FERRITH

Wraithwoods: an ever-shifting maze of pale birches, haunted by the remnants of mortals who lost their way in Faerie. Here, souls do not rest— they lie in wait.
– A Compendium of Faerie Flora and Terrain

It was a harsh descent, falling from the village's golden-haired darling to a man regarded as little more than a joke in Faerie. In Larkspur, Ferrith had never questioned his place. Once the sun of his small world, he'd never quite appreciated how power or lineage didn't matter in his village, as poor as it was. It was wit and warmth that shaped a man's standing there.

Neighbours trusted him with their fences and to herd their livestock, and hoped he'd come in for a brew. His friends at the tavern saved him a seat by the hearth. Village maidens made excuses to pass the fields where he worked. Mothers whispered about him as a good son-in-law. Old men slapped him on the shoulder, and it almost made up for his father's endless drinking.

He belonged to the rhythm of the village, as integral as the scent of Maren's mother's baking drifting down the lanes or the bell that rang to close the tavern. He listened well, laughed easily. So it was a sharper kind of displacement, now, to walk Faerie's twisted paths, where no one saved him a place, no one looked twice, and even the sky was unfamiliar.

In Faerie, the rules bent like heat haze. Smiles were often threats. Wishes bloomed like flowers and withered just as fast. Gold rusted here, and bones gleamed. Sleep came fast, but didn't guarantee waking. And rain sometimes fell in colours no eye could name.

All the things that had once made him sure of himself —his strength, his relationships, the dependable rhythm of his days—were rendered meaningless. No one cared that he could sing a folk tune or patch a roof or charm a room.

They thought of him as not just a fool, but a villain. The comparison clung to him like nettles. But he wasn't a villain. He had been more black and white since Vixora, since his mother's passing and his father's alcoholism. He didn't like feeling helpless; he needed to believe that evil could be fought, that it could be obliterated.

He now rode through a realm under the weight of indifference and scorn. He felt it in how Maren acted with contempt towards him, when a few days ago, she'd been flushed and happy in his arms.

They rode in uneasy tandem. Maren guided the speckled horse with more confidence than caution, her posture regal, shoulders stiff with tension he'd once known how to ease. The glamours disconcerted him more than he expected: his own and hers.

He kept a deliberate space between them, hands resting against the back of the saddle, not at her hips, not just because of their discord but because his hands were Zephyr's hands, her hips were Ysa's hips. The space between their spines felt colder than frost.

"Do you think we can pull this off? It's not like we know Liora Bramick very well," he ventured.

He didn't much like being near dragons. He hoped the glamours would wear off before they encountered any. He worried that any honourable dragon would set him and Maren alight simply for wearing the lie of a glamour.

Not even the whisper of their presence sat comfortably under his skin, and he had been glad when Kazimir's dragon had left Ebonspire. Ferrith couldn't really believe that dragons could be benign after all he had seen that day on the battlefield, his mind still reeling with the concept of Faerie.

But then his first experience of dragons had been Tanuhja's rotting white one, strung together with bone and blight, reeking of death. Sometimes, even now, the scent of it returned to him without warning: salt and sulphur and turned milk. No incense, no fresh air, not even Maren's perfume could cut through that phantom stench when it rose in his mind.

Wraithwoods loomed like a half-forgotten dream. The air was thick with the faint buzz of unseen insects. Overhead, the canopy of overreaching birches filtered light into moody silvers and greens that painted the mare's hide with restless shadow, almost as if he were Zephyr after all. Zephyr, with all his arrogance and conviction.

They'd been warned to skirt the boundary rather than enter the woods on the way to the Court of Nebulas, and after surviving alone in Faerie for a time, Maren seemed unfazed about her chances of completing the journey, with or without him.

"You can know people since childhood, and it can still go awry," she said. "Trust doesn't always grow the way you think it will. Sometimes it splits down the middle."

He winced and shifted in the saddle behind her. "I didn't mean to hurt you."

She kept her eyes ahead. "Well, you did."

Ferrith's stomach knotted. As much as her coldness hurt, he was glad to have time alone to figure out how to bridge the distance between them. There was no doubt that he had let her and Ysa down, but no matter how hard he tried, he couldn't figure out how to fix it, and he certainly couldn't stop thinking of himself as a liability.

How could he offer protection to a woman who wielded starfire in her hands? What did he have to offer, in a realm where his heart beat too loud, too slow?

Pity rose in him, and he shoved it down. He was a man, not a boy. A soldier had no time for pity.

"Maybe you'd be better off without me."

She twisted slightly in the saddle, meeting his gaze with fire under her lashes, even though her eyes were Ysa's. "You think I haven't considered that you'll age and I won't?"

Ferrith exhaled through his nose, hurt caught somewhere behind his ribs. "You think I haven't thought of that? That one day, I'll be wrinkled and grey."

Maren scoffed. "*That's* what you worry about?"

He frowned as a second set of hoofbeats seemed to

echo theirs—just once—then went silent. "What have *you* been worrying about?"

"That I won't be able to give you children. Mostly, that your body can be broken like a twig."

"Great. Thanks."

"And that you'll never be happy in Faerie because it took Vixora."

His throat scratched. "I worry about how to even exist in your world."

"I assumed you were too busy snooping to dwell on such things."

"And that you'll wander off with a fae male."

She turned away again, blinking hard. "You're an idiot."

"What if I only got a fraction of your years and you have to bury me?"

"That's a romantic notion," she said tartly, before sighing. "All your dalliances, and you still don't know the slightest thing about the opposite sex. All I need is honesty. And for you to think before you act."

He'd been so flattered that King Azeem had trusted him enough to make him a lieutenant in his army and send him into Faerie, so flattered to be needed by a monarch. But now, the betrayal—even though it had really only happened in his thoughts—seemed cheap, and he was bitterly ashamed.

The self-hatred within him for this was equally weighted to the hatred that flushed through him for Loxley. That blasted fae had hauled him before Zephyr and the others so quickly that he hadn't had time to examine the doubts in his own racing heart.

Maren pulled inky hair over her shoulder,

subconsciously impatient given how she always wore her own hair shorter. "You didn't tell me things about your time with King Azeem that you should have. You let your fears fester instead of being open with me. You endangered something I've worked towards my whole life. Ysa's safety."

Then Ferrith said, "I was scared I'd lose you if I said too much."

Her voice was quiet again, almost wistful. "You lost me anyway."

They rode in silence for a moment, the woods thickening in their peripheral vision, his shoulders slumped. Somewhere behind them, a twig snapped, and the hair on the back of his neck prickled, and he shook his head at his jumpiness, though he couldn't shake the feeling that they were not quite alone.

He said, almost in her ear, "You told me Faerie doesn't work like Larkspur. That secrets are protection."

A tree moved, just slightly, of its own volition. Ferrith flinched. He'd heard the stories, had no desire to have his courage tested against things he didn't understand, although he would put himself in harm's way for Maren and for Ysa, too.

The women he loved had always had that effect on him. He'd sprinted after Zephyr at the edge of the Shrouded Forest, but that was before he had seen the things he had seen. And Wraithwoods was a place that breathed without lungs. And watched without eyes.

She didn't even react to the shifting woods. Her red head tilted, sharp as a falcon's. "You sound like Thiago."

He looked away, jaw flexing. "You scare me sometimes."

"Do you think I don't need you, just because I don't shatter in your arms?"

Stilling the horse with a flick of her fingers, she kicked out of the stirrups and leapt down to face him properly. She planted her feet apart on the ground like she was about to challenge him to a physical fight, wincing only slightly when she remembered the glamour that had been cast, before regaining her momentum.

And it was odd for him, too, to see her character pour from Ysa's body, so odd not to see the freckled face and fiery hair he loved so well.

"What would you rather? That I dim myself so you feel more useful?"

Her barb stung. He remembered how much she liked it when he brawled with bawdy villagers who slighted her and how she murmured in bliss when his body curled around hers in sleep.

"I'm trying to be what you need."

"Try harder because Faerie will kill one or both of us and spit us out if we aren't singing the same tune."

The speckled mare grew skittish with the raised emotion, and he knew better than to dismount when Maren was spoiling for a fight, though he was tempted to haul her over the saddle or his shoulder, but she was a long way from laughing at his antics, and this time he couldn't kiss away her ire or tease her into laughter.

"I've never minded when you bested me."

"I hid my true self most of my life. That was mine and Kazimir's burden to bear. I'm sorry for lying to you and Ysa, I really am, but maybe I'm asking the impossible for you to love me as my true self. Maybe you should go home to Larkspur."

"I'm not scared of you," he said, when he should have said I love you.

For a moment, there was only the wind through the ferns. Then her eyes sparked. "Really?"

A single flame rose from her skin, violet-blue and trembling like a wish. It grew upwards. Then she added another, and another, until her palms were full of starfire. The air smelled suddenly of ozone and wildflowers after lightning, and the mare pranced on the spot, uneasy.

They looked at each other across the brittle air. Maren was dangerous, and he was not.

But the truth was that even with all the kisses he'd stolen from village maidens—behind haystacks at Bloomtide, under lanterns at feasts, by the creek where the fireflies gathered—it had always been Maren he was waiting for.

Maren, with her star-shot gaze and flame-laced temper. Maren, who didn't simper or swoon, who met him blow for blow with words sharper than any sword. He hadn't known it with the clumsy longing of boyhood, but she was the perfect fit for him.

Her fiery nature to his laidback one. Her certainty to anchor his doubt. Her wildness to draw out what was restless in him. With Maren, he was never a sweetheart or a prize to be flirted with. He was simply himself: maddening, mortal, messy.

Except he didn't even know how to make her laugh again. Instead, he stuttered, "If you had told me when we were children, maybe I wouldn't find...our differences...so hard to accept. You and your mother must have laughed at me."

"We did no such thing, and I won't apologise for surviving."

The trees shivered. From somewhere deep in the Wraithwoods came a voice he always missed: soft, pleading, lost.

Ferrith's head snapped up. "Did you hear that?"

He hadn't believed the souls of lost mortals could be trapped in the forest until now. Hadn't believed that Faerie could upend the terms of life and death so easily, in addition to everything else.

Maren paled. "It's not her. We need to keep riding. Hoist me up. Now."

Instead, he leapt down from his horse. She sounded so real. "I can't. Maren, I need to see her."

"Ferrith, you heard what the others said. You can't help the lost. They're already gone."

He handed her the reins. "Go, Maren."

He'd never had the chance to say goodbye to his little sister, and what if she was still in there, waiting for him to come and get her? Maybe that's why fate had brought him this way. Maybe his pain—him being in Faerie— had a reason after all.

"What do you mean? I'm glamoured as the calligrapher's daughter. It's not believable that I'd be out here alone." But he understood that she was far more worried about him than herself, that this was just her way of getting him to stay.

His ears strained to hear that voice again. "You don't need me. Go, and don't look back."

"You're wrong, Ferrith Namara," she hissed. "I've needed you my whole damn life. Don't you—"

It was almost funny now, how maybe he hadn't been built to take orders after all, seeing he pretty much disobeyed all commands, royal decrees, lovers' pleas, his father's damn wishes. Any one of the others would have had a better chance of holding him back with their magic, but not Maren.

She couldn't hold him back without setting the woods alight, because that wasn't a risk she was willing to take. Not here, where flame might awaken sleeping spirits or call the trees themselves into furious motion.

And Maren had always loved nature. Her starfire ran too hot, too wild, too eager to consume. It was glorious in the open, devastating in battle, he could be sure, but here, it was a blade with no sheath.

His chest heaved. "I love you," he said, in case he didn't see her again, even though her face wasn't her own, and it hurt.

Her fists were tight, volatile things, tinderboxes waiting for a single spark: the living match to her wildfire soul. "I despair. You're a doomed, foolish mortal with a big heart and no sense."

Her words rang in his ears as he ran into the goddamned Wraithwoods, ignoring every single warning he'd been given, ignoring even his own hard-won logic. The edge of the woods blurred as soon as he passed through, path and horizon alike swallowed in a hush of silver fog. Pale birches rose from the earth in mournful columns, bark like flayed parchment.

But Ferrith only focused on his little sister's sweet voice beckoning him onwards.

ZEPHYR

Icebound Wraith: translucent form, chilling breath, frosted talons. Once Eira Snowbright of the Court of Languish, sister of Lyra, gifted in granting peace to restless fae before their death.
— The Secrets of Faerie's Veiled Beasts
by Zephyr Ashmoor

T he fallen prince, whom the Binder called *Fatebreaker,* stood on the blackened cliffs near Ebonspire, where he had always found peace. For the briefest moment, his heart knew contentment, and he thought he was home. That somehow, in his disoriented state, he'd slipped through shadow and back to Ebonspire, where Ysa and his kin waited.

But something was wrong.

He rarely ventured this way without Mythros. Without his brothers. His pulse spiked. The wind tasted of iron, not salt. The cliffs always smelled like sage and sea, but today they smelled of jasmine and decay.

The waves crashed in the same pattern, over and over. What was more, the path down the cliffs should have been west. As a youngling, Zephyr had known that path so well that he had attempted it blindfolded and received a hiding across the backs of his legs from his father, before Veda had intervened.

But when he turned, the path was not there. His hands reached behind his back, but his dual swords were not crossed there, and his dagger was not at his thigh. Instead, he wore his sword—one with a stranger's hilt—on the wrong hip.

"Ysa?"

Nothing.

He had called out across the cliffs a thousand times as a child, before monsters roamed the Court of Lore, and yet this time there was no familiar echo. There was no answer either when her name rolled from his mind across the bond.

She had such a beautiful name. *Ysadora Silberquill.* The river that represented her still trickled through his mind, but it was flattened. There were no currents, no texture, as though the bond was a poor imitation, drawn rather than lived.

His emotional responses felt wrong, spiking too high, or too muted, or disjointed somehow, rising at the wrong time or too late. Almost as though he performed someone else's reaction in his skin. Fear snaked along Zephyr's spine. Ysa was in trouble. Why else would she leave him in silence when she knew that silence was what he feared most?

Except he had never told her that. Why had he never told her that?

He clutched at the threads of what was true. They had been on a mission to Gloomhaven with Tanuhja. He was almost sure of it. The thought flowed through his mind like driftwood he couldn't quite hold on to.

His mind was like quicksand, but he fell into the rhythm of being a mercenary. He'd lived that life for so many orbits that it was instinct. It comforted Zephyr to go through the drill. First, he needed to get the lie of the land.

Darkness curled from his boots as he shadow stepped. But each time he sank into darkness, he snapped back. Inexplicably, the passages beneath the veil remained sealed to him. He tried with force, although he had practised his shadow step since he was a youngling, and it had never required any more than breath and will.

Still, nothing. When Zephyr sent out shadow scouts, they refused, sticking to him like a second skin instead.

A curse sprang from his lips that Loxley would've been proud of, but it wasn't satisfying without his kin to hear.

In the end, he took the ridge at a jog. When sweat pooled on his brow and down his back, he threw down his cloak and increased his pace, following the cliff line until the rocks began to repeat, noticing the same twisted tree, the same patch of lichen, a ravine shaped like a crescent moon, his cloak pooled on the floor.

The sun didn't change its position in the sky, even though his exertions without Mythros and shadow-stepping should have taken long enough for his own shadow to lengthen. Wherever he went, Zephyr ended where he started, as though he slammed into a flat pane of dream. As though the blackened cliffs were a theatre set designed for him, not the old Court of Lore land he knew so well.

This was a cage, and Tanuhja had crafted it. But it was so difficult to hold on to logical thought. Exhaustion made it easy to forget that Ysa needed him, so he took a sharp rock and drew her name into his forearm, but his skin smoothed over the minute he had finished.

His skin prickled like static. Zephyr's hand tightened on the hilt at his side, and he turned slowly, scanning the warped cliffs. One shape stirred in the fog. Then another. He knew the curve of a horn, the ruined limbs, knew them from the Ebonspire dungeons, though he could have sworn he'd brought these outcast fae to safety.

"Stay back," he called out, in case they could understand. His chest burned. He had unwillingly killed a slithering monster, too, and he had no desire to end more lives, to carry more guilt. "I don't want to hurt you. Please."

He rarely said please. Power didn't beg, but desperation had a way of humbling even the sharpest tongues.

The first creature had legs too long for its body and antlers twisted backwards like hooked knives. Its skin was stretched taut over protruding bones, grey and thin as wax paper, but beneath it pulsed veins of slow, blue fire. Its face had once been beautiful—regal in the way high fae wore their grace—but now its jaw hung slack, one eye clouded, the other too wide.

When it lunged, it made no sound. No snarl, no screech, just the soft sound of displaced wind and the rattle of its taloned feet. Zephyr caught it in the ribs with his blade and felt no resistance.

The monster collapsed into the dirt and then rose again.

The second followed, screeching. She crept from the shadow of a boulder, crawling first, then unfolding. Her limbs bent the wrong way, knees inverted like an arachnid's, and her back arched unnaturally as though pulled by unseen strings. Her skin was sometimes bark, sometimes bone, and verdant green wept from her eyes.

He hesitated just for a breath. It was nearly enough to die.

Or worse, get bitten and become one of them.

So he drew shadows up and over his arms like gauntlets. He barely deflected her clawed strike. The cliffs burned black around him, jagged and steep. When he flung himself sideways, rolling across broken ground, she skittered after him. He struck back, and her spine twisted, resisting the rules of physics and pain alike.

More and more monsters came with the scrape of too many limbs over stone, their cries tearing at his soul. Zephyr's blade found them. He cut cleanly through wings laced with rot, ribs twisted into cages, mouths too wide and eyes too knowing.

They roared with the same frequency, tore with the same teeth, smelled indistinct, then they stood again, crueller, faster, wiser. They circled again and again. By all rights, they should have died from his blows. They should have crumpled. But the monsters reassembled, as if bound by narrative rules not flesh.

"This isn't real," he rasped out loud.

But the sweat down his spine was real. The ache in his sword arm. The despair blooming in his chest.

He had no choice but to continue. He pivoted,

dodged, struck, until his single sword shook in his hand, until he fought with his left hand instead of his favoured right one, until his blade grew dull and he fought with fists and staffs and rocks foraged from the landscape. He couldn't save them. He couldn't free them. He couldn't kill them.

They overwhelmed him, pushed him to exhaustion, but they, too, never dealt a killing blow. Claws raked across his chest. He stumbled and looked down at the wound. This wasn't how he bled. His body registered the pain, but though his skin was sliced, his wounds sealed as if the dream demanded an alternative destruction to mere physical pain.

This place wanted to unmake him, piece by piece.

He wasn't meant to die here. He was meant to break.

He staggered back into the rocks, heart hammering, hand to the slick wall behind him, fingers raw. Then, to his eternal shame, he ran like a hunted thing, dodging gnarled roots that shouldn't have existed on cliffside rocks.

His boots pounded the earth, and the wind howled through the crevices like a mourning song. No shadow path opened. No horizon shifted. When he had looped the landscape countless times, a wail rising in his body, when blisters had formed on his feet and his limbs grew leaden, when he was tempted to give himself to the waves, to dive through the seabed to escape the cage, a sound echoed in his ears that made him stop short.

It was a sound that never failed to make his heart swell: hooves alive with the rhythm that he knew intimately.

Zephyr looked up at a crack in the seams of the world as Mythros leapt towards him from a stained-glass sky, his mane like ribbons of storm cloud. He had rarely seen a creature so beautiful in all his centuries.

Zephyr stumbled towards his horse and pressed his forehead to Mythros's flank. "You found me."

Mythros neighed, full of pride, and dream-smoke rose from his skin. There was no panic in him, only deep calm, the kind that had carried them both through wars. His flank was warm, solid, real.

Zephyr remembered then, whispering to the stallion in the forecourt of the Chaos Queen's castle. He'd asked Mythros to search for him in the dreamscape if necessary, because dreams and shadows shared a language, and Mythros understood the spaces between. He had never dipped alone beneath the veil before, but in the Court of Chaos, boundaries frayed, and Mythros had always known when Zephyr needed him most.

The fallen prince knew in his bones that the rules of the dream had shifted.

That he might win against the foe who had trapped him here.

And in that moment of self-belief, his enemy stepped into the landscape. The dreamscape grew dusky, as if painted in ash and suspended breath. He knew something was coming. He'd always paid attention to the hints the world gave before it caved, although sometimes he was blinded by love. The wind was loud in his ears, but not loud enough to drown out his pounding heart.

He couldn't bear for Mythros to be hurt. "Go!" he urged the warhorse that his sister had once prophesied.

The stallion stamped his hoof, gloriously stubborn to the last cell.

His enemy didn't walk so much as emerge into the

space, as if the dream accommodated her presence. Though she was beautiful, there was cruelty in the curve of her lips: a slow, indulgent smile that didn't quite reach her eyes, as if she were watching a stray dog perform a trick it barely understood.

Recognition cracked through his haze. The Chaos Queen. He snarled. "You."

"I admit, I didn't think you'd last this long. But belief in the impossible has always been your flaw, hasn't it?" Her violet eyes lingered on Mythros for a moment. "Steady your horse."

Zephyr took up a warrior's stance in front of the stallion, sword drawn and caked with blood, but in this world, the threats didn't always come from in front. This was the Chaos Queen's world.

Behind her, cages fell from the clouds like rain. They were as delicate as bird bones, as dark as wrought iron. They landed with a resounding thud that rattled Zephyr's teeth. Inside each, the monsters he had fought writhed. He steeled himself. He hated bearing witness to their distress as much as he feared having to battle them again and again.

The Chaos Queen's eyes slid towards the cages. "You know these souls, don't you?"

It was true. Zephyr did know them, and melancholy fountained in him. There was an icebound wraith, a horrorsap dryad, and a green bane boar, its tusks like jagged stones. In the cage nearest him, a wretched creature wept acid tears into its claws, and Zephyr recognised his mother's gardener, whose skilled care took fruit trees from blight to bounty.

A stooped, snorting thing dragged its wings across the

bars, who had once commanded sonnets with a voice that shook crystal chandeliers. There was a creature—half moth, half rodent, with wizened incisors—who used to sell candied starfruit to fae younglings before performances at the amphitheatre. This was the fae woman who had championed Veda's art and told younglings stories while their guardians shopped at his gallery.

Zephyr's breath tore in and out of him. "Why are you doing this?"

Her voice was dipped in honeyed rot. "To help you collect stories, of course."

Of course. Why else would they be there?

Mythros gave a plaintive whinny, and Zephyr knew he shouldn't collect more stories, though stories were as intrinsic to him as shadows. What better salve to honour pain than story? The tug in him felt like a river. A river that whispered he was already on the cusp of losing himself. But the monsters weren't an illusion. They were the Court of Lore fae. He wanted nothing more fervently than helping those he loved, especially those who were lost.

Bodies were homes, and these fae had been exiled from their own. To lose the architecture of your limbs, the familiar cadence of your breath, the skin that once bore freckles or runes was a deeper form of exile.

It was a disorientation not just of mind but of memory. How did the monsters anchor themselves when even their limbs no longer functioned as they had, when their voices became strangled roars?

He imagined waking in such a shape: teeth where none should be, hunger that wasn't his, trying to be himself in a strange skin. How did you remember kindness with a mouth that only knew how to snarl? How did you remain gentle when your very presence inspired fear? No wonder the monsters raged. No wonder they clawed. They had been evicted from themselves.

But somewhere beneath the twisted muscle and unnatural limbs was still a sliver of self, watching. Trapped. Something beneath the monstrous veneer still remembered how to be held, how to dance, how to rest.

Zephyr discerned it in a flick of a gesture, a tilt of the head, a shiver in the presence of the moonlight. It made their torment crueller. It was a dislocation of the soul. A prison of flesh too broken to house them and too alive to let them go.

It terrified him that it could happen to anyone. Even him.

He would rather give up on himself than them. His throat was dry as bone dust. "I'll take their stories into me, but only if you give me a way to unmake what you've done to them. No riddles. No guesses. Just clarity."

A look of gleaming satisfaction passed over the queen's face, the kind worn by a puppeteer watching a marionette twitch to life. "Then step forward, and I will tell you all I know about curing them."

He walked to each cage in turn, eleven in total. The memories struck like a tide with no moon to restrain it. They arrived all at once, a thousand doors flung open in his mind.

A child weeping over a stolen toy. A male whistling beneath moonlit vines. Blood on the amphitheatre steps. Laughter in the library. Fingers dirtied by paint. A home in flames. Oranges sliced with a silver blade. A kiss goodbye on a hay bale. A cart tipped sideways. Charred portraits of a family with sun-bright smiles.

Too many. Too fast. The monsters' grief became his grief. Zephyr dropped to his knees as their lives poured into him like rich wine into a cracked cup. His own name felt like a myth on his tongue.

Who was he? A calligrapher's son. A knight. A husband. A brother. No, that wasn't right. A thief. A beloved prince. No, that seemed wrong, too. A statue cracked open by grief. A soldier who couldn't follow orders. A mask worn so long it believed it was a face. Confusion made the world tilt.

"Gallant fool." The queen crouched beside him and stroked back his sweat-damp locks, pity in her tone. "One person's memories are enough to break us. Who told you that you were whole enough to carry more? You are no match for my daughter."

There was another in his past who had offered carrot and stick, but he knew how to stay the course.

There was something this queen said she would tell him. Something important.

Zephyr's eyes darted to the cages, and he knew the captives as friends. "The cure?"

Her words came like scripture, flat and certain. "What is broken cannot be fixed."

He frowned. He knew that wasn't true, not only because of the sting of the Rune of Unveiling on his hip, but because he had been broken. He had lain in ruins more than once, although he couldn't remember the specifics. Irritation flared in him. If only he had been careful with Faerie semantics, but his mind had been too hazy to think about the pitfalls of promises and bargains, and to be precise with wording.

"Their names were unspoken too long. Faerie has forgotten them."

But he hadn't forgotten, and he took a measure of comfort from that. When the horse nudged him, he heaved himself into the saddle, though he had nowhere urgent to go. The queen gave a joyous laugh, the kind that cuts and soars at the same time, but the horse did not rear.

He remained stoically on his path even when other monsters came. They rode. They rode hard and fast, bodies moulded together like they belonged. The horse's hooves ignited sparks across the dream-warped stone. Zephyr leaned low against the horse's nape, trusting the beast to carry them both forward.

He decided he liked riding. It was a kind of meditation.

After a time, a female flashed into his mind. She had eyes like twilight and hair like ink. In her hands, she held a crimson quill, and her skin was butter soft. And her heart was generous and brave. Her name, like his own, danced just out of reach. He pinched his eyelids shut, his mind dizzy with absence.

"Please." His voice cracked. "Remind me."

But the horse only continued his gallop.

YSADORA

I do not recognise the mother I've become. Every breath brings a new horror. Will our daughter love me when we finally meet? Or are my arms fated to remain empty?
– Tanuhja's letter to her former lover, Kazimir

Zephyr lay discarded in a crater of black glass and ash, his breathing shallow, his mind caught in a cage woven of old fears and new griefs. He was small in a way my Zephyr had never been. This was the male who had faced monsters with steel in his hand and shadows at his heels. A male who had survived the death of his mother and the fall of his court, who had survived the spymaster's manipulations, and found the strength to rebuild his home and create a new family. A male who could turn a battle and our bedchamber into a dance.

Witnessing his vulnerability at my mother's hand, when I'd never seen him laid so low, unravelled a fundamental piece in me. The bond was quiet—so hauntingly quiet—that I wanted to shake him, to cry out, to demand that he come back to me. He had always been sharp edges, artful cunning, and defiant strength, but Tanuhja had stripped that all from him.

I wouldn't let her see either of us destroyed.

Rage burned through me, indistinguishable from love. I didn't know how to bargain with a court built on ruin and wild dreaming, only that love seemed the only steady thing in all this madness—her love and mine.

My mother had mistaken love for weakness. But love was never weak. It's what taught me to rise. She would learn now that my love for Zephyr was stronger than the distrust born of her heartbreaks.

This was what love meant: not firelight and lover's bliss—though his slightest touch was always enough to ignite my skin—but the unbearable ache of seeing Zephyr undone and knowing that I wouldn't survive if he didn't.

Zephyr had taken my ink-stained fingers, my thousand second-guesses, and my fragile heart, and believed I could venture into Faerie and belong. It had been with Zephyr that I'd dreamed the unimaginable, that I'd dared to be fae, dared to be bigger than my small life of lies, dared to believe that we could change Faerie for the better together.

Fatebreaker, came the whisper in my mind, and for a moment it almost sounded like the Binder.

But I didn't know how to help him. Every decision seemed laced with risk. I'd have given anything for the Binder to illuminate the path forward, but she remained elusive. The Binder felled stars and then watched while the world cratered. She had no answers; only paths and choices.

Even if I wanted to ask for her aid in that moment, I didn't know how to. Our encounters had never been initiated by me. Was Zephyr doomed if she didn't emerge from the unseen? How could I stumble across the right threshold, the hidden place where the veil between worlds thinned and Lunarys strung up stars? Was there a secret trail to her doorstep or an ancient oath to utter to summon her? Was there a wish I could whisper into the wind, or should I burn herbs under a dark sky?

No, it wouldn't work. Lunarys was always the seeker, never the one who was found.

Without his kin, without the Binder, there was no one to save Zephyr except me.

I would not leave him to rot in the dark. Ink flared from my quill, and chaos coiled at my back as I stepped into the crater. It was both a sanctum and a battlefield. At first, the dream didn't notice me, but Zephyr's shadows did.

They parted for me alone, allowing me closer. Their caress of recognition gave me hope. My mother neared, and the darkest shadows peeled off and lunged at her, snapping like feral dogs suddenly off leash, but that was her battle, not mine. The dream, the nightmare—whatever it was that kept him from me—can't have captured him fully. I had to believe that.

The air rippled as I knelt beside him and kissed his damp forehead. He was so damn beautiful with his lashes against the chiselled lines of his face. I needed to see those storm-cloud eyes light up at the sight of me again.

"Wake up, Zephyr. I need you. You don't belong to her. You belong to me."

When he didn't move, panic rose in me, thick and suffocating.

Tanuhja's voice was tight and thin. "You do not command this dream, Ysadora."

"Maybe not, but I will. My mate told me I'm a quick learner."

"You are the culmination of two forces the world couldn't tame. Why would you tether yourself to him?"

"I don't want to be protected from love. I want to live it. Bleeding, burning, breaking. All of it."

Maybe she didn't understand love at all because even when Zephyr had imprisoned me at Ebonspire, I'd known more freedom than I had ever had in the life she and Father had designed for me. But she had taught me something, as Wylda had hoped: she had reminded me that I was made by two opposing forces. So I opened myself to both the stars and the void. I breathed in: my father's meticulous love in one lung; my mother's painful yearning in the other.

My mother's violet eyes narrowed with suspicion. "The Binder gave you hope. Hope kills us, Ysadora. The fallen prince served his purpose. Now, only I can protect you."

Raw power hummed beneath my skin, both wild and precise. My ink flowed like liquid thought, while chaos crackled beneath it. Tension snapped within me, a fierce dance between control and surrender, like riding a tempest and hoping it wouldn't swallow me.

"You're wrong. I can protect myself. And I can protect my mate."

Maybe it was Father's memories in the ancient stone, ancestral magic, or a nudge from the Binder. It didn't matter. All that mattered was that my belief in our love, innate knowledge, and instinctive magic blended just enough that I could see a path.

It struck me that dragons were the bridge between nebulas and chaos. Dragons remembered the world before it hardened into rules. They were too vast for time and didn't follow the laws that governed lesser beings. Their hearts beat to rhythms older than music, older than gods. They did not yield to gravity or logic. They were memory and forgetting in a single breath. No compass could track them. No map could chart them. Which meant they could be a way to disrupt the dream. Thanks to Father and Zephyr, I had Caldoron's flame-kissed blade sheathed at my thigh.

I was still kneeling in the dirt. I drew the dagger— ignoring my mother's hiss of recognition—and it hummed in my palm, faintly warm. The dragonfire embedded in its edge was not heat but hunger, and it sought release. Above Zephyr's head, I carved a single rune into the skin of reality. Not into paper. Not into stone. Into the thin fabric between worlds.

The dream faltered because dragons did not believe in cages. Neither did I.

The dream tore, and I uncapped an inkwell from my pocket with a flick of my thumb. I deliberately chose ink harvested by Wylda, rather than drawing from the earth as the river sisters had taught me.

Magic required balance, and intuition told me I needed both chaos and nebula magic. Father had chosen firevein to write his message in the snow when he thought all was lost: firevein that burned words onto parchment and stone, maybe even dreams; firevein that bound itself to the writer's intent, making it nearly impossible for my tricky mother to alter once written. It pooled in the space between us, suspended.

Forlorn hopelessness seeped from Tanuhja. Her damn crown was still in her hands. "Choose me."

My answer was pure intuition, pure love. "I choose him."

She didn't try to stop me.

Then my ink flowed up, not down, swirling in chaotic loops. Galaxies shifting beneath my skin, stars collapsing and forming, my magic turned aware. It circled the space like a predator and then softened to touch the hollow of Zephyr's throat like a lover before spilling into the seam the dragon-kissed blade had made, the pair to Father's quill. Both instruments seemed in that moment to be utterly mine.

Instead of writing to create, I wrote to unmake.

I wrote backwards, upside down, let the ink lift from my palms and spin in midair, letters fluttering like unanchored roots. Lacing my ink magic with recollections, I weaponised intimacy: how the world quieted around Zephyr and me at Bloomtide; the warmth of his cloak and his heartbeat as he carried me through the Shrouded Forest; our bodies nestled close while riding Mythros together; the brush of his calloused fingers in the silence before he first ravished me on the cliffs; the weightless calm that had settled over us on the long journey back from Larkspur; the times he pushed me to be more without ever making me feel less; the times he had shared his past with me.

I wrote those moments into the fabric of the dream, not as weapons but keys. I made them roll like thunder across the dreamscape. They cracked the false heavens and poured in like molten truth.

Zephyr stirred in the crater. His breathing grew deeper. His fingers flexed in the crater dust. A wrinkle of confusion folded across his brow. The colour—stars, the colour—rushed back to his tawny face like dawn breaking across his skin.

The bond between us hummed with awareness. Somewhere inside him, the lie began to unravel. My mother said something then, but the magic whirled so deeply that it almost swallowed me up, and no one existed but me and him.

I continued, writing lies that undid truth: you are not trapped; you are already awake; the door to the dream is open. Each phrase flickered in and out of existence, refusing coherence, denying finality, demanding more life and growth. The inked phrases weren't neat. Chaos didn't beg for structure. It danced with ruin.

Then I felt it: the final, delicate thread snapped. The dream tried to hold him—Tanuhja tried to hold him—but I was chaos and creation entwined. *This* was my inheritance.

Not obedience. Not even rebellion.

An instinctive understanding of the pinnings of Faerie.

The dream buckled, and Zephyr's shadows receded. He woke like a storm dragging itself back into motion. He was slow at first, disjointed, the fault-lines of the dream still stitched across his brow.

His breath caught in his throat, a rasp like torn silk, as he heaved himself upright from the crater. Zephyr blinked as though caught between what had been forged and what was real. Then his storm-cloud eyes locked on mine, and he cast off the remnants of the nightmare like a second skin and stood at his full height.

Tanuhja's crown shattered in her hands. Its iron vines turned brittle, crumbling like dry branches under frost, and the sapphire swallowed its own gleam before dying into grey stone. What once writhed fell inert through her fingers. I thought about how my mother and I were alike after all. How there was darkness in both of us.

"Ysadora," Zephyr growled, voice frayed but iron-edged. His gaze slid past me, towards my mother.

"I'm here," I told him as the last of the crimson ink curled into the air like smoke.

Zephyr's hands reached for the crossed swords on his back, instinct tugging him towards violence, but when he grasped their hilts, the tension in his jaw eased, and he tilted his head towards me instead. *Your mother, your decision.*

I sensed through the bond that it would have been a different matter if she had hurt me. He would unleash his anger if I asked him to, but he wouldn't dishonour me by stealing this reckoning. And stars help me, I loved him for that restraint more than I ever could have loved him for fury.

Tanuhja's lips parted, wrought with confusion and maybe a smidgeon of pride. "How?"

The runes still burned above us, bright and righteous.

Fatebreaker, the Binder called him, and I wondered if she had seen this path and hoped for it to come to pass. But I said only, "Dreams bind those who believe. Love makes them disobedient."

A vein flexed in Zephyr's jaw. "Is there really no cure for the cursed fae?"

My gaze snapped in his direction. *I'm so sorry. We'll find another way.*

The faerie queen, who was my mother, gave a bitter laugh. "I didn't curse them consciously. The river sisters told me the monsters are the result of my breakdown. You see, grief is love weaponised."

I looked at her in horror. I had never known someone so broken.

"Will you stand with us against the Spymaster?" I asked, quietly.

"No." Tanuhja's violet gaze burned. "You chose your mate over me and my crown."

I gave a single nod. So our alliance was dead in the water, but I had mastered some of the magic I had come here to learn. Enough to gain a foothold in the Court of Chaos, if not a throne. I had no regrets.

It had been easy to choose Zephyr. His love didn't seek to possess, only to witness. Standing in that cold hall with my mother, I realised she had never known anything like it. She loved like a drowning woman grasping at driftwood: fierce and fast and doomed. I pitied her.

What tragedy it was to command the chaos of dreams and still never be held gently in the waking world. The impact of her pleas had been entirely erased by how she had first used Zephyr to her own ends, then discarded him like she had the outcast fae.

Still, I couldn't bring myself to break her already broken spirit. "If there's anything left between us, it can wait."

"So quick to dismiss me." Melancholy laced her voice. "I worried once that you'd never survive in Faerie. I was wrong. But know this, daughter. Only dragon riders have ever secured lasting peace in Faerie. In my dreams, you never succeed at *Kindling*. You fall from the lighthouse. No good can come of travelling to Nightblaze Isle."

Kindling. My mind filled with the old dream in which I stumbled over parched ground amongst skeletal trees, the luminous flower at my feet and the crooked lighthouse swaying in a turbulent storm.

Zephyr glowered. "I won't ever let her fall."

"But you do, shadow prince. Why do you think I tried to remove your piece from the board?"

I bit my lip. "I'm sorry that you can't see that Zephyr saves me even when it costs him."

"Males, even in this realm, find helpless damsels more appealing than when females find their power. You will discover the truth of it soon enough." She plucked a letter from the air and pushed it into my hands. "Kazimir stopped accepting my letters eventually. He tired of how I turned from helplessness to rage. Still, perhaps this letter will convince you that I, too, was soft once."

I stared at the letter, but all I wanted in that moment was to hold Zephyr.

When I looked up, my mother had left without a farewell, and Mythros was leaping over the cracks in the Court of Chaos towards us.

ELOWEN

*Beloved, to guard you in this realm, I carved a
shadow from my side and buried it beneath
twisted roots of the Wraithwoods. Your voice
now has teeth. Sing and let Faerie remember
whom you married.*
– Thiago's love letter to his wife Danaë

She sat with her thin shoulders pressed to the damp
wall, her severed finger bound in a strip of her own
torn sleeve. The cell was hewn from the dark grey
stone, and not for the first time in her life, Elowen missed
colour.

There were no tapestries, no silks, no carved
adornments, none of the usual conceits of fae elegance.
There was a narrow stone bench, more slab than seat or
cot, and a scratchy blanket that a hound might have
claimed as a chew toy.

The only light came from a crescent-shaped slat in the

door, too high to reach, and too narrow to permit more than a blade of silvered illumination. No servant dared enter this level.

Elowen heard him before she saw him. Silence folded the air like velvet, the shadows at the threshold darker than the cell itself. The mouth-binding spell cracked, not audibly, but with a shiver in her teeth.

Then her father stood before her, pale eyes glimmering. "Your betrayal is despicable."

Her tongue felt foreign, her mouth sore. "So is you binding me. But you enjoy that well enough."

He leaned forward, eyes glinting like knives. "Secrets have weight, Elowen, and you are hoarding them. If I fall, what do you think will happen to you and Xaire? To your mother, who some have not accepted as of this realm?"

Again, the old fantasy of his death comforted her. One day, she would be strong enough to have him on his knees before her. "You underestimate how much I am willing to lose."

The scuttling outside her cell told her his spiders waited, males armed with whisperings and steel, trained in the arts of silence and pain.

The Spymaster looked with distaste at the finger he had severed. "If you will not tell me your secrets, perhaps I will tell you one of mine." He settled back against the opposite wall, shadows flickering across his sharp features. "I have painstakingly gathered intelligence while you and Xaire sit in the lap of luxury."

She hated his meddling ways with a fury that frothed. Her finger throbbed as if every pulse drove infection deeper, and she was bitterly aware that her pain was the entry fee to prising open his confidence.

"The fall of the Order of the Glyph upended the balance of Faerie, yes. But that was accelerated by the Chaos Queen's breakdown. Tanuhja is what the Grimoire calls a reality anchor. Look how well that turned out."

Her voice rasped. "Why are you telling me this?"

Each word was weighted with cold certainty. "Ysadora Silberquill is the calligrapher's daughter with the potential to rewrite the Grimoire, but what most have forgotten is that she's also the daughter of the Queen of Chaos, with her mother's capacity for destruction. Ysadora's magic grows stronger each day. Do you understand what her combination of magic means?"

Foreboding made her even more lightheaded, but when she said nothing, he continued as if she had answered.

The shadows in the cell deepened as he spoke, responding to some emotion he kept carefully hidden. "Ysadora doesn't understand what she is yet, but I do. A corrupted reality anchor of her ilk, born from the Court of Chaos and the Court of Nebulas, is more dangerous than a thousand suns. Her mother nearly destroyed Faerie with chaos alone. Imagine what Ysa could do with the power to literally edit the cosmic order."

Her chest grew tight at the magnitude of what he described, but it didn't change who she loved and who she did not.

"I've spent decades preparing for another reality anchor's emergence. Building networks, gathering allies, positioning pieces on the board. And yet here you are, my own blood working against me. Just like your cousin."

Her slim brows furrowed. "This is about Zephyr. About destroying what he loves."

The Spymaster's smile was cold as winter moonlight. "No, Elowen. This is about protecting this family. You're going to help me save Faerie from her."

Elowen felt the blood drain from her face. "You want to kill her."

"I want to control her. There's a difference. Better to control such power than let it run wild again. But if control proves impossible...yes. Better one death than the destruction of everything I've built."

But her father had never stopped at one death. He'd always lusted after more.

She forced her expression to remain neutral, even as her mind raced and her father watched for signs of her capitulation. This was the moment to betray Ysa or face whatever torment he devised next. "And if I refuse to help you?"

"Then I'll take another finger. And another. Until you understand that your loyalty belongs to family first." His veined face glittered with cold promise. "I am not without patience, child. But I'm not without limits either."

She pushed her shoulders back. "Then you'll be disappointed."

Her father held her gaze. "What a pity for you that your meagre magic doesn't even allow you to save yourself. Pathetic. The daughter of a faerie king who can communicate only with her twin."

But Elowen knew she could do so much more. And she would be more effective if she bided her time until the right moment.

"I'll give you time to consider the wisdom of cooperation. The next time we speak, I expect better. One severed finger is nothing compared to what I can inflict."

The shadows swallowed him as he stepped into the corridor.

Elowen released a ragged breath as the cell sealed shut and wondered if her mother knew of his threats and if she approved, or whether she dared to raise a small voice against him, a little sign that she cared.

Alone in the darkness, Elowen allowed herself a small, fierce smile. Her father thought her weak, but he'd made a crucial mistake by telling her exactly what Ysa was and how powerful she could become. How could she get that information to Ysa and Zephyr from the confines of the cell?

Her mind was already working, already planning.

Let her father think he was winning.

She had secrets of her own.

YSADORA

Mythros was gifted by Rowena Ashmoor, Faerie Queen of the Court of Lore, to her son Zephyr on his 21st birthday, as foretold by his sister Veda. An ink black warhorse of a fierce and stubborn temperament, sired by Umbra from the Shadowfell plains, he is uniquely attuned to the prince's magic and rumoured to be capable of slipping beneath the veil.
– A Tapestry of Courts and Crowns

Zephyr folded me into his arms as if anchoring himself to something real. His breath was ragged against my neck, his shoulders shaking with fury and relief. My nails curled into his back, and I buried my head in his chest. He smelled of musk from his saddle and crushed jasmine. Only now, in his arms, did I allow myself to believe that we had escaped unscathed.

"Stars, I hate what she did to you."

"I'm still here. Still yours." His forehead dropped to mine. The dream still clung to his skin, sticky like the residue of a fever.

"Do you think she's ashamed of what she created?"

"Who knows. Maybe? Or maybe she would do anything if it meant saving you." He went quiet then, as if he was considering what sins he'd commit to save me, then he said, "We might have her alliance if you'd chosen her over me."

"There was no other choice," I said simply.

He looked at me as if he didn't deserve my utter loyalty, as if love were something earned in clean victories, not clawed from the wreckage. Not knowing that every scar on him only deepened my devotion.

When Mythros cantered to our side, still tacked up and wearing the saddlebags, he bent his head low and brushed his muzzle against Zephyr's shoulder with a tender, commanding touch. The stallion's breath steamed warm against the cool air of the Court of Chaos.

Zephyr's fingers trembled as they slid into Mythros's thick mane. His throat worked around words he didn't say. I ran a hand over Mythros, and the stallion nickered. My brow furrowed at how his coat was slicked with sweat even though the stables were not far. Constellations flickered just beneath the surface of his inky coat, and I could smell the faint tang of lightning, as though chaos had kissed him too.

I kept my voice soft, watching how Zephyr swayed slightly, exhaustion evident in his too-bright eyes. "You should both rest, and then you can tell me what happened in the dream."

He glanced at the decimated throne room, the fractured sky that blinked like a wounded eye, and the white dragon that circled still, then gave me a crooked smile. "I'm not sleeping in the Court of Chaos again, not even for you, Inkheart."

Through the bond, I sensed his yearning for Ebonspire, though he didn't speak it. The court was quiet now, yes, but though my mother and the half-life statues could not be seen, something still watched. "Then we ride."

Without another word, we mounted, though I checked for my quill and dragon-kissed blade first. Once assured they were secured, I settled in the saddle between Zephyr's legs and leaned my head against his chest. A shudder ran through him, and a breath later, Mythros was trotting, sure-footed and strong, as if he too understood what it meant to leave but not retreat.

The Court of Chaos did not turf us out. The three of us rode into it, fleeing not in fear but in defiance. It exhaled, releasing us like a fist opening, as if we had passed a test and won safe passage. The once changing ground now unfolded in silk-smooth silence beneath Mythros's hooves, and the landscape rearranged itself in soft gradients, ribbons of violet mist, and long shadows. The sky, once painted in kaleidoscopic hues, was a glorious blue.

No one challenged our presence or demanded tolls or tithes. No monsters slithered out to greet us or cawed from the skies. Not even the white dragon. The wind stirred, ruffling my hair and tugging the edges of Zephyr's cloak.

I searched the waters for the river sisters, scanning for the glint of an eye beneath the current, for hair like reeds and chatter riding the ripple. But the sisters did not appear. I searched for my mother too: for a trap sewn into the fabric of our path, for the sharp edge of her magic pressed into the air like a blade just shy of skin. But she was nowhere or everywhere. She hadn't meant for me to walk away with my mate's hand still warm in mine, but she let us go all the same.

We rode east towards the Court of Luminosity—Zephyr mused that my bargain with Esolas meant he would turn a blind eye to our presence until the hour of the meeting of Faerie rulers arrived—to avoid Frenzi, the largest settlement in the Court of Chaos, a tangle of tilted towers and slanted bridges.

There were smaller settlements that were half startling and half sublime. A lantern lit by screams. A horned female walking backwards. Tadpoles sucked into clouds. Dancers made of glass waltzing on obsidian ground, shattering with every pirouette and reforming with the next.

A sleeping giant's hand half-buried in violet moss. A long-haired male in a pin-striped robe offering tea to a tree stump. Younglings running barefoot through impossible geometry that flipped mid-air, only for them to begin again.

Still, no one saw us, as though the Court of Chaos itself had turned its face away.

We rode on. Mythros's hooves made barely a sound, as though conscious not to draw the queen's eye. Zephyr sat tall in his saddle with effort, eyes flicking to every tree hollow, every slanted oak as if deciphering their language, though I heard nothing at all. When I touched his wrist, his pulse ran as fast as a hunted thing.

"Talk to me," I whispered in his ear. *Through the bond.*

His voice rasped, rough with remorse. *I don't want the nightmare to seep through the bond to you.*

So he pulled his shadows close around us. The darkness obeyed, reluctantly at first. His magic was worn thin, but still, the shadows came: not as a wall, but a veil as delicate as fog and just as consuming.

They folded around stallion and riders, layering like gauze, dulling the world beyond us and our words from the world. Beneath that cocoon of darkness, it was just us and the hush of closeness, Zephyr's breath against my cheek, and the slow, thudding beat of his heart finding its rhythm again.

We were still riding at a trot, and I turned to ask him quietly. Cocooned in the shadows, our voices didn't echo or drift; they curled around ears, around collarbones. "What did my mother put you through, Zephyr?"

He didn't meet my eyes. The wind tugged at the ends of his dark hair. "It was the cliffs around Ebonspire. Well, almost. Not every detail was right. There were monsters, but they didn't die. Court of Lore fae." He hesitated. "I wanted to save them, but I couldn't even save myself. Tanuhja didn't even have to lift a blade."

I frowned. "Then how? How did she get the upper hand?"

His lips twisted in self-disgust. "I agreed to absorb their stories in exchange for a cure. I'd tried to prepare for something like this, of course. I told Mythros to find us if anything happened. It's easy for those who turn fae into beasts as punishment to forget that even beasts love and hold memories." A heartbeat passed before he continued. "Even though Mythros broke into the dream ready to carry me out, I forgot my own name. I almost forgot you."

"You would have found me again if you did."

He looked away, voice low. "Maybe."

"There's no maybe about it."

His knuckles were white around the saddle pommel. "I wasn't there when you needed me."

The shadows caught and held my words. "You told me once your shadows would always find me, and they knew me. Even when you didn't know yourself, your soul knew mine. You were the one who showed me that my magic acts in defence of the people I love. It's never stronger than when you're at risk. You made it possible that I succeeded, even on my own."

His breath ruffled my hair. "I had no idea it was a dream, not even when Tanuhja appeared. I was riding Mythros in an endless loop. Ancients, Ysa. His hooves were wearing down, and I didn't think he could carry me any further. Then the dream began to stutter and glitch." His tone was matter-of-fact, but the star that represented him in my mind winked in and out, and I knew how much he wanted to bury this moment in his past. But he chose to share it with me. "Then the sky bled, and I thought that was the end. For him and me, and the Court of Lore fae she had put into the illusion."

"I'm so sorry."

"Then I realised that it was crimson ink, and the mate bond kicked in. Our surroundings rippled. Trees folded in on themselves like paper and reformed as archways and staircases. Mythros refused to go any further. I had to decide which stairs to take. To consciousness. To you. I chose to walk towards the chaos that shimmered with contradictions. Soft where it should be sharp, wild where it should be cruel. Then Mythros was gone, and you were there."

"The dragon-kissed blade was a conduit for chaos."

He gave a shaky exhale. "Your mother said there's no cure for broken things, but she's wrong."

"Yes, Zephyr. She's wrong in more ways than I can count."

After that, he let his shadows dissipate and didn't speak again for a long time. His silence wasn't cold, only full. He held my palm to his heart, and the chaos in me stirred, and I remembered that for all the court's quiet now, part of me belonged to it.

Eventually, the land looked almost ordinary. Grass grew long and wild like at Ebonspire. The sky held its shape and had deepened into a deep blue with the evening, with familiar constellations emerging.

The air smelled of wet earth and loam, of pine resin and wood chip crushed underhoof. A stream greeted us further along in the hush of dusk-washed hills, honest water with reeds nodding at its edge in the breeze. Here, the Court of Chaos loosened its grip entirely.

It was a place we could breathe and recover.

Mythros halted without command, and we dismounted, bodies stiff with weariness and filth.

"There's soap in the saddlebag," said Zephyr.

I retrieved the bar and broke it in half—one of Wylda's concoctions scented with lavender and pine—while he unburdened Mythros of the saddlebags. We undressed by the stream's edge, backs turned shyly to each other.

The stream was narrow, but deep enough to wade. We stepped into it slowly, feet sinking into the sandy bed, water licking our ankles, then calves, then thighs. Mythros lingered nearby, beneath a low branch, watching with solemn, ancient eyes.

The water was bracing and cold, and I shivered, thoughts turning to Maren and Ferrith and evenings swimming in the creek. Tension coiled low in my belly as I considered what might have befallen them and whether they'd cope without the whisper rings.

But this wasn't Larkspur, and Maren commanded fire. Ferrith was brave and loving, even though he could be foolish. And stars, I needed Zephyr's touch to heal all that was broken in me. My teeth chattered as I scrubbed exhaustion from my skin and splashed my face, relishing the sting.

When I reached up to wash my hair, my mate was suddenly beside me.

He looked at me like I was the fixed star in his ever-spinning sky. "May I?"

My breath caught. Zephyr was waist-deep, his dark hair clinging to his neck and temples, his eyes two pieces of night sky. "Yes."

He stood behind me, working the soap into my tangled hair with careful hands. He massaged my scalp into a lather, rinsing with palmfuls of water and combing out the knots. Then his fingers stilled against my scalp, and the soap slid through his fingers.

He touched my shoulder and the nape of my neck. When I closed my eyes and leaned into his touch, he groaned with pleasure. Water flowed around us like a blessing. The world dimmed. Only breath remained. Only skin.

Through the bond, his thoughts slipped into me like rain into parched earth. *I missed this.*

Then what are you waiting for? I sent back.

He laughed low. *You're so damn beautiful. My mate, with ink and ruin in her veins.*

His hands trailed down my spine and around my waist before cupping my breasts, playing with them as he nuzzled my neck and nipped at my ear. I was already a molten pool of heat, already wanting to loop my legs around him and ask him to enter me hard and fast so everything emptied from my mind but him. But Zephyr didn't want that. He wanted to worship me, there in the water as twilight fell.

"Slowly, Inkheart," he murmured, or maybe it was in my mind.

You tease. I turned to face him.

I couldn't think or perceive; all I could do was react to his touch. Zephyr worshipped me like I was water and fire and the thread that held his ribs together. All my fear and guilt melted in those waters as our bodies met.

Zephyr's hands were no longer trembling. They were certain, sliding to the small of my back, where his thumbs pressed into the hollow. He pulled me against him, and I straddled his lap beneath the surface, thighs ghosting over his, water slipping between us like breath, his hardness pressed against my belly.

Zephyr's mouth found my neck, slow and deliberate, tracing the line from jaw to collarbone with lips that barely touched—just enough to burn. I gasped as he bit down, gently, and his chuckle rumbled through his chest into mine.

My fingers tangled in the wet lengths of his hair, pulling him closer, needing the weight of him against me. The press of him beneath the water made my thoughts dissolve. Stars, his touch. It undid me in the best ways.

I arched into him, shameless, breath catching as he dragged his thumbs over my nipples, tracing the wet line of my ribs, my hips, my buttocks, my calves. Every movement was drawn out, aching, the river lapping around us like applause, like prayer.

I met him with everything I was—ink and fire, flesh and belief. He kissed me then—open-mouthed, consuming —and I forgot the world, the crown, the nightmare, everything but each other's names.

There was only skin and pulse, lips and tongue, the heated press of muscle and desire beneath the shallows. The water darkened with night around us, hiding everything but the way we moved together—slow and sure, like we had all the time in the world. Like the clock wasn't ticking.

He entered me then, pushing deep inside with our eyes locked on each other, and through the bond, I felt his desire for me and his fears that he hadn't forgotten at all that something might keep us apart: family or strangers, crowns or the dark whims of Faerie.

We moved together in rhythms older than language, our sighs swallowed by the rippling stream. My mate claimed me with deep, long strokes that melded us together, my nails scraping lines down his back, him pausing to tease the peaks of my breasts as the water sloshed around us, his hands grasping my thighs until I was wide and open for him and his cock had brought me to such exquisite pleasure that I begged for release.

I could have lived every day like that and every night.

When the storm inside us broke, we did not cry out.

There was just a trembling stillness as we held each other, slick with water and shadow, the bond humming between us.

I kissed the corner of his mouth. "You're my beginning."

"Ysa," he breathed, like a vow. "You're my refusal to end."

We lingered a moment more in the stream, our limbs tangled, warmth flickering between us even as we became more aware of the cold water.

My eyes widened. "The soap."

He grinned. "Long dissolved."

Then Zephyr threaded his fingers through mine, and we waded towards the bank, droplets pearling on his skin. He hoisted himself out, then helped me up the bank. He found a towel, fresh clothes, and a blanket in the saddlebags, some fruit, bread, and our waterskins.

We dressed, stealing glances that made us both smile like fools. His eyes lingered on me as I twisted my hair up, and I flushed despite having bared body and soul to him.

We found a hollow beneath a tree, its roots forming a cradle in the moss, and sated our hunger and thirst, to a low chorus of crickets and the hoot of a distant owl. Mythros grazed in a nearby glade. Zephyr watched him with a haunting tenderness that wasn't one-sided. Even creatures born of wildness knew when they had been seen.

Then he turned to me, tenderness replaced by a furrowed brow, the sharp gleam of schemes returning to his eyes. "We have to be careful. Tanuhja said at Gloomhaven that there are things in Faerie that have been kept a secret even from my uncle. You are still so new to Faerie, Inkheart. There are powers here older than any crown. Secrets buried so deep they've slipped past history and into myth. Something is stirring." His storm-dark eyes searched mine, troubled. "I don't like being blindsided, Ysa. Whatever happens at that meeting, we have to control it."

I swallowed the knot in my throat, the fear of an unsung chord waiting to be played. "I miss the others."

He tugged me closer, his fingers pinching my waist in mock anger. "Am I not enough?"

I bit his lip in retaliation, and he laughed, rumbling and low. "Oh, you are."

The teasing evaporated from his eyes, and worry tightened his jaw. "We have to trust our kin to take care of themselves."

Coming from Larkspur, it wasn't easy for me to have my loved ones spread so far and to have no impact on their happiness and success. I tried not to let the old resentment rise about how Loxley had become the axis on which Maren and Ferrith's strivings turned. Instead, I bit my lip and pulled out my mother's letter.

"Are you going to read it?"

"I'm not sure I want to." For all my curiosity about the world and its workings, uncovering my history was painful.

"Then don't. But Inkheart, I've shied away from knowing my father better, and all it creates is deeper wounds."

I clutched the letter a moment longer, eyes distant. Then I smoothed out the parchment, drew up my knees and began.

My dearest Kazimir,

The nights have grown longer in your absence, and each one swells with memories of our child. I find comfort in knowing she is safe with you, beyond the reach of Faerie's dangers, but this distance wears upon me like a cruel shadow. Every dawn reminds me that I am here and Ysa is not.

I fear Ysa will remember nothing of me in the short days we had together. I fear she will forget my scent, my touch, the songs I sang to rock her to sleep. She won't know how starlight shimmers upon the lakes of Faerie and how dragons once soared across our skies. It cuts me to ribbons that she will recognise neither my voice nor my face. Does she miss me as I miss her? Or has she already settled into that world, content without me?

It is a thought that claws at me, no matter how often I tell myself that her happiness is what matters most.

Maybe I could endure this unnatural separation if only I had certainty that you are both thriving, but how can this be when the balance of the realms has been destabilised and food grows scarcer in the mortal realm?

Tell me, dearest, am I selfish to dream of a day when you both might find your way back to me, to Faerie? I find myself standing at the veil between worlds, whispering your names into the chaos, hoping that somehow she will sense my love, even from afar.

I carry this ache, and perhaps someday I will grow stronger beneath it. Promise me you will keep her safe. Promise me that one day this terrible sorrow will end. Promise me that one day you will hold me close, as you have before.

Yours,

Tanuhja

When I was finished, I passed it to him.

He skimmed the lines in silence, then sighed.

"Her love doesn't fix anything." Her love made my messy feelings about her harder to justify.

Zephyr didn't make excuses for her, and he didn't cosset me. He simply gave me honesty. "I know. You don't have to forgive her. You don't even have to understand her. You just have to carry on doing what you think is best."

I was glad. Gentleness would have cracked me open. "You've thought about this before."

"I think about it most days," he said, eyes dark. He dropped a kiss on my head. "But there are others who love you. An old calligrapher in the Court of Bones, for example."

My heart leapt. "You mean for us to go to Father?"

He nodded. Neither of us mentioned the strategic reason he had suggested the plan, but it loomed in both our minds, the unspoken hinge on which our path might turn. I had learned enough about the workings of my mate's mind to know that every kindness came with a calculation, every mercy a motive: never cruel, but never careless.

There was one niggling subject we hadn't yet had the courage to discuss: dragons, and with it my mother's conviction that only dragon riders had ever secured lasting peace in Faerie; and her warning that I wouldn't survive *Kindling*.

But mothers—even the worst of them—were born to worry, and Father knew dragons. Not in theory or from stories, but from experience. He'd spent decades in the deep reaches of Faerie, where drakes slumbered and sky serpents danced between cloud and thunder. He'd help me. Not because he thought it wise or believed I was ready. But because I was his daughter.

I had asked nothing of him for so long, and now I needed him.

Queen Thalindra at the Court of Bones was our ally, thanks to Liora Bramick. It was a good plan.

"I've missed Father more than I can say."

"I know. We'll go via the Wastelands. With any luck, the others will have made it there." He gave me a wicked smile. "But before I have to share you with our kin again, we have tonight. Now open up those legs, Inkheart, and let me ravish you."

Later, much later, after he had found all the buttons in my body that made me moan his name, after he murmured in my ear all the things he wanted to do to me and fulfilled some of those promises, he warned me to stay still in his arms lest my curves distract him again.

When my body was tired but my mind full, he made me vow to practice my chaos magic on the journey. I pretended to grumble and nestled my head against his chest, a smile playing on my lips at the calm rise and fall of his breathing.

Mythros settled in the grass nearby. Zephyr sculpted shapes from shadows to bring me to ease—a lotus blooming, a wolf cub playing, our favourite tree at Ebonspire—and my eyes grew heavy.

Soon, I would see Father and our friends again. The night was brushed with stars, vast and ancient. The kind of sky that forgave and invited new beginnings. We slept like we hadn't slept for a thousand years, tangled in each other's arms.

This time, sleep felt like sanctuary.

ELOWEN

With me, you will have children of your own.
They will carry your voice in their veins
and my silence in their bones.
Faerie itself will hush to witness their becoming.
And they will belong to no one but us.
– Thiago's love letter to Danaë,
delivered by whisperwind.

Days passed, but Elowen couldn't tell how many. She jumped at every noise that penetrated her cell, every skitter of an insect that she feared might be shadow, terrified that her father would come back for more fingers.

To her shame, the dominant stench was of her excretions into a lidded pot, placed as far away from her perch as she could manage. Here, close to the foundations of the keep, the stone wept, and sometimes she was forced to lick the stone to alleviate the desert dryness of her lips and throat.

It galled her to have her pride punctured in such a way, but she was no stranger to survival. Moisture gathered in beads along the ceiling and dripped at intervals into a rust-stained bucket in the corner, and sometimes she cupped her hands and stood beneath it.

The sound was maddening, out of sync with her heartbeat, adding to the rising dread that gathered like a storm in her body.

She did her utmost not to look at her finger except when changing the dressing with slow, wincing movements, adding the soiled one to a pile in the corner of the cell. It was absurd, really, that she missed the whisper ring as much as the finger it had once adorned.

The metal had dug into her skin some days, irritated her in the sun's warmth, and yet now, without it, she felt half-unmade. Her wound had congealed, but the ache remained, throbbing like a cruel metronome.

Her father's revelations about the impact of Ysa's dual heritage circled in a loop in her mind.

She wondered if her love for Ysadora was foolish. It didn't feel foolish, but she wasn't experienced in such matters, with the exception of Xaire, and he hadn't come for her. Hate and estrangement had always been more familiar friends than love and loyalty.

The first night, she passed out and woke to find a canister of healing tea in her cell, sent by her mother. It was incapable of reversing what her father had done, either in body or memory, but her mother had at least addressed the risk of infection.

Her mother's accompanying note on jasmine-scented

and monogrammed parchment—both in deed and tone—
was woefully inadequate to address Elowen's continued
suffering:

> *Drink this tea to ward off infection.*
> *In time, a glamour will hide the injury.*
> *Give your father the information he craves*
> *and you'll have a seat at our table again.*

Elowen balled up the parchment and deposited it in
the pot of excrement, hate bristling in her as she drank
every drop of the tea. Her mouth, bound the first night,
had been unshackled now that her screams of fury had
become silence once more.

Her father didn't just prize silence; he weaponised it.
The walls swallowed every breath, every thought that
dared venture beyond her skull. She tried to speak to
Xaire through telepathy, but he didn't answer. Her cell
had been built to silence her father's assets and
enemies: she was simply another risk to be managed
and muted.

When the door to her cell creaked open for the first
time, she didn't lift her head, afraid it would be her father,
coming to make good on his threat, or one of his spiders,
master manipulators made in his image, intent on drawing
out her secrets. Bracing herself, she wondered how much
pain and humiliation they would inflict. The hinges
groaned shut again, and the light dimmed behind
whoever had entered. Shuffling footsteps came towards
her.

The Spymaster and his spiders didn't shuffle. They
loomed. They slithered.

A scrape of wood against stone followed, and the soft clink of crockery. Elowen released her breath. A meal, then.

"I brought you stew," said a voice rarely heard within Echohold. "Still warm, if the tunnels haven't leeched it cold."

Hunger clawed at her ribs, but she kept her back stiff, her gaze pinned to the opposite wall. "Oh, good. Let me just freshen up, and I'll be right there." Of course, they'd send him. Of course, they'd send someone she had no use for at all.

Her uncle cleared his throat softly. "It's mushrooms with black barley. You used to like it."

Her eyes flicked towards him. "You don't know what I like. Not anymore."

She didn't miss the shock painted on his face at her appearance. There was no courtly politeness quick enough to mask the expression in his slate-blue eyes or the pinch of his nose. Not when she looked like this.

Her dignity hung in shreds. Her silver-blonde hair was matted to her scalp, and she desperately needed to bathe. Her skin itched beneath her soiled, torn dress. Dried blood crusted her hands and nail beds. The regal bearing she'd worn had slipped, piece by piece, until she had nothing left.

"You're right. I haven't been a good uncle, Elowen. I want to change that."

Orin sat on the stone slab next to her, thick ankles awkwardly crossed, gnarled hands kneading his knees. His shadows were cast softer and more askew than her father's. Her father boasted that either could have taken the throne, but he had schemed to win the crown before his older brother even realised what was happening.

Elowen flexed her maimed hand, and shooting pain made her regret the impulse. It irked her that he noticed the adjustments she made to avoid knocking it. "You're not here out of some noble impulse. You're here because they didn't trust a servant to keep their mouths shut."

Orin shrugged. His shoulders sagged not from age, but from yielding too often. Whereas her father's hair gleamed like lacquered night, Orin's was sparse and threaded with grey. "True. But I volunteered."

She narrowed her eyes at him. "Why?"

He hesitated. "Because I've been in your position many times."

Her lips twisted in cynicism. "You still have all your fingers."

"I'm not made for open defiance. Thiago was always stronger." His brow furrowed, and she wished she could read his mind, that her magic had some offensive use, any use, that would help her escape her fate. "He cultivated a network of spies, flattered courtiers, planted lies about my weaknesses, and reshuffled castle staff with loyalists before I even realised he meant to take the throne. I'm no match for him."

Caustic sarcasm bloomed on Elowen's tongue, but her voice lacked the strength to deliver a punch. "Supper must have been harder for you than for me. Yet, you still managed to blend into the drapery. So what good are you to me here?"

That stung. Elowen saw it land in the small tremor in his hands, but he didn't scuttle out like a servant dismissed.

It piqued her interest that he stayed, and she picked up the stew. The first nourishing bite made tears well in her eyes. He let her eat in silence, fidgeting only slightly. Her father's stillness was the silence before a strike. Orin's silence was the quiet of someone who's been talked over for decades.

After some time, he said, "Xaire is worried."

Elowen froze, spoon halfway to her lips. "He told you that, did he?"

"Not in so many words. But you stirred the still water. For all his faults, he cares for you."

Like Zephyr, Orin had a melancholy to him, a gentleness tucked in the creases of his mouth. Neither ever quite fitted into the roles they were born into. She supposed she shared that trait with them, too. She wondered if her father had ever told him a secret or if she was special that way, in what she had achieved.

"What do you want from me, Orin?"

"I want to help." He said it without flourish or plea, a male who didn't expect gratitude or forgiveness.

Elowen turned her head just slightly, enough to see her uncle's face in the dim light. 'Why?" she asked again.

Orin bent his chapped lips to her ear. "Because my son asked me to."

FERRITH

I was too much of a coward.
I hope it's not too late to tell Maren I love her.
— Ferrith's diary

Vixora had been seven to Ferrith's thirteen orbits when she disappeared. There had been something wild in his little sister, no matter how their mother tried to comb the wildness out of those golden curls.

Vixora had that kind of brightness that made adults nervous: sun-touched curls that bounced with every step and eyes the colour of calm seas hiding deep currents. She was curiosity and mischief dressed in ribbon—always just a little too fast, a little too far ahead, always chasing something that shimmered at the edge of reality. Even before she vanished, she had followed birdsong at twilight and strangers at fairs, and been thoroughly scolded for it.

Ferrith still loved her with every breath.

Even as a young boy, he'd been proud of how she wrapped her fingers around his thumb as she walked, more tumble than stride. He never minded that she tried to tag along when he snuck away from chores to be with his friends or that she'd once braided flowers into his hair while he napped.

In the back of a drawer in Larkspur, he kept acorn caps wrapped in cloth that she had presented to him like treasure. He could never throw them away.

He thought himself old enough to be her protector.

That naïve belief had not shielded her.

As best they could guess, ten orbits hence, she had wandered off into the Shrouded Forest when she should have been playing in the orchard. His father found her ribbons tangled in a hawthorn bush, one shoe half-buried in mud, and then, nothing.

For weeks, the men had searched while he had stood helplessly by, trying to console their mother, trying not to fall apart. Eventually, he'd stormed through the forest as though he could force it to give her back. It hadn't worked.

He'd been too young to understand that guilt like that never leaves you. That it hollowed into bones and echoed in him, no matter how much time passed. That his mother's dying would only add to his guilt, although it hadn't been his job to look after Vixora that day; it had been his father's.

He would never know if Vixora might have become difficult, or grown sharp like Maren, or loved him less as the years went by. It was possible that they would have grown apart as adults, but Ferrith didn't think so. In any case, in his mind, Vixora remained his bright-eyed, relentless little companion. She never aged. She never left him.

And so, when her voice called him from the depths of the Wraithwoods, it hadn't been logic that propelled Ferrith forward. It had been sheer instinct and a yearning for answers. The forest shifted as he ran, trunks rearranging like chess pieces. Silver birch limbs bent low, trailed their fingers across his shoulders. Voices flurried around him, dozens of lost souls whispering in his ears— pleading, discussing, weeping—but he ignored them all.

Vixora's bright voice cut through the noise like a girl calling her brother in from the fields for supper, threaded with a giggling that could only be hers. *Ferr, come on, slowcoach.*

The hairs on his arms rose. Vixora was the only one who had always called him that from all his kin. He sprinted faster. Her voice was his beacon.

Ferr, come find me. I'm hiding.

His feet moved before reason returned, drawn step by step into the tangled hush of the Wraithwoods, as if Vixy had only ever wandered slightly ahead and he'd been slow to catch up all this time.

He heard her just off the path: a faint, breathless *Ferr!* like she'd tripped and needed him.

The kind of sound that cuts through years and logic. His heart lurched as he scanned the endless shifting trees. He couldn't lose her again. Light dripped through the canopy in impossible colours—violet, gold, ink-black— and each step felt like stepping deeper into a fever dream.

He moved with that old ache blooming in his chest, the familiar guilt heavy in his limbs. One stride. Two. The third stride felt like falling, and her voice flitted ahead, too real, too close; it was almost unbearable how much he needed his little sister in his arms. What if he failed her again?

You promised you'd find me, remember, Ferr?

He had. He would.

Suddenly, there she was before him, and his chest couldn't contain the elation and the pain that filled him. She hadn't aged a day, still seven orbits old. He absorbed every detail hungrily.

She wore a dress woven from bark and spider silk. Moss clung to her bare feet, and when she walked, the forest leaned inwards, trees bowing like courtiers. In one hand, she carried a lantern filled with will-o'-the-wisps, and strange symbols burned across her small palms.

There were other changes. Vixora's movements were too smooth, too deliberate, and her eyes blinked a half-second too late. They softened at the sight of him.

Her voice still held the lilt and impudence of childhood. "Took you long enough."

How he had missed her. "Vixy." Ferrith dropped to his knees and opened his arms.

She didn't move into them. She guarded her distance instead.

She wasn't the same. Ferrith could see that now. "I can still see the child you were," he said carefully.

"I can say the same for you, Ferr."

He glanced down. It was true. Wylda's glamour had vanished, and he was himself once more: the mortal who had lost his sister. He was unendingly grateful that he'd found her, even if things weren't as they should have been. "I never stopped looking."

"You just didn't look in the right places. None of you did."

The failure would haunt him until the end of his days. "What happened to you?"

She shrugged. "The woods. I'm not the first. The woods just like me the best."

The way she said it, so lightly, chilled him, as if being claimed by a cursed entity was a passing inconvenience. Ferrith wondered if it was a good thing: if being liked meant that the woods eased the transition to this new kind of life or merely marked her for something worse.

He hoped that whatever his sister had experienced, she hadn't been afraid or lonely or in pain. For the blink of an eye, her hair hung in tangled curtains, threaded with burrs and the delicate bones of birds, and then she was herself again, curly and blonde and plump and pretty, and he wished never to see the other her again.

"I'd rather that the Wraithwoods don't claim you, Ferr. Really, I do, but I couldn't let you pass without asking you to come in. I wanted to see you, and I have been waiting for so long. I knew you would come one day. I knew you wouldn't forget."

His throat hurt. "I didn't forget you, Vixy."

She brightened. "I still remember, too. All the little details. Mama helping me make daisy chains and bake my birthday cakes. You hoisting me onto your shoulders at the village fair and tickling me when I was grumpy. Father dancing with me in the rain and sharpening his tools before a day in the fields."

"Father's not the man you remember. And Mama is gone."

She blew out her plump cheeks. "I know."

Ferrith already sensed the need for them to separate, but he wasn't sure he'd survive it this time. "Can you come with me?"

"I belong here, Ferr. To these woods and the lost."

He had been trying not to notice the lost. They hovered around Vixora like breath on a winter pane, shifting in and out of visibility. Some tall, draped in the remnants of once-fine silks now melted into trailing mist; others hunched, eyes like bioluminescent tide pools. They were wary of him, eager for something still to come, something to befall him.

Goosebumps chased up his arms. "Vixy, please. I don't want to lose you again."

"Maybe you will. Maybe you won't," his sister said in her sing-song voice. "These woods are shaped by grief and wild magic. They always demand something, Ferr. Sometimes it's blood, a piece of your name, a memory, or a secret you never meant to say out loud. They measure what you're hiding. What you're scared of. What you love most. You're no exception."

The trees listened. Ferrith felt their cold curiosity curling through the mist like a hand at his throat.

Then a tremor passed through the clearing. One of the gnarled trunks creaked, then tore itself apart with a sickening snap. From the exposed cavity, a mirror slid forward and jerked upwards, strung up with roots like obedient serpents.

Ferrith inched forward, drawn to it despite himself. His hands—so steady in Larkspur—trembled at his sides. The reflection glimmered with silver and sentience. It didn't show the man he wanted to be. Instead, it showed the man he was when guilt and doubts surfaced, all the shine and swagger scraped away. It showed him as Faerie saw him: imperfect, mortal, fragile.

Shame swarmed in. Then came the memories, played out in the mirror as if it were a stage.

He glanced at his sister, heart pounding. "What does it want from me?"

"It wants you to look, Ferr. To really look."

The glass clouded, then cleared. This time, it didn't show his reflection. It showed his unravelling, memories he'd shoved deep because he didn't want to dwell on his flaws. Turning a blind eye to how others struggled to belong in the village, because he so easily did. Kissing girls he didn't care for to feel less hollow, even when he left a trail of broken hearts. Storming out on his father after a fight, over and over again. Not questioning King Azeem's cruelties, because he benefited from praise. Plotting to steal secrets from his host at Ebonspire when eating at his table.

Dozens of failures coalesced, each a thread of shame winding tighter.

"I don't want to see."

"But Ferr, no one survives Faerie without embracing the dark side of themselves."

He didn't look at her this time, scared that she would be that changed thing again, the thing he didn't recognise, the thing that had suffered. The air around him buzzed with cruel suggestions. That he should sink into quicksand or be strung between the birch trees. That he should have let the decaying dragon feast on his cowardice.

"I'm sorry." His thoughts were frantic, his eyes wide.

"How mortal to apologise when you could change

instead," replied Vixora. "The woods will give you a hand."

The mirror's edge glowed with eldritch heat before it convulsed, and hands erupted from it, each one grotesquely unique. Terror congealed in his throat as the hands grasped him. A child's hand with broken fingernails and ink-smudged wrists that he recognised as Ysa. A crone's fingers, thin as kindling, knuckles knotted like roots. A fae lord's elegant palm, fingers crowned with rings dulled like broken promises.

They came for every soft and hidden part of him, clawing for his doubt, clenching, pressing, drawing blood. One wrapped around his throat. Another yanked at his wrist, yet others dug into his thighs, his calves, his ankles.

He didn't know what they wanted, couldn't figure it out, didn't want to die, didn't even know how to live. Agony flashed through his limbs. His body was splayed between them like a marionette stretched too thin, a crucible of guilt strung across his own regrets.

"Let go," he rasped.

Vixora stood rigid to one side; her hands, etched with Faerie's sigils, were clenched. "You have to endure it."

The Wraithwoods waited as the mirror hands bent him out of shape, pinned him like a man being strung between sins. But then a shape moved through the mist, and then another. He knew those voices. Loxley emerged from the shadows like a hero stepping out of myth, an axe in his hand.

His eyes were dark with knowing. "I fucking hate cursed objects. Don't let it take you."

Ferrith's shoulders curled as an axe spun through the

fog and severed one gnarled hand from its wrist. Splinters of bark and bone sprayed across the clearing.

"Are you here to finish me off?" he stuttered.

"I'm here to save your arse again," said the fae male as he picked up his axe.

Disbelief, then relief, washed through Ferrith, although he knew that if he survived, the stories would be tall, the laughter at his expense great. Each of Loxley's chops was a drumbeat of defiance. But the hands kept coming, the severed ones twitching, spasming, regenerating.

The ground was slick with ichor. Talons crusted in moss. Long fingers, pale as moonlight. Monstrous claws, slick with sap and spite. One hand jointed backwards, folding around Ferrith like a spider. Another cracked open at the palm, crawling with insects. A girl's fingers twined through his hair, whispering of dances he should have led, then yanked his head back.

Bile rose in his throat. "They're not stopping!"

"I said," Loxley growled as he brought the axe down again and again. In Larkspur, his curses would have turned a maiden's ears the colour of boiled beetroot. "Don't let it take you. It's your trial."

Sweat beaded Ferrith's temples and dripped into his eyes. "Not got much choice here."

"If you ever bothered coming to training, it would have helped." He swung his axe, planted his boot on one wrist and crushed it, only for two more to scuttle past his legs.

The mirror snarled, and its reflection momentarily showed Loxley, all his worst deeds on display—battle, betrayal, blood—but Lox didn't flinch. Instead, he met the image with calm contempt.

Then Maren was there. Her face was her own, flame-red hair, gold eyes flecked with green that he'd become accustomed to, luminous skin scratched raw across one cheek as though she had fought her way to him.

She was his anchor, proof that he wasn't all bad. If Maren wanted to save him after all he had done, then perhaps he was worth saving, after all. She blanched at the sight of Vixora, and her hands sparked.

"By all that's scorched, you fight this, you fight *her*, or I'll never forgive you."

"I love you, Maren," he said, and his sister seemed to smile.

"You, idiot," railed his love, in tears. "Your timing couldn't be worse."

But Ferrith knew he might not otherwise have the chance to tell her.

Vixora traced a spiral into the moss with one bare foot, her palms upturned and her eyes glazed in a trance. The trees leaning towards her were no longer her acolytes, but her conspirators. She didn't acknowledge Loxley's brutalising of the hands or Maren's sharp warning, and his heart swelled for her.

"Don't worry, Maren. She's on our side," he said simply.

Nothing could have convinced him otherwise, because his sister was pure-hearted and she loved him and always would, regardless of whether she was mortal or fae or something else entirely. Something switched in him: belief in himself or Vixora, or the kin he had found in Faerie.

Ferrith breathed through the pain, through the shame and peered into the mirror again. This time, he saw children laughing as he repaired a swing. How he gave his coat to a widow—she'd never have survived the

winter otherwise—and how he'd tended to her
hearth too.

The colt he'd nursed back to strength when others had
given up. How he ran a mile through the rain to bring
medicine to a fevered child. Whispering Maren and Ysa's
names into the dark when he'd been with his army unit,
asking the universe for their safety. Vixora's pealing
laughter, and the way she'd always believed he could
catch the stars.

He forgave himself. He forgave himself wholly for
being mortal and making mistakes. For loving fiercely and
fearing too much. For trusting the wrong people, for trying
too hard or not enough, for saying the thing that drove
someone away, and not saying the very thing that might
have kept them close.

And in that moment, it was enough.

The mirror screamed high and keening. It sang, too, an
ancient dirge that held impossible harmonies, grief and
revelation. The hands rotted away, and the glass burst
apart into petals of memory and meaning. Each one held a
part of him.

Ferrith saw himself—young, afraid, arrogant—and saw
other selves that could have been, and somehow, he saw
who he could become, although he looked away then. The
petals floated upwards, dissolving into the trees like a
blessing, like absolution.

Then he was standing in the centre of Maren and
Loxley, facing his sister, the only one without a weapon to
hand or even wanting one.

Vixora stood beneath the birches, watching. "You
passed." Her eyes, for the first time, were wet. She glanced
at Maren and Loxley, and he tensed. "So this is your family

now. I could punish them for intervening, but perhaps there is another way. I am good at finding other ways. Maren?"

"Yes, Vixy?" she answered, cautiously.

"Some of the souls long for release. Will you burn them with starfire?"

"If you wish. But not you."

"No." Vixora gave a sad smile. "Not me. Not yet."

So Maren raised her palms, and violet starfire danced between them. Her brow furrowed, tears glinting at the edges of her lashes but refusing to fall. Around her, the lost pressed closer, drawn to the crackling brightness, their half-formed faces luminous with longing.

Then Maren's expression eased into something like serenity, and her hair stirred gently in the wind, as the being that used to be his sister beckoned the souls forward. Their forms shimmered in and out of substance, their outlines smeared like charcoal in rain. Close to sixty of them in total choosing release. They moved without sound, without breath.

"I give you peace," said Maren.

Ferrith's chest tightened, both humbled and determined to be deserving of her.

The fire between her palms wasn't gentle now. Magenta flames ribboned into the air, coiling like a dragon leashed by will alone. But still, she held it. Held them. As starfire touched them, the lost souls dissolved into embers on the wind, mourning songs rising then vanishing with them.

A woman with silver-streaked braids floated barefoot just above the moss, hands curled as though still kneading bread. A young boy gripped a phantom slingshot, eyes wide in eternal mischief. A bearded man paced in a circle.

Wraithwoods bowed in farewell to them all.

When the last of them was gone, Maren's hands dimmed, and her knees shook.

Ferrith caught her and passed her to Loxley, his eyes never moving from his sister.

"The cost is balanced." Vixora's cornflower blue eyes— so like his own—shone. "Thank you, Maren."

Tension remained in Wraithwoods, like a held breath between the trees, and he didn't want to stay in that wretched place anymore. He wanted to take his kin and leave, but that would mean leaving his past behind. And her.

"Letting go is a part of the natural order, Ferr," said Vixora. "I have one more gift for you."

He stiffened, thinking of the hands, thinking of the unholy trees and the songs of lament. "It's not necessary."

Her smile faltered. "It's rude to look a gift horse in the mouth."

Ferrith blinked. "I mean, I don't even have one for you."

"But you didn't know I'd be here."

"I would've brought the world if I had."

A second lantern appeared at Vixora's feet, swirling with a pale force. She clapped her runed hands in glee. "Faerie immortality and magic for your own. That is, if you give the hungry woods your memories of me."

His breath hitched. He drank in the sight of his sister, wondering how it would be to erase the pain of her loss, but then he wouldn't remember the joy of their eight years together, from when she was a babbling baby to the curious, giggling girl he'd known. He wouldn't remember the conversation they had today and how it had healed him, a little, to know that she still existed in some capacity.

"This gift was always meant for you." She chuckled in delight. "There was someone else who came here. A spymaster and his mortal wife. He offered secret after secret, but the woods were dissatisfied. Eventually, he traded part of his shadow to secure his wife's transformation. Without that part, he is vulnerable, because that shadow may be found and wielded…if you count a shadow wielder amongst your friends." She gave a wicked smile. "And after that, I planned how I could make you stronger."

He exchanged a quick glance with Loxley. So Thiago had a weak spot, after all, one that Zephyr could turn against him.

She continued, dropping her voice into a whisper that funnelled right into his ear, as if this time it was the two of them against the world, and he was her co-conspirator, not the birch trees. As if they were plotting to steal from their mother's cookie jar, rather than magic from Faerie. And he wanted so badly for life to be simple again. "Forget me, Ferr. Live."

"Answer this, Vixy. Are you happy?" And he knew the answer even before she gave it.

"I have purpose. I have friends. But no, Ferr. This is a kind of limbo, and I won't be happy until I find peace."

"Then, I'd rather carry the pain, too. Remembering you is more important than power."

Her smile was sweet, but also damning, as if she knew the toll. "Then take both." She pressed the lantern into his hands.

"Ferrith—" warned Maren as Loxley uttered a curse.

The woods sighed around them, and for a moment, they all breathed as one.

"Say thank you," she teased, but her voice wavered. "Say thank you, and I'll even replace those glamours before you go on your merry way."

"Thank you, Vixy," he said in easy sibling rhythm.

Then agony ripped through him like lightning through old bark, and Vixora was there, holding him at long last, bearing witness as he unravelled. She cradled him through every burning second. He thought, as his cells and self transformed, that the pain would be worth it if he could be strong enough to be of service to Maren and Ysa, to make up for his past errors and make their path smoother.

High above them, far beyond the highest boughs, dozens of lights dotted the skies, and they weren't stars: they were souls oblivious to the mortal who turned fae.

YSADORA

The Court of Silver Seas dwells where salt meets foam. Its members are merfolk, sailors, and sea creatures, bound by the ebb and flow of tides. They speak in siren song and command the currents. Time moves strangely in their domain, and the greatest amongst them vanish between moments like fish through nets.
– A Tapestry of Courts and Crowns

I woke, gasping, to a sharp pain on my ankle. Zephyr's shadows stirred as I pushed myself upright. The cloak we'd shared slipped from my shoulders, pooling in the dewy grass. I stared as the ouroboros on my ankle flared once, white-hot, then split apart, its tail unravelling from its mouth.

The loss hit me like a physical blow. My chest hollowed out, breath catching on the jagged edges of panic. The mark of my bargain with Elowen was gone, and with it, the ploy that had fuelled our closeness.

Except, it hadn't been contrived for me. And I didn't think it was for her.

Zephyr blinked the sleep from his eyes. The cold morning light peeled across the treetops and painted his face with light and shadow, turning his slate-blue eyes to mercury. "Inkheart, what is it?"

I couldn't form words. Breath locked in my chest, and I rubbed the skin where the ouroboros had been. "The mark of my bargain with Elowen is gone."

His brows pinched as he registered what had happened. Stilling my hand, he said softly, "Elowen freed you from your bargain."

"She wouldn't. Not voluntarily." I scrambled for my quill. "I have to check she's ok. What if it's gone because she's dead?" My voice broke. "What if I put her in danger? What if her father… She couldn't have meant to release me from it."

Zephyr gathered me against his chest and then tipped my chin up. "Listen to me, Ysa." He waited until my ragged gasps steadied. "If she's under scrutiny, you'll just put her in more danger. Thiago is capable of many despicable things, but he wouldn't harm his own daughter."

I hoped so with the fervour of a burning star. "How can we be sure?" My every instinct clamoured to find her. He still hadn't heard back from his father, and didn't know if Orin was capable of loyalty over self-preservation.

"We can't, my love, but it's possible to survive there. Neither Xaire nor Danaë would allow her to be hurt, even if my father remains a coward. The sooner we get you into a secure position, the sooner we can help." Zephyr was already moving, shadows curling close to his heels, packing what little we'd taken out for the night, his movements practised. "Acting prematurely ends badly for us all."

Through the bond, I sensed how he cared little for himself; it was me he was determined to protect. It felt so unjust that Elowen didn't have the same protection cocooning her.

I forced myself to breathe, to think. Panic would help no one, least of all Elowen.

The sky had just begun to colour, lilac melting into soft gold. Our camp was dismantled in five minutes, and it took five more to tend to Mythros and saddle him. Zephyr mounted first, and I took the hand he offered, swinging up in front of him as Faerie leaned into day.

Zephyr's shadows detached briefly to stretch over his fingers like oil, and he drew a rune directly onto Mythros's flank in a single arcane sweep. The stallion huffed in response, and the rune flared violet-black for a heartbeat.

My mate wrapped my hands in the reins with his. "This isn't ordinary travel. I can only do it for so long, but the speed means we'll be safer as long as you don't let go. For the love of lore, don't let go, Ysa."

I checked for my quill and dragon-kissed dagger, and braced myself, sitting tall against his chest. "Ready."

The word had barely left my mouth when the world folded around us. Mythros's hooves struck shadow instead of earth, and Zephyr gripped me as we plunged into the velvet dark, propelled by his shadow mark.

The air turned thick and close, pressing against my lungs. Mythros obeyed without resistance, his body vibrating just slightly. The sensation was heavier than when I shadow-stepped in Zephyr's arms.

The stream where we'd made love and the bank where we'd slept fell away behind us. We passed the Wraithwoods, their hunger kept at bay by the speed of our passing. I thought I heard Loxley's bellows echoing through the trees. Soon, the monochrome gloom was pricked by golden chinks from the Court of Luminosity, light splitting the dark like spilt honey.

We rested there, at the very edge of Esolas's territory, to water Mythros when his breathing grew shallow. I practised my chaos magic as Zephyr demanded: using my emotions as conduits to warp reality around me in small ways, finding that my chaos was stronger where nature showed its power in wild glades and at the edge of a surging river.

Then we rode again, through nebula fields filled with great swaths of clouds, where I longed for a glimpse of Ferrith and Maren. The shadow travel drained us both. Zephyr's magic frayed with each league, and my chaos answered in unpredictable sparks, brushing him like static. We used the shadow mark until it frayed in its entirety, spitting us out in the Wastelands, where ash hills rose cinched around us like a noose.

Zephyr's shadows snapped back to him, and exhaustion lined his face. "You okay?" He scanned the terrain for our kin, then slid to the ground and helped me dismount.

I nodded. My body was chafed and sore as if we'd travelled dragon leagues.

Liar, he said in my mind, as he offered me water before taking deep slugs from the waterskin himself and reaching into the saddle bag for a velvet fig for Mythros, whose usually sleek coat was dust-swept and dulled by the crossing.

I looked around. "Any idea where they might be?"

Gabor had taught me about the Wastelands. It stretched like a scar between three courts, scattered with residual curses. The sky was closer here, and Fae magic bent strangely. The air was thin and electric, and there was a crushing weight in my chest, as if the Wastelands resented being crossed.

My tongue felt dry as bone, and a shimmer of ink had flowed unbidden to the nib of my quill and now bled onto my tunic. I quenched and reversed the flow. The soil was grey and brittle in parts, with silvered dunes in others. Yet, rare flowers bloomed in cracks, stubborn and bright as rebellion.

"A short trek that way, between tangled briars. They all know the place."

I gave him a rueful look. "Without Lox, Maren and Ferrith might have struggled to find us."

"Sometimes, we're too close to see the path clearly," he said lightly.

Mythros chomped the fig, and then we walked, shoulder to shoulder, alert to any change in the environment. Zephyr held fast to Mythros's reins, his other hand laced with mine. Overhead, false stars blinked on and off like the eyes of gods, though noon had not arrived, and the horizon coiled, never quite where it had been a breath before.

My messages still hadn't reached Father. "It's a shame we can't summon Caldoron."

"Yes, let's ask an ancient fire-lord to collect us like a

donkey," drawled Zephyr.

"You're right. That was a terrible idea."

A vault cracked open in my mind, and Father's memories poured out like smoke through stone, scenes from his younger years snapping into focus when he requested trivial favours from the dragon: Caldoron wouldn't light a bonfire, or warm his tea, or roast his meat. He wouldn't gather kindling, provide flames merely to light the dark, or ferry friends like common travellers.

"Have you been here often?"

"Often? No. Once only. Even then, Cyp and I didn't linger. These are paths forged by ancient bloodshed. They don't like being disturbed." His shadows had quieted, but they were never gone—a flicker beneath his collar, a slither at his heel—and his swords were within easy reach, crossed at his back. "Not much further now."

We kept walking as the Wastelands breathed strange truths into the world. Magic turned inwards here and devoured its own. I thought of daughters trapped by their fathers or manipulated by their mothers, lovers driven to hide in gnarled forests, fae warped by exile until they were half beast, half memory. The horizon wavered, quivering like heat from an untended forge, and our boots sank into silvered dunes.

I'd never felt further from Larkspur, here in this place.

Maybe we fuelled each other's emotions through the bond because his worry was a velvet weight against my chest. I didn't know how to live up to Faerie's needs of me. I didn't know how to save Elowen or even myself, or how to persuade a dragon to be mine.

Perhaps Faerie, in its devious way, had decided that we were prey. Perhaps the faerie kings and queens would come for me, or the monsters, and they would use me to rewrite the Grimoire, fight over me like I was the final sigil to complete some ruinous spell rather than a girl made of bruised hope and borrowed ink.

We crested a low rise between tangled briars, urging Mythros over an endless expanse of scorched soil and jagged rocks, bleached bones half-buried in the dust. And there they were.

Three figures sat around a small, smokeless fire in a natural hollow sheltered by twisted trees, and Wylda's chestnut gelding nosed brittle stems nearby.

The mate bond filled with joy. "Go!" I laughed, taking the reins from Zephyr.

Cyprian's head sprang up, his dark head with its patches of silver caught the strange light. Time seemed to hiccup around him: a telltale sign of his magic stirring in response to emotion. Then he and Zephyr were moving across the distance to crush each other in an embrace that spoke of days of worry.

"Finally. Thought you'd gotten yourselves killed or worse," Cyprian breathed.

Wylda rose, her warm smile was like sunlight, as if the mission had done her good, as if Esolas's attack hadn't happened. She pulled me into her arms. "Ysa, we've been so worried."

"We've been waiting since nightfall. I hate this cursed place," said Sequoia, not moving from her place around the fire, though her wings flexed behind her as though perhaps she wanted to embrace us after all.

"Good to see you too, Sese," said Zephyr, and something passed between them, old and understood and settled.

His shoulders had relaxed, even though we stood in the Wastelands. These people were safety. They were home.

But even as relief flooded through me at seeing them safe, a cold knot formed in my stomach. I looked around the hollow again.

"Where are the others? Where are Maren, Ferrith, and Loxley?"

Sequoia grimaced. "We were hoping you could tell us."

My heart lurched. "They're not here yet?"

"They had the easiest mission, surely? The Circle of Emberlight would never let anything happen to them." Small thorns sprouted from Wylda's fingertips as her control frayed. "Unless the glamours landed them in trouble?"

"No need to jump to any conclusions," soothed Zephyr. "Loxley can handle himself. So can Maren, for that matter."

The silence that followed was loaded with meaning. My chaos magic prickled along my skin, ink bleeding unbidden from my quill again.

"There's no way Ferrith would jeopardise us again. They'll be here soon enough." Stars, I hoped it was true. When it came down to it, I didn't care a jot about the outcome of the mission. I just wanted them safe and reunited with us.

They'll be fine, Inkheart, said my mate through the bond. *Loxley will make sure of it.*

Sequoia's wings folded tighter against her back. "At least those three are good at improvising."

"Is that what we're calling it?" said Cyprian.

Zephyr shot him a warning glance. "Briefing. Now. We have much to discuss while we wait."

We settled by the fire in a loose circle beneath the sagging sky. I tucked my legs up, and one of Zephyr's shadows detached to rest in the small of my back. Zephyr sat beside me, with Sequoia to his left, and Cyprian and Wylda sharing a fallen log opposite. The fire between us burned without the usual snap and crackle of normal flames. The horses found a patch of stubby grass and cropped it with determined optimism, a constant in this place where nothing felt real.

"We'll start." Zephyr went into command mode, omitting all but the most important details. "Ysa can siphon ink from the land now. Tanuhja took us to Gloomhaven. There, she offered Ysa her crown and trapped me in a dream in which I almost lost the threads of who I am."

"Oh, shit," said Cyprian. "How?"

"*Almost* being the operative term." Zephyr sighed. "By playing to my vanities about saving the cursed fae. It's okay. Ysa figured out how to harness chaos magic and rescued me."

Sequoia's eyes sparkled. "Oh, your male ego had to have loved that."

Zephyr rolled his eyes at her. "It's recovering slowly. Send flowers. Oh, wait, that's your sister's talent."

Wylda pressed her hands together, but the thorns still multiplied. "I'd never have forgiven myself if I had sent you there just to be trapped."

The shadow at my back pressed closer at the memory of the dream. My eyes met Zephyr's, and I picked up the thread. "It was the right choice, Wylda. My chaos magic destroyed her crown." I hesitated. "We found out that the cursed fae are the result of my mother's breakdown."

Cyprian's hazel eyes shifted towards gold. "Is there a cure?"

Zephyr's jaw tightened. "None, she said."

Sequoia's eyes narrowed. "Do you believe her?"

"I think *she* believes it, but she's wrong," I said fiercely.

Ancients, I love you, said my mate through the bond, and his tone grew wicked as though he was making a concerted effort not to dip into despair. *Although I think maybe the briefing should include our interlude at the stream.*

Behave, I replied. "And so you see, we didn't achieve our goal of allegiance, but I do understand my magic better."

"*Better* is an understatement. You're beginning to own your power," said Wylda. "Let them think you're a damsel in distress. I like our odds more and more."

I touched my ankle where the ouroboros had been. "You say that, but this morning my bargain with Elowen dissolved."

"Dissolved?" Wylda's voice sharpened. "Or was severed?"

My stomach churned. "I don't know."

Sequoia's wings shifted behind her. "Assuming the girl is still on our side, you have thwarted the intentions of more than one faerie ruler. This is when we double down in bravery and strategy."

Zephyr nodded. "Agreed. How did your mission fare? Tell me you were able to sway the Faerie King of Silver Seas?"

Sequoia and Cyprian exchanged a look.

Cyprian's expression darkened. "Not quite. We arrived

to find him already entertaining an envoy from the Spymaster."

Tiny mushrooms sprouted and withered at Wylda's feet. "Not just hosting them, but celebrating with them. A feast in honour of their new partnership. He was already bought."

My pulse quickened. "He's allied with Thiago?"

"The bastard Spymaster has been playing multiple games from the start. Just like with Esolas, he offered the King of Silver Seas a position as his right hand, power beyond imagining, all for the return of the High King's crown buried deep in the ocean." Sequoia gave a grim smile. "We feared their alliance had already advanced to the point where our pleas would be snubbed, but we sensed an opportunity. We arrived there the evening prior to the handover of the crown. So while the king and his court drank faerie wine and dizzied themselves in their celebrations, we did what we do best."

Cyprian grinned. "We stole and we killed."

The old me would have been horrified. This version leaned forward eagerly. My morality had already shifted in the short while since my goodbye to Larkspur.

Zephyr groaned. "I'm almost jealous I wasn't with you." *Sorry, love.*

I elbowed him, then gave my full attention to Cyprian. I wanted to hear whose blood they had spilt and whom they thwarted and what spoils they had managed to bring back to our family.

"Tell us everything."

Cyp's hazel eyes gleamed. "I'd rather show you."

He turned his palm upwards and pushed into nothing. His hand sank in to its knuckles, and he pushed further, until he was almost at his shoulder joint. Time magic, I thought, older than his bloodline, older than Faerie itself.

Cyprian threaded his hand through time as if parting strands of silk. When I carved a seam, the world shuddered. Chaos didn't ask permission: it broke, reshaped, rewrote. But Cyprian's hand vanished between moments, and I only felt a subtle lurch, like something ancient had been disturbed and barely noticed.

A ripple passed over us, light as a sigh. Then Cyp's hand emerged, and in his palm sat a circlet of metal so dark it seemed to devour light, sound, and hope, set with stones that carried the silence of deep oceans. Runes skated across its surface like oil on water, never still, never safe.

"Now you know why our thieving is legendary," he quipped. "Voilà, the High King's crown."

"Stars and shadows." Zephyr's lore magic sparked through the bond with his reverence for history and his knowledge that it was powerful, sometimes too powerful to meddle with. "How?"

But the moment the crown emerged, the Wastelands stirred in answer. Dust lifted without wind, and the horizon beat slowly as if it were an enormous, invisible heart. Mythros snorted and backed away, his eyes rolling white, though the gelding Torven was of calmer temperament.

The crown pulsed with power, and I felt my magic respond despite myself. I reached for my quill, and ink flowed, forming symbols in the air that dissolved almost as quickly as they appeared.

"Ysa!" Zephyr's voice cut through the rising pressure, an anchor amidst the storm.

Cyprian cast me a worried glance. "What the hell was that?" He wrapped the crown carefully in what looked like ordinary cloth.

The moment it was covered, the Wastelands exhaled, and the oppressive weight lifted from my chest.

Are you okay? Zephyr searched through the bond, trying to gauge the aftershocks running through me.

I didn't like how that felt. The bond vibrated like a plucked string.

How did it feel? he asked, gentler now.

As if an ancient eye had opened, and I was already catalogued within it. I trembled even though the crown was hidden.

Then we don't let it see you again. Zephyr's thought came like a shield slamming into place, but there were things even he couldn't protect me from and some wounds that were worth bearing.

I echoed Zephyr, "How?"

Wylda's soft brown eyes skipped between us. "The compass helped, and so did King Havriel's giddiness for power. The celebrations were so vast that the king bestowed the favour of water breathing from sunset to sunrise on all those in attendance, from the Courts of Silver Seas and Silence alike. The enchantment wrapped around our lungs like silk. Both courts assumed we belonged to the other."

"Hubris," drawled Zephyr. "Forever a weakness of faerie rulers."

Wylda nodded. "You taught us well. The frivolities were wild, with dancing beneath the folds of the sea and under vast kelp canopies that swayed to the music. Courtiers drank wine from shells. Those without an affinity for water dove with abandon through coral arches and ancient shipwrecks. Their voices mingled with the songs of whales. Seafolk drifted in bubbles rather than boats. Some swam in mother-of-pearl gowns alongside schools of glowing fish, while others gathered in underwater groves to share stories or have sex." She laughed. "If we hadn't had to work, I would have stayed. In any case, they were too enraptured to notice us slipping away."

I still couldn't take my eyes off the bundle in Cyprian's hands.

The mercenary's eyes shifted to full gold. "I slowed time so we could survive the pressure of the depth."

Wylda added with quiet pride, "Not easy, given how deep we had to go."

He gave her a fond glance. "Let's just say, I hate the Wastelands, but I needed the rest once we got here."

"We followed the compass to a trench no light dared enter. The bottom of the Cerulean Trench. There were a few false starts." Sequoia retched, and I wondered what had befallen them, but she didn't dwell. In fact, she gave a sly smile. "But we did it. We fought six merman waiting for the return of the true wearer of the crown."

I frowned. "But you convinced them?"

Sequoia shrugged. "They didn't much care for our interpretation. So we fought them, three against six. Cyp kept rewinding time, giving us chance after chance to learn their patterns. What was your count, Cyprian?"

"One, as you well know."

Sequoia winked. "Mine was three."

"And mine two," said Wylda.

"How many times did you rewind time, Cyp?" Zephyr

asked quietly. Fifteen seconds was as far as Cyprian could stretch.

"Eleven," Cyprian admitted.

Zephyr cursed. "For the love of lore, that could have killed you."

"It could have." A grim smile crossed Cyprian's angular features. It didn't reach his eyes. "But we needed that crown."

Storm-cloud eyes glinted. "And now we have it, which means my uncle doesn't. Reinforcing that Ysa is not one to be controlled. Rather, he is."

Stars, I hoped Elowen could hold on. I hoped she knew we were coming. "But we also have confirmation that the Spymaster is offering the same deal to multiple courts."

The bond churned with fury. We didn't know whether it was even possible for us to best a faerie king so resolutely that he wouldn't rise again, let alone ruin him if he managed to amass such power and allies.

Cyprian nodded. "If Havriel and Esolas were willing to trade, we have to assume others will as well. We're fighting a war on multiple fronts."

"We have the crown, but not enough allies to tip the vote," Sequoia observed. "And we're missing three of our own."

They'll come, Zephyr said through the bond, but I caught the thread of worry he tried to hide. *They have to.* "The mission was a success. I'm in your debt."

Cyprian shook his head. "We're family. There are no debts, brother."

Except there were. Zephyr had an armful of bargains to show for it.

I had Esolas's bargain on my wrist still, compelling us

to attend the meeting of faerie rulers, and Elowen's bargain besides. It might have faded, but I wouldn't abandon her, no matter the cost.

I looked around at these people who had become my family, gathered in this desolate place that felt like the end of the world. Dancing shadows from the fire reached towards us with grasping fingers. The wind whispered through the tangled briars, carrying with it the scent of old magic and older regrets, and above us, the crushing sky reflected our fears. Even so, we had something Thiago wanted desperately. It had to be enough.

But as we sat there around the fire, and my mate turned to whisper in Sequoia's ear, I couldn't shake the feeling that somewhere in the distance, the other faerie courts were making choices that would reshape Faerie in ways we couldn't predict or control.

I might have been pacified by our hopes and successes, but the crown remembered being worn.

Worse, it knew who I was. Perhaps even better than I knew myself.

33

YSADORA

I dreamed of a quieter life for you and Veda, but fate has other plans. Though your path is steep and thorned, the certainty that you will rise to meet your destiny fills me with a pride that even the greatest poets capture in verse.
– Rowena Ashmoor's letter to her son Zephyr

We waited for Maren, Ferrith, and Loxley in the bleached cradle of the Wastelands, and the pressure whistled through me like steam. My fingers itched for parchment, for ink, for the order of letters and lines.

But chaos required more than order. That portion of my magic, jagged and bright, searched for a seam where it could slip free. Zephyr and Cyprian sat around the fire together, brows furrowed in identical frowns as they colluded on strategy.

I paced the fringe of the tangled briars and caught the look that passed between Wylda and Sequoia: the look that said I needed an intervention. I hoped they wouldn't act on it, but they came towards me anyway, nudging each other like they were drawing lots as to who should speak first.

Neither Maren nor Ferrith would have hesitated, and stars, I missed them.

Zephyr's gaze lifted briefly, tracking me. The firelight played across his face, illuminating the hollows beneath his eyes. He didn't speak, but I felt the low thrum of him in the bond, a silent anchor against my storm. Still, his mind remained tethered to the matter at hand: battle routes, uncertain allies, the coming clash that we all anticipated in our bones.

Wylda drew the short straw and approached. "The waiting is hell. How are you bearing up? It's a lot, we know."

My chaos magic sparked along my fingertips, leaving tiny burns in the air. "Do you, though?"

"You're tempted to burn down the Wastelands. Honestly, it might be an improvement." Sequoia's feathered, raven-dark wings folded tight against her back. "Do you know how many times I've waited for Wylda to return from missions that should have been simple? Seventeen. Seventeen times I've paced just like you're doing now, convinced she was dead in a ditch."

"I still throw up if Sese doesn't check in at the agreed time." Wylda scanned the horizon like she expected it to lurch open. "Sometimes loved ones make choices that terrify us. Loving people in Faerie means accepting that you might lose them."

I folded my arms over the ache in my chest, thinking of Father and Tanuhja, Maren and Ferrith, Elowen alone out there, of how Zephyr had almost been swallowed by the dream. "Love is just another death sentence."

"Of course," said Sequoia. "But we choose it anyway. Otherwise, what the hell are we even saving?"

I nodded, swallowing the lump in my throat. For all our differences, Maren, Ferrith, and I had that in common with the mercenaries, and I was fiercely glad to have them in my corner.

Wylda glanced at Zephyr and Cyprian, legs outstretched, heads bent together in quiet conversation. She hesitated. "Ysa, Zephyr's teetering. We can all see it."

My heart hammered. Zephyr's attention shifted towards me through the bond, drawn by my rising panic. His concern wrapped around me like a warm cloak, and I fought the urge to run to him. "He's managing. Recording his stories helped. So does reliving his own memories. He's strong."

Sequoia's dark eyes held mine. "Yes, he is. But what if he spirals? When his family died, he almost didn't make it through, and this time, his lore magic is overburdened by the outcast fae and all this talk of the High King. The stakes are higher than they've ever been..." Her gaze held both admiration and judgment.

I flinched, and the air crackled and the dragon-kissed blade heated in its sheath. "You think he'll take me with him. You think *I'm* the danger." It was the plain truth. I couldn't argue with them.

"Yes," said Wylda, quietly. "Your chaos magic is still volatile."

My eyes narrowed. "What are you trying to say?"

Sequoia crossed her arms, wings rustling. Damn, she was beautiful. "You love him. We're not questioning that. You're mates. Bonded for life, as Veda foretold." She sighed, as if there was still part of her who imagined a future with him.

My stomach dropped. "You want me to leave him?"

Wylda blinked. "Leave him? No, of course not. The mate bond isn't a mortal binding to discard at will. We're saying we need a contingency in case he spirals. You love him, but you should love yourself enough to know when to reach for us."

Sequoia gave a tight nod. "If he does spiral, we'll help carry him back to you."

"Okay," I said. "What do you suggest?"

"Let us teach you how to block him from your mind to protect yourself," said Wylda.

I glanced at him. Even here, even now, his beauty took my breath away. But then, it'd been like that from the moment I saw him at Bloomtide. Who he was, how he walked through the world, meant I couldn't imagine being apart from him, and the bond felt true. To impede it was an act of harm to us both.

"But we promised each other we would never do that." A curl of shadow wiped away the tear that rolled down my cheek.

At the fire, Zephyr's whole focus shifted to me, and there was only me and him in the world and no one else, his storm-cloud gaze full of love and resolve. *It will be worth it, Inkheart. Even this. We have to plan for every eventuality. I need you to be safe.*

I tore my gaze away from him, understanding. "He put you up to this. That's why you were whispering."

Sequoia nodded. "He thought you'd hear it better from us."

I gave a wry smile despite the ache in my chest. How well he knew me. I'd never have agreed had he asked me himself.

All I wanted was certainty. They couldn't give it to me.

Wylda waited, ensuring that Zephyr no longer listened. "I'll help."

Sequoia gave Wylda a grim look. "Leave us to it." To me, she said, "She's the healer. I'm the breaker."

"How do you know how to do this?" I asked as Wylda reluctantly joined the others.

Sequoia's almond brown eyes grew distant. "Our parents were bonded mates. It's why their relationship came above everything. Sometimes that kind of love destroys as much as it builds. Mother blocked Father's rages often. She taught me how it worked."

Vulnerability was rare for her, and I wondered what in their past made the sisters so different, whether she had always shouldered the harder tasks to spare Wylda. Zephyr's star glowed in me: warm, aware, waiting. In a few short weeks, I had learned to rely on that tether. Doubt curled cold in my gut.

"I don't know if I can do this."

"You can do it. You just don't want to."

Skies above, she would cleave a priest mid-prayer and still sleep soundly after. "Is this really about keeping me safe?"

Her expression didn't waver. "You think I want him for myself."

The silence between us pulsed louder than any denial.

She met my gaze with something like pain. "I care

about him a lot. And I care about you a little. If that makes this complicated, so be it. And if you think I'd use our situation as a stepping stone to get closer to him, then you don't know me." She huffed a breath. "Just let me teach you how to block him. Okay? Find the part of yourself that wants space. Even if it's tiny. Even if you hate it. This won't break the bond, just dim it. It's a shield, not a knife."

But every part of me already felt like it was bleeding. "Let's get this over with."

"This isn't about magic, it's about focus." She tapped the centre of my chest. "The bond lives here. But it breathes through your thoughts. Right now, your mind is open. You're letting Zephyr take up every corner of it."

"Did he take up every corner of yours?" I asked, and then immediately regretted it.

"Yes, yes, he did," she said sharply. "But he's not your mind. You need space to think, not just feel. So give yourself a room inside your head. Walls, floors, windows, a door. Put him outside it."

"That feels—"

"Cruel?" Her eyes didn't soften. "Only if you never open the door again. Go on. Try it. Start closing the room off. Windows. Doors. One by one. He won't love you less. But you'll be strong enough to fight beside him, not just for him."

I clenched my fists and did as she said. At first, I still sensed Zephyr, but faintly as if through a veil. Then, with the closing of the door, there was a howling absence that eventually quieted. I hated that quiet, and so, I flung open the door again.

His words rang in my chest, moon-bright and fierce as a vow. *You did it. I never doubted you.*

Wylda came to stand between us. "You taught her the basics?"

Sequoia gave a sharp nod, jaw clenched.

"Then that's enough. Come on, let's eat and give thanks that at least Lox isn't cooking tonight."

I hugged my arms to my chest and went to sit beside Zephyr at the fire, and he laid a loose arm around my shoulders, and I wanted more, wanted to crawl closer until we were skin on skin, breath to breath, in that desolate place.

I already grieved the loss of the bond, although it hadn't happened yet.

Wylda had produced bowls of stew from our supplies, the scent of herbs and preserved meat rising in the thin air. The others ate with quiet efficiency, but my stomach churned. I pushed the food around in my bowl, eyes trained on the horizon as the others talked in low voices.

Years of mercenary work meant they ate and slept as the mission schedule demanded, regardless of nerves, looming threats, or the scent of blood still fresh in the air. Hunger was not a weakness; it was a background hum, tuned out like the ache of old wounds.

They had learned to chew through adrenaline and swallow around dread, to sleep with one eye open and fingers curled near the hilt of a blade. Soft beds were a myth. Warm meals were a luxury. They'd rested in treetops, on frostbitten stone, beneath war banners, and beside corpses.

Routine dulled fear, and necessity eclipsed preference. The body was just another weapon to hone, and the mission always came first.

But not for me. I still hesitated. My mind outran my

body, circling worst-case outcomes. I hadn't trained myself to rest beneath the weight of dread. I hadn't taught my hands to eat while the sky threatened war. Where the mercenaries had discipline, I had questions. Where they had silence, I had ink and thought and fear.

"You need to eat," murmured Zephyr, spooning some of his portion into my mouth.

I focused my attention on him and swallowed, surprised by the sudden tenderness. "You'll make me soft."

"Then let the rest of Faerie fear a soft woman who could end them."

For him, I ate. The fire crackled, and in the silence between bites, a movement caught my eye: a spill of ink looping along the ground in an elegant script, although I hadn't used my magic. The letters formed and reformed, our names drifting further apart with each iteration:

The Calligrapher's Daughter and her Fatebreaker

    The Calligrapher's Daughter...and her Fatebreaker

        The Calligrapher's Daughter......and her Fatebreaker

Cyp choked as he studied the writing. "What in the seven hells—"

My heart jolted into a staccato rhythm. "I didn't write that."

Zephyr's jaw tightened. "Faerie did."

Wylda's hand went to her spear as her gaze pivoted between us.

"We can stab it or just finish our stew," said Sequoia drily. "At least it's not trying to kill us."

But my meagre appetite had evaporated, and I glanced again at the ground and the low sky. "Those are the Binder's names for us. It feels like her here, doesn't it? Desolate, powerful, as if she could be close?"

Zephyr studied my face. "Yes. Yes, it does."

I set my bowl aside. "Do you think…" My intuition told me maybe we could reach her.

"Ysa," warned Zephyr, as the others stiffened. "Do you really want to summon one of the most dangerous entities in Faerie?"

"What harm would it do? We're waiting anyway. I need answers. We all do."

Faerie didn't respond to linear logic, not in the way the mortal realm did. I'd witnessed time and again that this realm didn't reward control: it rewarded paradox, not precision, high emotions, not balance.

And with Zephyr, I was capable of things I had no language for. The mate bond was a kind of magic older than Faerie's courts, deeper than dragonfire. There was something in the rhythm of us, some ancient alchemy that dared the stars to watch.

"Maybe, like the stars, Lunarys doesn't answer to symmetry. Maybe she responds to flux and turning points. Gabor said something in my lessons about the Wastelands—a place abandoned by rule, but not untouched by longing."

Zephyr held my gaze. "If anyone could survive an encounter with her, it would be you."

Cyprian stood, bowl forgotten. "Your confidence is admirable, Ysa. Your recklessness is less so."

"Better to bleed with friends than flounder blind," Sequoia countered.

"It *is* a risk," said Zephyr. "Summon a fate, even someone disposed to help us, and she'll demand something in return. For all the nudges the Binder has dared to give us, she must be careful to be neutral."

Sequoia's eyes narrowed at the firelight. "We all know our history. The Binder might ask for a strand of fate. A literal strand of your future. Your child. Your death. A victory you might one day win."

"She might not even take it immediately," said Cyprian. "We know she's patient. She could call it in whole orbits from now."

"I don't know. I think Ysa could be on to something," said Wylda. "Lunarys might be averse to mapping the future, but perhaps she'll give us some clue about what has already occurred. A clue to where Loxley and the others are. A clue to how Elowen fares."

"Even past information comes with a price," said Zephyr, and I knew it was the monster histories he was thinking of.

"That terrifies me less than the cost of ignorance," I said quietly. "If the Binder has even a shard of insight, I want it."

Skies, I wanted it so much. I could pose a question that could provide assurances about our kin's safety, or perhaps focus on loyalty, flushing out our worries about Ferrith and Elowen, or Loxley, who had not shown Ferrith the kindness I wished, or Tanuhja, who pretended to want the best for me, but whose heart was dark, or Orin, who lurked in Thiago's court but whom Zephyr—revealed in his tight silences and furrowed brow—clearly still loved.

I wanted a way to help our kin, to aid our vision of Faerie, and to prevent any severing between Zephyr and me somehow.

Perhaps he read my thoughts, because his expression shifted—conflicted, proud, afraid. Finally, he gave a reluctant nod. *As if I could ever refuse you.* "Then whatever the Binder demands in return, it better be worth the truth."

Cyprian shook his head. "You're going to do it. You're really going to do it?"

"Let's hope she arrives in a helpful mood." I paused. "Hide the High King's crown in time, Cyp. Then brace yourselves, because my magic is impatient for release."

The crown called to me, like a fishhook reeling me in, and then it was gone. I closed my eyes and reached for the rawest emotions churning inside me, just as I had learned at Tanuhja's court: the helpless fury for Elowen, my yearning for Father, Maren, and Ferrith, and the bone-deep desperation of asking myself if I could save Faerie on my own terms.

My chaos magic responded like a starving animal, pouring through my veins with savage hunger. Ink erupted from my quill without my conscious will, streaming into the air in violent spirals. It wasn't the controlled flow I'd learned to manage: this was chaos incarnate, black ribbons that writhed and twisted, forming symbols that hurt to look at.

And the Wastelands—they turned hostile. Above us, dark clouds shifted in a sickly rhythm, and the horizon snapped into brutal focus before beginning to twist in slow, nauseating spirals that made my stomach lurch.

Silvered dunes began to ripple outwards from where I stood. The air pressed against my lungs until each breath felt like drowning. The ink didn't just write in the air. It carved reality, leaving tears in the fabric of Faerie that made our kin gasp. But still, I continued. My chaos magic fed on the mounting fear—mine, Zephyr's, the mercenaries', even the horses' animal terror—growing more uncontrolled with each passing heartbeat.

Zephyr's voice was strained. *Ysadora—.*

His shadows writhed uncontrollably around his shoulders, responding to the chaos magic like oil meeting flame. Mythros reared suddenly, his eyes rolled white as he pulled against the reins, his hooves striking sparks from the cursed ground. *Easy, easy,* murmured my mate, and I didn't know if it was me or the stallion he addressed. My magic was loud in my mind, but he found a way through. He didn't give up.

Ysa, you need to stop. He reached for me as Mythros broke free, bolting several yards away before wheeling to face us.

I stopped, gasping, my hair damp with sweat and glanced at our terrified friends standing in a semi-circle behind us.

The air tasted charged, as though someone had struck a match in the bones of the earth. Faerie had yet to decide whether it would burn or bloom. It held a thousand unseen doors, each with its own cost, its own wonder.

The suspended ink suddenly stilled, hanging like a storm cloud. Then it began to fall. Where it touched the sand, the granules turned black as midnight, and in that darkness, footfalls multiplied around us like a plague.

What started as a few scattered prints became dozens, then hundreds: a writhing mass of impressions that crawled across the corrupted ground. Some prints walked in perfect circles, trapped in loops. Others staggered and stumbled. The worst were the ones that dragged, long gouges in the dirt where something had been pulled unwillingly towards an unseen fate, fingernail scratches alongside the drag marks.

A chill pooled in the hollow of my throat as I clutched my quill, and Zephyr reached for a hilt at his back, shadows gathering like breath. Cyprian, Wylda, and Sequoia drew their weapons too.

Then the footprints disappeared, leaving a single pair beside our own that sometimes walked ahead and sometimes behind: delicate and full of grace. Then the air creased like paper, and it was the Binder who stepped from the seam, her face shining and bright, her violet robes stitched with stars.

Her arrival washed over the Wastelands like a cool balm, easing its oppressive air pressure and allowing air into my tight lungs. The horizon ceased its nauseating spiral. The silvered dunes settled back into their natural state with barely a whisper of displaced sand.

Fuck, it worked. Zephyr grabbed my hand in an iron grip.

We were no longer just trespassers in the Wastelands.

We were the bold ones who had summoned an ancient being who extinguished stars.

34

KAZIMIR

Sometimes, when the wind shifts, I still expect to
hear the beat of dragon wings. Caldoron would
never bow to grief. He would soar above it,
waiting for the wind to change.
May he be untouched by ruin,
flying across the skies we once shared.
– Kazimir's entry to the memory stone

Mere seconds passed between the calligrapher's vault onto the dragon's back and flames crackling against the ramparts. Caldoron's haunches flexed beneath Kazimir, his long tail lashing against the stone like the thudding of a war drum.

Sunlight caught the ridged membranes of his bronze wings, casting the courtyard in molten shadow. Queen Thalindra's shouted orders were lost to the scream of wind and fire, and bone soldiers and tomb guardians ducked and scrambled in response. But Kazimir found a strange clarity that had always been his in the sky.

His blood rose with the heat radiating off the dragon's scales. *Let them taste what they have stolen, old friend.*

Then hold on, calligrapher. I will not be gentle, replied Caldoron.

The dragon's fury was a slow, ominous pull reverberating through him in rumbling growls, the echo of something older than kings: the kind of fury that remembered the betrayal of those who once called dragons allies, and later carved their bones for power.

The fire wasn't only Caldoron's; it burned in Kazimir, loud and bright. It sickened him that the Circle of Emberlight had bartered sacred dragon bones as if they were nothing more than mineral, spice, or coin.

The knowledge sat in his gut like rot as his thighs gripped Caldoron's spine, his throat raw from smoke and sadness. Healing had returned his strength, but not his peace. That would have to be won.

A cry rose below, and the distinct twang of crossbows cut the air.

They dare to attack us when the grave injury is ours? Caldoron snarled.

Justice is always slow until there's fire behind it, said Kazimir.

The bolts clattered harmlessly against the dragon's hide, apart from one that embedded in the softer scale near his hind leg, a thin rivulet of dark blood trailing behind. Caldoron reared up with a thunderous roar, smoke curling from his nostrils.

His voice rasped in Kazimir's mind. *We will scatter the bone soldiers like dry leaves in a storm.*

Kazimir knew there were other considerations—Ysa was always forefront in his mind—but he was not Caldoron's master. They were but equals, and only a fool attempted to temper a dragon's wrath.

The Queen of Bones had wronged dragonkind, and there would be consequences, and the calligrapher did not seek to throttle Caldoron's fire. Instead, he steeled himself to ride the storm, shoulders squared beneath the burning court.

He was not the reins, only the whisper within the tempest, listening to the dragon sing his pyre-song. If Thalindra had forgotten what it meant to awaken a dragon's ire, she would soon relearn the lesson, etched in smoke, seared into stone.

The dragon's roar split the clouds above. Kazimir clung to the bronze neck, pressing low to the glinting scales, as Caldoron folded his wings in tight and dove. The dragon's rage was a furnace beneath his ribs. He could feel it in the tremor of the beast's spine, in the flex of massive talons eager to rake, to rend, to punish.

The air convulsed with heat before his flames reached the ground. Beneath them, a few hundred bone soldiers stood in grim formation, their rune-carved exoskeletons glowing with deathlight, heads turning in eerie synchrony to meet the descending shadow.

Without breath to quicken or blood to chill, they did not flinch.

Then fire bloomed, a deluge of molten gold and blistering heat, and still quiet reigned, beyond the lick of the flames and the snap of Caldoron's wings, and Kazimir's own ricocheting heart. The bone soldiers didn't scream. There were no lungs to fill, no voices to articulate their panic, no emotions to rend.

The fire hit them like a verdict, scorching through rune-bound joints and war-welded sinew. Those who raised their weapons found their bones blasted from their sockets or melting at the seams. Line after line, they advanced, to meet the same fate: a wave of malformed death-guardians marching through the inferno, their broken grins undeterred.

One leapt impossibly high on its stilt-like legs, but Caldoron was ready, even without Kazimir's warning, veering to the left and whipping his tail through the air, catching the creature midflight. It splintered on impact, bones raining down like ivory hail.

So the bone soldiers do burn, said the calligrapher. *Another victory to add to your triumphs.*

The dragon had done his work. Fire laced the sky in serpentine ribbons. Marrow shattered like brittle glass beneath claw and flame. And still, the Queen of Bones did not come. Kazimir peered through the fog. She watched, instead, from the high black balcony of her sanctum, her silhouette unmoved against the stark sky. He wondered why Thalindra had not unleashed her magic or sent the trio of bone knights with their pikes that he had witnessed on a battlefield long ago.

The dragon's gaze shifted before he changed direction. They were both covered in debris and soot.

Don't, please. Kazimir warned as the dragon's attention tilted towards the balcony. *We need her. We can salvage an alliance.*

Caldoron's lips peeled back from yellowed fangs. *An alliance? After all that has occurred?*

He growled low in his throat, not in protest, but in betrayal. Then he launched forward without warning, turning at the last moment away from the queen on her balcony. A massive bone sentinel, half-buried in the ground, turned its head slowly to follow them, but did not act.

Kazimir barely had time to adjust his grip before the wind slapped him sideways. Far beneath them, more bone soldiers clustered in the courtyard. The dragon didn't level his wings or offer stability. He barrel-rolled, then angled into a near-vertical climb that stole the calligrapher's breath and had him praying to the stars for mercy. He clung to the ridge at the base of the dragon's neck, teeth gritted against the sudden force of ascent. The scorched ground fell away beneath them like ash from a dying fire.

Caldoron didn't circle back. He angled westwards, towards the jagged line of Dead Man's Ridge, a wall of small peaks that clawed the edge of the Court of Bones. Kazimir braced against the cold slicing across his face and let his mind reel, though his body instinctively worked to maintain his perch.

Dragon-riding was perilous, never more so than when a rider and dragon first chose one another, or when discord grew between them. It required a harmony of mind and instinct, between two egotistical species, a surrendering of ego in the face of something far older and fiercer for the common good.

Now, grievance was thick between him and his beloved Caldoron, clear in the dragon's sharp, agitated wing strokes, the lurching angles of ascent, the whip-fast turns with no warning. The dragon's displeasure rolled off his bronze scales, hot as forge fire, cold as betrayal.

The calligrapher would not have dared to speak with the dragon in this frame of mind, even if it had been possible. This was not the flight of a reunited pair.

One misstep and the dragon might not catch him.

But even fury was a kind of love. So he clung on, as the wind and forces threatened to tear him loose, as the dragon's scales became slick with wind-swept condensation, making his grip even more precarious.

The peaks approached fast, looming like the jaws of Faerie itself. The light thinned, casting the sky in shades of pewter. Anxiety knotted Kazimir's belly. He knew that if he couldn't face the reckoning the dragon sought at Dead Man's Ridge, he might never fly again.

Caldoron spiralled down in a controlled glide, but his descent was tight, unforgiving.

He landed, talons gouging deep trenches in the stone, sending tremors rattling through Kazimir. Then the dragon bucked strongly enough to toss his rider. Kazimir was thrown sideways and landed in a crouch, his palms scraping stone, his boots skidding on loose shale as he hit the ground. The dragon stepped away, tail twitching like a whip of disdain.

Kazimir fought to draw calm breaths as he stood. The air was dry. He could still smell the scorched bone lingering in the dragon's nostrils and the distant, acrid scent of burning. *You don't seem to mind if you kill me, old friend.*

You brought us here, not I. Deep-set golden eyes gleamed, pupils slitted and narrow. *The dead will not be forgotten.*

He loved this beast. Even now. Even with anger spiking

the air between them, in this place they didn't know. *The thought of an alliance angers you. But that was our mission, regardless of what we learned. We have meted out punishment, but it was always the way of the Order of the Glyph to bind the disparate parts of Faerie together. Have you forgotten our oath?*

Calderon flared his wings wide—not to fly, but to dominate—casting a titanic shadow that swallowed Kazimir whole. *I have not forgotten. I was there when we stood on the cliffside and inked that vow into the winds. It is you who has forgotten.*

Kazimir's gut twisted. So this wasn't about the bartering between Thalindra and the Circle of Emberlight. This was about him. Here, away from the carnage and cold indifference of the Court of Bones, there was only them: two remnants of an old war.

He could listen now; he could learn. *Then speak. Say what has been festering.*

The dragon's golden eyes narrowed to thin, unblinking slivers. *Have you even once considered the others of my kind who survived what was done that night?*

Kazimir's chest tightened as the old memory came to his head: dragons falling from the sky like stars being snuffed out. The bond between him and Caldoron was electric with betrayal and mourning. *Tell me why the dragons chose to fall.*

Caldoron's roar shook the mountaintop and the marrow in Kazimir's teeth. *Today is not about my fallen comrades. It is about you and me, calligrapher. About your abandonment when I was true. Have you once dwelled on how I survived when you were gone?*

Kazimir withstood the urge to step back. He had been

the only calligrapher left standing, and the dragons had needed him. *I failed you. I failed you all.*

There was no doubt in his mind that they had deserved more from him, and he was desperately sorry, although even now he wouldn't have changed the path he had taken.

The dragon's lips curled back to show the glow of fire building behind his teeth: a reminder of restraint. *You asked me to save them, to give everything, and I did. I stayed with you as long as I could. After you left, you didn't call for me. Not once.*

Kazimir flinched, just a twitch in the jaw, but Caldoron saw it. *I never meant to leave you...*

Smoke curled from the dragon's nostrils. *I waited under stars you once named for us. I waited while Faerie warped, changing all we put in place together. You broke your oath.*

The calligrapher whispered, *I'm sorry.*

The dragon and rider bond is sacred. One claw curled and uncurled into the stone, sending cracks spiderwebbing out, as if Caldoron needed a physical outlet to keep from boiling over. *You gave away Shadow, the blade I blessed.*

Not to just anyone. To Ysa, replied Kazimir.

Caldoron's tail lashed left. *Of course. For the babe in arms you left Faerie for. Left me for.*

A stillness expanded in Kazimir's chest. He hadn't asked Caldoron's forgiveness for all the time he had been gone, never once considering that he perhaps should have asked permission to have left in the first place.

He'd simply left, believing that the broken heart he nursed was his alone. *I thought of you every day, my friend. I had nothing to offer but silence.*

The dragon turned his gaze to the horizon as if Kazimir were a flicker beneath his notice. *Your thoughts are no salve.*

I'm ready to fight now, said Kazimir. *To mend what is broken.*

Caldoron snorted. *It is the Spymaster who dragged you back to Faerie.*

Then I am grateful to him, because he freed me from the trap of my own making, said Kazimir. *Although on my return, I did wonder if it was my broken shell of a body that you could not abide.*

The dragon's roar rolled through the cold air. *I would carry you if you were flayed skin and bones, Kazimir. What matters are your mind and spirit. You abandoned me for Ysadora, and now you've surrendered that fight too, bowing to the shadow prince.*

Perhaps he had stopped fighting against fate, perhaps he had tired of Faerie schemes. The thought was painful enough that he knew it was true. *I am sorry, old friend. I will be sorry until the day I die for separating from you, for not consoling when your kin and mine died. My daughter is my hope, just as you are my fire.*

A huff of warm air blasted past Kazimir's ear. *I do not need your guilt. I need your cunning.*

You have it. The silence between them stretched.

Then Calderon's serpentine neck arched lower, and lower still, until dragon and male were nose to nose. *Then we begin again, calligrapher. But remember, such decisions are ours to take together.*

We begin again. Kazimir repeated, looking up into the slitted gold eyes. *You are certain that the rest of the riot know nothing of what Liora Bramick bartered on behalf of the Circle of Emberlight?*

The dragon's chest rose and fell in a slower rhythm now. *They do not know. If they knew, the women would be ash by now.*

Sensing consensus and renewed rapport, Kazimir inched closer. *Liora Bramick must be deposed.*

Agreed, said the dragon. *If the rest of the Circle of Emberlight riders are involved, they must burn, too.*

Kazimir sucked in a breath. *Agreed.*

And the Queen of Bones? asked the dragon.

A rare smile broke across the calligrapher's face, the most genuine smile that had graced his expression since his reunion with Caldoron and Ysadora. *I have a bargain for her. One she cannot refuse.*

The dragon lowered his body to the ground, wings folding like a great bow drawn back. *Then let us return to the citadel, calligrapher, and you can tell me your schemes.*

I'll tell you everything, old friend. But I warn you, some of it requires a leap of faith.

The moment his hand touched Caldoron's side, old instincts surged. He scaled the dragon's back with fluid movements honed long ago, slipping between the familiar contours of muscle and bone: no reins, no saddle, only the bond between dragon and rider, reignited.

A rumble of affection shook the dragon's body. *You will need another quill, calligrapher.*

He nestled within scales already moulded to his body. *That I will.*

Kazimir no longer felt like a trespasser on the dragon nor feared that the next sweep of Caldoron's wings might send him plummeting. The sky welcomed them as they rose, and Faerie shrank beneath. Kazimir wanted this so much for Ysa: to know someone would catch her if she fell;

fly beside her when she soared; this inviolable safety, not caged but coiled around her like armour. He dared to believe his daughter might achieve it, with his help, if only he could somehow reach her.

But first, he and Caldoron had a tricky negotiation to execute.

This time, Caldoron did not punish him with speed. His flight had smoothed, his angles less razor-sharp, as if he'd permitted peace to settle in the spaces grief had gnawed hollow. Kazimir unfolded his schemes, and the dragon chuckled, a gravel-edged rumble like boulders shifting in a canyon.

Above the jagged peaks, below the pewter sky, they moved like ink on parchment.

35

ZEPHYR

The line between love and destruction blurs. I am
fracturing beneath this weight. Monsters crawl
from the chaos I cannot tame, and yet still, you
do not write. Tell me——is our youngling well?
Does she thrive?
- Tanuhja's letter to her former lover, Kazimir

Zephyr clutched his Ysa's hand, determined not to let go. The raw edge of her magic, dark and wild, bit against his restraint. He held his shadows tight against him, fighting the instinct to extend them to her. Then he sheathed the swords he'd instinctively drawn, and his kin followed suit. For a breath, Zephyr wondered if he'd taught his mate enough to survive, but she stashed her quill between her breasts, and his chest eased. Insulting the Binder was to invite obliteration.

Lunarys could not be bested; only navigated.

Ysa stood with her spine straight, ink-dark hair over

her shoulders like a spill of shadow made silk, as if she were writing herself into legend. Her heart-shaped face was both defiant and too soft for this realm. There was power in her stance, yes, but there was fragility too.

He'd spent over a century learning to read battlefields, to assess threats and weaknesses in the span of a heartbeat. But watching Ysa face down cosmic forces sent him into a spin. He hated Faerie for asking her to be more than human. He hated it when she released his hand. This was Ysa's choice. Her summons. He had to trust her to handle what came next, and he would endure any pain for the privilege of standing at her side.

Zephyr had witnessed battlefields drenched in blood, witnessed mercenaries fling themselves into fire for coin or cause. He'd watched faerie kings and queens tremble beneath crowns too heavy for their heads.

Yet it was the calligrapher's daughter—raised in the mortal realm, where magic was myth and courage was quiet—who dared to call Lunarys like a prayer flung at the stars. The current of the bond told him that it wasn't self-preservation that drove her, though she was the one his uncle coveted; it was her sense of kinship for them all.

His mercenary family held their positions in the stillness, but Zephyr could feel their collective tension at his back.

Then the Binder stepped through the seam. Mythros heaved, as if uncertain whether to kneel. Her eyes met theirs, brighter than stars, older than song, and the weight of her knowing settled over them like a mantle. She smelled of fire and first snow.

She didn't look best pleased. "Ysadora."

Ysa's smile of greeting wavered at the Binder's

expression, and the bond filled with uncertainty. "Lunarys."

Zephyr resisted the urge to step in front of her. It made complete sense to him that the Binder's first word was his mate's name: Ysa was the point around which all else tilted.

"This is the first time I've been summoned. I can't say I like it."

Fingers tattooed with waxing and waning moons were black at their tips, and the Binder's robes were discoloured at her knees, as if she'd been crouched in a pool of liquid night, folding darkness with her fingers. Her gaze raked across the others, and dread rippled through him.

She said to Wylda, not unkindly, "Your healing powers will be required before the path ends." Next, her attention fixed on Cyprian. "Ah, the one who turns time. I've met you before, and I'll meet you again, though you won't remember me either time." Finally, her gaze passed to Sequoia. "And you, raven-winged guardian. So protective. So certain. Would you break their hearts to save their souls?"

Sese's throat worked, and Zephyr willed her not to provoke, a common but useless wish. "You know the answer already, Lunarys. Why ask the question?"

A small smile ghosted across the Binder's luminous face. "The future does not hinge on knowledge. It hinges on choice, even when the knowing burns brighter. I am ever curious to see what shape a soul takes when tested."

Ysa's tone was carefully even, "I wouldn't have dared summon you, except you set my journey in motion and disappeared."

"Disappeared?" Sapphire eyes shimmered with

knowing too vast for comfort. "I've watched from afar as you carved your path, besting the Spymaster, absorbing the meteor's magic, discovering your capacity for chaos and navigating trust in Faerie."

Ysa's fingers flexed as if she longed to call her magic. "We could have died many times over. Now our friends are missing, and I have not heard from Father or Elowen despite my ink magic."

Fear wrapped its fingers around Zephyr's heart. But ancients, he loved her for not crumbling beneath this pressure, for refusing to shrink in the face of cosmic forces. *Careful, Inkheart. Don't rile her.*

The Binder's eyes narrowed, ancient calculation flickering across her face. "But you didn't die. And there is more to you than ink magic, as you have proved by bringing me here. I'm not a herald of tidy endings but a weaver of potential. Neither do I walk every thread I weave. Some paths must be taken blind, or not at all."

Must be a gift. Enough distance to stay blameless, but just close enough to watch the fallout, said Zephyr through the bond. He couldn't help speaking up in support of his mate. "Survival is not the same as safety, Lunarys."

Ysa's eyebrows shot up. *What happened to not riling her?*

She likes you better than me. Me disappointing her is par for the course, drawled Zephyr.

"There's more learning and compassion in survival than safety, *Fatebreaker*. You know that better than anyone. Sometimes the broken can be trusted more than those who believe they are whole. The old order would shatter. I've waited centuries for such an age for the old order to shatter. Just imagine what Faerie could be."

One corner of his mouth twisted in a wry smile. "Shift the scales, and they'll only tilt again."

"You haven't believed that since you met Ysadora."

He stilled because it was true. The optimist in him had died with his family, but Ysa's arrival and her sheer stubborn hope made possibility stir in his chest again. "I loathe Faerie for not deserving her."

The Binder tilted her head like a bird. "Love and anger aren't opposites. You don't loathe Faerie, *Fatebreaker*. What you feel is grief. Grief is love, bruised and bound. I was pleased you found some common ground with your mother, Ysadora."

Ysa gave a dry laugh. "Common ground? She burned any we found."

The Binder's expression flickered. "I've often wondered if I hung her star wrongly or whether my sisters play me at my own game." She sighed. "I am fond of you, Ysadora, but your chaos magic called me here rudely."

The ground around Zephyr's boots darkened with shadows as he watched for any sign of a threat to his mate. His gaze never left the Binder's face.

Ysa lifted her chin. Her resolve lit up the mate bond. "We have questions."

"Of course you do. But to ask a question of me after a summoning is to offer your throat or something equally as precious." Cerulean eyes shone, and Zephyr couldn't tell anymore if Ysadora remained a favourite of hers or whether his mate was just Lunarys's pawn, like so many others over the centuries when she had intervened. "I'll allow you one question about the past. Either a triviality about your kin. That I'll answer for the price of a sleepless night. Or a crucial piece about the two of you. But be careful, foreknowledge isn't always a blessing. It's your choice, Ysadora."

Behind them, Cyprian muttered, "There are no fair bargains with Fates."

For all her wiles, Lunarys is Father's ally and our ally, Ysa said through the bond. *Do I ask about our kin to set our minds at rest?*

I'm glad you're so sure. Zephyr's strategic mind assessed their options. *Asking about the threat to our kin would ease your heart, but leave us blind to the larger danger.*

The Binder inspected her darkness-dipped fingertips. "Hurry, Ysadora. I have stars to hang."

Ysa's thoughts whirred through the bond, and Zephyr felt the exact moment she made her choice: not the safe one, but the brave one. *Hasn't the sum of my learning from Lunarys been that if I don't like the paths laid before me, I can choose another?*

He trusted her more than life itself. *I love how you think. Yes, bend the rules. We don't follow the stars, Inkheart. We reroute them, even if we walk off the edge of the map together. Remember, wording in Faerie is everything.*

Ysa drew in a shaky breath and looked to the Binder. "Then I ask the question that costs the most, but I won't choose between love and loyalty."

The Binder's eyes grew moon-shaped. "I expected nothing less. Go ahead, daughter of Kazimir."

"My question is what past truth connects the danger to our kin and the danger to our mate bond?"

"Clever girl. The calligrapher would be proud." The Wastelands hushed further, and the stars in Lunarys's eyes wheeled like distant galaxies. "Even questions formed of love can unravel the fabric of things. But fair is fair. You asked what connects the danger to your kin and the danger to your mate bond. Tanuhja told you that the cursed fae are the result of her breakdown. What you don't know is that your mother is a reality anchor. Throughout time, reality anchors have been born into different courts, with the potential for catastrophic error as well as the promise of realm-altering potential. You, too, are a reality anchor. It's why the Spymaster is so invested in your potential for creation or destruction. It's why your bond with the *Fatebreaker* is more than the sum of its parts. More than romance. It's a magical safety mechanism, the balance of bonded equals. And that is why I orchestrated your meeting against my sisters' advice."

Every protective instinct Zephyr harboured suddenly made sense. Magical safety mechanism. He almost laughed at the clinical term for having his soul completed. The universe could call it whatever it wanted. He'd still choose Ysadora Silberquill in every lifetime.

There were layers and layers to the Binder, and he was sure there was information she still kept hidden from them. Again, he felt that old tug: the need to tell Veda how powerful her painted prophecy had been. "Did you feed this foretelling to my sister?"

"No," said the Binder kindly. "That was all her own work. I was sorry that her star was extinguished so soon."

Ysa's breath hitched, but she didn't look away. "So Father's leaving hastened my mother's fall?"

"It was complicated. I didn't piece it together for an age. They weren't mated, you see." The Binder stared at the horizon with its low flicker of stars as if she wanted to tweak the canvas of sky. "Your mother's bond wasn't your father. It was you."

Zephyr's heartbeat thundered behind his ribs in response to the flare of Ysa's pain that transferred through the bond to him.

She shuddered. *I thought Father's leaving had set the fall of the courts in motion. But it was me.*

He hid his racing thoughts behind calm stoicism because that's what Ysa needed. Theirs was the deepest love he would ever experience, but it was also about survival on a cosmic scale.

You were a youngling, Inkheart. Now we make our own fate, remember? To the Binder, he said, "You kept this from us."

Lunarys regarded him solemnly. "What good are scare stories?"

He tried to keep his cool, and only his experiences as one of Thiago's spiders helped him hold the fraying threads of his temper and his wild worry for his mate and the realm. "It isn't just Ysa, although she matters most. What about the outcast fae? Is there no hope for them?"

For the first time, Zephyr saw something like sympathy in her ancient features. "The bond grounds the reality anchor, Fatebreaker, but alone it won't be enough. She'll need something older, something that remembers when reality was young. The dragons knew the first anchors. And the dragons may, if fate is kind, have a role in freeing the cursed fae."

His shoulders eased for the first time in hours. *There's a way.* The future wasn't only loss.

Ysa reached for his hand and squeezed it. *I told you there would be.* Her twilight eyes met his, and the echo of hope glowed in them, muddying quickly into something else. "My mother said I wouldn't survive as a dragon rider."

She sounded so forlorn, he wanted to wrap her in his arms and convince her that he would never let any harm come to her.

"There are many paths and many choices." Lunarys stood taller, and Zephyr's hand twitched towards his sword, a reflex older than thought, honed by every battle that had taught him how quickly a deal could sour. But Lunarys made no move towards Ysa, only lifted a pale hand. "Now hand me the High King's crown," she said, as if asking for a brew. "Now that it's no longer buried, it hums for all the power-hungry to hear. It's safer with me."

"It's our leverage." Cyprian took a step back to signal whether he should memory walk into the folds of time.

But this wasn't any old mission. "We bargained. The choice is made," Zephyr replied, his chest tight.

Every fibre of his being willed him to refuse giving up the piece of history his kin had risked so much for, but he'd learned the difference between foolish pride and strategic surrender. Sometimes the best way to protect what mattered most was to let go of a lesser priority, however much it wrecked him. For his sins, he trusted the Binder, although he didn't like her.

For a beat, no one moved. Then, with a muttered curse, Cyprian's hand disappeared into the temporal fold, and Ysa flinched as he pulled out the crown. *Inkheart, Inkheart,* cooed Zephyr through the mate bond, *you won't have to endure it for long,* as ancient runes skated and twisted along the crown's band like minnows beneath ice.

The Binder tucked the High King's crown into her violet robes with the casual disregard of a thief on market day, and Ysa sighed with relief. The Binder said, "It's much safer with me. Ysadora, what was my wish for you at birth?"

His mate didn't miss a beat. "You wished for me to have courage, discernment, and love. And you told me to choose carefully who belongs in my inner circle, because my life depends on it."

Lunarys's pink shimmer lips curved in approval. "Well remembered. I suppose my neutrality is already compromised. When you meet Liora Bramick, please ask her what became of the young dragon rider who questioned her... I'm glad I answered your summons, Ysadora. Although I didn't come for you." The Binder locked eyes with Zephyr, sharp as struck flint and soft as dawn. "I came for the *Fatebreaker*."

Realisation dawned, and Zephyr's heart pounded as silver-blue light spilt from her fingertips and wrapped around him and his fellow mercenaries, stifling Zephyr's rising shadows, Wylda and Sequoia's vines and roots, and even Cyprian's sparks of time magic.

The magic felt like being wrapped in starlight and inevitability, gentle but utterly implacable. Zephyr's heart thudded, gaze colliding with Ysa's. They needed each other now more than ever, and he would have never agreed to the summoning if he had known this.

Horror filled the face he loved with his entire being, and in it, he saw the same terrible understanding. Ysa didn't have her father, or Maren, or Ferrith, and now she didn't even have him.

Her voice broke, "No."

"Others are arriving presently to speak with you, Ysadora," said the Binder. "Time, my dear, is thinning for us all. May your mate bond hold. For all our sakes."

"Inkheart, when trust is low, use the Rune of Unveilin–," said Zephyr, before his mate was ripped from him.

Then he was reeling through the universe, with his mercenaries and Mythros in tow, leaving the calligrapher's daughter alone in the howling Wastelands. There was no question in his mind: he'd tear through every trial to make it back to her. As the light claimed him, he pleaded with the universe for his mate to be brave and cruel enough for what came next.

36

YSADORA

Rider: Araminta Silberquill,
The Circle of Emberlight
Dragon: Vireza (Novawurm)
Characteristics: calm, observant, independent
Skills: silent flight mastery, cold endurance,
pathfinding in the skies
Known alliances: Kazimir Silberquill
(estranged brother)
Whereabouts: Last seen in Celestiva
– The Dragons and Riders of the Nebula Court
(second edition)

Faerie swallowed Zephyr in a cruel trick, and the mate bond stretched as thin as silk, as though he was nowhere my eyes could discern. The silence where he had been was a wound in the world.

My chaos magic responded instantly, erupting from my

quill in torrents of black ink that carved the air like scythes. When that wasn't enough, I took the dragon-kissed dagger and tried to peel back the light and shadows to reach him. I shouted his name into the empty air and hurled everything I had at the pocket of air, where he and the Binder had vanished: symbols that burned to look at, reality-warping spirals that made the ground buckle and split.

The Wastelands turned savage again, as if I were Tanuhja's daughter more than my father's. The horizon twisted into impossible knots, and the ground erupted outwards in violent waves that scattered the rare flowers blooming in the cracks of grey soil.

Fury and desperation clawed up my throat. He was gone. *Gone.*

But there was no target for my rage, no Binder to strike, only a vast, desolate emptiness. The slices I carved sealed themselves with mocking ease. What was my chaos magic compared to hers?

The Binder hung stars in their constellations and wove fate into patterns across the heavens. She didn't just wield chaos; she was its architect. As powerful as I was, as much as the faerie kings and queens wished to control me, my power meant nothing against her will. My frantic attacks were nothing more than a child throwing stones at the moon.

I sank to my knees, clutching my quill and dagger in my white-knuckled grip and the brittle, grey soil bit through my trousers. I was more alone in that moment than when Father had been taken from Larkspur.

At least then I'd had Maren and Ferrith. At least then I'd had the sense that the world was compact and full of friends, rather than wild and boundless and brimming with monsters. But as my rage ebbed, Father's memories swept through me.

Solitude can be a forge as much as a prison, he'd once whispered to himself long ago. He'd stood alone beneath alien stars without his brothers from the order, without his dragon, with only his wits and his quill. He had survived, and so could I.

Despite the heavy price for summoning the Binder, as the mercenaries had warned there would be, I had the missing piece of information I'd asked for: I was a reality anchor, just like Tanuhja, with the capacity for both creation and destruction, and my mate bond with Zephyr was a magical safety mechanism. A lifeline to keep me anchored. I clenched my fists, my nails making tiny moons in my palms. No wonder I felt so unmoored without him. What destruction might I bring if I lost control?

Lunarys had given me exactly what I needed to know, even as she'd torn away what I needed most.

The taste of salt and dust lingered on my lips as I pushed myself to my feet, wiping tears from my cheeks with the back of my hand. I counted each inhale until my heartbeat steadied. Odd that of all our allies, it was Liora whom she had drawn my attention to.

When you meet Liora Bramick, ask her what became of the young dragon rider who questioned her. I wondered what truth lay buried beneath the feathers and beads and courage of the Circle of Emberlight.

The wind stilled. And then, the sky answered.

A deep percussion rolled through my chest, a rhythmic thunder of wings that I recognised from Caldoron's time at Ebonspire. Next came the rush of displaced air, warm and heavy with a scent I had grown to love: ozone, starlight, and warm, leathery skin, wild and ancient as Faerie itself.

Dragons.

Three distinct shadows slid across the cracked wasteland like dark water. I looked up through the shimmer of sand and dirt that rose to see their wings spread wide against the low sky, their riders sitting astride them.

My heart thudded in a haphazard rhythm, and I found myself shrinking back, raising a hand to shield my eyes from the whirlwind of sand and debris kicked up by their landing. So this was who the Binder had meant when she had said that others would be arriving.

The first dragon to land sent shockwaves through the brittle ground. Liora's mount was a behemoth of metallic black and deep purple scales, each one palm-sized and pitted with craters from battles survived. The membrane stretched across its wings was translucent enough to show ink-dark veins beneath, even in the strange light of the Wastelands.

Liora leapt down from between its shoulder blades with practised ease, boots hitting the ground with authority. Her silver-blonde hair was braided with leather cords, and her face bore the kind of stillness that came from watching horizons. A deep green scarf wrapped around her lower face, and her deep grey eyes were visible once she lifted her flight goggles.

Two others rode with her.

The second rider, Phaedraen, had visited Ebonspire before, but here in the Wastelands, she seemed more on edge, with none of the easy smiles she had shared with

Cyprian. She was young and muscular, with feathers that hung from thin braids in her dark hair. Her golden drake was smaller but no less imposing. When it settled beside the first dragon and turned its wedge-shaped head towards me, I caught a glimpse of teeth like curved swords.

The third dragon descended with deliberate slowness, so I turned my attention to Liora. I had lauded the Circle of Emberlight as heroines, swooping down to help Father and Caldoron fend off the white dragon, and for their kind-hearted attempts to unravel hints of my chaos magic at Ebonspire. But now, with the Binder's warnings echoing in my mind, I wasn't sure their arrival was a good omen, after all.

Even so, I made a split-second decision not to portray enmity and arranged my expression into wonder. Lunarys had determined that a dragon was essential to our success, and the Circle of Emberlight's arrival was a chance to find out how Maren and Ferrith fared.

"Liora, Phaedraen, how did you find me here?"

Liora pulled down her scarf and embraced me as her dragon watched. "Thank the skies, you're in one piece. We found Ebonspire deserted, with signs of a skirmish, and have been tracking you for days. In hiding from your foes, you hid also from your allies."

I pretended I had no doubts about her, when my keen awareness of precisely how many millimetres separated my quill and dagger from my hands told another story. "Did Maren and Ferrith not find their way to you? We sent them with word."

"I'm afraid not. It could be that the sisters who remained at court have since welcomed them." Her face grew tight. "But we know from Thalindra about the meeting of the faerie rulers called by the Spymaster."

My chaos magic flickered at the mention of the meeting: a brief shimmer that made the air around my hands distort. I forced it down. "He would rather be High King than Spymaster, and this time he gathers allies from across Faerie to strengthen his position."

"So I hear." Liora's voice carried the clipped authority of someone used to giving orders midflight. "The Court of Luminosity turned on Ebonspire, and I hear the Court of Silver Seas is also for Thiago."

I searched her face, but I gave nothing away about what I knew of the mission to the Court of Silver Seas. "So you're here to help?"

Her lips quirked. "Why else would we have come?"

"Say it plainly. Say you'll stand with me and Zephyr against Thiago."

For a blink, weariness flickered, and then her mask of diplomacy returned, so carefully worn that I couldn't discern whether it hid aid, mercy, or ruthlessness. "I stand with you, but don't expect lockstep obedience. There are some things you don't yet understand about Faerie," said Liora, and the Court of Lore rune on my hip stung hot and bright with her blunt truth.

Frustrated, I turned my attention to the third dragon landing. It was beautiful, with pink veins streaked through its purple scales like sunset clouds, and forked horns swept back from an elongated skull.

Its rider was much older and new to me. Her scarf was a working brown that covered hair dyed a faded blue, dust-stained from travel, and where it had loosened around her wrinkled throat, there was intricate beadwork in shades of silver.

"I haven't met your third rider."

"That's Araminta. Give her a moment. She prefers dragons to people."

Araminta. The name stirred something deep in my father's borrowed memories, but I couldn't grasp it. The older woman dismounted, her movements careful but not frail. Dust flared as she jumped the final few feet to the ground, and she rested there a moment, one weathered hand resting on her dragon's neck as if drawing strength from the contact.

She inclined her head slightly at me, but said nothing, although I had the distinct impression that there was plenty she could have said. Her dragon's molten silver gaze didn't waver from my face, and I found myself wondering what secrets were written in the lines of my expression that I didn't even know I was revealing.

Liora tilted her head to one side, studying me with the same intensity as her dragon. "What are you doing in the Wastelands, Ysadora?"

I weighed up how much truth to offer. "I'm on my way to Father at the Court of Bones."

Araminta's hands, which had been carefully adjusting her dragon's harness, went completely still, and the three dragons formed a loose circle some distance around me, blocking any escape route across the silvered dunes.

My heart hammered. The absurdity of running from a dragon was clearly why I needed one of my own. Even at rest, they dominated the landscape. Lunarys had said the dragons knew the first reality anchors. Did they sense what I was? The way their ancient eyes studied me felt like recognition, though whether that boded well or ill, I couldn't tell.

Liora's dragon shadowed her movements as she stepped closer. "Of course. It was clever to come this way. Even warrior fae prefer to avoid the Wastelands. I'm sure Thalindra has healed Kazimir by now. We will take you there as soon as we are finished here, and test your stomach for the skies. But where is Zephyr Ashmoor, if not with you?"

My chaos magic hummed under my skin again, responding to the ache of his absence, thinking of what he might be enduring. "Your guess is as good as mine."

Her eyes narrowed, and her dragon's nostrils flared as it sampled my scent, and I understood why Ferrith had such an aversion to them. "If he's beyond the reach of your mate bond, then he's vulnerable. And if you're uncertain of his whereabouts, that puts us all at a disadvantage."

I bristled, exhaustion and grief making me snappish. "My mate would never put me at a disadvantage. Zephyr is not known for straying by accident."

"I like you, Ysadora." Liora's lips thinned into something that wasn't quite a smile. "But there's no room for romantic declarations when Faerie is being rewritten. I don't believe in males or mates."

"You don't have to believe in him, but I do." The words came out fiercer than I intended, my voice cracking with the strain of defending someone I loved who wasn't here to defend himself. "I know the difference between absence and abandonment. If he's not here, it's because he's buying us time, carving a path we can't yet see, or bleeding in a place none of us can reach. He's never careless."

"I hope that's true. Because if the two of you fail, the

Spymaster will make you his servant." She sighed and exchanged glances with her sisters from the Circle of Emberlight. "You wanted me to speak plainly. Emberlight governs the Court of Nebulas only in the absence of its rightful ruler. We do not have a vote at the meeting of the rulers. But we can help in other ways. All this talk of belief. What I believe is that certain females are born to ride, Ysadora. And the Spymaster's plans make it a necessity. You may be a hard person to find, but you're exactly where you need to be, here in the Wastelands."

Goosebumps trailed up my arms. "What do you mean?"

Araminta spoke for the first time, her voice like crackling stars, "The girl has not been trained."

Phaedraen huffed a breath, and her golden drake echoed the sound with a snort that sent sparks dancing through the air. "Neither were we, Araminta."

Araminta ran her fingers over her scarf beads as if they were a talisman. "We lived amongst the dragons. We bided our time. She had her nose in books in the mortal realm."

"There is no time. It must be now," said Phaedran, urgency colouring every word.

"She will take the test," said Liora. "The old bones will determine if she can proceed to *Kindling*."

All the while, the dragons turned their great heads to eye me with disdain: Liora's dragon had a calculating, exposing gaze; Phaedran's sunflare drake was more overtly hostile, releasing a controlled burst of light that sent spots dancing across my vision; worst of all was Araminta's, which seemed to catalogue every breath I took, every flutter of my pulse.

Phaedran glared at her dragon, which responded by

lifting its chin in what could only be described as aristocratic disdain. "I would say they're not usually this unhelpful, but that would be a lie."

"Dragons sense what we can't. They don't yet consider you one of us, although I hope that will soon change," said Liora.

They must have sensed the way lingering chaos magic hummed under my skin like barely banked coals, and the residual distortion it had left in the Wastelands' fragile reality. However much I tried to hide my emotions from the Circle of Emberlight, the dragons could probably taste my grief and disquiet.

"Are you willing?" prompted Liora. Her dragon shifted its weight, and I felt the vibration through the soles of my boots.

Watching the three riders and their dragons, I understood something fundamental. Each partnership was a fusion of will and power that transformed both dragon and rider into something greater than either could be alone.

Much like my relationship with Zephyr. It was more than companionship: it was symbiosis. And if I were to protect myself and those I loved, I would need this kind of partnership. While I was with them, I would probe deeper into the reason for the Binder's warning.

"I am willing. I will do your test. And then you'll take me to Father."

Liora's smile was wolfish, and behind her, her dragon's lips pulled back to reveal teeth like black daggers. "I told you, Araminta. She has courage in spades."

Araminta finally met my eyes, and in them, there was satisfaction where I had expected scorn.

ZEPHYR

Hollowsight Gargoyle: stone body, eyes like hollow voids, three-inch talons. Once Seraphine of the Court of Cavernous Dreams, sister of Faelen, gifted in tunnelling caves and hiding secrets in stone.
– The Secrets of Faerie's Veiled Beasts by Zephyr Ashmoor

Lunarys's light engulfed them, and Zephyr was reminded of how accustomed he had become to shadows and why Ysadora's void didn't unsettle him. Darkness held him without asking him to shine. It didn't pretend to purify. It simply allowed him to exist. He didn't show panic—he never did—but his separation from Ysa overcame him like silence in the wrong key.

Gone was the creeping numbness when a loved one left, the instinct to pull back that which had become core to his identity after his mother and Veda died. He told himself Ysa could handle herself. He told himself she was strong. Both were true.

The third truth was less noble: he needed her.

Not as a crutch, not as a shield, but as the only quiet in him that didn't hurt.

With the bond quiet, every step felt unmoored, like he was walking through a world that had forgotten its shape. Time was thinning for them all, Lunarys had said, and Zephyr felt the pressure in his bones to line up all the pieces on the chessboard of Faerie to ensure his mate came out as the winner.

And then the light released them, and it was mercifully dark again. Ysa had described Lunarys's starry plains to him. Still, as gifted as his mate was with words, she hadn't prepared him for the way the starry plains existed outside the normal flow of time.

Zephyr was over a century old, yet here he was, experiencing wonders that were entirely new, all because of his mortal-raised Inkheart. Beneath his boots, the ground crunched like crushed diamonds. The sky stretched wide and fathomless above them, not black but a saturated navy blue that hosted a riot of constellations wheeling in slow, impossible orbits.

Some stars hung so close he could have reached up and plucked them like fruit. One bright star blinked and tumbled through the air, and the Binder caught it in her bare hand, tutting before pinning it in place again. The air smelled sweet and metallic, hinting at beauty amidst inhospitable places, but he couldn't help but think how easily fire and fury could spark here.

His kin sensed it, too, because they landed around him in practised formation, knees bent, alert and ready.

Mythros and Torven's hooves clinked gently against the diamond plain, their breaths misting out in silver coils.

Wylda dropped into a crouch, rope vines spilling from her wrists. "This place. It's too open for comfort."

Sese's feathered wings extended wide, her eyes scanning for threats in a place where none should exist. "Stay close."

Cyprian straightened slowly, fingers already working through temporal calculations that faltered the moment he glanced skywards. "Well, brother, we've certainly had some adventures together."

They looked to him for orders, for certainty, but Zephyr's mind, honed by orbits of war, fell utterly silent.

"You can't think about Ysadora." The Binder materialised beside them and began the intricate work of pinning up stars, as if she didn't have a moment to waste. "And you have work to do, *Fatebreaker*. You all do."

Zephyr growled, "You told us I was her magical safety anchor, and then you separated us."

The Binder's hair rippled as if caught by some celestial current, though no wind stirred the star-strewn air. She turned to face him fully, cerulean eyes pained with the weight of a thousand reckonings. "*Fatebreaker*, have you still not discarded the illusion that fate will ever be gentle? This isn't punishment. It is preparation. Anchors must sometimes drift to test the strength of their chains. What is forged without pressure is rarely strong enough to hold when the cosmos tilts. Your love is not destined to be ornamental. It must be capable of bearing weight."

"Be that as it may, I can't feel her."

"He was never this attached to me," said Sese to Wylda.

"The timelines are knotted here," said Cyprian. "I can't get a clear read on anything."

The Binder ignored them both. Her silver hair shone against the canvas of the night sky, and she raised one long-fingered hand, dipped in night, and caught another falling star before lifting it overhead and pinning it into place, her other hand already preparing the next.

"You can't feel her, you say, but are you truly listening?"

He bristled and then centred himself, and the bond was there after all: a whisper when it should have been a song.

Lunarys smiled and lifted one dark-tipped hand, fingertips trailing starlight like ribbons. The constellations shuffled, rearranged into patterns he did not understand: sigils, maps, destinies still developing. "Satisfied?"

Zephyr gave a curt nod, and his heart bloomed with its own symphony.

"Now if I were you, I'd make a start on all the work you promised."

His voice came out rougher than intended. "What work?"

She indicated the bargain lines on his arm. "You'll need your merry crew of outcasts to finish on time."

"Merry?" scoffed Sequoia.

Zephyr's jaw tightened as he looked at the bargain lines etched into his arm, now glowing faintly with the light of the celestial plain. They whispered of debts still outstanding, of oaths only half-kept. He rubbed them, suddenly aware of how many promises had been made on blood-slick battlefields, in smoky taverns, the backrooms of Faerie courts, beneath falling stars and cursed trees and in the rain-soaked ruins of old keeps. Each bargain line burned with the memory of grunt work traded for sanctuary for the cursed fae.

"There are too many in this realm who have forgotten that true kindness breeds loyalty. There are many turning points ahead of us yet, but given a splash of grit and a sprinkling of destiny, the remaining courts may be more amenable to honouring old boundary agreements unravelled in the Grimoire. I should like to see hopeless souls find their place again." The Binder lifted her gaze to the heavens.

Zephyr stood transfixed as silvered script burned itself across the starry plains, each phrase honouring the past of a cursed fae, marking out a path that could have belonged to any one of the mercenaries had they not found one another.

He flies still, but not towards home.
She conversed with rivers, now floods them in rage, her children turned to kelp.
The knight grew antlers and forgot all but his hunger.

Lunarys caught Zephyr's stricken look, but said only, with a voice like wind through bone, "When you absolve your bargains, do not forget the Thorn King."

"The Thorn King reads intentions like we read battlefields," said Cyprian. "You would have Zephyr go to him?"

The Binder dusted her palms together as though brushing off cosmic residue, with the weariness of one who'd seen a thousand crossroads chosen poorly. "The *Fatebreaker* will need help from you all. Choose this path or not. The decision is yours."

But Zephyr wasn't thinking of the obstacles in his path, only of the ones Ysa might face. He didn't dare to ask about his own fate, but there was nothing he wouldn't do for his mate. "What did you mean when you mentioned Liora Bramick and the young dragon rider who questioned her? The Circle of Emberlight is pivotal to our prospects. Liora is an ally."

"Liora is...complicated, but that is a problem for your mate to unknot. One soul, two paths."

Frustration frothed in him. How was he meant to protect Ysa when he was navigating blind, while his uncle sat on reams of knowledge like a dragon hoarding gold? Every question he asked splintered into two more, and still the answers came wrapped in riddles or silence. Protection required clarity and strategy, not half-truths buried beneath Faerie politicking.

"What did the first reality anchors sacrifice, Lunarys?"

The Binder stilled, and galaxies whirled in eyes rimmed with paper creases. "Their humanity. Their connections to the world they were trying to save. They failed because they forgot why reality mattered. But you are a master of histories, Zephyr Ashmoor, and that is no small thing."

Cyprian pursed his lips. "And Ysa isn't like the previous reality anchors."

Zephyr nodded. "Her family, her community, is everything to her. Maybe because she was brought up in the mortal world."

"The two of you are similar that way, *Fatebreaker*. There is nothing you won't do for those you love, and love is all there is left, even when the stars are dust. So you understand why I agreed to hide her in the mortal world and also why it was essential that your paths crossed? Now she is in Faerie, the mate bond means she stands a narrow chance of tipping the scales of Faerie the right way. But love can be a chain as easily as it can be a foundation." Lunarys paused. "I would very much like your mate bond to be a love story rather than a cosmic funeral pyre."

Zephyr's lashes dropped to hide the expression in his storm-cloud gaze. His voice was quiet, almost resigned: "I would too. But I've only ever seen love end in ash." Beneath the practised detachment, his heart leaned towards something brighter.

"And yet, for all your own history, you practice love in its many forms well, *Fatebreaker*." Lunarys paused. "I sense the horses would like very much to run wild beneath the stars if you would like to leave them with me."

Zephyr growled, "Mythros stays with me. He's more than a mount."

"Torven, too. He doesn't like change," said Wylda, although he never baulked, and she meant that he was family.

"Of course. The dragons will smell the starlight on the horses. Either way, if they survive their curiosity, they may well earn a legend of their own. Now go." Light ribboned from her fingers in radiant, undulating waves.

Zephyr closed his eyes against the brilliance. It wasn't painful, but it pressed, passing through him rather than over him. He heard the soft creak of Cyp's leathers. Wylda called out to Sese, soft and low. Sese herself took a quiet breath, like she did when she steadied her aim. Mythros whinnied.

Then Zephyr opened his eyes, and the impossible vastness of the starry plains had vanished. The sky was once again where it belonged: high, distant, and blue-grey with dawn, though with the Binder gone, the sky was dimmer. The ground beneath them no longer shimmered like diamonds, but held firm, cold and real, the scent of damp earth rising to meet him. He was relieved that the warhorse and gelding remained with their group, where they belonged.

The transition from the ethereal to run-of-the-mill Faerie seemed to him like coming down from a fever dream, only to find the world still wrong. Zephyr's shadows, which had been subdued in the starlight, spread eagerly across the familiar terrain.

With a weary breath, he turned to his kin. "I can do this alone."

Even as he spoke, his shadows scattered like scouts, skimming over stone and root, but his fiercest one peeled away, and he sent it threading back through the veil towards the Wastelands. Towards the half of his soul still out of reach.

"Not a chance," said Wylda. "I've rested enough."

Cyprian gave a hollow chuckle. "We can rest when we're ash."

Sese stretched her wings, testing her readiness. "Same song. Different battlefield."

He didn't show them how grateful he was, but they knew. "Then, you heard Lunarys. We have work to do."

Face set with grim resolve, Zephyr pulled the map from the saddlebag and rolled it out with a crackle of parchment. The map steadied him in a world that had become too fluid, and he traced his finger from their position over a suggested route that both fae and horses would weather, even at pace. Then with fierce love in his heart, he and his kin trekked into danger, like they'd done a thousand times before.

They worked without rest and without the compensation of coin, which Loxley, in particular, would have found difficult had he been there. Though they were accustomed to working in different pairings and without their full contingent as necessities arose, it felt to them all —with the exception of Sequoia, who tolerated community rather than embraced it—that their circle was incomplete without Ysa, Loxley, Maren, and even Ferrith.

As the date of the meeting of the Faerie rulers drew uncomfortably closer, Zephyr and his remaining mercenaries spent precious hours in blazing fields, culling the rot-touched deer that threatened one court's sacred groves, in exchange for sanctuary to the gilded night crawler who had once been Roderick Sunsinger of the Court of Starry Flight. All the while they waded through ankle-deep decay, courtiers sipped wine and pretended the blight didn't exist.

"Cowards." Wylda wrapped a scarf tight around her face against the stench, though she did not falter from their task.

But Zephyr barely heard her. His shadows moved with mechanical precision, cutting down the diseased creatures with the same detached efficiency he'd once reserved for battlefields. Each strike was perfect, emotionless, his body moving on instinct while his mind went somewhere else entirely. Somewhere that didn't ache with Ysa's absence.

"Zeph—" Sese's voice cut through his trance as she grabbed his sword arm. "The deer are down. You're hacking at corpses."

He blinked, looking down at the mangled carcass

beneath his blade, not remembering the last dozen strikes. His chest felt hollow, scraped clean, and he longed for the river of the mate bond to surge once more.

The next bargain required them to wade through putrid wetlands, dragging bloated corpses from the ceremonial pools. Cyprian used his temporal magic to speed up their task. Still, their hands reeked of death and bog water, but a sharp-nosed faerie queen had offered the mirror stalker, once Silva Glasstrill of the Court of Madness, sanctuary for their efforts, and so the mercenaries endured.

Zephyr worked with grim determination, hauling body after body without pause. Exhausting himself physically was easier work than using his lore magic and taxing his saturated mind, and for that, he was grateful. He had come so close to losing himself in Tanuhja's dream and shuddered still at the thought that he might have lived centuries more, unable to put Ysa's name to the face that haunted him.

Better to be dealt a quick death than that, better to die toiling in killing fields than for his lips never to form the shape of her name again or to taste the toffee sweetness of her tongue.

They cleaned rot from the bellies of sleeping giants, half-submerged in glade grasses. The giants' dreams leaked into Zephyr's saturated mind, a balm somewhat: visions of younger days when the world was green and whole.

For the next obligation, they crossed into wind-flayed highlands, where shrieking wraiths had made a nest in a ruined watchtower, to free it for a faerie king who had agreed in return to provide sanctuary to Nyra Silverbough of the Court of Wild Ferns. Wylda baited the spirits with her blood and sealed the stones with salt and sigils.

On and on, the mercenaries toiled, each task revolting yet purposeful. They hunted root-leeches the size of wolves in a grove where light did not penetrate and spent a full day in darkness, killing blind.

In the absolute darkness, Zephyr found a terrible peace. His intensity bordered on reckless. Here, he could pretend the world had shrunk to just his blade and his breathing. Here, he could forget that somewhere across the realms, his mate was facing dangers without him.

"Brother." Cyprian was gentle but firm. "You're scaring us."

Zephyr looked at their faces, asking himself when he had become someone his family had to fear.

They entered a vale, where the trees wore the faces of the dead and moaned with unfinished farewells. For every echo they calmed, Zephyr felt the weight of his own unfinished business with his mother, with Veda. But also the growing certainty that some farewells could be peaceful, that love didn't always have to end in reproach.

For every echo they calmed or tree they felled, they won a day's sanctuary for the cursed fae. They stood knee-deep in red snow under a sky that refused to thaw, carving out the bones of an ancient war beast entombed in ice, that one king dreamed of resurrecting. The cold bit through their armour, but Wylda's vines bloomed with spring flowers, a reminder that life and beauty persisted.

He and his kin endured each degrading, soul-staining task willingly, because the broken deserved sanctuary. No rot, no blood, no crawling thing could turn Zephyr from the path. He'd scrub bones in silence, wade through carrion, choke on smoke and shame, whatever the bargains demanded.

Each act of service was a small rebellion against the injustice of the fallen courts. If their work earned just one more outcast fae a place to rest, a sliver of dignity, a chance to live, then he would kneel in filth a thousand times. In that willingness to serve and sacrifice, he found not humiliation, but strength.

The kind of strength that came from choosing love over fear, hope over despair, and connection over isolation.

Faerie had turned its back on the outcasts, but he wouldn't. In refusing to abandon them, the mercenaries created a vision of Faerie in which power was something that didn't dominate but protected, and to Zephyr it seemed like some of his mother's hopes had survived her death.

Still, the monsters' stories were louder now. Cyprian called his name more than once, but Zephyr's head was full of teeth and wings and gnashing and sobbing. It was like being buried beneath the bones of everything he had learned.

As though he were parchment: written on, rewritten, torn and singed and stitched back together. Sometimes he couldn't hear his own thoughts over the cursed fae voices anymore, and he knew he needed to find a way out for himself as well as them, or he would no longer be whole, no longer be the mate Ysa deserved.

After the tasks were done, when Mythros and Torven grazed and the others slept, in abandoned cabins or desolate groves, or beneath the canvas of sky that the Binder had dotted with diamonds, Zephyr sent out his shadows to look for Loxley, Maren, and Ferrith, but he never found them. But the searching itself became a kind of prayer, a way of holding space for the missing pieces of their family.

His other shadow did not return, but it comforted him to know that his mate lived and that she was not alone. The bond was muted across the vast distances, but he dared to hope that the Circle of Emberlight would keep Ysa safe. He was beginning to understand that the bond wasn't just about needing her: it was about choosing to build something together, even when apart.

Only their visit to the Thorn King remained. Then he could find his mate, like he promised he always would. He could haul her into his arms and pray to the ancients to gift them a few precious moments together before Faerie realigned along its godsforsaken fault lines.

The two of them deserved that at least: time to breathe in the scent of each other's skin, to taste each other's lips, to tug her body like a jigsaw against his, where she belonged. He held that hope in the big expanse of his mercenary heart and felt only a little rash for needing the calligrapher's daughter so much that he'd gladly give up his name to any mortal fool who asked.

It struck him that he hadn't been hopeful before Ysa. Now that he was, he loved her all the more for it. Hope was more than loving her; hope was becoming worthy of her love. Of somehow creating sanctuary for others, how Ysa had created it for him.

Although Zephyr yearned for Ebonspire with a strength of feeling bordering on madness, he rued how long it had taken him to understand: safety was found in people, not in a place.

It was found most of all in his mate.

38

YSADORA

Species: Astral
Appearance: ridged horns, vast wings with
tapered edges, silver and blue colouring
Characteristics: proud, merciless, clever
Abilities: fire-breathing, navigation, telepathy
with their rider, immense speed
- The Dragons and Riders of the Nebula Court

" The old bones will determine if she can proceed to *Kindling*," said Liora, whom the Binder had pointed a night-dipped finger at.

Even so, I followed her and her sisters from the Circle of Emberlight, with their beaded and braided hair, deeper into the Wastelands, as if we were merely off to the maypole. The silence stretched between us like a taut wire.

I wanted to ask what the test would involve and what the old bones had said of them, once. I wanted to ask if the sisters from the Circle of Emberlight remembered who

they were before they were dragon riders, but the
Wastelands swallowed questions. So I kept walking
behind Araminta, who favoured her left leg with each
step, and kept my questions caged as my legs wearied and
my clothes stuck to my skin.

High above, silhouetted against the bruised sky, their
dragons wheeled in quiet circles. They did not intervene.
They did not descend. But my attention tugged towards
them and their heat across the distance, like breath
through a keyhole. Their circling cast flickers of shadow
across the broken ground, brief eclipses that cooled my
skin for only seconds before the dry heat returned, heavier
than before.

Liora and Phaedran did not look back, but Araminta
did sometimes.

Father's memories twanged in the depths of my mind,
and I couldn't help feeling there was more to her than met
the eye.

Phaedran began to hum a low and rhythmic tune, like
a song meant for marching, and the other two riders joined
in, their voices thin and reedy against the wind, but
something in the harmony made my chest tighten. There
was sorrow in it, and loss, and perhaps hope buried so
deep it had nearly forgotten itself.

Still, I walked, because to turn back was to admit I
feared the truth of myself more than I feared dragon flame.
I didn't. Not yet. Zephyr could love monsters, and even if
the duality of nebula and chaos turned me monstrous, I
could match his hopes for the future with my own.

By now, the copper sky had dulled to grey, and I
craved water. The three riders were unconcerned. They
walked with the measured pace of those who had made

this journey many times before. After several hundred metres, a path took shape amongst the silvered dunes, laid with blackened bone stakes half-sunk into the shifting earth.

My pulse leapt to a jagged rhythm and then, like a mirage solidifying into something ancient and terrible, we came upon a dragon skeleton jutting from the landscape like a crown of bones. At the dragons' cry above, the bones twitched.

To my astonishment, the sisters of the Circle of Emberlight fell to their knees in the sand—Araminta more carefully than the others—and bowed until their foreheads kissed the ground. The bones were bleached white and vast, ribs arched like the ruins of a cathedral. My chaos magic flared, but the dragon bones did not stir again when the sisters beckoned me forward.

I hesitated, just for a breath. What I would have given to have Zephyr at my side. Then I stepped into the shadow of those ribs as the three females still knelt in the sand, though they now sat erect with palms on their thighs.

"Don't be afraid," said Phaedran, gazing at the skeleton with its hollowness returned as one might stare at an old lover turned to stone. "When the Order of the Glyph fell, many females wanted to ride, but dragon riding is not a whim; it's a calling that's written in the stars."

Liora nodded. "Unlike the Order of the Glyph, our sisterhood did not inherit centuries of dragon rider tradition. So we turned to this ritual as a necessary precursor to *Kindling*. A way to assess both legitimacy and survival. This site—where the first bonded dragon fell—is where would-be riders are judged. Pilgrims, under the

Circle of Emberlight's escort, present themselves to the bones to prove their purity of intent and magical compatibility. Kneel, Ysadora and open yourself to the old magic. If the marrow stirs, you'll be shown which dragon to approach at *Kindling*. If not, you walk away with nothing but dust on your knees."

My throat was parchment dry. "How many have attempted this rite?"

"Too many," said Araminta quietly.

Liora's jaw tightened. "Two hundred and thirty-one. Twenty-seven went onto *Kindling*, and ten make up the Circle of Emberlight's ranks."

Those were odds only the insane would take. "What happened to those who failed?"

Phaedran looked away.

"And the others?" I pressed.

Liora brushed sand from her sleeve. "Some were broken, bones snapped clean under the strain. Some were buried beneath the stars, left forgotten. Others burned by dragon flame, erased without mercy. Failure is absolute when it comes to dragons. Few live to speak of it. Fewer still are whole when they do."

Araminta gave a dry huff that might've been a laugh. She tapped the twisted scar just visible beneath the edge of her scarf. "She's not exaggerating."

I stared at the three of them, wondering if, like them, I would be deemed worthy. Perhaps the bones would tell me that I was too much or not enough. That dragon fire would never be mine to command. That I would burn or tumble or be crushed by the will or body of a being far greater than I.

"What if it doesn't choose me?" I asked, and there was

no mercy in their faces, only expectation and perhaps even thrill.

"On your knees, Ysadora, then place your palm to the sternum," said Araminta, as wind moaned low through the ribcage like the last sigh of a world lost. The bones there were polished smooth from centuries of initiates doing the same.

I knelt slowly and pulled my damp hair over one shoulder, then laid my palm against the cool sun-bleached bone. How would it weigh me—the girl brought up in the wrong realm and still trying to make this one hers?

Magic gathered at the edges of my skin like frost, and the earth beneath me pulsed once, faint and slow. The sisters chanted in old fae, and their words moved like calligraphy set loose on vellum: looping and sharp, beautiful in form yet laced with danger as if binding fate to the page of the world.

The dragon bones creaked as if shifting their weight in deathless slumber, and beneath my hand, the cool bone warmed. Was this what the Binder meant about dragons knowing the first reality anchors? The warmth felt like recognition. I gasped, wanting Zephyr, wanting Father, wanting Maren and Ferrith.

Power crackled around me. For a single moment, I wasn't in the Wastelands. I was in a mind as old as time, and she showed me a dragon with ridged horns that curved like ink strokes against the sky and vast wings that tapered to sharp edges, with silver veins across deep blue like a living constellation.

That dragon, its clever reptilian eyes like mirrored moons, opened its jaws and spoke my name in a hiss of starlight: *Ysa. Reality anchor. Child of ink and chaos.*

Then I was back in my body again, my palm tingling with residual magic as I pulled it back. The three sisters, strangers all, watched me with expectant faces, and loneliness was a physical ache in my chest, whether for Zephyr or the dragon whose name now fizzed on my lips, a gift from the old dragon bones. What if I failed? What if I burned? What if I were too much chaos and not enough light?

"And?" prompted Liora as the three dragons— Satharion, Sindrosira, and Vireza—landed heavily behind their riders, fracturing the light and kicking up sand that rasped in my throat. Her deep green scarf had barely shifted, and the stillness in her face was eager now, though she tried to hide it. "Did the bones gift you a name for *Kindling* or did they leave you empty?"

I met her gaze and exhaled the name I hadn't known a moment before, "Ryvaris."

Phaedran gave Liora a sharp glance. Araminta stiffened.

Only Liora smiled, and the curve of it cut like glass. "Ryvaris is unbondable."

"Perhaps, but the bones are never wrong." Phaedran's throat bobbed with unease.

"Perhaps Ryvaris has been waiting for her all along," said Araminta quietly.

Liora stood. "We ride for the Court of Bones to prepare Ysadora. If Ryvaris answers, we'll all bear witness. If he doesn't, Faerie will forget she ever knelt at this altar."

I met Liora's gaze and nodded once. The prospect of seeing Father filled me with a giddy, child-like joy. But inside, something coiled tighter. I had seen my dragon's clever reptilian eyes and witnessed the bonds between dragon and rider. I would ink my name into the sky if I had to. Ryvaris would rise for me, because without him, the future Zephyr and I hoped for would disintegrate like parchment in flame.

Though the Spymaster still coveted my abilities, he would soon find I was no longer his to bend or barter.

I would secure my freedom and Elowen's, and watch Zephyr unseat Thiago from his throne.

39

ELOWEN

If I lose myself in the magic Vixora granted me,
what remains of my mortal self?
- Ferrith's diary

Her father did not return to take more fingers.
Elowen was spared that much at least,
although it was cold comfort. The stench in the
cell clung to her skin and lodged in the roof of her
mouth until even breathing tasted like rot.

There were no fresh linens, no soap, not even a basin
for washing. Elowen's skin was bruised and sallow, and
her soft blonde hair was matted with grease and neglect.
She had always been slight; now her finely tailored
garments sagged from her body, stained and crusted with
blood.

She was filth in finery: a daughter turned prisoner, a
noble turned waste.

The nub where her finger once was had healed into a puckered scar, no thanks to her parents. If she was careful not to brush the tender flesh, Elowen could move her hand without wincing. But every time she did, her mind filled in the phantom weight of the part that was gone.

It was a reminder of ownership: how every part of her had been claimed by her parents.

She imagined carving hateful truths into the walls of her cell to shame them with blood from the nub of her freshly torn finger, if she had to. Each groove a curse, each smear a warning. But Elowen was done performing grief in private. Her pain deserved an audience.

When she named their sins, her voice would thunder before witnesses, too loud for silence or comfort.

Her cracked lips curved. Or perhaps she would indulge one of her many violent fantasies.

For now, the solitude in her cell pressed in from the corners. There was no voice to soothe her, no acknowledgement of her pain. The absence of touch became its own form of starvation.

So Elowen's thoughts echoed alongside the dripping ceiling. She counted every crack in the stone until her mind rebelled, counted every crumb from the bread and slivers of fish and fruit to take her mind off her severed finger.

Time folded in on itself. Without sun or stars, days bled into nights without clear delineation. Her sense of reality frayed at the edges, but then in recent memory, only Ysadora had given her cause to hold on. Every sound in the corridor spiked dread. She lived in the pause before pain, a kind of limbo engineered to break will.

Her father's meticulous cruelty had taught her

something valuable: how to endure and how to hate with precision. Her voice grew hoarse from disuse, but not from lack of thought. Her mind raced, reaching for exits that didn't exist, for alliances that she hoped feverishly still existed.

She lay awake in the still dark, time shapeless around her, wondering what her father planned next. Why hadn't Xaire come to soothe or free her? Where were Ysadora and Zephyr? Her father was meticulous in his cruelty. Perhaps Ysa *was* capable of destroying Faerie. Even so, Elowen's love for her burned bright and unrepentant.

Uncle Orin had promised help, and he did, in small increments, never at a set time and always when her father's attention was turned elsewhere. He brought meagre offerings from the kitchens and sometimes rich meats in berry juices that she wolfed down, secreted away from the family dinner table.

Sometimes he brought a clean, moist cloth for her to wash, although he never went as far as a clean dress. Often, he wordlessly took away the bucket of excrement, and Elowen turned away her face in shame. Once, he swept her cell clean as she slept.

"You are so accustomed to silence that Thiago thought not to put more than simple enchantments in this cell." Orin's broom swept steadily, the scratch of bristles against stone filling the stillness. "But I know your father's tricks and I've undone them all. Speak freely."

"He thinks he has won." Her voice was winter itself. She hated the thought of her father's crowing arrogance, that making her feel smaller inflated his ego. "Where is he now?"

"Pursuing alternative trails. The title *Spymaster* always suited him more than his own name."

"What of the bloodheart tree?"

"It still rains its crimson leaves."

A thrill of satisfaction ran through her.

Orin sighed deeply. "I must tread carefully. Thiago does not take well to open defiance. I can do more for you if he believes you are serving your punishment. My brother's ego is vast and quick to bristle."

Elowen gave a bitter smile. "I tire of playing the part he demands. But let him think he wins, for now." She paused. "What of my mother and Xaire? Do they suffer as I do?"

His eyes, so like Zephyr's, filled with regret, and Elowen was reminded how her cousin was the better male in all ways that counted. How long ago had Zephyr offered her an escape route that she had refused? "Your mother is trapped in her own shadows, and Xaire walks a dangerous path between loyalty and survival. A path that I know all too well."

Elowen's eyes sharpened. "Then you understand more than you let on. Are you truly on my side, Orin?"

Orin set down his broom and leaned against the wall, his usual bumbling manner stripped away. "I am. I have not told anyone of the bargain mark on your ankle, have I?"

She had little leverage in the cell, but it had been her test to ascertain whether her uncle would weaponise knowledge against her. "No, you haven't. And it must never be revealed."

He nodded. "If Thiago knew the extent of your interactions, he would break you beyond repair. Our survival means choosing battles carefully. This game requires patience. I have an idea, if you'll consider it."

His use of *our* made gratitude swell in her, and Elowen dipped her head to hide her sudden tears. How quickly she would have once disparaged Orin for his tentative phrasing. "I'm listening."

"Trick your father by releasing the calligrapher's daughter from your bargain."

Elowen sucked in a breath. Clever. She'd underestimated him. For a blink, she wondered what the Court of Silence might have been—what her own life might have been—if Orin had won the throne and not her father. Then she said, "I can't let her forget me."

Orin's expression softened, and for a moment, he looked more like the benevolent uncle he had been before her father withered his soul. "I have found that fear of loved ones forgetting you often speaks to our mind rather than theirs."

She was bereft to lose the mark that was proof of her connection to Ysadora, and doubts bobbed in her mind: Ysa would let her rot in her cell, that Ysa would be relieved to be rid of her obligation, that no one would ever love her by choice. But Orin was adamant that keeping the bargain would bring greater wrath on them all, should her father see it.

In the end, the logic was clear: Elowen had nothing further to lose, while Ysadora and Zephyr remained at risk.

So, Elowen agreed and released Ysadora from her bargain, though severing that lifeline was a bitter sacrifice. The psychic wound cut deeper than any blade. And with the enchantments lifted, she did something else.

She reached telepathically for her twin, although his abandonment had made her tender heart stone. The connection, when it came, felt hollow: like shouting into a void that swallowed her words whole.

Xaire's mind was there, but walled off: no acknowledgement, no warmth, nothing of the twin bond that had once sustained her. But that didn't stop Elowen. She listed every grievance, every betrayal, every moment he'd chosen their father over her or turned his back on her when she needed him most.

I needed you, Xaire. I still need you.

She didn't know if the words reached him. She didn't know if he flinched, if he heard her voice tremble in the space where their connection once pulsed bright in the wretched silence. But she poured it all in anyway: the fury, the sorrow, the cold truth of her loneliness. She hurled her pain like stones into a still lake, hoping something— anything—would ripple back. And still, he did not answer.

But now, at least, he knew.

TIME SLIPPED FORWARD AGAIN, knotting and folding over itself like fabric in a storm. When her father's voice came like thunder through the walls of the cell, Elowen startled. Relief came first, quickly soured by dread. She hated the part of herself that still listened for his voice, that still remembered when it had once meant safety. Now his voice was just a reminder: the walls had never kept him out, only her in. He was merely her king and had relinquished all rights to call himself her father.

But what of her mother?

Desolate skies, she yearned for another of Danaë's notes on monogrammed paper, anything to confirm she mattered. She didn't know what to name her. Coward? Victim? A warden in softer clothes? She wondered if her mother wept behind closed doors, or if she turned away, practised at pretending her daughter was never there at all.

Some days, Elowen hated her more than her father, because at least Thiago never hid the knife. She had learned that silence could be just as sharp as cruelty.

In the hallway outside her cell, her father did not restrain his anger. "Imbecile. What am I to do with them?"

A nervous subordinate stammered, "Two of them were glamoured to look like your nephew and the calligrapher's daughter when they went into the Wraithwoods, my king. None of our party wanted to enter that place, but we did it to please you."

Thiago's voice dropped to a deadly whisper, "So you lost half your party to the Wraithwoods, even though I mapped them out in exquisite detail for you, and you did not deem it necessary to verify who you dragged back to me?"

A hesitant breath. "We…thought the risk of delay outweighed—"

Her father cut in, dangerous even in his restraint. The heel of his boot drove into stone. "Your thinking is precisely the problem. You expect me to parade a false *reality anchor* at the gathering of courts?" The hallway went quiet but for the sound of cloth shifting, a gloved hand perhaps curling into a fist.

There was a yelp and the sound of shuffling feet. "No,

my king. They fooled us all. The red-haired male is known to be a companion of your nephew's. Even the hounds didn't scent the difference."

Victory blazed in Elowen's chest. Her father's perfect plans crumbled.

"First Esolas failed, now my spiders. The bloodheart tree bleeds my authority drop by drop, and still you make a fool of me." Her father's voice crackled like fire catching dry leaves. "If you cannot tell flesh from glamour, perhaps you deserve to be replaced by something conjured. Perhaps you don't deserve that whisper ring."

"It won't happen again, my king."

Her father snapped. "You've humiliated me before my allies and enemies. Find my nephew and the calligrapher's daughter before the meeting. Or next time, I'll feed you to the Wraithwoods myself. These three can join my daughter. Let her sit in the company she so craved. Let her choose between crown and conscience, between family and sentiment. The three pawns will be useful as leverage when my nephew and the calligrapher's daughter arrive."

"Shall I bind their magic?"

"Bind two fae detached from their court magic and a mortal, all of whom are lodged in the foundations of this keep?" Thiago scoffed. "No. Let them keep their little tricks. Power without a plan is nothing. They'll flail, waste energy, and reveal exactly how far they'll go." The heavy fall of his cloak brushed the stone. "But post guards. Discreetly. I want no surprises."

"G—guards?" stuttered the spy. "A shadow would surely be preferable?"

Her father's pause stretched so long that Elowen could taste his indecision. "Shadows are too dear. Steel will do."

To Elowen, it sounded like he had come up against the limits of his reach, although she couldn't be sure what had happened, only that for all his posturing about the failed efforts to capture Ysadora and Zephyr, he was rattled.

She thought maybe she would taunt him about the slow weep of leaves from the bloodheart tree, that for all his efforts still prophesied a change of king. Bracing herself, she sharpened her tongue, but her father's boot heels retreated.

Elowen pressed her scarred hand against her knee, the missing finger a constant reminder of his power over her. She trembled as adrenaline and tension eased, but a quiet part of her ached that he hadn't cared enough to check how she fared.

The sound of approaching footsteps made her heart hammer against her ribs: heavy boots, multiple sets, growing louder. She longed for the company of fellow captives as much as she feared it.

The cell door groaned open, and Elowen raised her eyes. One of her father's spiders shoved in three figures, travel-worn and grimy, the stink of the road clinging to their cloaks. The sudden influx of bodies made the already cramped cell feel suffocating.

One swore under his breath, and she recognised her cousin's friend Loxley under his overgrown beard, who had clowned around at court. The second, a red-headed female with fire in her eyes, stumbled, wrinkling her nose at the stench, and was caught by the most beautiful, tall blond male Elowen had ever seen. Something about him felt strange: a shimmer at the edges, although she could have sworn Ysadora had said the male kin she had brought to Faerie was mortal.

The door slammed shut, and the four of them exchanged glances.

Elowen knew of Ysa's kin from their ink messages, and in that moment, she desperately wanted them to like her. But instead of showing warmth, she straightened her spine and said coolly, "Welcome to my father's hospitality. If you're here to rescue me, you're terribly late and clearly under-qualified."

Loxley flashed a grin. "Sarcasm. The true sign of nobility in captivity. This is going to be fun."

The red-haired woman—Maren—lifted an eyebrow. "We made it further than anyone else, didn't we, Elowen?" She softened after a beat, although reluctantly. "Ysa will be over the moon that we found you. She was worried sick when she couldn't reach you during our last days at Ebonspire."

Elowen's breath fogged the stale air. "You left Ebonspire. Of course you did." Her last sanctuary, gone.

She must have been more tired than she thought, overwrought, or even hallucinating from something slipped into her food, because there, the blond male replicated across the cell. Three perfect copies materialised like the snowflake paper cutouts she made as a child.

Each wore with the same tattered cloak, golden hair tousled the same way, sky-blue eyes with the same calm, kind expression, yet they felt different. The first carried sorrow deep in the shoulders, the second held barely contained energy as if he might rip off the cell door, and the third stood with a stillness that spoke of newfound strength rather than hesitation.

Elowen blinked hard. "I'm losing my mind."

Maren offered a half smile, and worry flickered in her eyes. "Takes some getting used to, right?"

"A stroke of luck that you kept it together in front of Thiago and his spiders," said Loxley. "You're going to have to learn how to control it better."

"I'm aware." Ferrith's smile didn't quite reach his eyes despite the bravado. "But by all means, keep reminding me."

Elowen's spine pressed against the cold wall. "Is it…a trick of the light?"

Loxley clapped the middle Ferrith on the back. "You're not hallucinating. Our golden boy got himself blessed by the Wraithwoods, because apparently, he can't ever decide where to stand in a fight."

Then there was only one of him again, and he stood taller, shoulders squared despite their predicament. But Elowen caught the way he swayed slightly, one hand bracing against the wall. Whatever magic he'd just wielded had burned through him.

"That magic cost you something," said Elowen, thinking of her mother and the Wraithwoods.

Ferrith's jaw worked for a moment before he answered. "Anything worthwhile costs something." He paused and forced strength into his voice that his body clearly didn't possess. "I'm Ferrith."

Her breath hitched. "I know. Ysadora told me all about you. Are she and my cousin all right?"

Maren's face was grim in the dimness. "We wouldn't know, with your maniacal father after them."

"He is not *my* anything. Not anymore. I would've helped them if I could."

"Maren," said Ferrith. "Look at her hand."

423

Loxley's eyes sharpened as he took in her bandaged stump. "Fuck, that changes things." He studied her face with new respect. "Takes guts to cross the Spymaster."

Humiliation bloomed hot across Elowen's collarbones. She met Maren's gaze, ignoring the throbbing nub of her finger. "I know what he's capable of. If you're here to fight him, then I want in. I'm done being his."

Ferrith's eyes warmed. "Ysa loves her," he said, and Elowen's heart swelled. "That's enough for me."

Maren's tone was sharp, testing. "Pretty words, but they won't keep us alive when her father comes for us. You say you're done being his. But are you ready to be one of us?"

Loxley shrugged. "She was never one of them, not really. Why do you think I agreed to your idiotic plan to come here?"

"We have a way to stop him," said Ferrith. "It won't be easy, but I've got something to prove myself."

Loxley rolled his shoulders. "I've wanted to tear your father a new arsehole for entire orbits." He met Elowen's gaze. "I've watched him ruin too many good people. He won't ruin you, too. Not while I'm breathing."

A flicker of surprised laughter escaped her, brittle at the edges. "That's the stupidest thing anyone's ever said to me, including my twin."

Maren frowned. "We need proof we can trust her. Ysa's word is not enough for me. Not on this. Not with her being Thiago's daughter." And Elowen remembered that Maren was close to Kazimir and would protect Ysa above all else.

They were brave, these allies of her cousin's, and Elowen wanted to belong to their group, but the cost of rebellion was far greater than they could imagine, and she didn't know if they could ever see her as anything other than the daughter of the faerie king who held them captive.

The question lingered in her mind: would they accept her enough to stand by her side when it mattered most, even without the bargain she had made with Ysadora? Or would she still be alone when the dust settled, with even her twin silent, serving his own carefully veiled ambitions?

In reality, she had no choice but to take this leap of faith with these strangers. Hope was too fragile to carry alone.

Elowen allowed herself a thin, crooked smile. "I have someone on the outside."

Loxley's brow furrowed. "Who?"

She glanced at the locked door. "Orin."

There was stunned silence. Then Loxley threw his head back and laughed: loud, maniacal, incredulous laughter that echoed around the stone cell. It was the kind of laugh that bordered on madness, the kind that dared the world to defy it. It scraped at the silence her father had forced upon her, clawed into the cracks of the stone and made something come to life in her again.

Elowen didn't try to stop him. She let him laugh. She let her father hear.

Let him wonder what she was becoming in the dark.

Maybe Ysadora was the rising storm, but Elowen was the quiet knife.

YSADORA

Do not shun your shadows, dearest.
You have not yet learned that shadows
may provide comfort as well as stir fear.
- Rowena Ashmoor's letter to her son Zephyr

P haedran braced her step against her dragon's
scales and extended a hand. "Up and be quick
about it. Sindrosira is most likely to tolerate you,
but she's not glad about it."

Her dragon had seemed ready to incinerate me earlier,
but perhaps none wanted to carry me. It didn't matter.
My desire to see Father was stronger than caution. I
checked for my quill and dagger before grasping
Phaedran's palm and clambering up behind her onto the
dragon's back.

Sindrosira swung her head round, nostrils flaring, maw
yawning open to show her curved teeth: a reminder that I
was prey tolerated only by alliance. Her taupe-red scales

were warm beneath my palms, their surface ridged like armour hammered in dragon fire.

As I settled behind Phaedran, Sindrosira's breathing shifted from sharp huffs to something steadier: not acceptance exactly, but maybe she'd decided I wasn't worth the effort of throwing off.

"Hold tight." Phaedran pulled down her goggles and adjusted her scarf. "And don't look down if you're prone to sickness."

I didn't know how I'd fare because I hadn't ridden the skies on Caldoron when he'd been at Ebonspire, although Father had suggested it, because Caldoron had turned his head away when I neared him. The stiffening of his wings and his flare of smoke said *no* more clearly than words.

I had pretended not to mind, but I had stood under the star-strewn sky that night and wondered what it would be like to be welcome on a dragon's back. Until Zephyr had found me and carried me to bed with a twinkle in his sea-mist eyes.

I could still feel the barely-there pulse of him through the mate bond, distant but alive. Proof that he was still breathing. Still out there. Still mine. What would he make of me on dragon back?

One thing was for sure: despite our unease about Tanuhja's warning, Zephyr had always believed in me, that I could break the rules of Faerie or rewrite them. Where others saw limits, he saw possibilities. He was the reason I kept moving forward when fear threatened to root me in place.

I tried to suppress the worry swirling in my belly. My mate was powerful. He and the others would be okay. The least the Binder could have done was steer him towards a streak of good fortune, preferably one paved with coin, a reunion with Loxley and zero life-threatening detours.

I barely had time to complete my thought and wrap my arms around Phaedran's waist before her dragon's muscles bunched and we launched skywards into the falling night. The world fell away. My stomach dropped, tumbling somewhere in the silver dunes while the rest of me rocketed up.

The wind shrieked past my ears as we climbed through clouds and veils of falling darkness. Pure terror and exhilaration crashed together in my chest. This was why dragons ruled the sky, why it was dragons that would turn fate in our favour, and I revelled in the terrible exultant joy of it, utterly absorbed by wind and wing and the potential for destruction.

"First flight?" Phaedran shouted, and I could hear the grin in her voice.

"Yes," I managed, though the wind stole my breath.

"It gets easier. Or you get more reckless. Hard to tell which."

Below us, the landscape began to change, the shimmer of silver dunes giving way to darker land, twisted and dry, veins of black magic scarring the surface. To our left and right, Liora and Araminta rode their dragons in formation, but my attention kept drifting to the name that buzzed in my mind like a living thing.

"Tell me about Ryvaris," I called to Phaedran.

Her shoulders tensed. "He's an astral dragon," she said finally. "Bred when the magic of Faerie ran deeper and wilder than it does now. He's fast, merciless, and clever in ways most humans never expect. His navigation and speed are unmatched. Every rider who's approached

Ryvaris has done so believing they will bond, but he has a habit of burning them to ash."

Gooseflesh crawled up my arms. We were flying into shadow, but not Zephyr's familiar darkness. This felt *wrong*. Below us, bone sculptures jutted from cracked earth, not random bones, but human femurs twisted into spirals, ribcages woven into thorny crowns. Trees stripped bare reached up like skeletal fingers begging for mercy that would never come. I drew a breath that tasted like dust and old blood.

"Sweet merciful stars," I whispered.

"Yeah," said Phaedran grimly. "You'd think Thalindra would've improved the place with all the magic she has gained. But no. Bleak charm it is."

Sindrosira caught a downdraft, and we descended, the last light of day fractured and crawled like fingers across the desolate ground. To our left, Liora's dragon began its descent, wings angled low. Araminta followed a beat later. Below, the court stirred: shapes moved among broken arches and crumbled ramparts, their movements synchronised like marionettes guided by the same hand.

Suddenly, I didn't know whether Queen Thalindra was friend or foe.

But she had healed Father, and so I gritted my teeth as torches guttered to life along the broken parapets, guiding our passage. Sindrosira let out a low growl, not of fear but recognition. She circled once before gliding down, her great wings folding with practised menace as we landed hard on the blackened stone with a bone-jarring thud.

Dust swirled, and I waited for it to clear before I slid off the dragon's back and hit the ground with less grace than I hoped. My legs trembled from the flight. The air here tasted of old death and newer hungers, and the name Ryvaris burned brighter in my chest, as if responding to the nearness of so much concentrated magic.

Liora dismounted beside me, calling out something about stable grounds, but I barely heard her because there, beneath an archway carved from what looked suspiciously like a giant's ribcage, was a figure in black silk robes that I would have known in any realm, in any form. My heart stuttered. For a moment, we simply stared at each other across the ashen ground.

Then we were running to each other, he straighter, less gaunt, than I remembered, as if this court had given him back his youth. His limbs carried him with a grace that was both wonderful and wrong. We collided like stars falling into orbit, and his arms came around me with desperate strength.

"Father." The word came out broken against his chest.

He cupped my face, thumbs brushing away tears I hadn't realised were falling. "My brave, reckless Ysa. What are you doing in this cursed place?"

Before I could answer, footsteps approached across the stone. Araminta emerged from behind her dragon, pulling off her riding gloves. "She came for you, Kazimir. And for a dragon. But the real question is, brother, are you still having trouble with yours?"

"Brother?" The word scraped out of my throat.

I jerked back to stare at Father's pale face, then at Araminta with those same sharp cheekbones, those same brown eyes, the same elegant way of moving. And then the vault of Father's memories from the ancient stone cracked open in my mind: a brother and his older sister racing each other up the rocks, dreaming of flight, both obsessed with dragons; a hatchling resting its head in the sister's lap and the brother watching with envy poorly disguised as a smile; two younglings kneeling before a dragon too old for time, their eyes bright with hope and though the dragon turned its gaze to the older girl, only one sibling was destined to enter the Order of the Glyph. How had I missed it?

"Oh, yes." Araminta removed her scarf to show the deep scar on her throat. "Did he never mention his dear sister?"

He didn't deny it. He just looked at me with that same weary sorrow I'd mistaken for wisdom all my life.

As my gaze shifted between my beloved father and my dragon-riding aunt, I realised that in Faerie, the past wasn't mourned, it was weaponised. Love was just the prettiest blade.

41

YSADORA

The Dance of Marrow is performed at the Court of Bones only during times of transition or fragile alliances. The femurs, taken from long-dead warriors, are said to carry the echo of their final breath, and the clashing of bone summons their silent witness. Each strike is a vow. Each stomp, a warning: remember who died so this court could rise.
- A Tapestry of Courts and Crowns

At supper, long tables stretched beneath vaulted ceilings and every bench was filled. Druids draped in ash-stained robes murmured blessings into their cups. Shamans with bone runes painted across their throats passed platters of charred meat between them. Blacksmiths still wearing aprons lined with soot clinked goblets heavy with spiced root ale. The scent of food and incense mingled, rich with old magic. On an ivory dais, Queen Thalindra sat on her throne, her circlet of antlers glowing in the firelight.

Nothing escaped her notice.

Father and I sat halfway down the main table, eyes darting every so often to the dragons circling the skies or standing sentinel in the vast courtyard visible through dull windows. The food between us was strange and austere: mushroom pies braided with nettles, bony game hen, segments of blood apple, steamed roots tossed with bone salt and cold cheese aged in cave darkness. None of it was familiar. All of it tasted like a memory trying to be something new.

We had deliberately taken places away from the sisters of the Circle of Emberlight. Even though Father was acquainted with more than a few of them, the interactions were fraught, as if the sisters were loyal to Araminta or harboured their own hatred against the Order of the Glyph.

Araminta's posture was rigid, almost stubbornly so, and her jaw set as if holding back old grudges. Every so often, her gaze swept towards us, a flash of something unreadable in her eyes: pride, regret, or warning.

Father's eyes flickered briefly to his sister before lowering his gaze to the table. He tapped a quiet rhythm against the wood, and I missed the scent of lavender and sage oil he used to protect his hands in the mortal world.

Abruptly stopping the tapping, he turned to me. "She rides. Did you see?"

I nodded. "Araminta? She's formidable. Completely in tune with her dragon."

A faint smile ghosted his lips. "She was always like

that. Born to fly, as if the skies themselves chose her. But it wasn't allowed." His voice thickened. "The Order of the Glyph had rules. Old, unyielding rules. And Araminta broke them."

I searched his eyes, and the flicker of pain in them was unmistakable. "Is that why she carries the scar?"

He gave a heavy nod. "A reminder. A punishment, some say. But to her, it's a mark of survival. A badge of honour."

A servant approached, bone runes gleaming on his throat, carrying a platter of meat so red it still seemed to pulse. His voice was like gravel. "The queen's finest game. Those felled by your very own dragon's tantrum."

Father smiled politely and accepted a portion. I followed his lead, nodding my thanks while my heart still hammered from his revelation. The servant lingered, eyes curious, before moving on.

Only when he was out of earshot did I whisper, "Tantrum?"

"The queen and I are calling it a misunderstanding."

I frowned. "So you have her alliance?"

"In a manner of speaking, yes."

Relief flooded me, but I paused, tracking back our conversation. "Did you sanction Araminta's punishment?"

Father's goblet hovered near his mouth as he sought to keep our conversation private. "Of course not. But I didn't stand in their way."

His words stung. "Why didn't you tell me about her?"

"Because I chose to leave her behind, and given the choice, I'd probably do it again. We were kin, but we were never cut from the same cloth. She was wild, untamed, driven by fire and rebellion when I was forged by duty and restraint. Our paths diverged before either of us could fully understand the cost."

How easily he spoke of leaving Araminta behind, like casting away slippers that didn't fit. A storm of anger and sorrow swelled beneath my ribs. "Would you do the same to me, if it suited you?"

A flicker of pain crossed his face. "No. You're my hope, not my burden." He reached for my hand, but I pulled back.

Hope, not burden. As if people could be sorted so easily into useful and useless piles. I realised that he had abandoned my mother, too, in a way, although they had agreed on their plan together. It didn't make it any better that he had not abandoned me, and I remembered with dread how Sequoia had told me of how Father had broken mate bonds for the Order of the Glyph and had possibly done worse.

Chaos surged within me, squeezing my lungs and snapping at the quiet like a wildfire licking at dry branches. The clink of goblets and soft chatter faltered as those nearby stole glances.

I pushed back from the table. "I need air."

Father followed as I walked to the tall windows overlooking the courtyard. Dragons wheeled overhead, their wings cutting shadows across the stone. We stood side by side, watching Caldoron land with a thud that shook the glass.

After a moment, Father said, "I forget sometimes that you are part Chaos, part *hers*."

A shiver ran down my spine. Yes, I was the calligrapher's daughter, but also a daughter of Chaos, and I had to believe that gave me a chance of surviving what others sometimes didn't. I gripped the hilt of the dragon-kissed blade in my pocket, its weight grounding me amidst swirling uncertainty.

"You deserve Araminta's anger, Father. And even Tanuhja's."

He drew in a sharp breath. "Yes, I suppose I do."

I swallowed the knot tightening in my chest. "You hid so much from me."

"But I gave you the key to my memories."

"You know as well as I do that your memories arrive as a trickle, not a flood."

He nodded. "For good reason. It took Lunarys and me a long time to find the right vessel. Stone porous enough to hold memory but dense enough to keep deeper truths sealed until you need them. Memory isn't meant to be forced."

I dragged my gaze from the dragons, and we returned to the table, where he busied himself filling first my plate and his own. In Larkspur, that would have been my daughterly duty. "Eat, please, Ysa. You need your strength."

I toyed with a piece of the pie, picking out the bones, but didn't eat it. I'd never complain about Loxley's food again. "Every dish looks like a test."

My father's smile twisted. "The shamans are waiting to see what you do with those bones. Everything in Faerie is a test. This court just doesn't pretend otherwise."

We lapsed into silence. I ate a few small bites, then pushed my plate away. "I don't know if I can do any of this."

Father put down his cutlery, and the words burst out of him, like he'd been holding them back. "I expected Zephyr to be here, standing behind your chair like a well-placed threat. Where is he, Ysa? He promised me he would never let you stand alone. Where are Maren and Ferrith?"

I met his gaze without blinking. "The Binder took him. No...don't pity me. He doesn't follow me like a shadow. He walks beside me. And sometimes, we divide our strength." I had to believe it. And even as I said it, I wished he filled the chair at my side. "Maren and Ferrith are with Loxley, I think, but no one has heard from them in days."

"Then I will take to the skies with Caldoron."

"I need you here to help me prepare for *Kindling*. That's the only way to beat Thiago, Father."

He winced, as though he believed it should have been his job to deal with his old enemy and not mine. I knew that the psychic hurts about Danaë still lingered, though he had been physically healed in the bone milk pool.

And I knew that tonight wasn't the night to tell him about Tanuhja's fierce, broken love and how I pitied her. I wished bitterly then to be a child, when he had mopped my tears and I didn't have to navigate the complexities of his emotions as well as my own.

A wretchedness came over him, and he thumbed Caldoron's scale that he wore around his neck to soothe himself. "I fear that I've been gone too long from Faerie, grown too distant from my dragon, to be of use to you in preparing for *Kindling*."

"Will you tell me about your own *Kindling*?" I held my breath, hoping that he wouldn't refuse, and as he spoke, the memories in me unspooled to give me accompanying images, as if they had been waiting for this very moment.

His brown eyes grew distant. "There were—and to the

best of my knowledge, still are—three parts. The Flame
Offering, in which you place an object into dragon flame to
prove your lack of pride. The Walk of Ash, when you walk
alone over dragon bones and the bones of those would-be
riders who failed before you, and face their memories.
And the Sky Ascent, which is really a falling that a dragon
may save you from."

My heart pounded. "Starlight, save me."

"For my own *Kindling*, I placed a sword into the fire
that accompanied me in my first battle, and I had carried
as proof of my worth. On the Bonefield, I walked through
the burning bone fields accompanied by the memory of a
brother from the Order of the Glyph who begged me for
help mastering the delicate loops of a calligraphy spell.
The lack of mastery of the specific spell cost him his life
during *Kindling*." Father's throat bobbed. "During the Sky
Ascent, I folded my arms across my chest but left my eyes
open wide, and then stepped from the ledge without a
word or cry. Caldoron caught me before gravity could
claim its due, sealing a bond born of faith rather than
force."

I nodded slowly, steadying myself. "I'll remember that
when my time comes. You still won't help me?"

Father slumped, beaten down by his choices. "Won't?
It's not that. I've just learnt an old male's limits… I will ask
Araminta to help you. It will go some way in making
amends for me to admit that, for all my training and
experience with the Order of the Glyph, she is perhaps
more accomplished than I."

"Do you think she'll speak to me?" I asked quietly.

His smile was too sad to be reassuring. "She will, but
on her terms. And when she does, be ready to listen and

watch carefully, because *Kindling* is unforgiving, Ysa, and you are too precious to me to gamble against something as cruel as the ancient dragon rite."

"You can't ask me to request the counsel of someone you've written off. Either Araminta matters or she doesn't."

"It's her that's written me off. Why would she want anything to do with me, when I turned my back on her?" He was quiet for a long moment, watching the shamans dance. "Araminta and I...we disagreed about fundamental things. About the Order of the Glyph's rules. About what dragons owe us and what we owe them. But you're right. She's formidable, and more importantly, she never lost her connection to dragon magic the way I have."

"Lost it how?"

"Distance. Time in the mortal realm. Fear." He gestured towards the windows where dragons circled. "Look at Caldoron when he's near me versus when he's flying free. There's a hesitancy now that wasn't there before. Dragons sense doubt, and I've had too much of it for too long."

"And Araminta doesn't?"

"Araminta has many faults, but doubt isn't one of them. She rides like she was born to it because she believes she was. That kind of certainty is what you need for *Kindling*. Once it took place at the Court of Nebulas, but the dragons made Nightblaze Isle their home after the fall of the Order of the Glyph, and the Circle of Emberlight is now more trusted as their kin and keepers."

"Still telling stories about me, brother?"

We both turned. Araminta stood behind us, filling the space like smoke from a forge.

Father made to stand up. "Araminta, it's good that you have come. Let us reconcile."

"You're more adept at breaking ties than mending them."

"Please, sister," said Father.

"Don't." She held up a hand. "I've heard enough." Her gaze shifted to me, measuring. "I am pleased for you, Ysadora. You're the precious daughter he kept. The one worth more than dragon loyalty." She stepped closer to me, ignoring Father completely. "*Kindling* isn't a game, girl. It's dragon fire and old magic and the kind of pain that leaves marks. Meet me at dawn in the dragon courtyard. We'll see if you're worth the trouble you've caused." She walked away without another word, leaving Father and me staring after her.

"Well," said Father quietly. "I suppose that's settled."

I sighed, needing to breach the distance between us. Father belonged to my nearest and dearest, always. "I'm sorry that this is complicated. And I'm sorry I waited to tell you that I missed you. I'm glad you're healed."

Warm brown eyes met my violet ones. "I'm healed, almost too well, but some parts still ache when I look at you."

Through every hardship, my love for him held fast, like a flame refusing to be snuffed out by the cold winds of fate. Despite his mistakes, I saw the quiet moments where his love broke through: the acts of care, the pride in me, the risks he took.

We clinked glasses after that, soft and almost ceremonial: a moment of peace that felt too much like a farewell.

We watched a group of shamans begin a rhythmic

dance, each clutching a femur like a baton. Their bodies twisted and stomped in sync, striking the bones together with sharp clacks that echoed in the vaulted hall, and the faerie queen smiled and joined in. Though the tone and mood and colours of the dance were nothing like the maypole at Bloomtide, I was reminded of home.

I turned to Father and said, "I miss Larkspur."

He sighed. "The pattern of books on the shelves in the bookshop, knowing where each item belonged. The smell of bread from Anja's bakery. Even the cracked bell tower that never rang on time."

I nodded. "And the swan that kept attacking Hilda's little brother."

He huffed a laugh. "That urchin deserved it."

"I thought that Faerie would replace Larkspur. I love Ebonspire, but I was driven out from that home, too."

"We might not find home again, Ysa. Or we might have to make one." His voice was soft and rough, like it had worn down from holding too many things for too long. "You carry Larkspur in you. Every kindness, every stubborn hope. That's what makes you dangerous to Faerie. You still remember what it means to belong."

I leaned my head against his shoulder. We sat like that, in a court built on bones, talking about a place made of bread, maypoles, and old cracked bells. For a while, we were just a father and daughter, remembering home.

Then, as the night grew more raucous and the faerie queen returned to her throne, and the dragons circled outside, I told Father of most of what had transpired since our parting: Esolas's attack and Ferrith's betrayal, my fears for Elowen, how I had mastered chaos with the help of the dragon-kissed blade and siphoning ink from the land, what the Binder had told me about my place in Faerie and how maybe, an astral dragon called Ryvaris would be mine.

Father listened with growing alarm, especially when I told him of the High King's crown. He went deathly pale, the lines on his face deepening. "If that falls into Thiago's hands. It's more than a symbol. It's the keystone of Faerie's fragile peace. We're standing on the brink of chaos. If only the brotherhood were still here to maintain the Grimoire. If only I were strong enough to hold lines together myself."

I saw clearly then how deeply he clung to the old ways, trapped by duty and legacy, blind to the fact that I embodied both creation and destruction, intertwined like a fierce dance. He longed for stability in a world that demanded change, and in that tension lay the fragile hope of what I might become.

I said only, "We need allies and strategy, cool heads and dragon flame."

Father nodded and took my hand. In turn, he told me about how he had lost his dragon's trust and regained it, how Liora Bramick had built an alliance with the Faerie Queen of Bones by trading dragon bone dust—and how even after all this time, he knew Araminta would never have played a part in this—and how the dragons' fury about their desecrated remains could be the key to more than winning Thalindra's alliance at the meeting of the rulers.

At the mention of her name, the faerie queen shifted on the dais, and I felt her attention like a note struck in the bones of the room. She rose from her throne, goblet raised high. The entire hall fell silent, shamans freezing mid-dance.

"To old alliances," she called, her voice carrying to every corner, "and new possibilities."

The queen's toast echoed in the vaulted hall, and through the windows, dragons called to each other in the night. Liora was the first to raise her cup, and we followed, along with everyone else.

As the bitter root ale slid down my throat, I met Thalindra's eyes across the hall. Her scrutiny burned through the revelry, a reminder that in Faerie, every alliance was a promise, and every promise, a seed that could grow into either salvation or ruin. Tonight, beneath the surface of celebration, the currents of power were shifting.

I set down my goblet and turned to Father. "I should rest before dawn."

He nodded, understanding, and stood to accompany me to my chamber. Around us, the feast continued, but the weight of tomorrow pressed down on me: it would bring dragon fire and old grudges, and I would face them without Zephyr at my side, and somewhere in the darkness beyond these walls, enemies gathered strength.

"Remember to take the quill and the dragon-kissed blade," said Father, when he left me at my chamber, and I thought he might ask to hold them, but he pressed his parchment lips against my cheek and bade me goodnight instead.

That night, for the few hours that I slept, a shadow caressed my cheek, and to me it almost felt like one of Zephyr's.

42

YSADORA

*A rider must have three things: A spirit
unshackled by pride. A spine that will not bend.
A heart willing to burn.
– The Dragons and Riders of the Nebula Court*

The bed chamber I was allocated was too still, too cold, each breath a visible mist. The hard stone bed offered no comfort, and I longed for a night on the hay bales in Ebonspire's stables, when Zephyr's attention chased the thoughts from my mind. Rest was impossible: my mind tangled with thoughts of my kin, my enemies, and Ryvaris.

Unable to bear the quiet, I drew my quill and traced the dragon's name into the stale air. R-Y-V-A-R-I-S. Each letter shimmered as it left the quill's tip, iridescent and alive with flickers of heat. The name rippled with latent power, curling and uncurling like smoke from a slumbering beast.

The R pulsed like a heartbeat.

The Y forked outwards, as if reaching.

The V beat once, twice, like wings flexing against a storm.

By the time the S looped into existence, the letters had begun to rise of their own accord, dancing like dragon wings across the room before dissolving with a burst of energy that ruffled the blankets and snuffed out the lone candle by my bed.

Silence rushed in, louder than before. I held my breath.

Then, just as I turned to lie down again, a deep, resonant roar echoed across the clouds, low and long, as if something ancient had stirred. I didn't know if it was real or a dream, but a thrill of hope and fear laced through me like static before a storm.

My chaos magic reacted, rising to the surface like a tide, and I was learning to live with its strangeness, learning to understand that light wasn't always good and dark wasn't always monstrous.

Whatever waited ahead, it was coming fast, and it would see all of me.

Eventually, I slept for a short spell, and in that thin sliver of rest, the stars whispered secrets in a tongue I almost understood, and the old dream of falling from the lighthouse returned, as if Tanuhja was making a last-ditch effort to turn me from my path.

At dawn, I woke with the phantom touch of shadow still lingering on my skin and dressed for what might be my first true reckoning with dragon fire. Doubts plagued me about what had led me to require Araminta's help when she had every reason to hate me.

I still hadn't discovered why the Binder had urged me to ask about the young dragon rider who had questioned

Liora. But my morning training sessions at Ebonspire had prepared me well for walking into trouble, despite doubt.

So, I braided my thick hair, thinking of how much Zephyr loved it. Then I fastened the last buckle on my leathers, slipped my quill and dragon-kissed blade into place, and exhaled.

Three days remained until the meeting of the rulers.

Three days to consolidate our kin and allies.

Three days to win the allegiance of a dragon that hadn't answered to anyone in an age.

The bone-coloured light of morning spilt like smoke through the narrow windows of the Court of Bones, laying ghostly trails across the flagstones, and I steeled myself for what lay ahead. Faerie had taught me harsh truths: that love wasn't safe, power wasn't pure, and even family could fail you.

But I'd survived the ruin of innocence, and in that wreckage, I'd found belief in the family I chose, and in the world we might still make.

Araminta was already waiting in the dragon courtyard when I emerged into the rosy hue of dawn light. The air tasted of salt, char, and the deep-buried magic of the world before. In the courtyard, dragons stirred, wings rustling, reptilian eyes narrowing, old gods remembering their hunger. The sound of claw on stone set a wild, reverent fear loose beneath my ribs: part dread, part wonder. These creatures had once bowed to no one.

I wouldn't run, and I wouldn't fear Ryvaris, whose name was already etched onto my soul.

At my footsteps, Araminta didn't turn around from her task of bundling dried brush into her arms. "You're late."

"I'll help." I stooped to gather my own bundle.

That earned me a sideways glance, the faintest twitch of approval hiding in her mouth. She harrumphed. "Your hands are too soft, but they won't be by the end of today."

My stomach clenched. "*Kindling* takes place today?"

Araminta hefted her bundle and glowered. "The old bones believe you are capable, despite Kazimir's influence. But the old bones see only possibilities. I see the daughter of a celebrated fool who abandoned his dragon and the Chaos Queen who created a dragon in name, but which is nothing more than a skeletal, diseased thing."

I forced a steady breath. My aunt's animosity merely sharpened my resolve. I was unsure if she wanted me to succeed or whether my failure would bring her Schadenfreude and cement her superiority over the brother she loathed. But it didn't change my path.

She beckoned me to follow with my haul, and as I did, I glanced up at Caldoron and a few other dragons I knew slumbering or staring down at us from perches across the Court of Bones, realising they waited for their riders. But there was no dragon here that matched what the old bones had shown me of Ryvaris.

I wanted to meet him but feared it in equal measure. "Will you prepare me here, at the Court of Bones? I thought we might go to the Court of Nebulas or to Nightblaze Isle, where the dragons dwell."

Araminta snorted. "You wish to prepare for *Kindling* in sight of the dragons you wish to impress?"

My cheeks warmed. "I guess not."

My aunt sighed. "This place is as good as any, and it has the bones we need to replicate some of what *Kindling* entails." But the rune on my hip heated, telling me she didn't trust the bone court.

I didn't attempt further conversation then, discouraged by the proud tilt of Araminta's head and the slight furrow in her brow. I couldn't help staring at her, at the muscles in her legs and shoulders from orbits of dragon-riding, at the faded blue hair beneath the hood of her cloak and the handful of silver beads that brushed the scar on her throat. She moved with a silent discipline, her steps deliberate, her shoulders squared, with no attempt at niceties.

Despite her coldness, I couldn't help but admire her.

We went a little further before we arrived in a courtyard in the far western side of the Queen of Bones's keep, where a fire pit had already been dug and ringed with blackened stone. There, four other sisters of the Circle of Emberlight waited, their cloaks pulled tight against the dawn chill: Liora, Phaedran, and two others called Serayne and Iskriel, who had dined at Araminta's side the previous night.

Liora nodded once in approval when I laid down my armful of sticks and gestured for me to step out of my boots. The ground was warm through my boots, already smouldering. A trail of hot ash and bone fragments stretched across the courtyard like a spine of flame.

My mouth went dry. I looked down at the fragment of a long vertebra visible in the dirt.

"This path is walked barefoot," said Liora. "The pain teaches you where your fear lives."

Araminta tossed her bundle into the fire pit. "Start walking, Ysadora. While you do, we'll teach you the difference between nebulite and aetherian, between a sky beast and voidstalker. If you can't hold dragon lore in your mind while your feet burn, you've no business asking for Ryvaris."

I nodded, then bent to undo my boots. Tiny skeletal forms circled the courtyard, and at first, I mistook them for insects: fluttering bone-winged things barely the size of a finger. But they moved in perfect intervals, and I realised, the faerie queen's trust only went so far.

She granted the Circle of Emberlight access to her court and space for ritual, but not privacy. These delicate, drifting creatures were not pests; they were her eyes. And everything they saw, they carried back to her on bone-thin wings. I resisted the urge to stomp on one and instead moved forward on bare feet to the bone trail.

The moment I stepped onto it, pain bloomed up my legs. Araminta began reciting names of dragon breeds, their physical traits, and personality quirks. I walked, skin burning, blisters forming, each step an echo of those who had come before and failed. But I listened. I listened and catalogued the information she gave me.

I pretended I was still in our bookshop in Larkspur or the cellar, reading about a wild adventure.

I pretended that this was all a dream that I would soon wake up from.

WHEN I HAD WALKED over hot bones and embers for what seemed like hours, and my mind brimmed over with knowledge of dragon kind, the sisters of the Circle of Emberlight called me to the remnants of the fire.

Phaedran and Serayne took my feet into their laps and applied balms to my scorched arches. Blisters had bloomed across the soles of my feet, some already split and leaking. Char and ash clung to my skin, embedded deep.

The flesh was raw in places, peeling in others, the angry red of ritual sacrifice. The sisters didn't wince at the sight. They merely exchanged glances as if measuring my worth. I hissed once, when they bound the worst of the injuries in strips of cloth that smelled faintly of silverroot and dripped in bone milk.

Their touch was brisk, and I missed Wylda's kind touch and friendship and longed to be reunited with my chosen family.

But the pain was nothing compared to how hollow I felt. What remained was an aching truth: the dragons did not want a flawless rider. They wanted one forged, scarred, and proven, and I didn't know if they would allow me to soar or let me fall.

"Pain is a good offering." Serayne smoothed the bandages. "But it is pride you must offer in the first trial of *Kindling*."

Araminta stood nearby, arms crossed, unreadable as ever. But I felt her gaze settle on me, weighty and sharp. "I did not hear a whimper, and that is a small thing, but it is not nothing."

"Come," said Phaedran, moving my foot from her lap and tapping the spot beside her. "Rest a while here before we make the journey." She pressed a cup of dark liquid into my hand. "Drink. Not for pain. For clarity. *Kindling* burns more than just flesh."

Liora nodded. "It's time for introductions. If you survive today, you will be one of us."

I drank. The liquid tasted of sage and smoke, and each sip burned its path down my throat. Liora talked, but I found myself drawn to Araminta instead, to the way she held herself apart from the others, the careful distance she maintained even while sitting close enough to share our fire.

"We are five of ten. The others guard elsewhere this morning. The Circle of Emberlight doesn't travel complete unless the need is dire," said Liora. "There's me, of course. My word is law in the Circle of Emberlight. Phaedran is known for flying into storms and other dares. Her dragon is lightning-marked. Araminta, once thought unfit to bond, now rides the oldest living beast."

"Thanks," muttered Araminta.

"That was meant as a compliment."

Silver beads clanked as Araminta threw more brush on the fire. "I didn't take it as one."

A smile ghosted over Liora's lips. "Serayne's dragon is blind but never misses. Iskriel veils her ruthlessness in gentility."

Iskriel's smooth brown head turned her way. "I'm with Ara. If that's how you describe us, no wonder we number only ten."

Liora laughed, and in the skies above, her voidstalker's cosmic purple eyes reflected the firelight like distant stars. "Tirithwyn is as graceful as falling ash. Caedra is a tactician, feared not for her strength, but for how little she reveals before she strikes. Zavréa speaks little, but commands the fiercest loyalty. Virelya once fell from her dragon and rose again, wrapped in flame. And Nimareth is the keeper of the Circle of Emberlight's northern watch."

The sisters of the Circle of Emberlight unpicked their leader's descriptions of them as I hobbled over to Araminta at the edge of the fire, surprised that my feet had already partially healed. The sun now blazed across the Court of Bones, and the fire was thankfully almost out, despite my aunt's stubborn attempts to keep it going. As if summoned by the dying flames, a shadow passed overhead, then another, and another.

Swallowing down my trepidation, I weighed up how best to approach my aunt. Loose strands of her faded blue hair had escaped the leather cord binding it beneath her hood, and a few strands curled against her cheekbones. The early light made it shimmer, more smoke than sky. Her boots, scuffed and cracked with years of dragon-riding, were stained with soot, and the soles warped slightly. She grumbled as I sat beside her.

"My father is sorry for how he treated you."

She blinked at that, surprise flickering behind her guarded eyes. "He has a funny way of showing it."

I clenched my hands in my lap before I forced them still. "I think he hopes to make amends."

Her expression shuttered into practised neutrality, as if she sealed away her softness aeons ago. "Some bridges burn too thoroughly ever to be crossed again."

I looked away for a moment. "I understand." A pause. "Will you share your own experience of *Kindling* with me?"

"No. I don't think I will," she said, "because you need to forge your own path, like I did, and we are not kin, only allied by necessity, not by love."

And I cringed, swallowing the sting. Some fires had to be faced alone, even if I wished otherwise. I turned my gaze to the other sisters of the Circle of Emberlight, wondering if I should move places, dreading the moment they deemed *Kindling* would begin, in case Ryvaris did not choose me.

A burst of raucous laughter flowed over us from the group. It cracked through the morning air, bright and irreverent: a reminder that life went on, even here, amidst bones and fire. For a moment, I envied their ease.

"Liora," Araminta muttered, "would snip the scales off a sleeping dragon if she thought it might serve us."

I gave her a sharp look. "What became of the young dragon rider who questioned her?"

Araminta scowled, her gaze flicking towards her leader, then back to me. "Who told you that?"

My shoulders rose with the weight of her scrutiny. "The Binder."

At that, she paused. "Lunarys strung up the stars that shine atop the lighthouse on Nightblaze Isle herself, one dim star for every dragon breed to light their way after the Order of the Glyph fell. She wanted them to have a home."

"And the young dragon rider?" I prompted.

Araminta's scowl deepened, and she lowered her voice. "The young dragon rider you speak of was Jirelle. Brilliant, reckless, outspoken. She was reassigned to patrol the borderlands. It's dangerous work. Isolated."

"A punishment dressed up as honour?"

"Worse than that." Araminta checked that the others were still occupied. "Jirelle's reports stopped coming after three months. When Liora finally sanctioned a search party, we found her body, but it wasn't wild magic that killed her."

"What do you mean?"

"Have you ever seen someone die from bond

severance?" Araminta's eyes were haunted. "It's not quick. It's not clean. Jirelle's fingernails were torn away from clawing at her own skull. The healers said she'd suffered for days as her connection to her dragon was dismantled layer by layer. Thought by thought, as though by dark magic."

My blood chilled. "Skies, that poor rider."

Araminta's voice cracked. "I don't think Liora wanted her dead, but I am almost certain she was behind it. She wanted Jirelle and us all to understand exactly what happens when riders asked too many questions. Perhaps she even wanted Jirelle to feel every moment of her dragon's confusion, his terror, as their souls were ripped apart. Her dragon spent those final weeks circling the borderlands, calling for her, growing weaker as the bond bled away."

"What happened to him?" I almost didn't want to know.

"Some say he flew into the sea, as if it were his choice. But I know better than that," Araminta said, her face pale. "He fell. The bond severance destroys a dragon's ability to navigate, to think clearly. Perhaps he kept trying to reach her even after she was dead, kept following the phantom pull of a connection that was no longer there. We never recovered his body. He doesn't even lie in the bone field."

The silence stretched between us, heavy with horror.

I bit my lip. "So Liora killed a rider *and* a dragon."

"I believe so. But not one of my sisters dares to speak it aloud." Araminta's mouth twisted, something between a grimace and a smile, and I understood that my aunt valued obedience even less than Zephyr and I did. "You're clever, like him. Like my brother," she said, not looking at me. "Kazimir believed cleverness could protect what he loved. It didn't."

Her words landed like ash in my lungs: dry, choking, true.

She turned to me then, finally, fully. Her brown eyes were sharp, sharper than Father's had ever been. "Listen closely. Liora is loyal, yes. But to the Circle of Emberlight, not to you, not even to individual riders. She wants you to succeed today, but only because it strengthens the Circle of Emberlight's position. You might well be getting out from Thiago's yolk, just to earn another."

The air between us grew colder, heavier. It was a bitter lesson that freedom might be another form of control. But a small voice inside me whispered that not all bonds were chains.

Araminta glanced at my feet, still tender but mostly healed. Around us, the other riders had grown quiet, their conversations trailing off. My aunt gave a small nod, as though she had been tolerating our conversation, rather than valuing it.

"Don't read too much into healing. The pain always comes back before it's done teaching." She shifted, rising with a fluid movement that belied her years. "It's time."

The sisters from the Circle of Emberlight looked up at her and readied themselves, shedding their cloaks, tightening their boots, and tying their scarves. Then they raised their gazes to the sky, and from the swirling haze, five colossal dragons came, each a masterpiece of shimmering colour and brute strength.

I scrambled for my boots, awestruck as I watched their descent: scales glistened in hues of cosmic purple, burnished pink, deep forest green, fiery crimson blending with smoky charcoal, and midnight blue speckled with star-like silver.

A low rumble shook the courtyard as they landed, their talons crushing bone and stone beneath them, their great wings folded with a soft, leathery rustle. Their eyes locked onto their destined riders, and the air was thick with the scent of ozone and ancient magic.

My aunt's cloak billowed like wings. "Now we go."

Now, we would find out if a daughter of ink and chaos could join the ranks of female dragon riders or if I—like so many others before me—would leave my bones on an island of dragons.

My heart clenched as I reached for the comfort of the bond, and found Zephyr too distant still, even for a goodbye. Because my mate had known the pain of incomplete goodbyes, and I had also: the kind that left words fossilised in the throat.

I didn't want that for either of us. And so I wrote Zephyr a message in wisps of ink imbued with the fierce love I felt for him, even though Father had told me that the Queen of Bones stopped unsanctioned communication to and from her court:

Zephyr,
I don't know what will become of me at Kindling
but if I fall, know that I flew because of you.
Wait for me, love. Or come find me in the fire.
Your Inkheart.

I drew the dragon-kissed blade with shaking fingers and carved a thin, glimmering fold in the veil. The air split with a hiss. The dragons roared, and the roars seemed close and a world away, and the scent of ancient magic stirred.

My message hung suspended for a heartbeat, then slipped through the tear with a crackle and the veil sealed. The dragons watched me now with eyes like burning coins. I glanced at them, keeping my head bowed, and the sting of isolation deepened.

Whatever awaited me beyond this moment, the path forward was mine alone to walk or to fail.

43

YSADORA

The crooked lighthouse can be found on
Nightblaze Isle. It is lit by a circle of seven
dimmed, captured stars, their purpose not to warn
ships, but to guide dragonkind.
It is said the star-circle cannot be extinguished
unless Faerie itself falls.
- The Dragons and Riders of the Nebula Court

I rode with Phaedran on Sindrosira again, and the dragon was no more welcoming the second time, but the flight to Nightblaze Isle was short, shorter than my wild beating heart wished it to be. The wind tore past us in ribbons, thick with ash and sea-brine, as the dragon isle rose from the mist like a jagged tooth of the world.

Below, the sea boiled with thermal vents and primal magic, glowing faintly beneath the waves like veins in the skin of Faerie. Sindrosira flew like something summoned from an age before stories, her wings beating with a rhythm older than language. The lighthouse came into view: tall, crooked, pulsing with a strange, star-fed radiance.

Around it, dragons circled.

I gripped the saddle harder, pulse quickening. I could already feel the isle's heat, taste the metallic promise of fire in the back of my throat. This was where I would stand bare before them: no names, no lineage, no mate to shield me. Judged only on what I chose to offer, and whether they found it worthy.

My mate would have said there was comfort in that: to live or die on one's own merit. But standing alone had never felt like freedom to me, and I bitterly wished my kin were with me.

But there was no time for longing. The dragons above wheeled about the clouds in solemn silence, watching as though we were a gathering storm: wary, but largely unmoved. Sindrosira gave a sharp hiss as she landed on the black rock near the edge of the isle, her claws cracking against the brittle stone. She barely waited for Phaedran and me to dismount before she launched into the sky again to join her kind.

"The rest of us will wait in the lighthouse. There, behind the viewing pane."

She was going to leave me alone any minute. She was a stranger, not even a friend, and I didn't want her to go. "How long will it last?"

"Until it is decided." Phaedran pinched the bridge of her nose. "I hate *Kindling*. It brings it all back. Good luck, Ysadora. You remember the oath?"

My mouth was dry. "A spirit unshackled by pride. A spine that will not bend. A heart willing to burn."

She nodded. "I hope you succeed."

I stiffened as she brushed a kiss against my cheek and took off at a steady pace towards the lighthouse. Araminta was waiting for her by the spiral steps upwards, and she raised a hand in acknowledgement, expression grim, and then vanished into the tall tower.

Then I turned to look at the site of the first trial, *The Flame Offering,* that Father and Araminta had taken pains to explain to me. There it stood, not fifty metres away, an eternal dragon flame housed in a brazier of scale and bone. It sat atop a plinth at the edge of the isle and required an offering to prove lack of pride.

This was where it would begin. Or where it would end.

I moved forward on legs that seemed carved from smoke, aware of every eye on me, dragon and fae. The wind tugged at my hair and cloak, as if trying to pull me back, as I walked to the plinth, my footsteps steady over the uneven ground.

A few minutes later, I stood before it and tried to ignore the fear-inducing beat of dragon wings and the transfixed faces of the sisters of the Circle of Emberlight pressed against the viewing pane in the lighthouse.

The flame was unlike any I had seen. It did not flicker and cast no warmth, despite its red hue. I had no need to climb it: magic was allowed in the first and second trial, but not the third. So, I removed the dragon-kissed dagger from its sheath and considered for a moment.

Unlike Father, I did not intend to offer my blade to the flame.

I offered a part of myself instead, a part that I had come to love since my mortal glamour had fallen away.

My heart beat a defiant rhythm in my ears as I gathered my hair to one side, fingers trembling. There had been a time I thought little of it. In my mortal years, my hair was just something to tame, to keep out of my eyes while I read, or to bundle on top of my head when I swam in the creek with Maren and Ferrith.

But after my mortal glamour fell, the hair grew longer, richer, unmistakably fae. How I enjoyed my body then, how I claimed it. The slender limbs that bent like reeds but held the force of rivers. The twilight gaze that males and females alike so admired. And stars, the dark waterfall of my hair streaked with molten strands that shimmered like ink.

I enjoyed playing the seductress. Not in the way mortal songs speak of conquest, but in the quiet knowledge of power: the curve of a smile that lingered a breath too long, the brush of a shoulder that turned heads, the heavy weight of a gaze returned without apology. I learned the shape of my hunger and the joy of being hungered for. I learned how to unfasten a bodice with confidence and look my mate in the eye while doing it.

I learned how to wield softness as a blade.

And Zephyr—skies—he looked at me with reverence. Like me, he took pride in it. I had seen how Zephyr looked at me when my hair spilt down my back, his fingers tangling in it. He grasped it during the wildest of our nights, tugging it sometimes when he wanted me closer. He wove idle patterns through the strands while we lay entwined with each other. He threaded it through his hands like he could learn me by texture alone.

In the dark, after he returned from missions to find sanctuary for the outcast fae before we left our home, he'd buried his face in my hair, breathing in the scent like it grounded him, instead of waking me. Although I did wake. His fingers knew every knot in my braid, every path down my spine.

I closed my eyes as I remembered. That was what I was giving up now to sate the flame. Not just the hair, but the power it had come to represent. The pride I had wrapped around beauty and want. To sever it was no small gesture. I lifted the dragon-kissed dagger, its edge catching the strange starlight that poured from the top of the lighthouse.

"This is an offering of meaning," I whispered. "Not just matter."

And I cut. The blade hissed through the strands with startling ease. My thick braid fell into my hands, heavy as rope, and I held it for a breath. Then I tossed it into the brazier, wielding my quill to send wings of ink to carry it the last few inches and manoeuvre it into the heart of the dragon flame.

For a moment, nothing happened.

The flame merely licked around the offering, curling red tongues against the dark strands. Then, the fire changed, inhaling the hair and flaring gold, rising in a tall, twisting column that painted the isle in molten light.

In the skies above the lighthouse, colossal shapes slowed to a near-hover, the dragons suspending their titanic wings in a tableau of elemental might. They let out a keening wail that rolled over the isle like a mournful hymn.

Their eyes—fiery embers, shards of ice, pools as dark as the voids my chaos created—burned into me like a brand. This was no casual observation: they were dissecting, judging, measuring every breath I took.

The weight of their gaze pressed down like the cold grip of the grave, and though I had seized their attention, a chill crept up my spine. I wasn't sure I wanted to be known so completely. Through the viewing pane, the sisters broke into smiles.

Only my aunt remained impassive.

My heart pounded. I had passed the first trial.

I was not yet worthy, but I was seen.

The golden blaze still shimmered in my vision as I turned from the brazier and knelt to unlace my boots. My soles tingled in anticipation of the searing path ahead for the second trial, the *Walk of Ash*. I jogged towards the Bonefield, barefoot, cursing myself for not waiting to remove my boots, my already-sore feet gauging the temperature of the ground and how it warmed as I neared the Bonefield.

Each step pulled me deeper into the old magic, into the trial that would test not what I could give, but whether I could endure. My stomach lurched as I stood above it. It was less a field than a pit I had to jump down into.

I jumped down, the impact rattling up through my legs. The drop wasn't far, but it felt like falling into another world. The heat hit me immediately: dry, radiating from the bone-littered floor like a living thing. And I was glad for the practice I had endured that dawn, even as I noted how in reality nothing could prepare me for this.

The Bonefield stretched out before me like a battlefield

long after the war had ended, silent but never at peace. Fae bones lay scattered in half-buried clusters, scorched and splintered, their brittle edges fused to the earth by dragon fire. Femurs jutted from the ash like signposts of failure, and ribcages, warped by heat, curled inwards as if still trying to shield their last breath. Here and there, the tarnished glint of a melted glyph pendant or a cracked piece of armour marked the final resting places of would-be riders.

But it was the dragon bones that truly unsettled me. Colossal ribs rose in sweeping lines, not unlike the hulls of sunken ships, half-consumed by earth: monuments to beasts who would never fly again. Skulls bigger than my body lay half-sunken in the ground, eye sockets dark and gaping. Their teeth—twin rows of curved ivory—still gleamed, some snapped mid-roar. A few still glimmered with residual enchantment, a whisper of the power they once held.

At the far end of the field stood a bone tower, built from skulls, vertebrae, and broken wing and tail bones, too many to belong to one dragon alone. Vines crept up it, curling around bones, and to me it seemed like a shrine. The structure leaned slightly, like a monument forgotten or defaced. I didn't go near it. Something about its stillness felt sacred, and sacred things were not to be approached lightly by the unchosen.

I stumbled on the second step across the field and caught myself with a whisper of a curse. My breath turned shallow. I forced myself to move, fearing that my soles would melt into fleshy gloop if I stood in one place too long.

With every step, phantom voices grew louder in my

ears, voices that belonged to the bones beneath my scalding bare feet. The heat beneath my feet grew in increments: first like sun-warmed stone, then the smoulder of coals, then sharper, hungrier, like flame gnawing at my skin. I hissed through my teeth but kept walking, the Bonefield rising before me in a shimmer of heat and memory.

The world narrowed to each step, each flash of pain and the silent scream of nerves firing in my calves. In the skies and behind the viewing pane, I was being weighed for my bravery and resolve.

I thought of Father and Caldoron and their unending love story, I thought about Araminta's quiet adoration of her aeons-old dragon Vireza, I thought of Zephyr, his laughter in the bond, and how he would have paced beside me, helpless and furious. But he wasn't here, neither in shadow nor flesh, and the bond was a mere whisper.

A sharp sting lanced up my heel. The ground steamed. My breath came ragged. But I did not stop.

As my thoughts stilled and I focused on placing one foot in front of the other, the phantom voices found me.

I tuned into the voices drifting up from the blackened jaws of long-dead aspirants, unwillingly, helplessly, as they curled up from the scorched ground like tendrils of smoke, fragments of voices, thoughts, regrets that weren't loud, but intimate:

She said if I screamed, the dragon would turn away. So I bit through my tongue when the flames carved trenches down my spine, swallowing blood instead of sound.

I offered my father's war helmet. The flame spat it back. When I reached to retrieve it, it took my life as well as my hand.

I stood before them, chin raised like a queen. I asked to be chosen. I should have asked to serve.

The moment I saw the golden-winged dragon, I knew she would never stoop to catch me. Leaping anyway was a kind of freedom.

I faltered. Just a breath, just a step. But the bones sensed my hesitation and punished me for it. A gust of heat rose to meet me. My skin was slick with sweat. My heartbeat thundered against the cage of my ribs.

How could I hope to endure what so many had not? The question clawed at me with every step across the scorched bones. My foot hovered above a cracked femur, and for a moment, I couldn't bring myself to step down.

Their hopes, their desperation, the last moments of their lives clung to the scorched earth like smoke to skin. Some had likely been stronger, wiser, and more ready than I.

And still, they'd fallen.

If this place had devoured them, what arrogance to think that I could pass untouched. All I had was breath and belief, and even those were thinning. My chest ached with borrowed grief. But without me, what chance did my kin have against Thiago's reach for power? How would they stand against his desire to become High King? The Binder had brought Zephyr and me together for a strange kind of alchemy, possible only in Faerie: the chance to create a kinder realm than we had inherited.

So I walked, hands curling into fists, as whispers of dragon thoughts plagued me.

I bore him through the stars before he fell. He clutched my horn as if it would change fate. In the end, he bellowed my name and let go.

Two moons I lay pinned, watching my kin circle overhead, too afraid to land. The rockslide took my body, but their cowardice killed my heart first.

Brothers wheeling through the skies for aeons, and then he chose to fall. What choice did I have but to follow?

I took step after agonising step, tears trailing my cheeks, my pulse a war drum, my heart a flame. I kept walking, even as the soles of my feet blistered and wept, even as my body swayed from the heat and the weight of borrowed sorrow. These weren't taunts. They were the remnants of those who had come before me: fragments of courage, of desperation, of terrible beauty.

They didn't want me to fail. They wanted to be remembered.

Ashes clung to my skin, heat climbed my calves, but I listened.

Neither did I give up. I didn't lie down amongst the bones, though heat, pain, and loneliness warped my mind, and I was tempted. I set my gaze on the edge of the field and pressed on, blistered and burning, knowing that if I stopped now, I would become another voice threaded with regret.

I couldn't bear the weight of their unfinished endings, so I gripped my quill in my damp hands and placed one foot in front of the other, concentrating hard. My bare feet burned, but my hand was steady as I wrote the whispers into the hot air. With every thought I honoured, the air grew a little lighter, the field a little less hungry.

My ink magic danced, drawing out each soul-scrap like poison from a wound. Each line of ink rose and lifted like birds startled from a tree, then vanished like breath into the bone-warmed mist. I gave their fear and failings form.

As I reached the other side of the Bonefield and clambered out of it, legs trembling, hands blackened by ash and ink, a warmth that was not pain washed over me: gratitude, maybe.

I straightened slowly, my breath ragged, thanking any star that would listen for my luck in surviving the second trial. But then, my gaze was drawn upwards, as if some invisible tether had cinched tight around my eyeballs and pulled.

That's when I saw him. Ryvaris.

Perched on an outcrop of obsidian rock above the field, half-wreathed in mist and the rising heat of the isle, was the dragon the old bones had shown me, and he was as magnificent as the vision had foretold.

His horns spiralled like dark calligraphy etched against the dawn, and his wings stretched wide, tapering into blades of midnight edged with veins of molten silver. His eyes found me at once: molten moons, unblinking and vast.

I couldn't look away. Ryvaris's stare pinned me like a blade pressed to a pulse point. Something stirred in my chest, as though a piece of me had been waiting to be seen by those eyes and only those.

Ryvaris did not move. He did not roar or flare his wings. He simply watched me, weighing every breath I took. And though he said nothing, I gleaned his meaning like a word written on the inside of my ribs.

Soon, said the dragon. *Soon.*

I swallowed hard, the words forming at the edge of my mind: I am ready.

The dragon's eyes narrowed almost imperceptibly, and then he took to the skies. His wings beat with a sonorous roar, and he ascended like a shadow cast by a comet. Only when he had faded from sight did I look at the viewing pane.

There, the sisters stood in silent awe, and my aunt's austere face broke into the glimmer of a smile.

44

YSADORA

I wish for a storm of love that sweeps me off my feet and anchors me in the chaos, not one that unravels at the first tremor.
— Danaë annotations in her Faerie books

S oon, Ryvaris had said, but I was a wreck and not ready to face my doom or my destiny.

I needed to breathe without ash in my lungs and to recuperate enough that my pulse drummed without dread crowding it. The crooked lighthouse that housed the final trial loomed in the near distance, but I had no intention of making my way there yet.

What I wouldn't have given to lay my head in Zephyr's lap, just for a while, and enjoy the marvels of the world around us: to doze in a meadow of wildflowers and watch the clouds, rather than ominous shapes within them, to take comfort in each other's bodies and feel the rising heat that had nothing to do with dragon flame and retribution, but love and desire instead.

I was delirious with the need for Zephyr, and perhaps some infection had set in, but I didn't dare look at my feet, knowing that their state would match the horrors of my imagination, and this time, I had no salve or linens to tend to them.

Instead, I limped over to where I'd left my boots. Each step was a grim shuffle on ruined feet, my muscles quivering with exhaustion. I sank onto a flat rock at the edge of the isle with a groan and stared out over the sea, keeping a wary eye and ear out for dragons I might irritate with my presence.

Salt clung to the wind, and I parted my lips, hoping it might scour the Bonefield from inside me. The sea water swirled with secrets and I looked out across the water, sending desperate wishes to those I loved—to Father, Maren, Ferrith, Elowen, to the mercenaries, and my mate, most of all—to stay safe, to always be safe, whether I walked away from this isle or became part of its myth.

My hair was tangled with soot and sweat, the severed ends crisp and uneven where I had used the dragon-kissed blade to sever my braid. I ran my fingers through the strands, feeling strangely lighter, and startled at careful footfalls behind me.

"I'm forbidden to intervene in your healing," said Araminta. "But you may heal yourself."

I had no way to heal myself with chaos and ink, and there were no plants I recognised on the isle. "Is the third trial soon?"

"Not until dusk. Dragons prefer twilight. They say the light is truer then."

"Why did you come if not to help?"

Araminta settled beside me with a heavy sigh, her weathered hands folding together. "So you can close your eyes. The dragons will not bother you while I am here." Her voice carried the weight of someone who'd witnessed too many trials, too many failures.

The gruff softness in her tone surprised me. I nodded and leaned back against the warm stone and let my spine release its tension. With her there, I let myself rest. The kind of stillness that is earned.

Ryvaris's moon-silver eyes haunted the darkness behind my lids. Watching. Waiting.

Eventually, sleep claimed me. In my dream, I stood at the mouth of a river, and Tanuhja was there, though this time I had short hair and hers was long. She touched my cheek, and her violet eyes were serious.

My headstrong girl, you attempt Kindling despite my warning, and fate is not always kind. I have sent the river sisters to revive you when the time comes. Even courage needs gentleness.

She kissed my brow, and the dream shifted, flowing like water over rock, dissolving into a hush of waves and a strange, sweet chanting. I woke to coolness on my feet. Salty sea water poured by hands that were not quite mortal.

Blinking against the light, I propped myself up on one elbow, heart pounding, uncertain if I still dreamed. Sea-slick and glistening, the river sisters knelt over me, their touch light as foam. They wore wrappings of braided seaweed and scraps of silver-scaled fabric that glinted like fish-bellies in the dusk. Their limbs were long and jointless, but elegant, and their faces were as translucent as blown glass, revealing flickers of movement beneath as though prophecy swam there.

Araminta stood not three feet away, arms folded, not intervening, but not indifferent. Her face was unreadable, save for the way one hand clenched slightly at her side, a dagger glinting in her grip as the river sisters continued their work, cupping my arches, pouring water over my burns, scouring with sea salt. There was no mischief to them this time, only a quiet fortitude that verged on sorrow.

"We are not here to save you. Your mother sends us with love, only to remind you: you are not alone," said the first.

"The one who sees you watches still. His hunger is old, but his heart may yet bend," said the second.

I touched a third one in silent gratitude, and she paused, the lines of her body trembling like a reflection disturbed in still waters. Her fingertips brushed mine— cool, weightless—and in that instant I saw rivers winding through starless groves, and a woman's voice calling her child through mist.

Then she offered me a single strand from her seaweed-wrapped wrist, laying it across my palm. A blessing, perhaps. The others finished their work and rose in unison, and the river sisters melted back into the sea. But the third's opal eyes, fathomless and still, met mine for the briefest beat before she vanished with the others, a pale shape swallowed by the surf.

"Well, Ysadora." Araminta's tone was wry as she sheathed her blade. "It seems you have your father's luck."

My father's luck. That twisting, thorned thing that had

won him dragons but lost him so much more. I didn't know if I wanted it. Above us, the dragons grew impatient, their flight becoming sharp and angular, carving patterns of agitation into the sky. Flames flickered at the corners of their mouths: restless heat barely restrained.

Tentatively, I flexed my toes, and when they didn't hurt, I checked one foot and then the other. There was no blackened, brittle, or raw, weeping skin. No blisters or sliced flesh. Instead, my feet were pink and whole and revived.

I pulled my boots back on, laced them, and turned to my aunt. "It's time."

THE LIGHT HAD SHIFTED. Not just the sun lowering over Nightblaze Isle, but the air itself thinning and tightening, as if Faerie held her breath.

Liora's voice rang sharp with authority as she called the others to attention. "Positions, everyone. The dragons grow restless."

She rang the bone-chime that hung beside the lighthouse stairs, and the sound was high and mournful, like wind through a hollow ribcage. The dragons heard it, also. Their wings stirred the dusk as they descended in anticipation to the roof of the lighthouse.

"This trial requires surrender," said my aunt of the *Sky Ascent*. "We will return to the viewing pane, but we will have no sight of what transpires above us. When the moment comes, you must leap without magic. We will know you fail only if you fall past us, or we'll know you succeeded if you rise on dragon wings."

"Be brave." Phaedran tilted her head, the beads in her hair catching the evening light like distant stars. "But without pride."

Liora's boots scraped against the stone as she shifted her weight. "We've staked much on your success, whether you asked for it or not. If you fail to secure a dragon bond, the Spymaster will assert his will on Faerie."

Araminta's expression flattened into something unreadable, like a door closing just before a storm. "Look up, and you'll see expectation. Look down, and you'll see fear. Look inwards, Ysadora, and if you find anything worth catching, perhaps Ryvaris will, too."

Iskriel nodded. "The air knows what belongs to it. Step when it calls. No sooner, no later. Anything else is death in disguise."

"Enough." My aunt was brusque, though worry flickered in her eyes. "Dragons do not wait for riders to find their courage."

Serayne gave me a soft, parting smile and led the others up the narrow stairwell. Only when the final boot cleared the stairs did I put the old dream of me falling from the lighthouse out of my head, shake the dread from my limbs and begin my ascent.

Father's quill and the dragon-kissed blade felt redundant against my skin. Still, I climbed. The spiral stairs rose ahead of me like a question, damp with the chill of evening dew, and each step tested my courage.

What if I wasn't enough? What if passing the previous trials had been mere luck? The whispers from the Bonefield lanced through my mind. Would I join all those who had tried and failed, their bones now part of the isle's foundation?

Even before I reached the top, I heard the dragons breathing, bodies shifting like boulders grinding against the world. The air was heavy with smoke and the musk of dragon hide, dense enough to coat my throat.

I emerged into the tearing wind and endless sky. I dared not look out over the breathless gulf between the edge of the platform and what might wait beyond it, not with dragon heads swivelling my way, like storm clouds gathering thought, sentience coiled in every breath.

Awe, terror, and reverence tangled in my chest. I felt smaller than I ever had, smaller even than the girl I had been in my father's bookshop, unknowingly drinking a potion to mask my fae self. Here, in front of the dragons, I was laid bare. I glanced at the circle of dimmed stars overhead that Lunarys had strung together for the lighthouse and centred myself.

Then, heart in my mouth, channelling my mate's belief in me as if it were my own, I walked towards the first dragon, a skybeast.

As my gaze locked with her citrine eyes, I bit my lip so hard I drew blood. She was huge—brutish, scarred, bronze plates over rippling muscle—a dragon that might once have been feral. Her tail lashed hard enough to send me over the edge had it come any closer.

She lowered her horned head to my cheek and inhaled deeply, and the rattle of her breath made my stomach twist. The heat of her nostrils made sweat bead across my forehead, and I fought the urge to step back, to run. Her jaw opened so wide, the air heated with flames lying in wait, and for one breathless moment, I thought she might burn me whole and leave the pickings of my body in the Bonefield. Then she huffed and turned her head.

Not rejection, exactly, but disinterest; I was not hers.

With feet like lead, I carefully made my way to the next dragon. The wind howled, and the abyss beckoned, and my heart hammered a reckless rhythm, questioning how I could possibly think a girl from Larkspur could claim a dragon in Faerie.

The dragon was a halo serpent, long-necked and narrow-eyed, sinuous green in colour like moss over wet stone. He tilted his head sharply as I approached, smoke curling from his nostrils. His gaze drilled into me, peeling away my courage like brittle bark.

I was exposed, every flaw illuminated, every moment of doubt magnified, as if he said, *You are nothing. You are no one. Why do you dare stand before us?* And then he exhaled a low, dissatisfied growl, launched into the sky and took up a higher perch, facing away.

Two rejections and cold fear in my chest spread like frost. What made me think I belonged here?

The third dragon was an aetherian, I thought, hulking and coal-dark, and Araminta had described them as determined and curious. But in his pupils, I saw not curiosity, but calculation. He hissed low, and I felt the spell of my offering unravel in the air, tasted the burn of pride I thought I'd left behind.

The dragon read me like a book, and he found every page wanting. The platform suddenly felt like a stage for my humiliation. When our eyes met, the dragon clicked his jaws together once, dismissively, and snarled loud enough for me to flinch. My pulse went wild, thinking that would be it, that the flames would come. But he lumbered away and didn't look back.

Three failures. The taste of defeat was ash on my tongue. I stood there, throat burning, my courage in tatters, three dragons gone cold. They had judged me and found something lacking. The taste of failure was bitter on my tongue, and I couldn't even turn my head—my movements small and incremental to avoid riling the beasts—to see if the dragon the old bones had shown me was there.

The fourth unsettled me more than those before. It was a nebulite in starry silver, every scale edged in a faint shimmer of purple, like frosted chaos. Her claws were too long, her body thin from age or choice, and her wings made no sound when they shifted.

I couldn't breathe under her strange gaze, and still, I held it until she turned her attention to my ink-stained hands. The nebulite's shoulder brushed my face. It left behind a chill like snowfall on bare skin, but there was something in her touch, perhaps longing. She made a sound like distant thunder, low and questioning.

That rumble drew another response: deeper, more resonant.

It broke her focus and mine, and we both turned towards the growl.

I felt his presence like a pressure in the chest, like gravity had tilted: Ryvaris.

He was perched high on the edge of the platform, an ink-horned astral dragon coiled like poetry made flesh, looking down on me in perfect stillness. He did not blink. Whereas the others had assessed me with ancient, ruthless clarity, his gaze felt like a question.

His mirrored moon-eyes shone silver, the exact colour of the veins that had shimmered across his wings. Recognition crackled between us, and possibility.

I stepped towards him without knowing I was doing it.

Though I wanted to bow, I didn't.

Ryvaris's gaze lingered on my hacked hair, on the pocket which held Caldoron's dragon-kissed dagger, on the cavity that hid my thundering heart. He saw everything.

And in my mind, as clear as breath on glass, he said, *You are mine.*

My pulse slowed. I wasn't afraid anymore.

He inclined his head, a movement so slight I could have imagined it. So subtle, it might have been mist shifting or the way stars nod just before dawn. And I understood that the *Sky Ascent* was in fact the opposite, and I was ready to fall in surrender.

I stepped to the edge and stood at the precipice. The wind howled up from the abyss, wild and alive, tasting of salt, ash, and endings. The sky was one of Veda's paintings, a vast canvas bleeding twilight hues, the bonded dragons circling like titans of fate.

My thoughts darted to that old dream of falling, and I accepted whatever outcome destiny had written for me. The dimmed stars crowning the crooked lighthouse bloomed like a bouquet of starlight gathered by Lunarys herself, and in that silver hush, I thought: perhaps I could surrender to the death, if it meant blinking out to wonder like this.

My boots tipped on the stone rim, feeling the pulse of the world beneath my feet. Father had not closed his eyes when he leapt, so I kept mine open, wide and wet with wind, and I let go. I fell backwards like a quill falling from a desk, an ink drop cast into the sky, small and meagre, only one cog in a vast realm of possibility.

Air rushed up to meet me, tearing the breath from my lungs. The stars above spun wildly. The lighthouse shrank. My limbs flailed once, then stilled.

I was falling,

falling,

falling.

In that terrible silence, I saw not one, but two dragons launch after me.

Ryvaris dove first, silver-veined and ink-dark, streaked downwards with thunderous power, his regal gaze trained on me. But the nebulite was airborne, too, ghosting in and out of visibility with every wingbeat, like a dream rupturing. She was pale as a dying star. Her wings were not scaled but gauze-like and stretched between moonlit bones.

She shrieked through her narrow maw—the sound of something ancient and unloved—veering hard so she cut straight across Ryvaris's path, a blur of gauze and claw. They collided above me. It was not graceful; it was chaos.

They were a tangle of scale and smoke, of talons and teeth. Ryvaris's claws raked the nebulite's shoulder, and silver blood scattered like stars. She retaliated by driving her fangs towards his throat, but he pulled back, his tail lashing to maintain balance.

I was still falling.

I tumbled beneath their battle, limbs splayed, breath ripped from my lungs. My stomach clawed towards my spine, and the wind and dragon roars filled my ears. Smoke exploded from Ryvaris's nostrils as the nebulite's wings coiled around him. She released him, diving towards me, but he slammed into her side, sending her spinning before she regrouped, silver eyes blazing with rage.

The battle had cost precious seconds. There would be no time for them to save me, not while they were at war with one another. I wondered if Father had ever fallen or Araminta. I wondered if a fall was survivable.

I wanted to reach for a seam of chaos. I wanted to make myself wings of ink, and I thought maybe I could if I had long enough. But the final trial could be won only through surrender.

So I fell, willing myself to be lighter, braver, to acceptance itself, but gravity had no mercy and no care for me.

This was not flight. This was the void.

The stars Lunarys had strung blurred into tears.

I was going to die here. Bones on stone. A voice of regrets.

Then there was a crack of glass or wards or stars-knows-what. Shadows lashed against the viewing pane, pouring through like water through a broken dam, strong arms—reinforced with dark shadows that in my dream I had mistaken for gloves—pulled me towards a centre of gravity my heart would always know: Zephyr.

The sisters of the Circle of Emberlight cried out, my aunt foremost amongst them. "No! You must not intervene! The wards…he broke them!"

But Zephyr, my *Fatebreaker*, reached for me anyway, reckless and furious with love. The bond was wide open, no longer a thread, but a torrent, a rush of light and memory and breath. And stars, his fear for me, his utter relief to hold me in his arms again. This was love, sharpened into something feral. He had seen me fall. He had thought it would end with broken bones and cutting silence. And now, to feel me in his arms again—even if only for a heartbeat—was too much and not enough.

Inkheart, Inkheart, said my mate in that suspended moment, as if saying my name might anchor me to the world, as if love alone might slow the fall. *Don't you ever leave me in the dark again.*

But before I met the bliss of his chest, before I could look into his storm-dark eyes and trace the dimple in his cheek, and drink in the forest scent of him, before I could feel the heat of his body against mine, the hitch in his breath or even speak his name, Zephyr's eyes widened in terror.

A dragon came like a living shadow, riding an unseen current. It struck the lighthouse wall with enough force to crack stone, claws finding purchase on the broken viewing pane. Its roar split the air. Talons wrapped around me like a second ribcage. A violent yank backwards, and I was ripped away from my mate, dragged back into the sky. Heat poured over me. The dragon's heart thundered with mine.

I looked up into twin moons full of knowing.

Through them, I saw not my fall, but my flight.

The air glimmered with magic as rider and dragon bonded. Then Ryvaris spread his wings and caught the evening wind, carrying us both through the star-scattered sky.

Somewhere, Araminta whooped, and pride—so fierce it made my heart sing—flared bright in the mate bond.

ZEPHYR

*No toffee in your pockets again? Truly, your love
wanes. I shall mourn until you make it up to me
with ten pieces and a kiss.
- Ysa's note to Zephyr on the morning of his
return*

The calligrapher's daughter, whom the *Fatebreaker*
loved beyond measure, had claimed her dragon
as he knew she would, almost as if it had been
written in the stars. He'd known his brilliant mate would
succeed, not because of any certainty offered by the cryptic
Binder, but because of his faith in her. But that didn't dull
the way his knees buckled when Ysa fell.

She fell with a stillness that terrified him, mouth parted
in something close to peace—no flailing, no magic—
trusting a dragon to catch her or nothing at all. For one
trembling blink of eternity, nothing existed but her falling
body and the thunder in his chest. He feared she had

already left him until the bond burned bright and he knew she was still alive.

Then his instincts and his magic slammed into action, and he almost had her, safe, against his chest, when the ink-veined blue wrenched her away, and his arms snapped shut on nothing but wind.

He sucked in an agonised breath as the dragon soared through the sky with his mate clutched in his talons like a prize. She looked impossibly small and heartbreakingly brave: hair hacked short (that, he didn't understand), leathers torn, skin streaked with soot. Zephyr braced himself to unleash night itself to defend her, until the mate bond flared with Ysa's wild joy.

And he knew: she had been chosen.

The relief that she was okay poured through him.

Ancients, he loved her more for her fierce heart than for her achievements.

The Circle of Emberlight had cheered around him, but Zephyr staggered back from the viewing pane and turned away from them. The sound he made was half sob, half laugh. His soul was too full of wonder and gratitude to be with strangers.

He pressed his hand over his chest, over the place where the mate bond flared. Then he closed his eyes and let the bond flood him with glimpses of Ysa's reality: the scent of scorched air in her lungs, the beat of ancient wings thrumming through her bones, the talons curled around her but never piercing, their path over cliffs to a wind-carved ledge where the dragon invited her to clamber onto his back. His mate gripped the ridges of her dragon's spine, and then they were airborne, scale to skin, not as master, not as burden, but as kin.

He pulled back from the bond then and let her have her moment, unobserved.

The shadow prince shuddered. Though he had encouraged Ysa to take risks to earn her place in Faerie, he realised that he had only ever meant for her to take risks when he could control the outcome, and that he was furious at Kazimir for allowing Ysa to face such trials alone.

Still, for all Zephyr's fiercely protective instincts, his mate was a star of her own making, and the Binder would be pleased that they had each followed their paths and met not in shadow, but in the blaze of their becoming.

His uncle thought Ysa fragile, but she had never been fragile, not even when she was mortal. She was strong. Even before she had touched the meteor, the calligrapher's daughter had been a myth, a youngling capable of stabilising Faerie.

He had witnessed her skill in building not only alliances but loyalty, navigating the path of fractured family with grace, making ink magic her own despite Kazimir's weaknesses, learning to bend pain into chaos when he floundered under the weight of it.

He had seen her refuse to cower before those more powerful than her and experienced how it was to have her love unmake him and build him back up again. She was a marvel, capable of rewriting the Grimoire to create the Faerie they dreamed of, and now with her dragon, she was a reckoning.

A wolfish grin curved Zephyr's lips, sharp and full of promise.

A dragon meant more than wings and fire. It was proof that Ysa was dangerous. It prevented their enemies from seeking her out, from thinking they could tame her. A dragon was also legitimacy. It meant that the old powers of Faerie had chosen his mate.

Their cause was no longer just rebellion; it was sanctified. And when Ysa absolved her bargain with Esolas, when she attended the meeting of the rulers, her dragon would land like a war banner.

For all his hopes, a chill ran down Zephyr's spine as he tallied the web of victories they had secured to give them the best chance of besting his uncle: the dragon, yes, but it had begun earlier, with the decision to leave Ebonspire, to cast off safety for strategy.

Bargaining with Esolas. Ysa's hard-won command of her chaos magic. Drawing information from the Binder. Finding the High King's crown. Forging alliances through bargains, daring, and sacrifice. Calling in the Thorn King's long-slumbering favour. And yet, there were so many unknowns that troubled him, including his own fragile mind with its tangled stories.

First amongst them: where the fuck was Loxley?

He drew a steadying breath, pulling himself back into the present moment, back into the room, back into the slow drag of breath and blood, realising he'd been adrift in the tides of thought and the weight of what still lay ahead. The reverent hush as Ysa had endured the *Sky Ascent* was gone, and they had forgotten their fury at his interference. After all, Ysa had chosen to fall without magic, and the veined blue had chosen her.

"The old bones called it true," said Liora. "Aurenza can't have thought she stood a chance against him."

Iskriel arched an eyebrow. "Indeed, his wingspan alone boded ill for her, let alone his fangs."

Phaedran nodded. "The others will be disheartened to miss a successful *Kindling* after so many previous falls."

Only the older one, Araminta, turned to him and said, "The dragon's name is Ryvaris, shadow prince, and he will keep your mate safe when you cannot."

"Then I owe him more than I can ever repay," said Zephyr. "And I'll still try."

A sliver of respect warmed her gaze. Her eyes lingered on Zephyr, just long enough to say: *you'll do well enough.* "You can start by providing coin to fix the viewing pane." Then she turned. "Sisters, to our dragons. The Circle of Emberlight has grown, and the sky awaits us." From the pouch at her belt, she drew a loop of beads and passed them to Phaedran. They shimmered, streaked with silver and blood-red, like molten sky.

Zephyr joined them as they trudged down the spiral steps, boots ringing against stone, although he resented the walls that curtailed his glimpses of Ysa, wanted to push past them so that he could look up. He didn't, of course, he hadn't ever forgotten the courtly ways his mother had taught him, even in his mercenary life.

Outside, the isle lay cloaked in full night. The moon hung high and bright, and the stars Lunarys had strung together for the lighthouse flickered pale against the ash-smeared sky. Kazimir stood waiting on an old volcanic outcrop beside Caldoron, who had flown them to the isle. The dragon's hide shone copper in the moonlight, gleaming like a leprechaun's treasure. Above them, Ryvaris soared through the air with Ysa, and Caldoron snorted a plume of smoke, as if he disapproved of such theatrics, and then the dragon's ember gaze settled on

Liora Bramick, as if he would like to flay her skin from her bones.

Zephyr filed away that piece of animosity, remembering the Binder's prompting for Ysa to question the Circle of Emberlight's leader.

He liked Liora. Her decision to intervene during the last battle with Thiago and Danaë had almost certainly tipped the odds in the mercenaries' favour. He was reminded how Faerie, in all its brutal beauty, offered no reward for virtue. Sometimes, it was necessary to choose baser instincts over grace to survive.

His mind flashed back to his desperate journey to reach this moment: Mythros slick with sweat, his flanks heaving, foam flecking his bit as Zephyr urged him on, the shadow mark burning dark and urgent at the stallion's shoulder. His steed's eyes rolled white with effort, hooves striking sparks against stone as they thundered the last ridge towards the Court of Bones, but still Zephyr urged him on, promising rest only when he reached the calligrapher. The shadow mark pulled like a storm tide, but he vowed to see Ysa again or die trying.

He made his way to the calligrapher's side. "Kazimir," he started, intending to make amends for his harsh demands when he had arrived, demands that had earned him one of Queen Thalindra's cool, arched brows, lifted in bemused reprimand. Ysa's inked goodbye had drowned all reason.

The calligrapher laid his hand against his breastbone. "I saw what you did, Zephyr. Were it not for you, Ysa would have—"

Zephyr placed his hand over Kazimir's. "Don't say it."

He couldn't bear for his worst fears to be given shape in words.

Kazimir stepped back, squinting upwards, his throat bobbing with emotion. "I never imagined that females would take to the skies. My own sister…" At that, Zephyr frowned, stealing his focus from the horizon, but the calligrapher continued. "Two dragons fought over Ysa… two. And Ryvaris, the fiercest amongst them, chose her."

Caldoron gave a low snort. His eyes glowed like twin embers banked low, older than the tide.

"Peace, old friend. No one's questioning your glory." Kazimir chuckled. "Oh yes, I'm sure the blade you blessed played a part in how foolishly Aurenza challenged Ryvaris. Perhaps she thought Ysa had your backing even though you deigned not to intervene in the rite."

At Ebonspire, there had been a strain between Kazimir and his dragon; whatever rift had existed was gone. The old fae stood taller, almost miraculously healed by Thalindra, and the dragon leaned into his rider, utterly at ease.

Zephyr allowed himself a quiet smile. Not all broken things stayed that way. Just as he felt the magnetised pull again to the starry sky, to his mate, a vast shadow passed over them and a rush of wind swept through the clearing, dry and electric, rattling the grasses and tugging at their clothes.

Dust spiralled upwards in glowing motes as a dragon landed. Zephyr's shadows seeped out to meet the threat, but then they quietened of their own accord, as if in recognition. There was only one soul they would do that for.

He turned, and forgot how to think.

Ysa slid down her dragon's foreleg, an entire sky in her twilight eyes. She was ash-streaked, wild-haired, radiant in her exhaustion. Every dream he'd ever whispered to her was written on her face.

And every plan, every worry, every breath he'd been holding shattered into nothing.

"Well, Zephyr?" She cocked her head, the veined blue formidable behind her, and he wanted to fall to his knees at the sound of his name on her lips. "Do you want a ride to the Court of Bones or not?"

But the mate bond said something else entirely. The mate bond said, *kiss me, hold me, be mine for all time.*

Zephyr didn't need another invitation. There, before her father and the sisters of the Circle of Emberlight, before their five dragons and Ryvaris, who was Ysa's, he kissed her.

His hands tangled in her hair, pulling her closer, as if he could shield her from every danger simply by holding her tight. Her hair smelled of smoke and starlight, the shortened strands between his fingers in need of soaping.

He kissed her like there would be no tomorrows, and for agonising hours when she had been imperilled, he believed that was so. He kissed her so thoroughly that his lips bruised and her cheeks flushed as if their passion belonged in the bed chamber and not here, for all the world to see.

He kissed her with the hunger of a parched man lost in the endless Wastelands, searching for an oasis, as if her taste was a promise of life, the only place that felt like home. Her breath came in shaky bursts, mingling with his, and for a moment, the chaos of Faerie faded, and only the fierce, electric pulse of their connection remained.

Not the calligrapher's daughter and her *Fatebreaker*.

Certainly not the reality anchor and her magical safety mechanism.

Simply lovers, soulmates, kin.

When they finally parted, his forehead rested against hers.

"Ah, young love, burning brighter than dragon flames," said Kazimir, earning another huff from Caldoron.

Araminta eyeballed the calligrapher, and Zephyr realised who his sister was as they bristled at each other. "Can't say the dragons didn't get a show, but let's get on, shall we? Lest they fly off in protest."

Amidst the circle of riders and dragons, with Zephyr at her side and the calligrapher's scowl deepening at Liora's every move, Ysa gave her sacred oath to the dragon who had chosen her. The oath was not spoken out loud because Ryvaris had told Ysa they would make their own.

Then Liora Bramick braided three strands of Ysa's hair with beads, one for every trial she had passed, and the Circle of Emberlight welcomed her into their order. All the while, Lunarys's circle of dimmed stars shone atop the lighthouse, and a nearby tower of dragon bones gleamed under the moon.

The night held its breath, and there was a lone luminous violet flower that pushed out of the cracks of rock at Ysa's feet. The scent of scorched stone and old storms filled the air. When the ceremony was complete, Ysa kissed her father's cheek.

Then she took Zephyr's hand, eyes bright with triumph and tenderness. "Shall we?"

He smiled and, through the bond, showed her exactly

what he expected on the other side of the flight. "Try and stop me."

Ryvaris turned his great head towards them and exhaled a curl of smoke in warning, but Ysa wasn't afraid. Laughing, she led him up the deep blue scales, where they settled on the saddleless curve of the dragon's spine.

Zephyr brushed his lips to the crown of her head. "I dreamed of you like this, Inkheart. Unbreakable, alight, sky born."

She turned her face slightly, brushing her cheek against his chest, then looked forward. "Hold on," she murmured.

His arms wrapped around his mate's waist, his chin tucked against her shoulder, and he swallowed a curse as Ryvaris launched into the sky, quicker and stronger than Caldoron.

His Inkheart was wild and shining, with beads in her hair. They were not alone in the sky. Above and below, dragons flew in formation: beasts of obsidian and copper, of pearly pink and duskfire.

Pride burst in his chest as Faerie unfurled beneath them. Stars scattered over the sea like silver coins. The salt wind was sharp against their faces as Ryvaris's muscles rippled beneath them. The other dragons' calls echoed across the night sky, and for a few blessed minutes, nothing chased them.

Not duty. Not danger. Only the thrum of wings.

YSADORA

*Let it be remembered: tending dragons is not the
same as commanding them. The old laws
preventing female riders must be upheld,
regardless of talents shown in menial tasks.
– A Short History of the Order of the Glyph*

My bedchamber at the Court of Bones had been too austere, too cold, the previous night. The faerie queen's generosity had not eased my loneliness. Ceilings carved from pale stone, a lattice of bone work over the windows that made me feel like a prisoner of fate, shadows tucked in every corner like forgotten promises from my absent mate.

But now Zephyr was here. His body, sprawled beside mine on the hard bed, was all the comfort I needed. He didn't just fill the space; he warmed it. He made it feel lived-in, his cloak and boots discarded on the floor, although neither of us had much in the way of belongings.

The long lines of his body were stretched towards me, one muscular arm bent behind his head, his other hand cupping my hip, so we pressed into each other. I could smell the storm scent of his skin, the salt of flight still clinging to him, and that quiet hum of the mate bond was golden and alive, wrapped around my ribs like a soft tether.

"Are you all right?" I asked gently.

He blinked at me, like he was caught in memory. "I am now that I found you."

His storm-dark eyes locked onto mine, and in their depths I saw the cost of loving me: the sleepless nights, the weight of command, the agony of not knowing if I would survive. His gaze was a tempest still, but quieter now, tinged with the weariness of someone who had waited too long for the promise of peace.

Stars, I'd missed him, this male who had held the sky open for me, again and again.

"I like what you've done with your hair," he said solemnly.

"Liar." A laugh burst from me, because I'd seen my reflection in the polished floors as we made our way to blessed privacy. I traced a finger over his bicep, noticing the bargain lines had gone. "That's where you went?"

He nodded and leaned in to nibble at my lip, teasing, the wretch, testing how much I wanted him and who would break first. He kissed the corner of my mouth and then dipped in his tongue, and I moaned, sliding a hand beneath the fabric of his shirt, mapping the planes of his chest, the strong beat of his heart beneath my palm.

The silence of the chamber wrapped around us like

velvet. Zephyr breathed my name like a spell, and I arched towards him, aching to be known, to be undone by him.

Zephyr's hands skimmed my sides, my breasts, my buttocks, and his cheeks dimpled as I bit my lip, not wanting to beg for more, knowing he knew the exact shape of my need through the mate bond.

A shadow encircled my waist like a caress, holding me in place as he pulled my tunic down and trailed heat along my collarbone before lowering his mouth to one breast, circling the soft peaks with his tongue, before giving the other breast the same attention, and skies, the sight of his dark tousled head there, the wicked grin on his tawny face as he looked up and caught the ecstasy on my face.

But two could play at that game. "Release me," I said, and Zephyr's shadows fell away.

The bed shifted as I stood and peeled off my clothes. His own garments disappeared in between my kisses, first on his torso, and then down to the sparse smattering of hair above his straining manhood.

Zephyr drank in the sight of me in the moonlight, and I did the same: his sculpted chest, the strength of his shoulders, his lashes casting shadows over his cheeks, his pupils blown wide with desire and devotion. I kissed my way up his thighs, smiling at the way he trembled beneath my mouth.

The tension in him was coiled, just beneath the surface, held only by will. "You're going to undo me."

"Good." I wanted him unmade for me, to peel back every layer of composure.

He tried to stay still beneath my touch, but his shadows betrayed him. They rippled like water, guiding me with all the want he wouldn't speak aloud. When I finally took him into my mouth, he cursed in a language I didn't know, his hips bucking instinctively before he stilled, giving me control.

I took him slower, deeper, savouring the taste of him—storm and longing—and when he stilled like he was nearly at his zenith, I pushed him back to sit on the bed and climbed into his lap, tracing a light finger over our matching runes.

He hissed through his teeth as I brushed my breasts against his chest. "Ancients, Ysa…"

"You always look at me like I'm sacred."

His breath caught. "You're everything the stars promised and more."

Zephyr gripped my hips when I straddled and lowered myself onto him. When our bodies aligned, his shadows moved with us, synchronised and knowing. They cradled me, pressing me flush against him, winding around my wrists and lower back in a dance that felt as much worship as it was possession.

We moved, fevered and fused, the bond pulling tight between us until I didn't know where he ended and where I began. It flared so hot between us that it could have melted bone. There was no rush. Only the low rumble in his throat when my nails skimmed his back. Only skin and heat, our breaths falling into rhythm, and his voice low in my ear, telling me I was his.

I savoured the reverent slowness of it, how we were both so tired, but this made us come alive.

"Do you feel that?" His brow rested against mine. "The world could fall away, and I'd still find you."

I nodded, breathless. "I believe it."

Later, hair mussed, he murmured, "Sleep now, Ysa. Tomorrow, we face the kings and queens of Faerie."

Limbs tangled, I relaxed, as if my body had been waiting for this certainty. Starlight spilt across the stone floor in a silver hush, and even the dragons slept. I memorised the soft heat of Zephyr's arm draped across my waist, the salt of his sweat still drying on my skin, the unguarded peace in his features. The rhythm of his breathing soothed the wild pace of mine, and we synced breath by breath.

Beneath the peace, a splinter of dread lodged in my chest that the world wouldn't let us have this again.

ZEPHYR and I made our way to the stables before breakfast to check on Mythros. Residual shadow magic thrummed in his bones, and neither carrot nor apple tempted him. I pressed my cheek to his warm neck, breathing in the familiar scent of hay and sweat and horse, and he shivered beneath me, uneasy. He skittered, stamping once, as if he could scent Ryvaris clinging to my skin like perfume. I murmured apologies into his mane, and his breath huffed out in something close to forgiveness.

My reunion with the mercenaries at breakfast was a raucous storm of rough embraces, curses and backslaps hard enough to bruise, their affection as unapologetic as their blade-work. I hadn't known how hollow I'd felt until I was wrapped in their wild, warm presence again. Even Sequoia, whose affection came wrapped in barbs, pulled me into a crushing hug.

"So now you can fly, too," she muttered, as if the words hurt her pride but swelled her heart.

My mate watched; a softness in his steely eyes. Then, shamans with their hoods drawn up led us to a solitary slab of basalt on a barren plain, where incense burned low in cracked skulls.

The Queen of Bones sat on a stone stool, ringed by smooth tree stumps. No guards flanked her. None were needed amongst allies. She was surrounded by flat bowls of salt and bone fragments—divining tools—and behind her, totems of elephant tusks dangled from crooked branches, rattling with the breeze. She was beautiful in layered taupe chiffon and her circlet of bleached antlers.

She did not rise or greet us.

A hush fell as we all took our places. Cyprian chose a tree stump furthest from the faerie queen, and Sequoia jostled for position beside him, leaving Wylda to file in next and Zephyr and me to follow. He was close enough for me to feel the heat of him under the thin court cloak he wore.

Others joined us at the queen's invitation: Father, Liora, Araminta, and the three Circle of Emberlight members who had accompanied me to *Kindling*, and a few elderly courtiers who from time to time consulted the divination tools.

Thalindra flicked her opaque gaze across the assembly. "The hour of the meeting of the rulers is nigh. Speak your truths, before the bones speak theirs. Let the bones weigh every vow, every grievance. And when the last word is spoken, we will call the dragons." Her mouth crooked just slightly at Father, and he looked carefully away.

A crease formed between Zephyr's brows. *Kazimir*

*assured me that Thalindra's support was certain. But did he
confide the terms of her allegiance to you?* he asked through
the bond.

*He's guarding something. Whatever he traded, it wasn't
small,* I replied.

No one spoke at first. Then Liora raised her voice, the
beads in her hair catching the weak sunlight. "The Circle
of Emberlight recognises Ysadora Silberquill, the
calligrapher's daughter, as dragon-chosen, trial-hardened.
Our sister."

Thalindra studied me, her lips neither smiling nor
frowning. Around her, the older courtiers whispered
softly, tossing shards and bones into their bowls, watching
the fall of salt with more reverence than most gave to gods.
I wondered what the dragons in the distance made of this
strange communion.

"This is a boon for our cause, but you are untested in
diplomacy or battle, Ysadora. We cannot be sure that your
presence and that of your dragon, given your untrained
bond, will turn the tide against the King of Silence."

Give her hell, smiled my mate.

I met the Queen of Bones's gaze, spine straight, the
weight of Ryvaris's flight still coiled in my bones. In my
chest, the dragon stirred: an awareness, a readiness. "I did
not come to be coddled. I came to be useful. And I think
you'll find that given that I am the sole reason why the
Faerie rulers are meeting, my *presence* is less ornamental
than most."

Cyprian guffawed and earned a stern stare from the
queen, and Father looked down.

Oh, she's not going to like that, drawled Zephyr.

Behind Thalindra, the diviners continued to sift bone

and salt, but even their movements slowed. The queen did not blink. Her gaze was the kind that stripped layers, seeking the marrow beneath. "Your father's steel, then. Or your mother's defiance?"

"Both." Zephyr's voice carried the practised cadence of someone who could move between courts both in light and shadow, though he'd never felt he truly belonged. "Perhaps I may paint a picture for the court of where we stand."

The queen's fingers trailed through a bowl of salt, slow, circular, thoughtful. "You may proceed, shadow prince."

I raised an eyebrow at my mate. *Very smooth.* I didn't like the way Thalindra's attention lingered on the males new to her court, and Wylda, too, noticed and caught my eye.

One of my many talents, Inkheart, is how practised I am at diplomacy. The other is distracting queens, but only one female has ever truly undone me. "You have ruled longer than most have drawn breath. You've watched courts rise, fall, devour themselves. No court is safe. Not even yours. The King of Silence doesn't care for borders or crowns, only conquest. But fortune is with us. The bloodheart tree sheds its leaves. My uncle is weak. We have traded sleep for strategy, struck bargains and roused dragons from slumber to strengthen our hand. This alliance isn't built on hope. It's built on sacrifice."

Thalindra's eyes gleamed. "And yet, my shamans tell me that the Court of Luminosity and the Court of Silver Seas stand with the King of Silence. The Court of Nebulas is fractured. Both the Court of Embers and the Court of Chaos are indifferent. Even with my vote, so cleverly won by Kazimir, this attempt is futile."

A shaman lit a second bowl of incense and placed it at her feet. The smoke wafted sideways, not with the breeze.

The sisters of the Circle of Emberlight whispered amongst themselves, like moth wings in the hush. Only Araminta remained quiet, her brown eyes darting from Father to the queen.

Oh, yes. You know how to charm her, I said sweetly through the bond. It might have been easier to sway the Bone Queen had we gauged her trustworthy enough to confide in her about the High King's crown. I was starting to suspect the reason Lunarys had taken the crown into her care was to prevent discovery by Thalindra's shamans.

I came to the same conclusion, said Zephyr. *But there are other ways to sway the game. What else would have kept me from you for so long?* His head dipped in a show of humility, but his voice remained steady, smooth as still water hiding a current beneath. "You do not need the smoke of incense to tell you that the time is ripe for change in Faerie. It is clear enough in dragon smoke. We don't need a majority. We need momentum. Enough to crack the foundations of his dominion and show the other courts he's not invincible. The rest will follow fear or the scent of victory, whichever comes first. Give us that foothold, Queen of Bones, and you won't just be remembered for your wisdom. You'll be remembered as the first who stood."

The horns hanging from the branches rattled above her head. "That is a speech your mother would have made."

Zephyr inclined his head, and the mate bond filled with melancholy. "Then I am honoured."

The ghost of a smile, too sharp to be kind, touched the

queen's mouth. "What makes you think my court won't bleed?"

Zephyr's jaw flexed. "Because I have bargained with the Thorn King."

One of the diviners drew in a breath through her teeth, muttering something under her breath in a language older than crowns. A shard of salt cracked in her bowl. The scent of the incense curled into my nose: earthy, bitter, metallic.

The Bone Queen's eyes widened. "Only fools and kings treat with the Thorn King. Which are you, shadow prince?"

Zephyr's shadows seeped from his fists. "If I'm a fool, I'm a dangerous one. And if I'm a king, I'll rule a realm free of monsters like him."

Thalindra met Father's eyes, and a shadow of understanding passed between them. "Then it is agreed. Let them think me theirs. We will play it as if Kazimir is my prisoner. Of course, I might need to break a few bones." Her voice was a purr of delight, and Father stiffened. "When the time comes, the Court of Bones will stand with you at the meeting, in voice, if not in blood. I shall travel by bone carriage, shadow prince, and perhaps you will ride with me, your stallion tethered to my horses."

Zephyr's smile curved with practised ease, that elusive dimple a mark of charm honed by too many noble rooms and too many dangerous females. "Mythros has no love for confinement, but I thank you, Thalindra."

Sequoia snorted, and I tried to keep my expression serene.

From the edge of the basalt plain, the sky stirred. Shadows peeled from the low-hanging clouds: vast silhouettes of diaphanous wings, their flight more glide than effort. The dragons had come to listen. My heart soared as Ryvaris emerged from the mist, ink-blue and silver-streaked, and then stuttered at the sight of Caldoron accompanying them, burnished bronze, the wind catching the edges of his wings and turning them to flames.

To me, the air tasted of sulphur and brimstone and old reckonings.

At the dragons' approach, Araminta raised her eyes to the sky, disconcerted.

But Liora had no such qualms, focused as she was on speaking on behalf of the Circle of Emberlight. "As neither rulers nor subjects to the bargain with Esolas, we are not sanctioned to attend the meeting, but we will stand ready with our dragons on disputed land just past Wyvern Reach in case of necessity."

Thalindra's voice dropped to a velvet murmur, soft, deadly. "I'm afraid, Liora, my dear, our alliance is over. Did you tell the rest of the sisterhood what you exchanged for access to the healing of my bone pool?"

Liora blanched and stumbled backwards off the stump. "They do not know. Please, whatever has changed…"

Thalindra smiled thinly. "Well, at least you have spared your sisters the fate that awaits you."

"Thalindra—we are friends."

"We are nothing. You turned a dragon's wrath on me."

Ryvaris's gaze landed on me—steady, searing—as if to say, *see how quickly thrones turn to ash.*

Then, finally, Father spoke. His voice was clear as cut glass, and Caldoron loomed behind him. "What you offered was not by consent. Dragon bone dust is sacred. You betrayed the oath."

503

Phaedran sprang up, red-faced, beads clinking. "It's not true."

Liora gave her a sad smile, and although her voice held venom, she staggered back towards her dragon. "I betrayed no one. I only made use of the remains. I only made my sisters safe. You benefited from centuries of tradition and training, calligrapher. You benefited from the bone pool. And yet you stand here and lecture me about the risks I took to keep my people safe?"

Serayne and Iskriel cried out, terrible understanding dawning on their faces regarding the price of their healing, and Araminta's hands curled around the arms of her stump-seat, knuckles white.

Beside me, Zephyr's shadows writhed low around his boots like smoke resisting the urge to rise.

"Tell that to the dragons," said Father coldly. Behind him, Ryvaris exhaled a plume of smoke, and Caldoron's tail lashed once against the basalt ground, and the others curled their claws into stone, as if they, too, would not forget the insult.

Stars, no. I knew about the bone dust, but for Father to use it like this… My chaos magic erupted, sending crackles of dark into the daylight.

But Zephyr whispered to me through the bond, and the fever in my blood cooled to a simmer. *Breathe, Ysa. Be ready to move if the dragons clash.*

And then Caldoron's eyes were aglow as he moved towards Liora. A low growl thundered from his throat, colder than fury, and heat shimmered from his skin. It was the sound of a dragon's verdict. Father did not stop him.

"Please," Liora begged, her sharp grey eyes clouding over, flitting not to the dragon looming before her but to her voidstalker, Satharion. I couldn't help thinking that she didn't have her scarf or her flight goggles, and that had we gathered later, Satharion could have spirited her away because he had the gift of night invisibility.

Satharion's muscles coiled, and he was ready to spring. But he did not, because Ryvaris was already there, as if by collusion with Caldoron, ink-dark wings folded, body coiled like a snare. And who was I to interfere in the justice of dragons? Who was I to tell them to forgive them when she had fallen foul of her oath?

Ryvaris barred the voidstalker's path with a guttural hiss. A ripple of pressure flattened the air around them, and Satharion whimpered, cowed. The voidstalker's eyes glowed faintly, caught between instinct and command, but it would not move. Ryvaris held him there, still as death.

And Liora knew. She held up her hands, hands that had tended her dragon and picked up her sisters from a thousand injuries. "I'm sorry," she said.

Caldoron lumbered closer, backing her into position. Each movement of his massive body was a song of inevitability: wings hissing against the wind, smoke gusting in heaves from his nostrils, heat rising. His tail swayed once, cutting a furrow into the ground behind him. All around us, silence gathered, vast and heavy. Even the shamans did not breathe.

And there, amid clanking bones and the perfume of bitter incense and scorched salt, Caldoron opened his jaw.

The fire came not as a roar, but as a whisper.

A spiral of liquid flame licked from his throat, gilded and terrible. It touched Liora's torso. Her scream tore through the silence like a blade, and I skittered back against Zephyr, and his arm flashed out to hold back Cyprian from intervening.

Liora collapsed, clutching her tunic as it blackened and curled, seared to her skin. Still, Caldoron did not relent. He exhaled fully, wreathing her in flame. The world fractured around me—bone, ash, and sorrow—splitting reality like torn parchment. My magic clawed towards a tear, wanting to spill through.

You are more than this pain. Zephyr's words knitted the broken parts of me back together.

Gods, the stench. It was foul beyond language: burned flesh and melting bone, a sweetness that turned rancid in the back of the throat. Liora's beads, once symbols of rank and pride, melted into bubbling black pearls.

The bones clattered in the bowls around the faerie queen, divining a fate already sealed. When Caldoron withdrew, the fire tapered off, drifting into the night air like steam.

The sisters of the Circle of Emberlight cowered around my aunt, their faces painted in horror, and I didn't know how our sisterhood would weather what had happened, how we would rise from this fracture, after watching our sister beg and learning the part my father had played.

My magic was a roar inside me, perhaps stoked by Ryvaris. The sisters of the Circle of Emberlight and I had been bound by shared purpose, by the understanding that we protected each other when the world would not.

Now, that bond was charred. How could we trust each other's choices when our leader's desperation had led to such betrayal? How could we stand together when some of us had benefited from her sins while others remained ignorant? Araminta's tight mouth told me what I already knew: The Circle of Emberlight was broken, perhaps beyond repair.

Father stood apart, motionless. His face held no anger, no sorrow, just a bone-deep weariness that aged him more than the white at his temples ever had. There was nothing for Wylda to heal.

Liora Bramick was already dead.

At last, Satharion moved. His muscles trembled as Ryvaris stepped aside, a silent release that was no mercy, only dismissal. A sound escaped him then, like mourning filtered through some eldritch gate, so mournful and wrong it raised the hairs along my arms. Satharion nudged her with his snout. And then he turned his head. Void-lit eyes met mine for a heartbeat. There was no challenge in them now, only bleak comprehension.

Only then did Ryvaris turn his head, silver eyes flashing like a closing gate. His voice was gravel and ember, a landslide whispered through fire. Each word was laced with heat that never quite burned, but always threatened to. *Not all who walk the path of Kindling are worthy of its fire.*

I know, I told him. *But she had led me to you, and I wanted us all to rise.*

Only then did I exhale and bury my face in Zephyr's chest, my pulse thudding like a drum of war in my ears.

The Queen of Bones averted her eyes from Liora's remains and turned her attention back to me. "Choose your sisters wisely, calligrapher's daughter. And if your father has not taught you the lesson, learn it now: power does not abide deception, only debt, duly paid. We will see what tonight brings. I have great hopes that I will not be disappointed." Then to the shamans, she said, "Throw

Liora's bones into the sea. She will no longer find peace here."

But Satharion had already gathered up what remained of his rider, and he carried her with keening roars to Nightblaze Isle and the Bonefield that waited for her there. As I followed the arc of their flight along the horizon, the truth blazed through me like a meteor. This miracle of flight and flame I shared with Ryvaris came at a cost that could burn us both out of existence.

47

YSADORA

*For one brief era, the thirteen courts existed side
by side, bound by accords older than memory:
each crown gleaming, each dagger hidden.
– A Tapestry of Courts and Crowns*

I needed air that didn't taste of politics and bargains, and Ryvaris sensed my need. His summons came not in words but in longing: a pull in my chest like silver thread drawn taut. I found him waiting on the cliff's edge where bone-white stone met endless sky, silver-streaked wings folded against his sides. He was silhouetted against the noon light, as if carved from starlight and shadow.

Approaching slowly, I marvelled at the shimmer of power around him and startled when he turned his head. He lowered it, and I reached up by instinct, or perhaps inspired by some suppressed memory of Father's, and placed my palm against the warm scales between his eyes.

The world tilted. Not physically—I remained standing on solid stone—but something fundamental shifted, like stepping through a door I couldn't see. I glimpsed the vast breadth of my dragon's consciousness: centuries of flight, the weight of dragon-deep knowledge, the fierce protectiveness that had chosen me.

You are afraid, he observed, not unkindly. His tail curled slightly, a gesture I recognised as gentle teasing.

A little, perhaps, I settled beside him, close enough to sense his radiating warmth. *Was it justice that happened to Liora?*

Dragon justice is not human justice. He flexed his talons, and I tried not to notice.

I needed to understand. *It seemed that Caldoron and you agreed on how to punish her. You blocked Satharion from helping.*

Caldoron is a solitary dragon amongst the riot since Kazimir fled Faerie, but on this we agreed. The other dragons were not consulted, but we knew they would not intervene. There was no cruelty in his tone, only the patience of mountains watching mortals scurry below. *Satharion's rider broke sacred law. But you mourn her still. Your kind sees shades where we see absolutes. In time, Ysadora Silberquill, you will learn to see the world from my eyes, as well as your own.*

Through our bond, I felt the complexity of ancient wisdom tempered by something almost like fondness for my moral struggles.

What comes next will scald perhaps as much as dragon fire.

Yes. Ryvaris's agreement rumbled through the bond. *But we do not fly alone.*

He crouched low, offering his shoulder, and I climbed up with hands that trembled only slightly. His scales were warm beneath my palms, each one perfectly fitted to the next like plates of midnight-blue armour. I sat just behind the ridge of his neck in a natural hollow shaped for me.

Hold fast, he warned, and we launched into the sky, and this time my stomach lurched rather than roiled.

Flying with Ryvaris was nothing like riding Mythros. The stallion was earthbound strength and familiar comfort; Ryvaris was pure elemental force. Each wingbeat thrummed power through his body and into mine. The world fell away, not gradually, but all at once, as if we'd stepped off the edge of existence.

Wind became my second skin. My dark, cropped hair, with its three beads, whipped behind me. We cut through clouds that parted like silk around us. Ryvaris's joy in flight kindled wild abandon in my chest, and my chaos magic responded, crackling along my fingertips where they gripped his scales.

Instead of rejecting it, he welcomed the energy with the satisfaction of a jigsaw piece sliding into place, letting it flow between us, and I wondered what perhaps we might achieve together. He did not swoop nor did he twist, but it was a deepening of trust.

We soared higher, above the Court of Bones, above the circling dragons, above my mate, until the world below looked like a map drawn in shadow and bone. Ryvaris was proud, but he wasn't vain: he simply knew that he was an apex predator, star-born and unmatched, and he flew with the confidence of a creature that had never met its equal.

In the skies, the political machinations seemed small and the clash with Thiago as distant as mist.

This is what I offer you, said Ryvaris. *Not just flight, but perspective.*

Why did you fight the female dragon for me? I asked him.

She would have claimed you like a bauble, a prize to flaunt. But I knew what you were. Not a conquest. A calling. A cold satisfaction flickered through the bond at how he had dispatched her. *I have been waiting for one like you. In you, I saw a reflection of what we were before the wars. Before the breaking.*

His words stirred the memory of our oath, vows that felt more real now than ever, the kind dragons and their riders had made since the first wars.

What was sundered, we mend. What was scattered, we gather, Ryvaris breathed like an incantation.

And my response, whispered against his warm scales, *Before you, I was ink without flame, words without flight.*

When we finally landed amongst the skeletal trees of the Court of Bones, I slid down from his back on legs that felt strange after flight, as if part of me was still soaring and sensed the dragon's contentment, like bedrock beneath rushing water. His silver eyes gleamed with the calculating intelligence that had melted armies into memory and turned aspiring riders to ash. I met his gaze, and calm filled me. Dragons did not expect stillness; they expected awe or terror.

In me, Ryvaris found only a rider who had rewritten fate with ink and chaos, and wasn't afraid to do it again.

48

YSADORA

The work withers in your absence, and so do I.
The last of the bone dust is spent.
Return to me and bring both the substance
and the solace I lack.
Yours in fire and want.
– Queen Thalindra's letter to Liora Bramick

I t happened quickly after that, as if the entire Court of Bones shifted into another plane of being.

Dragons circled above on sombre wings or perched on high ground, like predators waiting, calculating, watching the fragile threads of fate twist beneath them. Whispers tangled with incense smoke, salt hung heavier in the air, and those who intended to make the journey to Echohold prepared themselves, their footfalls muffled on the black earth.

Under the awnings and arches of Thalindra's keep,

smiths unfurled weather-stained hides and bone-wrapped bundles. They strapped heirlooms over queen's attendants, layered knots of ribs and sinew over forearms, etched collars with the names of the lost, fastened cloaks that had once belonged to the dead, and looped vertebrae pieces through padded leathers until they resembled walking mausoleums.

Although rumour had it that the Queen of Bones had no need for protection. She had control over bones, those of others and herself. At a glance, she could render an enemy prostrate before her, spine bowed to her will, or use splinters from her skeletal structure to shield herself. The darkest whispers told of a queen who could drain vitality with a touch.

Even the coach horses were tended like war-beasts, their flanks brushed clean with salt-water bristles, hooves darkened with ash, a bunching of ribs on their shoulders and chests and masks of lacquered skulls on their heads. They snorted at the weight, at the scent of dragons, at the heavy air of what was to come.

Ferrith would have baulked to see this theatre of war, a far cry from the structured drills of his past soldiering for the mortal king: magic twined with marrow, charms stitched with teeth, a soldier's preparation reeking not of steel and sweat but of rites and rot. He liked his battles clean, predictable, honest blood spilt by fist or blade.

We teetered on the edge of something irreversible.

The Bone Queen had commandeered Father's attention directly after the flaming, and then he and Caldoron had flown a while, but Zephyr and I sought out my father as soon as we were able. We found him near the hitching posts, where the coach horses were being adorned with banners. His hair was windswept, his brow drawn. All around him, the Court of Bones teetered on the edge of movement: shamans daubed ash sigils on the wheels of bone carriages, and messengers ran with last-minute orders pressed into their palms. Father looked solitary and strained.

I sighed as our eyes met, my stomach knotted. "What wranglings led to yesterday's flaming, Father? Liora bargaining with dragon bone dust is unforgivable, but what happened…"

Zephyr stepped in as my voice trailed off. "How did you convince Thalindra to stand by as Caldoron burned a key ally alive? Ysadora's ally?" The doubt in the bond told me he already suspected that Liora had not been all she outwardly presented.

Father straightened slowly, as if he'd expected this scrutiny. His eyes met mine, heavy, shadowed. "It was not an easy choice, but Caldoron would not be assuaged when we learned of the deed, and it was the leverage I needed to secure Thalindra's vote and her aid."

I frowned. "Her aid?"

His lips pressed together. "The only reason this court still functions is because of Thalindra's access to dragon bone dust, but of course, that cannot continue. The dragons, had they known, would never have allowed it. But our discovery of Liora's misstep…" He grimaced as though he preferred a stronger word, "…presented me with an opportunity. Caldoron will, at intervals, turn his dragon flames to old fae bones here in this court. In return, present and future members of the Order of the Glyph and the Circle of Emberlight will retain access to the bone pool."

My eyes widened, but I was not surprised. For all Father's fragility—he was not a warrior and neither was he brave—he had, of course, maintained the Grimoire and was amongst those of the brotherhood who were an expert at contracts.

Zephyr arched a brow. "That is some feat, calligrapher."

Father's face creased into a wan smile. "I'm not finished. Given the grotesque crime of desecrating and benefiting from dragon remains, Thalindra is now bound by oath to make reparations for her involvement by using her death magic and the bone pool, together with magic administered by the fallen Prince of Lore, to unmake the curse of the outcast fae."

Zephyr sucked in a breath. "You have outdone yourself, Kazimir. Did I hear correctly? You included that term, for me?"

Father nodded. "And for Faerie. To repay you for all you have done for my Ysa."

But I knew that he had done it for other reasons, too: to soften the sharp edges of his guilt for his role in Liora's downfall by securing the well-being of future dragon riders, including me; and, most of all, to make up for abandoning Faerie after the fall of the Order of the Glyph, for allowing the Grimoire to unravel and making no attempt to stop, or even slow it, and for his part in the creation of the cursed fae. He was not blameless, but he tried to make amends, and for that, I loved him and I forgave him.

I waited for a bone insect to pass and asked, "Did Thalindra readily agree?"

"She saw the wisdom in not enraging Caldoron more." Father thumbed the dragon scale around his neck. "I did not enjoy his wrath yesterday. I felt the wrongness of it, although I knew it was right."

I swallowed hard, recalling the scent of charred flesh and molten beads, how the terrible stench of it had filled my nose and throat until I had wanted to turn away and close my eyes, and beg Cyprian to rewind time. No one deserved such an end.

Except perhaps the King of Silence.

Then Father said to Zephyr, "Perhaps it won't work. But it is a chance for the cursed fae. For the monsters they now are."

Zephyr grasped Father's arm, and respect, hard-won and tentative, flickered between them. "I will make it work, Kazimir. You have my deepest gratitude."

Through the hopeful song of the mate bond, I knew that he wasn't only expressing his thanks for the gift of a rosier outlook for the cursed fae. He was grateful for how Father had, in his own way, protected me.

A breath passed between us, then I asked gently, "Have you spoken to Araminta?"

His face shuttered. "She will not speak to me. Though I have tried.

"Grief and anger make her crueller than usual," I murmured, brushing my lips against his cheek.

As Zephyr and I turned away and walked into the flurry of motion, we passed the sisters of the Circle of Emberlight, their faces pale and tight-lipped, eyes rimmed red. I noticed that other sisters had arrived, their dragons joining the riot in the sky and on land.

Araminta did not introduce me, and neither did Phaedran. Some stood with quiet dignity. Grief had turned into barely restrained anger in others. Still more huddled together, whispering urgently, casting suspicious looks, eyes darting to threats both within their circle and beyond, dragons a breath away.

I was no stranger to fractures deepening under pressure, but I didn't seek to bridge the ice between us. Weighing Liora's crimes could wait for another day. Relief washed over me as Araminta rallied the sisters, directing them to assemble their weapons for transport to Wyvern Reach.

But when she averted her gaze from my father, I knew that for all her practicality, her fury ran deep.

I had not heard from my mother, but I wondered if she knew and if she sorrowed for not being at my side.

My mercenary kin prepared also, counting arrows, honing blades, and rubbing oil into leathers. Armour lay in heaps beside us, patchwork pieces of leather and fae steel, ready to be donned at a moment's call.

Wylda laced her bracers with supple fingers, while Sequoia checked the tension of her bow strings, whispering to it like an old lover. Cyprian sharpened a dagger that needed no edge, his jaw tight.

Among the clatter of blades and dull thud of bones, I sat cross-legged and quiet beside them, oiling my quill, checking each pot of ink, ensuring none had clotted, then slid a second dagger into the sheath at the opposite thigh to the dragon-kissed blade: balanced weight for an unbalanced realm.

Mythros grazed nearby, unencumbered by the relics of war. We hoped to survive with careful diplomacy and veiled threats, but the shamans declared that blood would be spilt before moonrise, and Thiago lusted for violence like a wolf denied meat, whether against kin or foe.

I wondered how Elowen fared, and my heart panged.

After weeks of scheming, Zephyr was eager to move on from court games, see which of our carefully laid traps would spring first and let his shadows off the leash. He had already honed his weapons. His calm was only surface deep now, stretched tight over the molten hunger for vengeance.

I felt his need for justice through the mate bond, his shadows already primed for war, a simmer of retribution against his uncle that he had long postponed. But when he looked at me, his shoulders tensed, doubt trembling at the edges of him, as though he feared he might lose me and would prefer to lose himself.

Cyprian finished his task with steady focus, then joined Zephyr as he gazed out at the dragons on the horizon. "I don't like our odds, damn it. I hope Loxley's got something up his sleeve."

Zephyr's blue-grey eyes flickered as he turned, as if he had been listening to something else. Something no one else could hear. Then he was himself again, confident in himself and his kin. "When has Loxley ever let us down? He always finds a way, even if it's through a bog."

The two shared a brief, knowing look as Wylda, Sequoia, and I joined them.

Wylda made a noise in her throat, and I knew she was nervous to see Esolas again. "What I wouldn't give for us all to be at Ebonspire again. This is the moment the board either clears or catches fire."

"Let it burn," said Sequoia under her breath. "But the fact that Lox, Maren, and Ferrith aren't here means either something's gone wrong or they've found something too dangerous to walk away from."

My chest tightened, thoughts racing through every grim possibility. Loxley was clever, Maren was cautious, and Ferrith was stubborn, but even those strengths couldn't outpace death.

They'll come. Loxley's faced worse and walked away with a smirk and half a plan. The light caught in Zephyr's gaze, hard as flint, and his shadows writhed, feral things, trembling for release. "We're agreed…this ends today with Ysa's freedom and all our kin home, intact, with Elowen in tow?"

We all nodded, jaws clenched, eyes sharp, thinking of Gabor and not wanting to carry the loss that ailed the Circle of Emberlight. Whispers carried on ill winds, alliances shifted like sand beneath their feet, and the line between friend and foe blurred in the half-light. I wasn't afraid. Not with Zephyr beside me. Not with Ryvaris overhead.

But stars, the air tasted like endings.

Don't brace for loss yet, Inkheart, said Zephyr through the bond.

I gave him a soft look. *I'm not. I'm bracing to fight.*

He searched my face. *Good. Then I'm right beside you. No walls between us.*

Cyprian gave us both a long-suffering look and muttered, "Save your declarations for after the bloodshed."

As the queen climbed into her bone-lattice carriage and we prepared to move out, I searched the shifting crowd for Father and caught sight of him deep in murmured conversation with Sequoia. Their gazes fell on Zephyr, then on me, not in warmth but in calculation. Betrayal bloomed in Father's eyes, and I turned away, tension knotting low in my spine.

Father would rather damn himself than hurt me.

I was almost sure of it.

49

ELOWEN

*The way Elowen trembles in the cell reminds me
of Father after a binge, except this time, I stayed.
This time, I won't walk away.
– Ferrith's diary*

E lowen drew in a breath through the open window of her bedchamber, looking out over the bloodheart tree. The air was coppery and thick. From the crown of the tree, a slow weep of scarlet leaves drifted downwards. The ground beneath the tree had grown slick, a living wound spreading in concentric rings. No birds sang there, but then they never had.

Her father only liked to hear her mother sing. That's the way it had always been.

His spiders had removed the four of them from the cell that morning. They had grown pale together, starved together—for Orin could not steal as much as they needed from the kitchens—their strength leeched by damp.

But they had not broken, though Elowen's legs had trembled when she stood. Ferrith had insisted she pace the cell to keep her muscles from atrophying, and when she had said no, he had tugged her with him, muttering under his breath about keeping her spine from snapping like a frosted branch.

Maren exercised of her own accord, her green eyes watching every movement of the guards with the attention of a soldier still planning a war. Loxley had jested about breakfast and promptly gagged when they were presented with a pitcher of grey broth and a single bruised fruit.

She hadn't meant to grow so attached to them, and now her father had cruelly parted her from them, and sent them their separate ways, to be scrubbed clean and dressed, as if a few layers of silk could erase captivity.

She didn't scream or struggle as his spiders led her away. Her father would have taken that as a sign he had broken her. Instead, she walked, chin high, having already planned how she would show him he had underestimated her.

The attendants descended in silence, like carrion birds, their faces placid as they set to work scrubbing the dungeon from her skin. She let them. Their hands were brisk, gazes dispassionate, as though she were an inanimate object to be restored.

They bathed her in rosewater to mask the scent of stone and fear, scraped the dirt from beneath her nails, and oiled her skin until it gleamed with forced vitality. Her ribs pressed sharply against the inner seams of the gown, no matter how many layers they added.

The dress, a draping cloud of raven-black silk, could not hide the stark angles of a body that had known recent hunger. She was thinner than before, harder, sharper. A girl carved down to blade and bone.

Next, her matted hair was coaxed into civility, parted in the centre and smoothed straight down her back like a waterfall of ashen gold, glossed and pinned with jet combs that glinted like thorns. Her brown eyes were rimmed in kohl and shadowed in soot-hued powder, made larger, deeper, emptier. Rouge bloomed on her cheeks like bruises made lovely.

The attendants glamoured her disfigured hand, making flesh smooth and whole again, weaving illusion over what her parents deemed unsightly. But she would not allow it to pass unnoticed. She insisted on gloves: thick, inelegant, and as black as mourning. It was her little rebellion against her parents' expectation of elegant poise.

It gave her great satisfaction to imagine the gloves around her father's neck.

They had polished her into a vision, but the stink of the cell loomed in her mind. Before they left, as a parting gift, the most accomplished attendant, eyes vacant, bound her mouth like she had always known they would. Elowen allowed herself a small smile: they didn't realise that she could speak to anyone with her telepathy, should she choose. She could fell anyone.

And by the desolate skies, she would shatter the calm at precisely the right moment.

When they left, she stared back into the mirror and met her own gaze without flinching. She looked like a ghost fashioned into a queen, but beneath the paint and polish, her fury glowed steady.

Her father hadn't told her where the others were or if they were still alive. Faerie's Spymaster continued his games with the slow drip of information manufactured to control the tempo of panic.

The thought of danger finding Loxley, Ferrith, or Maren sent a sharp pang through Elowen's chest. They were more than capable of looking after themselves—particularly after Ferrith's encounter in the Wraithwoods—and it was difficult enough within the walls of the Court of Silence to guard herself.

Still, with Ysadora leagues away, the burden of their safety pressed down on her shoulders, even though Maren had informed her that Ysadora had no inkling of their whereabouts or that Ferrith had changed so utterly.

Elowen knew that her father's appetite for spectacle and cruelty meant no pawn was too precious to sacrifice. She had learned that bitter lesson herself. He would destroy Ysadora's kin one by one to gain control over her.

And yet, traitorous heart that she was, Elowen yearned for Ysadora to attend, more than she hoped she would stay away.

But even if she remained forgotten, the four of them, freed from the dungeon—in addition to Orin, who also had his part—would find a way to inflict damage today and escape in the aftermath.

After all, they had allocated roles and rehearsed for every eventuality: she would crush her father's mind at the most damaging moment, Orin would use his detached shadow against him, and the others had, according to their strengths, carefully carved out opponents amongst Faerie's rulers if they intervened.

Failure was an outcome too horrible to accept.

Still, a small voice in her agreed with Loxley that escaping from the room itself would be less difficult than escaping from the court. Elowen had used her isolation well. Faerie kings and queens were swift to recover and swifter still to wrath.

But she had spent each silent hour unpicking every problem Orin had laid before her, preparing for every scenario. Her mother, for instance, would almost certainly intervene the moment Elowen turned on her father, but her speed couldn't match her daughter's. Elowen's mind magic was razor sharp in precision, and required none of the rigmarole of lungs and breath, voice and lips.

The Wraithwoods had gifted her mother magic, yes, but not the deep-rooted power of one born fae. Elowen's telepathy made her the natural choice to be in command. For all her days and nights robbed of her power, she relished the chance to use it.

She flicked her glance to the bloodheart tree and sat primly on a chair as one she loved approached, overtly to show her disdain by not rising to embrace him, but actually because her legs wouldn't hold.

She'd sensed him from the moment she left the cell, his mind so familiar she wanted to rush to find him. Days she had convinced herself that he didn't care for her, but the curse of her telepathy meant that at least she could be certain that the opposite was true. Xaire had fought with their father behind closed doors, tried to bargain, to bluff, to beg. She felt every wordless spike of guilt that lanced through him, every sleepless night in his comfortable bed.

Xaire hadn't abandoned her, not truly, but that knowledge didn't erase the bruising silence.

He'd stayed free while she rotted.

Her awareness sharpened the moment his boots echoed down the dark corridor outside her bed chamber.

He paused at the door, and she plucked the thought from his brain. *May I?*

It took her so long to answer that he considered sending a shadow beneath the door to check she was all right. The banality of his being worried when she was in her bed chamber almost made her laugh out loud in scorn.

Enter. Elowen hated that her brother would see beneath the silks and cosmetics and know how much she had suffered, and that her suffering would wedge between them, despite how she handled it, because he had not prevented it.

Her twin came in and clicked the door quietly shut. He hesitated at the threshold, as though afraid her rejection might be physical, not just psychic. His silhouette was leaner than she remembered, as though shame had carved pieces from him. That easy, infuriating confidence she'd once resented had been eroded, and to her surprise, she missed it.

You left me in the dungeons, she said coldly in his mind, no hello, even though her soul longed to slip into their familiar patterns of old: him hurting her, her forgiving him. *You didn't stop him.*

I tried, his dark gaze raked over her face, her body, dropping to her gloved hand, before searching her eyes.

He was hopeless. Hopeless in his efforts and the dim light of his love. What was love without action?

She missed the lie that he would always be her companion. Her twin. Her shadow-self.

Her posture remained rigid, her voice in his mind, clipped. *It's okay. I did not expect more.*

He flinched. *I begged you to tell Father what he wanted to hear.*

Elowen didn't know whether to remain seated or strike him across the face. *Still, those same tired ways to pacify him.*

His jaw tensed. *You don't need to strike me, El. I've done a good enough job bruising myself over this. But if you need the release, I won't stop you.* He came closer, tentatively. *I almost asked for Zephyr's help, but he's got enough problems of his own.*

She snorted at that, her own fluids spraying against the mouth binding.

Xaire tried again. *I asked Orin how you fared.*

Her chestnut eyes flared. *Don't you dare spoil this for me, Xaire.* Her twin looked at her, confused, and she kicked herself for insinuating she was anything but broken.

His thoughts pressed into hers again, raw, uncertain. *Please don't hate me.*

She let the silence stretch, not to punish, but because the pain was still too raw to forgive, and even love could not mend a wound that still bled. *I don't hate you. But I'm not sure we can ever go back to what we were.*

Xaire's throat bobbed as if swallowing words he no longer had the right to say. "Maybe we don't go back. Maybe we learn who we are now," he said aloud. He waited for a flicker of response, but when none came, he nodded once, turned on his heel, and walked back through the door, closing it quietly behind him.

His footsteps were ghost-light on the floor down the hall, and his mind trailed after him like fog: grief-cloaked, full of words he hadn't said and memories neither of them could forget.

Elowen sat motionless and turned her gaze back to the bloodheart tree. There was another who had treated her like a sibling. Though it might have been sensible to resume contact with Ysadora, after having her mind silenced for so long, she was afraid her newly restored telepathy might betray her in front of the wrong minds. More than that, she feared Ysadora's rejection and worried that in reaching out, she would find that Ysadora had already let go.

Instead, she straightened her gloves and waited for the charade to begin.

ZEPHYR

The Court of Embers has smouldered
on the edge of conflict for millennia,
and never once taken a side.
Though it does not strike first,
its vengeance is absolute.
– A Tapestry of Courts and Crowns

T he procession of guests approached Echohold with the grim pageantry his uncle always demanded.

They dismounted in silence—Zephyr and Ysa from Mythros, Cyprian and Wylda from their wind-weary steed. Sequoia smoothed her wind-tangled hair after landing moments before. Not one of them acknowledged Kazimir, fearing even a look might crack the delicate lie of his servitude to the Queen of Bones.

Thiago hadn't simply invited the courts. He had choreographed them. Carriages rolled across the black-frost road, obsidian-wheeled and silver-draped, bearing emissaries and delegates from neighbouring courts, flanked by mounted guards whose spears glittered like icicles.

Some preferred to walk, cloaked in furs, although some had webbed feet, and others flew on wings of their own. Zephyr's own kin arrived on horseback, while the Court of Embers came on the backs of desert scorpions.

Danaë's snow leopards prowled on either side of the column, hateful beasts that had never warmed to him despite his efforts to befriend them. Their silence unnerved even the seasoned soldiers. One growled low as they passed, but Ysa didn't flinch. She was learning. Though her hand went to check for her quill and dragon-kissed blade, a nervous habit.

It helped that Ryvaris and Caldoron rested just beyond the reach of the Court of Silence, behind a ridge where Caldoron had first waited to rescue the calligrapher from Danaë's torture.

"Do you think Lox and the others are here?" asked Ysa.

"Knowing Lox, he's probably behind us," retorted Wylda.

They scanned the crowd for Loxley, Maren, and Ferrith, and found no trace. Elowen would likely already be in the meeting hall. A flicker of movement drew Zephyr's attention: one of Thiago's spiders, trailing them through the column. He wanted to be seen; otherwise, he would have worn his whisper ring. Zephyr kept his hand close to his sword, his shadows leashed tight as wire beneath his skin.

Sequoia, wings half-furled, flicked a glance at him.

"We're already surrounded. If they wanted us dead, it'd be done."

"Comforting as always," Cyprian replied, sharp-eyed.

The horizon didn't shift, flat and merciless, until Echohold's jagged silhouette emerged from the fog like a blade pressed to the sky. Zephyr was overcome by an intense longing for the rugged charm of Ebonspire.

As they neared the castle, Esolas stepped forward from beneath an icicle-fringed arch. Even in that cold expanse, tiny motes of light hovered like fireflies around him. He was draped in long white robes that shimmered like refracted sunlight on fresh snow. There was a circle of aides like a sundial around him, close enough to guard, far enough to grant privacy. The faerie king's eyes went first to Ysa, then to Zephyr. No warmth touched his gaze, and his spine held tension.

Zephyr moved half a step in front of his mate before he could stop himself.

Esolas inclined his head. "Calligrapher's daughter. Shadow prince."

The titles landed like chess pieces.

"Esolas," Ysa replied coolly, though a tremor of anticipation flickered through her.

"You came, as I prayed you would," said Esolas, and the bargain mark on Ysa's wrist shimmered once and vanished.

Part of Zephyr, the one shrouded in shadows and silence, wanted to smother the light of this faerie king now that Ysa was free. With their kin, they could fell this male and his aides. Then they could leave, hide in the furthest reaches of Faerie, where his uncle couldn't harm Ysadora. But Ysa had never been one for running, and dragons

TOWER OF BONES AND DIMMED STARS

were colossal creatures, too unwieldy to remain hidden from scouts.

The other part of Zephyr, which had been nurtured by his mother and loved stories, wanted to understand the Faerie King of Luminosity. Again, he asked, "What does the Spymaster have on you, Esolas. Why did you agree to his games?"

Esolas hesitated before he held out his tanned hand, beneath the icy arch, with the snow leopards drawing ever closer. Zephyr's grip tightened on the faerie king's wrist, and his storm-dark eyes became unfocused, breath catching, as he drowned in someone else's past.

His mind stretched, swollen with borrowed pain, as it absorbed the faerie king's secret: Esolas and his sister queen Aurielle had loved the same person, who loved them both back. But Esolas used his authority to force their lover to choose him. The lover ended his own life rather than betray either, and only Thiago—and now Zephyr—knew that the ultimatum had driven him to do it.

Zephyr dropped Esolas's wrist and staggered back. "This isn't just politics. It's blood and broken hearts."

Esolas's scrutiny would have made a lesser male crumble. "You do not judge me?"

"History is not mine to mould. I'm sorry for what my uncle holds over you."

A bitter smile. "Be warned, son of the Court of Lore. Thiago will kill your love if he cannot control her."

Zephyr's eyes darkened. "I'll burn the realms down before I let him harm her."

"I don't know what the King of Silence plans for today, *Fatebreaker*, but I hope he fails," said Esolas, making Zephyr wonder if he had crossed paths with the Binder.

The Faerie King of Luminosity cast one more look at Ysa. Something fierce and tender warred in Zephyr's chest. His mate stood proud, cloaked in calm, but he felt her pulse flutter through the bond. She had no idea how terrifyingly precious she was.

Esolas took his leave, and Zephyr murmured the faerie king's story to his kin.

A few minutes later, they were ushered into the atrium's yawning space, the hush thickening with each court's arrival. Above, the ceiling stretched into leaded crystal, panes shaped like jagged petals and eyes.

The light that filtered through bent into unnatural hues: bruised violets, blood-copper reds, decayed golds, that made courtiers appear otherworldly, monstrous or divine depending on the angle. One quadrant housed a greenhouse, as if laid out for theatre, filled with ink-giving plants sacred to the Order of the Glyph. As if to taunt Ysa and Kazimir with what had been claimed.

Ysa baulked at the sight of it, and Zephyr knew his uncle had hit his mark.

Zephyr loathed many places in the Court of Silence, but the Vaulted Atrium of Tongueless Praise deserved its own category of contempt. Here, he'd witnessed courtiers punished for speaking out of turn. Here, his father had been publicly rebuked and ritually humiliated.

A wall of ice now blocked the view of the bloodheart tree, his uncle's way of hiding the prophecy of his downfall from the assembled courts. Rumour had it that he had convinced the court that the shedding merely signalled his imminent ascension to High King, not his downfall.

Zephyr's lips curved in a feral smile. Decay preceded

collapse, not coronation. The air groaned with floral rot, soured nectar, and something metallic beneath.

His uncle had invited a small entourage from every court, handpicked for their gossiping tongues. Courtiers and emissaries filled the outer galleries, one section for each court. Each contingent brought its own dissonance: cymbals of scent, movement, suppressed power.

Zephyr recognised half the faces and trusted none. Veiled servants lined the walls, balancing trays of blood-red wine and bloated figs: compliance masquerading as hospitality, poison dressed as welcome. Beneath his boots, the polished darkwood absorbed light, making it feel as though he walked on deep water, taunting him with his reflection.

Every step forward felt like weights were chained to his ankles, and he tightened his grip around Ysa's hand, trying not to let his demons pollute the bond. She moved beside him, her steps precise, defiant. Her ink-dark hair combed in a style that exposed her neck, and the dragon-chosen removed not to spoil the surprise of Ryvaris.

Her chaos magic had begun to rise in her blood long before the outer gates. Now it crackled through the mate bond: anxious, curious, indignant. His shadows answered restlessly before he leashed them tight.

He met her violet gaze. Ancients, he wanted to spirit her out of that damned place. *Not yet, Inkheart.*

She exhaled softly and nodded. She needed to be strong for this. She needed him to be strong, too.

And he was. He was both resolute and prepared. He only wished that it would be enough to save those he loved.

They attracted attention as they walked. Their

mercenary kin fanned out behind them: Cyprian's gaze sweeping the rafters, Sequoia's wings twitching like she smelled a trap, Wylda already curling a rope around her hand as if to restrain herself from striking first. Zephyr's shadows retracted tight to his frame, silent and waiting.

Seven thrones lined the rectangular dais, beneath crystal domes that reflected distorted versions of those seated. The central throne sat at the apex, higher and more ornate than the others. There was a twin pair for the sibling monarchs of the Court of Luminosity. One would remain empty: though the Court of Nebulas had not fallen, and the Circle of Emberlight had stabilised it, they were not ordained rulers and therefore could not decide Faerie's fate.

But for the most part, the rulers of Faerie had come. Or rather, they had been summoned like players to a final act.

His uncle lounged in the central throne like he had already been crowned High King, fingers laced on the pommel of a blade that clearly wasn't just for show. Danaë stood at his right shoulder, holding a chalice as black as pitch. Her cool eyes never left her mate's face.

The Faerie King of Silver Seas smiled at them with sharpened teeth and jittering hands, and Zephyr knew he had not yet told Thiago he had lost the High King's crown. Another, the Faerie King of Embers, watched Ysa like she might upend the entire realm. He wasn't wrong. Esolas gave a clipped nod, lips tight, as if he anticipated trouble, and his sister laid a comforting hand on his. The Queen of Bones gave a knowing smile and turned to Kazimir as if he were a pet. Her robe of calcified bone flowed around her like a fossil caught mid-bloom, and at her feet was a scrying bowl.

Tanuhja's not here, said Ysa through the bond, looking at the empty throne of the Court of Chaos.

His heart panged. He, too, had looked for Orin. *No, but we will succeed without her.*

They were guided to a space directly opposite the dais, lower and isolated behind an ornate wrought-iron balustrade: a holding pen in all but name, positioned to remind everyone present who held the power. The space was too narrow for comfort, flanked by two of Thiago's spiders.

Zephyr sat rigid at Ysa's side, his shadows flickering faintly across the floor. Sequoia remained standing, one hand on her blade. Cyprian and Wylda glanced at the crowd, eyes scanning for allies.

Zephyr sent a silent prayer to Loxley, though it would not reach him. *Where are you, brother?*

And then, Thiago's voice cut through the atrium, soft and seething, "Shall we begin?"

Zephyr resisted the urge to bare his teeth, and his uncle turned his head a fraction, pale eyes skimming Zephyr like a knife.

Thiago rose from his gilded throne, and his voice carried across the atrium, deceptively soft, "I invited you here today to address a threat that could unmake our very existence." His gaze swept the thrones lining the dais before settling, with slow venom, on Ysadora. Zephyr's jaw locked. "The calligrapher's daughter sits amongst us. As you know, the queen and I extended our protection to the girl once before. She rejected it. And now, monsters run rampant across Faerie."

Wylda's brow furrowed as a ripple ran through the courtiers, muffled gasps behind gloved hands, jewel eyes exchanging sidelong glances. "He's blaming Ysa for the monsters?"

"He knows the power of a simple story." Zephyr's pulse roared in his ears, but he kept his posture loose, arms crossed, as if bored, though his shadows seeped from his boots. The mention of *the girl* was a deliberate diminishment.

Ysa tilted her chin up, calm as still ink. "I've heard worse." She did not look away from his uncle.

His uncle's voice flowed again, like oil on water. "Ysadora Silberquill came of age in the mortal world. She is untested and untrained." He turned to his old foe Kazimir, tone sharpening with cruelty. "Her father abandoned his sacred duty as Faerie's last calligrapher. And now the Grimoire is almost entirely undone."

Thalindra looked up from her scrying bowl. "Be careful how you talk about my pet. As you see, he is already paying his dues." She gave an elegant shrug and missed how Danaë looked sorely tempted to undo all Kazimir's bone healing with a choice song or two. "If the Grimoire is dying, perhaps it's not the fault of a girl with ink on her fingers, but of a kingdom grown too fond of silence."

"I disagree." The King of Silver Seas leaned forward, rings clicking against the crystal of his armrest, his pale mouth trembling. "We must consider containment," he rasped. His eyes, pale as salt, flicked from Ysa to the greenhouse behind her. "Before the chaos devours what little order remains."

"I've never been prouder of stealing from someone," muttered Cyprian. "Truly. It was worth every grey hair."

Thiago nodded at his fellow king, words falling like carefully placed stones. "My nephew and the calligrapher's daughter are mated, although he was initially charged with being her captor. He failed in that, and we must weigh his other failings, too."

Zephyr's eyes hooded. "This should be fun."

Thiago's gaze fell upon those gathered with almost fatherly concern. "Zephyr comes from a broken lineage. He stole artefacts of import. Defied this court. Refused to return Ysadora when commanded. Turned his shadows against me and the queen, who has been like a mother to him." Danaë, poised behind him in her widow-black gown, allowed herself a flicker of a smile.

Danaë, a mother to him? Zephyr almost choked on the absurdity. He'd fought his first wars long before she'd ever set foot in Faerie.

"I propose the following," said the King of Silence, descending two steps. The atrium stilled, and at the foot of the dais, the snow leopards stirred, purring like beasts sensing fresh prey. "Let the monarchs decide, on behalf of their courts, if Ysadora Silberquill may remain in Faerie… under my control."

Zephyr and Kazimir locked eyes, both united in the desperate need to protect Ysa.

Sequoia rolled her eyes. "Give me strength. They can't really be falling for this?"

"Oh, they are." Ysa's chaos magic spiked, crackling at her fingertips.

Steady, said Zephyr, though the Thorn King's absence scraped at his nerves and he hoped his calculations weren't just wishful thinking. *There are seven votes. As the proposer, Thiago may posture but not vote. The Court of Chaos and the Court of Nebulas are off the board. Five votes remain. The Court of Silver Seas is with him. The Court of Bones is against. The Court of Embers abstains. That puts the deciding power in the hands of Esolas and Aurielle, and Inkheart, he trusts us.*

On the throne dais, the Queen Aurielle of the Court of Luminosity folded her fan with a crisp snap that echoed like a challenge, prompting her brother to lean forward with a diplomat's poise. "Truth is not always held by the loudest voice. Should we not hear from the calligrapher's daughter and your nephew themselves?"

A murmur rolled through the room: some approving, others scandalised.

Thiago's gaze darkened with violence. "By all means, you may deliberate. But if the Grimoire fails, it is not only Ysadora Silberquill's life at stake. It is all of ours." A hush rippled across the galleries, a wave of suppressed murmurs that felt less like gossip and more like dread, and his uncle preened, his task nearly done. "But first, let me present a final truth. Proof that my nephew has planted spies within my court. That he is already beholden to his mate and has no control over her."

The atrium's great doors swung open. Xaire strode in, his dark hair catching the twisted light from above, leading four figures with bound hands: Elowen, gagged like a traitor, although it was no different to the treatment she had always endured; Ferrith, gaunt, dulled like a mirror dimmed by dust; Maren, bruised but defiant; and Loxley, impossibly, grinning like an imp.

Wylda stood frozen, lips parted. "Please tell me they haven't been here all this time."

Sequoia let out a breath like a blade sliding free, but Loxley didn't look worried.

"Uh, oh," murmured Cyprian. "Brace yourselves."

Ysa jerked to her feet at the sight of their kin bound like criminals, paraded like offerings before a court that didn't care for them, and he didn't blame her. Her magic surged in protest, chaos crackling at her fingertips, the greenhouse behind her shuddering in resonance. She barely registered the gasps around her or the shocked whispers threading through the outer galleries. All she could see were the people she loved most: battered, gagged, restrained.

And she *really* wanted to call Ryvaris. She wanted the ink-veined blue to burn down the atrium and all those in it, as long as their kin made it out of here alive. But that was her fear taking over, and his Ysa was made of love.

They had to stick to the plan. His Inkheart deserved to be the Queen of Faerie, and he would not let her make this mistake.

Zephyr was already moving, intercepting his mate with a hand at her waist before her chaos could spill uncontrolled. "Steady," he growled low into her ear, "or you'll give him the excuse he wants. Let him reveal everything first. Let him overplay."

But he was shaking. His pulse pounded at his temple as his gaze snapped to Ferrith. Something was wrong, and through the bond, he knew that Ysa gleaned it, too. Not just the thinner frame but the flicker of unnatural gold at Ferrith's temples. His skin was paler, too pale. And there was a quiet to him, not just weariness, but restraint. Zephyr's gut turned.

Ysa's thoughts roared in her mind. *This is what Thiago wants. A spectacle. A breaking point.* Her instincts screamed to run to them, to tear the bindings from their wrists, and her pulse thudded in her throat as she, too, noticed the difference in Ferrith.

Thiago's voice unfurled slow and silken, and he had never been so compelling: "My own daughter turned against me."

A shiver travelled like a wave across the pews, silks rustling, eyes widening.

A silent tear threaded down Danaë's face as he continued, "Make me your High King, and I will quell this threat. Make me your High King and I will control the calligrapher's daughter and make the Faerie we all deserve."

Loxley chose that moment to speak. "Gods, that was dull."

Maren coughed, a thinly veiled laugh.

Then the atrium exploded into violence, and his mate wasn't the one responsible.

YSADORA

The quill I now carry is no match for the crimson one in your hand, but I am quite satisfied. Your magic and your courage have long outgrown mine. It's only fitting that you keep the better tool.
– The calligrapher's letter to his daughter Ysa

E lowen met my eyes.

I blinked hard to hold my tears back.

After all the hours spent writing to her, fretting about her, waking in the night to a new torturous thought about what had befallen her, it was almost unbearable to not even know the precise shape of her hurt.

I didn't know what had been done to her in the dark.

I had imagined her broken, yes, but I had not imagined this. Even under the layers of ceremonial finery, the black silk gown, her smoothed blonde hair, I noted her hollowed cheeks, the tremors in her bones, her skin bruised in strange hues.

Pain had a scent. It had a posture. It had a silence that curled around the body like old smoke, unlike Thiago's cold silences. Elowen's silence was full. She wore it now like courtly attire, regal in the way tragedy is when it refuses to bow.

It appalled me that her parents had arranged her pain into something presentable. For themselves. Even now, they did not baulk at the sight of her, safe in their presumed knowledge that with her mouth binding, she could not shame them, that Xaire was her only translator.

My magic flickered at the edges of my control, and through the mate bond, Zephyr whispered to me, with words I could not process but a tone that soothed me like a balm. It slowed the unravelling. Not completely.

Courtiers shifted, startled by the ripple of power, and Thiago's spiders shifted their attention to me from Elowen. Deep in my mind, Ryvaris stirred, ancient fury coiling, ready to tear through flesh and stone to protect me and those I loved.

Even as I catalogued the quiet devastations in Elowen, I noted a sharpness that no dungeon, no spell, no father's betrayal had managed to dull. She was diminished, but not destroyed.

Joy lit her face like moonrise over ruin. For the first time in what felt like forever, her voice slid into my mind. *You came for me. Even after I released you from our bargain.*

She plucked the thought from my mind. *Of course, I came. Bargain or not, you're kin. You were always more than a vow.*

She turned from me, then, and met Thiago's gaze, bristling with defiance, resolve in every line of her thin body. Still, Thiago underestimated her. Still, he did not prepare. But I realised: Elowen was not waiting to be rescued; she was waiting to strike.

My heart thudded. *No, Elowen. We can end this without violence.*

But my revenge. Her voice in my mind trembled at the edge of fury and hopelessness. *I must have it. I can't let my pain go unanswered. I've rehearsed this moment a thousand times, and in none of them did he walk away whole.*

Stars, I knew what it was to hold pain tightly, to survive by sharpening grief into a new, stronger shape. So all I said was, *I understand.*

Elowen's spine straightened by degrees, as if drawing herself up from some invisible wreckage, her attention already elsewhere. She paused to say, *Ferrith isn't who he was, Ysadora. The Wraithwoods did something. He's changed.*

My heart jolted. Ferrith and Maren should never have ventured into the Wraithwoods, and now I was doubly grateful that Loxley had been with them. Ferrith, sunlight in human skin, with curls the colour of ripe wheat and eyes so vividly blue it hurt to look at them in summer. Ferrith, who had once laughed like the sky couldn't fall, before he found out that it could.

Instinctively, even metres away, I could tell he was different, different beyond the whisper of betrayal that we had discovered when I last set eyes on him at Ebonspire.

Skies, I loved him. They should have been somewhere safe. Yet, here he was, a mortal caught in the games of Faerie, and I should have said *no*. Should have told him that he should stay in Larkspur with Maren. That they could make their lives together there, even though had I left them behind, my heart would have splintered into shards too fine to count.

Elowen caught Ferrith's gaze, and one finger—oddly, not on her dominant hand—crooked, beckoning him forwards from where Xaire kept an unbothered watch.

Alarm sharpened Zephyr's voice through the bond. *She was in your head. She can speak to others besides Xaire?*

I nodded. *Elowen has been robbed of her voice for so long that it was her secret to tell.*

A vein throbbed in his jaw, but he returned his focus to what unfolded.

Then, Ferrith fractured. One breath, there was only him: golden-haired, bound, flicking his gaze to Maren as if to draw strength. Next, there were three of him. Identical copies peeled into being like mirrored flame, and the King of Silence stilled his performance, the faintest flicker of surprise cracking his mask.

It didn't matter that the original Ferrith's wrists remained bound. The others moved freely and fast. One freed Maren, her nebula fire sparking to life the moment her hands were hers again, so fierce she belonged on the throne of the Court of Nebulas herself.

Another reached Loxley, his beard overgrown, who looked like he was enjoying himself. The ropes fell away like ribbons at a forgotten festival. Then the copies returned to break Elowen's bonds and Ferrith's own, before being absorbed back into him.

It was like seeing a stranger inside my oldest friend, but I couldn't look away. Whatever Ferrith had become, it was beautiful and terrible: something reshaped by Faerie's darkest woods, touched by magic not meant for mortal blood.

Zephyr's shadows were eager to strike, to end this. His will held them in check, but barely. We all knew the cost of moving too soon. Power shimmered down the bond like a drawn breath. *He's not just alive. He's become something else entirely. Either way, he belongs with us,* said Zephyr, and my chest ached with the swell of love and grief.

Zephyr was right. He was still *ours*. Ferrith had chosen our kin over his fears of Faerie. It meant that love could survive transformation. That even twisted by magic, scarred by the wilds, and punished by Thiago, Ferrith had remembered who he was to our family.

"Forest be damned, have I taken too many mushrooms?" asked Sequoia.

They were waiting for my word, for Zephyr's signal.

Wylda had shifted her stance, putting herself between a cluster of terrified courtiers and the potential chaos. "No more than usual. But I'm almost certain that this trip's on Ferrith, not your foraging."

"You think mushrooms explain this?" retorted Cyprian. "Please. This is Faerie. There's always a worse explanation." His hand had drifted to the hilt of his sword, fingers tapping once: a signal that he was ready.

You should know, I said to Elowen, *I've changed, too.* I let her see a flicker of Ryvaris: the dragon's blue scales rippling like moonlit ink, teeth bared in protection.

Elowen didn't flinch. She tilted her chin at a slight upward angle that showed the blade's edge of determination, because with a dragon, escape was almost guaranteed. That kernel of knowledge gave her the courage to attack her father in front of the eyes who came from across Faerie, though he had shamed and broken her into a desperate little thing, and robbed her of her voice and self-belief.

Across the atrium, the stained glass above her fractured

her reflection into a dozen faces, but none of them looked afraid. She stepped forward, not towards freedom, not even towards me.

She stepped forward to confront her father.

The snow leopards slunk from the shadows, drawn by the scent of fraying power, towards the prey they remembered. Now they paused, uncertain, their hard eyes fixed on Elowen, before lowering themselves to the ground.

They remembered her, but they scented the predator in her. Their nostrils flared, and they edged closer, seeking a new mistress. Danaë had once ruled them with a single look. Her fingers twitched, as though calling the leopards back to heel, but they didn't move. Not for her.

But Elowen simply met their gaze and kept walking, unbothered by the slinking figures that had once caused her alarm.

The first leopard whimpered, ears flat, before backing away. The other followed, circling wide to watch her from the dark as she progressed towards the faerie king.

Thiago had, in his hubris, weighed Ferrith's intervention and decided that he was in no danger. Faerie's Spymaster opened his arms to embrace his daughter in a parody of paternal mercy for the court, but Elowen's intent was far from reconciliation. She was no longer the girl who had once longed for his approval.

As she reached him, her power lashed out: a mental assault that made her abuser stagger.

I wondered for a moment how different life might have been for Elowen had her father known that she was even more powerful than Xaire.

Zephyr clearly thought the same, because his flint eyes

narrowed, and he said, just once, *Gods, if Thiago had known, he would have weaponised her. Just think of how he could have played it, the harm she could have done.*

She was doing harm now, glorious harm. Horror twisted Danaë's elegant features as she watched her husband fall to his knees there, in the vaulted atrium, where he had dispensed his merciless judgment with cold, kingly disdain.

One moment, the Spymaster stood like carved frost— tall, unbending—the next, his spine arched in pain, one hand flying to his temple as if to claw the intrusion free. Emotions reeled over Danaë's face, clear to read. The husband, who had given her so much: her children, her magic, her place in Faerie.

I picked up my quill, gleaning that I might have to raise my magic against the once-mortal woman who Father had chosen to mother me when Tanuhja had sent me away. For all her sins, I did not wish her harm. Yet if she dared to hurt Elowen, I knew with grim certainty that my power would answer in kind.

I anticipated a shattering of glass and shredding of muscle and bone as Danaë turned her voice into a weapon, but her will unravelled beneath Loxley's magic. He was behind her, shaping her intent into something weak and passive, so she simply sank onto Thiago's vacant throne, her face an eerie mask of composure.

Elowen was magnificent. She stood utterly still, bound mouth silent, silver-blonde hair bound in a ribbon as dark as her purpose, as if her soul had sharpened to a blade. She looked like a painting of vengeance: hollow-cheeked, brown eyes unblinking, her beauty ethereal and bruised.

Her father's pale grey eyes, so calculating and cold,

widened with disbelief. Her mind pressed forward like the tip of a spear, lancing telepathic force that bypassed his defences entirely and rendered his shrewd cunning to jelly.

For all his ice and shadow, for all his dominion over silence itself, Thiago was powerless before her. His breath clouded in cold puffs, and his thin mouth pulled into a snarl of pain. She held him there, with nothing but thought and rage.

Even without a voice, in that moment, she was louder than any king.

Though Faerie was brutal compared to the mortal realm, even though I still nursed softness in me, I was glad to witness her revenge. Ryvaris clawed at the barriers of my mind, desperate to join the violence, to protect our kin with fang and flame. Every muscle in my body coiled with the effort of holding him back.

The monarchs stirred, exchanging uncertain glances, and chaos spread like a crack through the atrium's carefully curated order. Jewel eyes turned away, lest catching sight of Thiago's shame, condemn them to punishment. A few leaned forward, hungry for blood. Others let out scandalised laughs. Most hovered between awe and dread.

The rulers of Faerie did not lift a finger, or a blade, or a thread of half-arsed magic to help Thiago, nor did his spiders, because alliances and dependencies were not the same as friendship, and they all saw how they could benefit from the death of the King of Silence.

If the Spymaster fell, the balance of power would shift, and in that chaos, each of them might seize something greater for themselves. Unease rippled through me at the

Queen of Bones's expression and how she was recalculating our alliance based on every eventuality. Even she considered Elowen too broken and full of rage to be much better than what had come before.

Zephyr's jaw tightened, but he didn't look away—not for a breath. Through the bond, something surged, dark and golden, edged in vindication. Joy, cloaked in steel. "We had a plan. A vote. A legitimate end to this all. Ysa deserves more than an existence in shadows."

Cyprian crossed his arms, leaning back. "You know Loxley. Plans are always suggestions. Besides, we're mercenaries. None of us is suited to court politics as much as mercenary life. Aren't you enjoying this just a little? Let your cousin have her moment."

"She has clearly earned it," retorted Zephyr.

The Spymaster knelt, spine arched, one hand clawing at his temple, but he was not yet broken. Ice spilt out beneath him, and the courtiers were transfixed now to see a meek princess seek patricide.

ELOWEN

You seem to think, beloved, that Xaire is more in your image. I have come to believe that Elowen is your mirror: calculating, composed, always assessing, waiting to turn against the hand that holds her down. We have taught her well.
– Danaë's letter to Thiago

A ll her life, Elowen's father had presumed to think that he was the cleverest mind in Echohold, perhaps in all of Faerie. The legend of the Spymaster had merciless teeth, velvet-sheathed claws, and gore thick enough to drown entire courts. Younglings grew up hearing his name spoken only in hush or warning.

It was far worse being his child, gagged and groomed into submission.

Elowen could never be satisfied with the crumbs of affection that kept Xaire loyal.

She was far too proud, far too wronged for that. Now, she realised that it was a gift that her father had underestimated her.

Their father believed his secrets impenetrable, his will unbreakable, and his mind a labyrinth no one could walk but him. Pride stopped him from seeing that his daughter was the darkest secret at the heart of his court, but she would show him what he had created in the dark. All her suffering, all her waiting and plotting had led to this moment.

Elowen stood before him in the vaulted atrium and didn't hesitate to take her chance.

Her father had always crowed that control was power, and Elowen was very controlled, at first.

She tunnelled into the veined corridors of his consciousness and found nothing she could not decipher or twist to her will. She located the rooms in his dark mind, where he had replaced vulnerabilities with cruelties. His thoughts scattered like rats at her arrival, and he couldn't fathom in that moment how to stop her.

Elowen didn't whisper apologies. Slowly, deliberately, she thrust open doors of the rooms in his mind, flung down the curtains, smashed the stained-glass debts and bargains he'd accrued and unearthed secrets he'd buried like corpses in shallow graves. Each room held rot: cells and chains and quiet sobs of things better left forgotten. That fuelled her rage.

Her magic held a savagery that neither her father nor her twin could match. Where Xaire had mastered his shadows through combat and command, Elowen had studied pain. She had practised behind her gag, behind her stillness, letting fury ferment during each slight, each withheld kindness.

Xaire had practised at appointed times, but Elowen had wielded her mind endlessly during the dark hours of neglect and abuse. Those moments had forged her.

She didn't spare a thought for her mother, who had coddled her father and never protected her. Coward. Victim. A warden in beautiful clothes. She had given up trying to understand. If her mother had wielded magic against her, Elowen might have succumbed to it, so focused was she on her revenge against her father.

For a fleeting moment, she worried that Ysa and Zephyr and their new family might flinch from her, but even that thought could not prevent the outpouring of her fury. Fury that had been threaded through her by small and large acts of violence against her mind, her body, the very shape of her soul.

It felt dangerously good—glorious, even—to relinquish the reins and allow her magic to follow its will, her will. To stop pretending she needed restraint or permission. No longer stifled and compressed, it poured forth in eagerness, dancing to her triumph. And Elowen was finally, truly, unbound.

She let it shred through the grey matter of him, then, like claws through silk, twisting, splitting, razing. Her father fell to his knees in the waking world, and in his mind, she watched every clench of pain. His crown fell askew as he clutched his head and he tried to shield the most sacred vaults of his mind behind sigil-bound doors, but Elowen tore them open like wet paper.

He had always called her weak, but the damage she wrought was so easy, so joyous, that it was almost play.

Faerie's legendary Spymaster was reduced to mewling on his knees by the daughter he'd tormented.

It thrilled her that her father's undoing was not only painful but a spectacle. After all, he had projected strength from the moment he had left the cradle. It gave Elowen the single greatest pleasure of her life to peel it away.

All the ways she had envisaged wreaking havoc with him came to fruition then, and Elowen would have wept with delight, but she didn't want to give him the satisfaction. Instead, she revelled in every incision her mind achieved against his.

She did not speak to him. Let him taste the silence he had forced upon her. Let him choke on it. At long last, he learned the lesson he had so frequently imparted to others: mental suffering often rendered the victim mute.

His tongue moved more slowly than his thoughts, and even those were flickering, tattered things now. His mind asked short questions, as though he couldn't manage longer formulations. *How? Why?* As if he had the right to answers.

He deserved only her silence, and he would reap now what he had sown.

The atrium narrowed to a point. There were just the two of them: father and daughter.

It could all have been so different, but now it could only unfold one way.

She slid through the red velvet walls of her father's mind like a scalpel through brain tissue. She lit fires and watched his cells curl in on themselves like leaves under flame. She peeled back the layers of memory like old wallpaper until the walls of his mind sagged.

Neural pathways snapped under her touch. She found

the place where he hid his shame and carved her name into it. She stitched her rage into his thoughts so that he would know no peace, even in his final moments.

Her magic peeled his mind apart like old fruit, and she watched with cold delight as he realised too late that he had raised the very thing that would unmake him. She was a thing then, too delirious in her destruction to remember that she had a soul.

Her magic made art of his suffering, and she barely noticed the ice spreading beneath them.

She could have gone further still—collapsing language centres, refolding his grey matter, manipulating his brain connections like a puppeteer, garbling the commands he gave his body, perhaps even in time bending him to her will—but she wanted desperately for him to understand what was happening to him.

Really, what she was doing was not cruelty; it was balance.

She sought only to make an inverted cathedral, a sinking temple. Each crumbling wall was a monument to the times he had ignored her voice, her tears, her worth, or dealt her a quiet cruelty dressed in regal silk. Her obscene excuse for a father, who had never once bounced her on his knee, wiped away her tears, or given her fatherly advice that didn't serve himself.

Now he was nothing more than meat laced with knowledge and spite.

Only when a shadow fell across her father's convulsing form did Elowen know that Orin had stepped into the fray. Her uncle's face held no satisfaction, only the grim resolve of a male about to undertake work that should have been completed a century ago. Orin was perhaps her father's oldest victim, the one he had honed his cruelty on, and they had planned this assault meticulously.

Desolate skies, she wanted to be the one to kill her father. But Elowen wasn't guileless enough to think herself capable of killing a faerie king without help. Had there been any justice, Faerie itself would have armed her. As it was, a chink in the perception of her father's power was all that she could hope to create alone. Such a chink would hasten his downfall. Her lips curved upwards, though her mouth was still bound.

She was glad to have been the one to begin the feast, even though it would take others to finish it.

Orin had been practising, she knew. He raised one hand, palm open, fingers splayed like a summoning. The air around them thickened, and her father's shadow answered. It rose, coming from some distance away. It was hunched, roiling, recognisably him, but warped by separation. It snarled and pulsed, as though her father's cruelty had been given independent form: the part of himself he had severed to protect her mortal mother.

The shadow turned towards its former master with something like hunger.

Elowen's heart *sang* to see her father beaten and humiliated so. She only wished that she could be the one to end his sorry life. Still, watching him be consumed by his own darkness would etch itself into her memory like a dark hymn of victory.

YSADORA

If you're reading this, I've gone where your healing light can't reach me.
I deeply regret that I was too petty to share a love that was radiant, even when halved. I am not the brother you deserved, but perhaps the manner of my leaving will remind our court that you were always our finest hope.
– Esolas's letter to his sister Aurelie

Elowen exerted her power over her father, the faerie king, holding the assembly captive in stunned silence.

Then Zephyr stiffened beside me, his whole body locking as if bracing for impact. His shadows coiled tighter around him, ready to strike at the first sign of true danger. I followed his gaze to a figure emerging from the gloom at the edge of the atrium.

Orin. Not hiding. Not broken. But stepping forward with quiet certainty from the darkness of his own making, even though my mate had told me that his father had suppressed that side of himself, and had only ever cowered since Rowena and Veda's deaths. The shadows around him moved with purpose, not the hesitant flickers I'd expected, but deliberate tendrils that spoke of power concealed rather than lost.

A thread of stunned disbelief wove through the mate bond. *Ancients. He got the moth courier.*

From the shared glances between Elowen and Orin, it seemed Zephyr's father had not been idle. For all his silence, he had not ignored the request for help. There was a moment of recognition between them: a plan within a plan, something they had coordinated while the rest of us focused on building alliances, on growing my magic and the formal vote. His father gave him a smile like sunlight through winter branches, brief and unexpected, and Zephyr found himself moving before he could think better of it.

Zephyr ignored Cyprian's curse and the spike of my anxiety in the mate bond. Even with his shadows moving like instinct, Zephyr was a breath delayed. A slice to the hamstring of the first, a twist of shadow through the ribs of the other, closing the throat of a third with darkness.

As he fought, his father said, "This time, I will not choose you over my son, brother." The words carried the weight of old guilt, old choices that had haunted him. And the mate bond cracked open with grief and something fierce, like love dredged up from ash.

Orin took advantage of Elowen's hold on Thiago.

Elowen's focus dimmed for a split second to tell me,

Ferrith discovered Father sacrificed his strongest shadow so the Wraithwoods would grant Mother magic.

For a moment, Thiago's shadow obeyed. Orin turned his own brother's shadow against him, and I wondered if the elder brother would take the throne all these years after being usurped.

But his magic, whether from lack of practice or power, faltered. The shadow writhed when he attempted to turn it against Thiago, twitching in resistance. Then it thinned, dissipating at its edges like smoke, becoming half-formed, then collapsing into itself like nothing. And Elowen was waning. She couldn't hold Thiago forever.

It had been a dangerous gambit.

Though she wanted this moment to be hers, she was not enough to stop him. Her magic could never truly rival his: not in breadth, nor the old, terrible depth of it. Even now, with his allies silent and the court watching, with Elowen's will crushing down upon him, Thiago remained terrifying.

He was on his knees, but he was still a faerie king. That title was not just ceremony; it was myth, forged in bone-deep bargains and ancient rites. Power like his did not shatter easily. Even weakened, he pulsed with the echo of silence and winter, of kingdoms won and undone by a whisper.

Thiago moved like something thawing, not swift, not whole, but inevitable. His hands pressed against the slick, dark floor as if drawing strength from the bones of Echohold itself. He stood, not all at once, but like snowfall thickening into a blizzard, slow and silent until the world vanished beneath it.

Cold bled into the floor beneath his boots, and his

shadows thickened with every breath. His gaze found Elowen, and though red rimmed his eyes and she had wrought havoc with his mind, there was recognition in them, and disappointment, as if she were a cracked heirloom he'd once prized, now returned to him broken.

He didn't strike her. He didn't speak to her.

Instead, he dismissed her. Maybe—stars help us—he still loved her.

My muscles tensed, ready to spring into action. We were all poised on the knife's edge of violence, waiting for the moment when protection would outweigh politics.

A slow turn of Thiago's head, a flare of frost in the air between them, and then he looked past her like she was nothing more than a ruined plan.

But Orin was not ignored. The crystal above twisted Thiago's smile into something monstrous. The shadows gathered at Thiago's back surged like black surf. In a single, fluid motion, they struck: not with elegance, but with contempt.

A wave of darkness slammed into Orin's chest and lifted him from the ground, flinging him backwards through the air like a discarded cloak. He landed hard, his shoulder cracking against polished stone. The sound echoed, humiliating and final.

It all happened so quickly that Zephyr pivoted, one moment intending to stand shoulder to shoulder with his father against the King of Silence, the next changing his path towards his crumpled father.

He crouched down beside him, taking care not to turn his back on Thiago, shadows sweeping protectively around Orin as he reached out with hands that once would have hesitated. Every instinct screamed at him to turn those shadows into weapons, to strike back at his uncle, but he forced himself to focus on what mattered more: his father's safety, the bigger picture.

My heart ached for him and all the times he had endured here, at the Court of Silence, only for there to be more. And though there had not been softness between them for many, many years, some long-locked door between them eased open without a sound. Orin had faced worse than failure. He sat up with quiet pride, chest rising once as if to mark the attempt.

We can salvage this, I whispered through the bond to Zephyr.

But a cold dread curled beneath my ribs, gaze darting to Elowen, who stood with her mouth bound, eyes burning, magic pressed tight against the seams of her body. That had been their plan. Maren's green eyes locked on my father, desperately seeking a strategy. Ferrith's duplicates flickered and died until only the original remained. Loxley's impish grin faded. We had lost control, and it hadn't paid off.

I locked gazes with Father, and his fingers twitched, clearly missing his quill, missing the might of Caldoron, but calling the dragons now would only prove every fear about my danger, destroy any hope of legitimacy. The dragon's roar echoed in my skull, furious at my restraint.

Wylda moved forward, as if to help Orin.

But Cyprian shook his head. "Thiago has not done grievous harm. You know what Zeph planned. We have to win with legitimacy." His voice was steady, but I caught the way his knuckles had gone white around his sword's pommel. Even he struggled with the choice to hold back.

I hated it. I hated what Thiago made of Faerie and what he had made of us.

Around us, in the Vaulted Atrium, Faerie was watching, holding still, not daring to react lest Thiago's gaze find them next.

He didn't turn to them. Instead, he turned to Danaë, and she looked back, her lips parted in disbelief at their predicament. She was no longer fully dulled by Loxley's tampering. Her posture had returned, not regal, but present. Thiago's shoulders straightened a fraction. Devotion flickered in his pale eyes, and I wondered if it came from true affection or possession. Then that glimmer hardened. His fists curled, bones cracking softly beneath the strain. Power bled back into him with his resolve.

He was a king again, or worse, a male with nothing left to lose.

Unsatisfied with the spurt of violence against Orin, the Spymaster did what he had always done, which was to find an outlet to drain his pain.

He pinned Esolas with a glare, his voice a low chime of ice shattering underfoot. "I offered a place at my side, and yet you give opportunities for my enemies to strike. Did you think I would not realise?"

Zephyr stood, helping his father up, shadows gathering like knives. I sensed the moment he almost lost control: the terrible temptation to end this before Esolas could be hurt.

Esolas darted him a plaintive look that said, *stand down*, as if in premonition that weathering the force of Thiago's wrath might spare his sister queen. His hands remained open, palms bare, as though ready for peace he knew wouldn't come, and he addressed Thiago, his voice loud and clear for all to hear, "I never meant to betray you, Thiago. But I cannot blind myself to what you've become. Ruling with darkness is never as powerful as ruling with light. For all your power, the fae of this court and others love your nephew more than you. By tending to the cursed fae, your nephew earned something you never have: devotion. Your nephew showed mercy where we showed indifference, even though we bore the responsibility to act. Even if you win today, that debt will not be forgotten."

The room changed with those words. There was guilt in some expressions, grim admiration in others, and the monarchs shifted uncomfortably on their thrones, and I understood the Binder had been right to pressure Zephyr to continue the tasks he had begun.

Through the bond came a slow, steady breath. *Maybe we're not quite so alone in this fight after all, Inkheart.*

I smiled, our bond humming like a spell. I was so damned proud of him. In that, nothing had changed.

Thiago's eyes narrowed to slits. He turned to the gathered court. "My nephew aligned himself with traitors. He offered them shelter and gave them room to strike. By the ancient laws of Faerie, before the vote is cast, betrayal may be answered in kind. I challenge you to duel."

Esolas paled. "This is tyranny. Duelling is a tradition at the Court of Luminosity, meant to dazzle rather than destroy."

But Thiago just smirked, relishing the thought of retribution. Danaë brought her husband his blade: strong and forged from darkness and the memory of colder seasons. And again, Zephyr attempted to intervene, but Esolas gave a sad smile and handed both his staff and crown to Aurielle.

A moment passed between them, full of all the things they would never say. Then Esolas stood, as if his bones had stiffened in that cold place, and drew his own sword with far less flair, a slender length of starlight-steel. His hands trembled, but his spine did not bend.

He faced Thiago: two faerie kings, one crownless, the other not.

The atrium stilled, and then, like lightning off cold stone, the duel began, but not before Thiago said with slick enjoyment, "This male competed with his sister over a lover, and issued the ultimatum that led to the lover's death."

A ripple moved through the court: gasps caught in throats, fur cloaks pulled tighter, emissaries turning to whisper behind gloved hands. Those who had always held Esolas in esteem recoiled.

Esolas looked at Aurielle, his heart in his golden eyes. His voice cracked, "I'm sorry," but she turned her kind face away.

The cruelty of it hit me like a physical blow. Through the bond, Zephyr's rage burned white-hot. *He weaponised a private grief. He doesn't just want to win, he wants to salt the ruin.*

My eyes flicked to Father on the dais, still biding his time, and then to Elowen, Maren, Ferrith, and Loxley, frozen in place by thin curls of frost I had only just discerned. Though I hated myself for saying it, I replied. *Please, love, his fate is sealed by his own hands. We can't let his ruin become ours. Our kin need us.*

Intervention would damn us all, but it didn't make it any easier to stand by.

Thiago smiled as the first strike fell, then steel met

shadow. Light met ice. It was over in three heartbeats. Thiago moved like silence given form, too fast, too precise. Esolas's defence faltered, thrown by grief, by memory, by the knowledge he was already outmatched. The dark blade sang through the air and into Esolas's chest with dreadful ease.

The Faerie King of Luminosity gasped—not from pain, but shock—and crumpled like falling dusk. Blood bloomed across his chest like some final, horrifying flower.

Aurielle's scream split the air like a sunflare at midnight, a blaze of mourning too bright to bear. It unspooled into the hushed horror of the court, and her light magic guttered in her grief. Even Wylda wept. Around us, there was no applause, just the hush of a realm watching one of its brightest fall beneath winter's hand.

Ryvaris roared in my mind, a sound of pure fury that made my vision blur with dragon-fire. Every fibre of my being screamed to make Thiago pay for his crime, but I held back, even as my soul bled.

Zephyr stepped forward and, with a wordless look at Aurielle, shrouded the Faerie King of Luminosity in gentle shadow, despite all he had done, to us and his sister. He met his uncle's triumphant gaze, his voice like a blade on bone. "Call the vote."

For the first time in that damned atrium, Thiago spoke directly to Zephyr, his smile as sharp as winter's edge. "Very well, nephew."

Quiet devastation filled my bones. For all our cleverness and every sacrifice made, not just my freedom, but our dream of a fairer Faerie was in peril. What stung deepest was that our restraint, when every instinct yearned for vengeance, might be the only thing that could still save us.

YSADORA

*Any ink plant relocated between courts must
undergo intensive magical cleansing rituals to
strip away harmful magic or unstable properties.
Plants known to have been cursed, infected, or
otherwise corrupted (either by dark magic or
unnatural influences) are to be destroyed.
— A Short History of the Order of the Glyph*

"Call the vote," my beloved said, his voice flint-sharp in the thick, perfumed air of the atrium. He came to stand beside me then, and I'd never been more grateful for his strength. Shadows slithered behind him like blades unsheathed, but it was his stillness that drew all eyes. He wasn't begging. He wasn't bargaining. He was done waiting.

To me, he sounded like the rightful king.

The violence in him simmered, ready to break.

The silence that followed was not empty. It crackled

with magic, with old grudges and new calculations, with the taste of blood and the sting of grief. On the floor, Esolas's body lay still, his light dimmed forever, his spilt light magic pooling like wine beneath Zephyr's shadow-slicked shroud, mingling with crimson that was not wine. His fate showed the cost of speaking out in the King of Silence's court, but still, Zephyr was not cowed.

Stars, I loved him, and I gripped his hand and sent my love like a cocoon of protection into the mate bond. He showered me with warmth in return, and we stood there, with our kin all around, spread through that godsforsaken court.

Thiago, as the proposer, could not vote, but one by one, the monarchs answered the question of whether the King of Silence should control me and be crowned High King. Behind Thalindra, my father bristled with the need to protect me. For now, he could only watch, impotent, as others decided my fate.

My stomach roiled. Six votes—that was all that remained between us and failure.

Thiago returned to the apex of the dais to sit on his throne, ushering Danaë behind it. The tension in his shoulders betrayed the false calm on his gaunt face. His magic was barely restrained, a storm caged by protocol.

Danaë stood like a frozen portrait, her glassy gaze locked on Elowen. Her snow leopards did not answer to her when she curled her finger. They did not sit. They did not rest. Their feral intuition sensed the fracture in power, and the tension tightened like a noose around us all.

One twist of Thiago's pale, long-fingered hand and a crystal basin before him filled with six orbs, each representing a monarch's vote. The courtiers fell silent as the orbs levitated, and the voting began, swirling slowly before settling into two piles: light for *yes*, shadow for *no*.

The Faerie King of the Silver Seas raised his chin. "Yes," he said too quickly.

The Faerie King of Embers sat unmoved. "I abstain," he said flatly, as though even apathy carried heat enough to burn.

The Queen of Bones met my gaze. Her scrying bowl fizzed at her feet, but she did not look down. Her voice curled through the air like incense. "The calligrapher's daughter deserves the chance to prove herself without coercion. I vote no."

I nodded my thanks, but my heart stumbled all the same. One voice wasn't enough to steady the weight pressing against my spine. Courtiers and monarchs alike leaned in, waiting to see which side would outnumber the other. With the Court of Nebulas unrepresented and the Court of Chaos absent, only Aurielle, the newly bereaved Queen of Luminosity, stood between us and damnation.

Zephyr squeezed my hand, and his velvet voice came through the bond. *Even if they don't vote our way, know this—I would choose you, every time, in every realm.*

But Esolas had sided with us, and therefore, it was only logical that she would, too. All eyes turned to the Dawnmother. Her brother lay dead at her feet, his white robes soaked with the life he'd once held so fiercely. She looked at her brother's cooling corpse and the assembled members of the Court of Luminosity. She studied Zephyr, then me, chaos crackling around me. And I thought to myself, she didn't see me as a threat, but as a mirror: another female, asked to carry too much.

Tears slid soundlessly down her cheeks. Her voice was

dusk-light and breaking. "I'm sorry, but I cannot risk the fall of my court." Her hand trembled as it rose, but in mourning, in surrender. "Yes." And the white orb flew to meet the other.

Yes. Such a small word to seal my fate. The word struck like a needle, sharp and surgical, trying to thread me into a life not of my choosing. I could not blame the Dawnmother. We had not courted her favour, and her brother's violent, public death had left her with grief too fresh for reason or courage. Power, not justice, drove Faerie.

But still, I mourned the future of our imagining.

But my mate mourned me. Inconsolable grief and heartbreak poured into the mate bond, and I knew he would not willingly let me go, even though the vote was binding. *Call the dragons,* he said, his hand linked so tightly with mine that I thought he might pull me into shadow, even though the master of shadows stood mere feet away, enjoying our turmoil.

Thiago's triumph filled the space like poison, as Esolas's blood pooled on the crystal floor, seeping out from beneath Zephyr's shroud of shadow. The corners of the atrium darkened as he rose from the throne and kissed Danaë, as though her pearly lips were the seal on a victory long plotted. The faintest smile ghosted his lips, not of joy, but inevitability.

Our mercenary kin watched the Faerie King of Silence, eyes sharp and mouth tight. To blades-for-hire, arrogance was weakness disguised: an invitation for a kill, and my gut churned as I realised they would die for me without hesitation, just as Zephyr would.

My gaze was drawn to Elowen's dull eyes, as if some

last spark had finally flickered out. As if in that quiet collapse, she realised that just like her own freedom, her father had taken mine.

Maren was still frozen to the spot, despite turning bursts of violet flame against her feet. "Get her out of here. I mean it, or I'll haunt your mate bed," she called to Zephyr, low and fierce, and Ferrith's eyes flicked towards the crowd, his protective instincts sharpening. Loxley mirrored the tension, shifting his weight forward, a silent warning lingering in his posture.

Thiago sighed at her, like she was a pitiful thing, and spread his arms wide, a mockery of invitation. His eyes gleamed too brightly. "Won't you cheer?" he asked the gathered assembly. "For you have a new High King, and Ysadora Silberquill is no longer a threat, but a tool."

Call the dragons, demanded my mate. He turned sharply, gathering our kin with a swift gesture. The mercenary kin tensed, blades half-drawn, ready for anything, and Sequoia looked the fiercest of them all, her wings flared and eyes hard as obsidian.

But then chaos whispered through the atrium, calling to me. A flicker of unease shadowed Thiago's brow, as if some latent ward had faltered. The air shifted as the seam between logic and dream tore open, and my father's mouth fell open.

They had not seen each other since I was a few days old, and yet, here she was, my mother—the Faerie Queen of Chaos—stepping through a rift in reality. No guards flanked her, no banner announced her name, and yet none dared speak, the courtiers stilling as if pulled into orbit around her gravity.

She claimed the space, every footfall a sharp click, her

twisted crown reforged and encircling her head with its long waves of falling night. Even the Queen of Bones lowered her head a fraction, and the King of Embers blinked once, slowly, then inclined his head as if granting her legitimacy.

Zephyr grinned, a true, unguarded grin that cracked his solemn, steely façade wide open, as if sensing a change in fortune, and the mate bond lit up with radiant hope.

I held that hope close, as my mother passed, pausing only to stare in confusion at my short hair.

Then, she stepped over Esolas's body, climbed the dais, and sat on a throne. For all her desire to hand me her crown, she was haughty and contemptuous, born for the role of queen.

Only once seated did she turn to Thiago and say with a smile, "I trust I am not too late?" Her eyes gleamed as Thiago's lips flattened into a thin, bitter line, and she added, "My vote is no." Then Tanuhja simply rested back into her seat, violet eyes fixed on Thiago as if daring him to challenge her place.

Her silence was louder than any war cry.

The decision had been made, and the final orb darkened and joined Thalindra's *no*.

The Spymaster's icy face with its river of blue capillaries reddened, and a rustle moved through the court like wind through dry leaves. Ferrith and Loxley punched the air in mirrored movements, then looked at each other in embarrassment, and Maren and Elowen exchanged small smiles.

Amidst it all, Danaë watched Tanuhja not with fury, but with something resembling relief, evident only in the faint upturn of her lips. It was subtle, quick as a breath.

But I saw it, as if perhaps part of her rooted for me, and I realised that motherhood was perhaps more complicated than I ever imagined.

Sequoia let out a low whistle. "Well, I'll be damned. Maybe your mother's not the monster everyone made her out to be."

Wylda elbowed her. "Or maybe she is just the kind we needed."

A sob threatened to claw its way up my throat. In the very place meant to break me, I stood bolstered by the one woman who once abandoned me. It shouldn't have felt like a victory, but stars, it did.

Zephyr's shoulders relaxed for the first time since we set foot in his uncle's court, and in my mind came the psychic echo of a dragon's roar muffled only by distance. Ryvaris had felt the game of courts tilt.

A slow breath escaped Father, who had been pretending to be the Queen of Bones's pet all the while. His eyes closed briefly before he allowed himself an almost imperceptible smile, and in his brown eyes I caught a flicker of relish in anticipation of the havoc our dragons would presently wreak.

But our brittle calm shattered like glass under a hammer.

Thiago's lips curved into a cruel smile. "An impasse, then. How inconvenient." He scanned the court, his demeanour more composed than I hoped. "But rules are rules. And as proposer, I hold the casting vote."

But my mother wasn't finished. The Queen of Chaos lifted a brow with wicked poise. "How rude of me. Did I neglect to say? The *Fatebreaker* invited a friend to attend court today, one who knows the heartbeat of this land, one who walks this land by instinct, not invitation. He knows what belongs and what festers." She smoothed down the velvet of her gown and met Father's gaze with mock sweetness, as if to say, *I was as fit to raise our child as you.* "In light of…let's just call them monstrous *mishaps*…I granted him safe passage. He really has been rather angry with me. It felt only fair."

My heart pounded. *She rigged the game in my favour,* I said through the bond.

Not for the first time, Zephyr agreed, his emotions surging with vindication. *And she knows how to pick her moment.*

Loathing carved itself into Thiago's features, as if he had learned of the Binder's name for Zephyr and it was a festering splinter under his skin. The scrying bowl at Thalindra's feet trembled before cracks spiderwebbed across it in jagged lines.

Then the rift Tanuhja had not sealed widened like a fresh wound in Faerie's fabric. From the shadowed breach stepped a primal silhouette, half-male, half-forest nightmare, accompanied by his clicking beetle, glinting shiny and dark. His skin was cracked bark, streaked with veins of sap-green, crowned by antlers and black thorns, and he dominated the atrium, as tall as two males.

Ruby eyes glinted as his beetle companion tapped its pincers with impatient rhythm. Unease slithered through the crowd like a shadow, and the faintest tightening at Thalindra's temple betrayed her controlled exterior, a relic from Faerie's brutal past, a deposed monarch of her own court, returned to court affairs.

I shuddered, remembering how the Thorn King had separated Maren and me in the Shrouded Forest, how he had wounded me, and how Zephyr had cradled me in his arms so that I could heal at Ebonspire, how he had been a King of Bones once.

It's okay, Inkheart, he's not here for us, said my mate.

"Speak, Thorn King." Thiago looked up at his uninvited guest, nostrils flaring. "If you have words to cast into my court, do so now. Let's not pretend you came here in silence."

The Thorn King's voice rumbled like ancient trees groaning under their own weight. "Long ago, I forgot my name. The male whom I once knew as the Prince of Lore returned that name to me, which you knew but chose to keep." His gaze locked onto Thiago, and a shiver danced up my spine. "The old laws of Faerie are clear, and they will not be bent to suit petty ambition. When a vote is tied, it is rejected."

It is done, said my mate, and I sensed the euphoria of our kin around us.

But it wasn't done. It was only just beginning.

Thiago's jaw clenched so tightly the veins in his neck bulged, but his smile remained: a brittle mask stretched over fury. "You presume to lecture me on law?" he asked, his voice soft and seething. But the old laws could not be twisted without cost.

Courtiers stiffened in their finery, gazes flitting between the players in the games of Faerie, between the Thorn King and Thiago most of all. Some looked to their monarchs, others mostly looked afraid of what had been said and what might come next. They were right to be scared because the Faerie King of Silence addressed them once more.

His cloak of shadows curled tighter around him,

clinging like armour or fear. One foot slid half a step back, almost imperceptibly, but enough to suggest instability. His eyes scanned the court like a cornered predator, daring anyone to speak against him. His hand extended towards the gathered monarchs, inviting alliance. But his fingers curled, almost clenched. Like he already sensed their hesitation, and it burned. Danaë came forward to stand at his side, her chin angled with porcelain defiance, though her eyes shimmered with something dangerously close to doubt.

"Should I feel sorry for him?" asked Wylda.

Sequoia snorted. "Not one bit."

The King of Silence could have chosen to accept his fate, but he was not one for grace. He addressed the Vaulted Atrium of Tongueless Praise, where he had once been unmatched in power, "Ysadora Silberquill is dangerous. Pool your magic with mine. Bind her magic to mine, and you will be safe. I can still be your High King."

No one moved because Zephyr had not only made alliances but earned respect through the bargains that had lined his arm, burdens he had carried to keep us all safe. My mate had always understood that power without sacrifice was just tyranny dressed in silk. His uncle would never learn that lesson.

Now that we had legitimacy on our side, my mate's wrath surged through the bond, and though he never intended to let his uncle walk from that place, Thiago's threat against me and his violence against Orin and our kin sealed the truth: this could only end in blood.

But Zephyr was not above toying with his prey when it suited his strategy, and every notch that he drove his uncle's fury higher meant a weakness he could exploit to end his reign—and his life. The mercenaries sensed their leader's thrust, and they grinned like wolves scenting blood, their enjoyment barely masked beneath steel and swagger.

Zephyr prowled forward, shadows curling lazily at his heels, like predators at rest. His smile was slow and cruel, all teeth and venom-laced charm. The bond between us thrummed with satisfaction, as if this was what he'd been waiting for.

"Your dreams are for nought, dear uncle, because the King of Silver Seas has misplaced the High King's crown. There I was thinking that the legendary Spymaster of Faerie knows everything."

"The Prince of Lore speaks the truth. By ancient decree, the coronation of a High King or Queen," said the Thorn King as his beetle clacked, "cannot proceed in the absence of the sacred crown."

Through the bond, I teased, *This is going to be fun,* and Zephyr's grin widened, wicked and dazzling, just for me.

"Xaire," called out Danaë, ignoring his twin, as if Elowen's defiance had severed any belonging. "Come and stand with us."

Xaire approached with his languid step, his lips pursed in thought. He pushed the lock of dark hair on his forehead back, a male blessed with all the natural advantages of birth and good fortune, before saying with regret. "I stand with Elowen."

Danaë's face went ashen, one hand flying to her throat as if her son had struck her. She had come to Faerie because Thiago had wooed her and promised her children from her own womb, but she had lost them both. Thiago's pale eyes flashed with something beyond anger: a son's betrayal that cut deeper than the enemy's blade. A son he had nurtured as his successor, once Zephyr had chosen the Court of Lore over the Court of Silence.

Unmoved, Xaire raised his hand, and shadow magic surged, clean and sharp. The wall of ice encasing the bloodheart tree cracked down the centre, and the frozen curtain fell. Behind it, the bloodheart stood almost entirely bare-limbed and trembling.

A rustle moved through the crowd like breath, and even the monarchs, proud and aloof on their thrones, leaned forward.

Danaë's smile faltered at her husband's humiliation and their son's betrayal, then Thiago's violence cracked through the air, targeting not Xaire, but Zephyr.

And my mate—he was *pleased*. He tilted his head just slightly, like a predator hearing the last breath of its prey, and let the shadows curling around him deepen to knives.

The courtiers of Faerie scattered, emptying from the atrium like breath from a diseased lung. Fae of diverse courts burst into motion, ushered away from harm by their monarchs. The atrium erupted with the sounds of strained breath, swishing silk and rushing feet—webbed, hooved, bare—and the flutter of wings brushing against crystal walls.

Jewels and weapons scattered across the floor as fae tripped. The monarchs moved swiftly, even Thalindra, barking quiet commands as guards shielded them with blades drawn but unused. Now that the vote had concluded, there was no obligation to remain. They had no desire to interfere in the internal affairs of the Court of Silence, and they did not owe Thiago any fealty.

The Thorn King, too, retraced his path into the rift. The

beetle's pincers clicked softly as it followed, and they disappeared into the shadowed seam as silently as they had come. Only the Dawnmother hesitated. Breath-hitching, she stopped to cradle her brother's still form. Then, golden light burst from her palms, engulfing him. The light consumed Esolas swiftly: a final act of love in the midst of chaos, and I knew it was not the last time we would see fire that evening.

"Go," said Thiago to Danaë, and the hard mask of his pride slipped, allowing a glimpse of their ruinous love.

She brushed her fingers against the iron circlet at his brow. "I can sing," she said, when she meant *I can kill*.

He shook his head. "Lead our people to safety."

So, she did, pausing to kiss his temple, before calling the snow leopards to her, and not sparing a glance for her children. Even the servants did not stay, abandoning any pretence of hospitality, scattering like startled birds and fading into shadowed doorways.

Until the Spymaster of Faerie stood alone in the eye of the storm he had created, surrounded only by the spies he had trained, perhaps forty in total, more than five for each of us, although given the right impetus, my mate could fell those alone and so could I.

But Father had not fled the dais, and neither had my mother. In fact, Father smiled in relish as, at last, he sensed the moment to shed the illusion that he was indebted to Thalindra and become his own reckoning.

With a whispered word to Tanuhja that looked suspiciously like flirting, he slipped his new quill from his breast pocket, drew ink from a vial, and wrote such exquisite calligraphy into the air, that my heart faltered mid-beat, caught between memories from the ancient stone—at last, I witnessed with my own eyes—his calligrapher's magic for the first time.

His quill moved in looping arcs and sharp flicks, each letter cut into the air with the skill of a master swordsman, art and rebellion married in ink. Even though we stood in the Court of Silence, my father had written and maintained the Grimoire, and while he could not rival a faerie king's power, he shattered the frost-binding spell that held Elowen, Maren, Ferrith, and Loxley with a downwards stroke.

They stumbled forward, released, and scrambled for fallen weapons, Loxley like a youngling in a sweet stall. I caught Father's eye then, and we both called our dragons. I saw them in my mind's eye, the bronze and ink-veined blue shimmering in the stormy sky.

Father could not resist another flick of power at Thiago's back, who had, after all, once been his romantic rival, and my mother rolled her eyes and shooed him off the dais and out of danger.

Then Thiago exploded into violence, and the Court of Silence shook to its very foundations. The land itself answered Thiago's call. The dais groaned beneath the weight of encroaching ice and cracked atrium tiles. His shadows twisted and curled, warping the space and swallowing the edges of the room whole, a tempest of despair unleashed by a king who would settle for nothing less than total dominion.

His magic pushed back to the far reaches of the atrium, lengthening the battlefield, as if Thiago feared direct combat. His spiders surged forward like a tide of malice, blades flashing in cruel arcs, before they vanished. Even under the blanket of darkness, they wore whisper rings.

"Get their rings, Ferrith!" called out Zephyr, his shadows moving like a dark tempest incarnate to match his uncle.

"On it," replied Ferrith, and he was true to his word, splitting into multiple copies of himself that darted through the melee like phantoms, snatching whisper rings while Maren flared her flames ahead of his path, lighting the way, searing and disorienting their targets.

They could have slipped on the whisper rings themselves, but they didn't.

They fought openly, bravely, killing at least three while I watched with borrowed weapons and scalding flame, before my mate reminded me to focus.

Tight breaths punctuated his commands, his focus as sharp as the edge of the twin blades he had drawn. *Maren and Ferrith can hold their own. Focus, Inkheart. We are so close, now, to having everything we have dreamed of.*

I nodded and drew deep on my well of power to help my mate counter Thiago.

Shadows thickened, coiling into rope and slavering beasts, each one an echo of his will. They lashed at us, winding up our legs, seeking to gouge our eyes and mouths, desperate to blind us, silence us, consume us, wrench us apart.

The ground fractured, pulling us into grasping hands of darkness, and I used my ink magic as a tether to stay upright or found myself protected by shadows that I recognised immediately as Zephyr's. Thiago's shadows funnelled into spears and swarmed in curtains around us, trying to sever the mate bond with a silence so complete I would have chosen death.

Thiago continued his assault, channelling the brutality

of a centuries-old court, and every minute felt like an eternity as we fought our way towards him. His every motion sent ripples through the room: ribbons of shadow magic and frost spread across the floor and walls in fractal veins, coating even breath in rime.

I loathed the touch of his magic, even as I fought, its suffocating clutch of gloom and despair. Black ice stabbed upwards, cruel and glassy, spearing those too slow to move, and one of Ferrith's duplicates was caught, and I knew too little to understand if that iteration of him could bleed.

It crawled up pillars and across skin. The mate bond pulsed like a heartbeat in my throat. Zephyr was alive, near, fighting, and for me, that was both anchoring and unbearable: the mere thought of one of my kin dying fuelled my chaos magic.

He wanted us dead, of that I could be sure.

He hated that we were not only allies, but family, and he wanted to break us. Not for strategy, but for spite.

Together, Zephyr and I were a tempest: my ink and chaos, the bold magic of creation and destruction: his shadows, the cold grip of inevitability. He was devastatingly dangerous, threads of his shadows tightening into nooses that crushed and silenced.

His voice rang out, calm yet commanding, directing our allies with strategic precision, drawing Thiago into making mistakes and exploiting every crack in his defence. Each stroke of my crimson quill painted wards of protection around our allies, while with my dragon-kissed blade, I carved chaos.

Loxley looked every inch a madman forged in a dungeon, his ginger hair unkempt, beard wild, and fury honed by captivity. He was full of flair and bravado, his axe cutting down two fae with a broad stroke one moment, carving paths through Thiago's frost the next.

Cyprian moved like a ripple across still water, manipulating pockets of slowed time to create openings, then darting in with his blade. He smiled even as sweat darkened his tunic. His swordplay was elegant but unshowy, grounded in discipline rather than pride. Together, they were devastating.

"You good?" Cyprian called, breath measured, eyes molten as time bent around him.

"Would be better with a bath," Loxley muttered, cleaving through another foe.

"And a shave," Cyprian retorted.

Sequoia fought like a street brawler, all momentum and brute force, her wings tucked in tight, her dagger and fists gleaming with blood. She howled with delight every time she took down a foe, the sound stoking my own bloodlust. Next to her, Wylda's twisting vines snared ankles and wrenched weapons. They fought in tandem: Wylda's magic setting the rhythm, Sequoia landing the killing blows.

"Careful," said Wylda, as her vines caught an assailant midleap.

Sequoia grinned, blood on her lip. "Why start now?"

All around us, the fight raged. Xaire was there too, turning his shadows against the servants of his own court, even as he called out for them to stand down. Though he fought alone, with no one to guard his flank, some who slipped past his defences crumpled midstrike, clutching their heads in silent agony.

Through the chaos, I glimpsed Elowen pressed against

a pillar, brown eyes blazing with vengeance as she wielded her mind like a scalpel. Each spy who fell to her telepathic assault was another small revenge. Her mouth was still bound, but her power screamed for her.

And Thiago was so strong, even with his spies falling around him, even with their bodies piling up and catching us underfoot. A dome of silence descended, thick and unnatural, smothering shouts, cutting off commands.

Sword clashes rang hollow, like memories of war rather than war itself. The greenhouse that bloomed with ink plants shrivelled as the King of Silence's cold passed over it, as if he wanted to prevent me from using its wares.

But I had learned that chaos could make its own rules, and the river sisters had taught me how to draw from the earth, so I did, turning the land against its king. I gave the land my fear, my rage, my sorrow, and chaos answered.

The crystal floor beneath Thiago's feet spider-webbed, throwing off his balance. Phantom winds howled through the atrium, carrying the scent of ink and starlight, making the faerie king stumble. I imagined what would happen if Maren fell as Thiago fell to one knee and clawed himself back up. If Ferrith's laughter vanished forever. If Zephyr—

My mate's shadows curled protectively at my back, and our bond ignited. *You're fucking magnificent*, he said, and I was so glad that silence could not infiltrate our bond. His shadows struck outwards, not just as blades but as shields, catching barbed tendrils mid-swing, pushing back frost with warmth drawn from fury. *With me*, he breathed into the bond, and I nodded once.

I wrote in the air, each stroke of my calligraphy flaring with gold ink drawn from the veins of Silence. Binding runes. Barriers. Unravellings. My spells laced through his shadows like constellations in a midnight sky. Zephyr and I fought together—chaos and shadow, ink and pain—answering Thiago's dominion with defiance, inching forwards with every step.

And I revelled in our vengeance, in the rhythm of our rebellion, the way Zephyr's shadows met my ink in perfect synchrony, a dance we'd never choreographed but had always known. Each clash was a stanza, each step a brick in the path we built: darkness and light, fury and mercy, instinct and choice.

My chaos spat, erupting in silver-gold shreds that clawed at reality. It bent space, created light, and reformed truth, every spark a reflection of my pain, my love, my refusal to cower. It didn't obey; it demanded.

Glorious swaths of pure destruction and possibility tore through Thiago's summoned beasts, splitting shadows down the spine and leaving trails of stardust in their wake. My quill moved like a weapon, and my dagger like a song, our kin at our sides, my magic alive with all we'd suffered, all we still hoped for.

We pushed forward, not like soldiers, but like survivors.

Ferrith and Maren fought at our flanks. Ferrith's duplicates, each wielding a single blade, one shielding, one striking, one defending Maren, his golden curls sweat-dampened, not a note of fear on his face.

Maren was a violet firestorm, determined and cursing, like someone who refused to die quietly. Her magic scorched the air, sweet as burned petals, and the scent of charred shadows was thick in the air, like burnt wood and grave dirt.

Beneath it was the rot of congealing blood and wilted

greenhouse life. And then, a waft of ozone and sulphur met my nose, and I knew the dragons had arrived.

Just as we reached Thiago.

The dragons crashed through the glass of the atrium, and crystal and glass rained like glittering stars. Ryvaris and Caldoron soared through the collapse, their wings beating with a low, subterranean hum. Jaws opened with crackling flame, smoke curling from their nostrils, and they landed hard enough to quake the already broken ground.

In that moment, the King of Silence's face was a picture I wish Veda could have painted.

55

YSADORA

Mouth-binding is a technique favoured by
monarchs in the Court of Silence.
It stills the tongue, but never the mind.
It is particularly cruel in Faerie,
where words are weapons.
– A Tapestry of Courts and Crowns

A final flutter of crimson leaves floated down from the bloodheart tree like the last heartbeats of a dying thing.

Forty of Thiago's most trusted spies fought us on the battlefield, but when the dust settled from the dragons' landing and the moon spilt its light across the fractured land, only six remained. Even they fled, swallowed by the night.

Thiago did not turn his head to watch their escape or prevent it. His pale eyes were fixed on the dragons, then on me, as the realisation settled—slow as winter seeping into bone—that I was a dragon rider.

He stood a few inches from where Esolas's blood had flowed, looking at me with fear.

But no, that wasn't it.

Faerie's Spymaster was too proud for fear and too deadened to its many iterations, having caused so much of it himself. He had seen fae soil themselves at his feet, carved screams from them in interrogation chambers, bled them dry beneath new moons.

He'd weaned the truth from the lips of lovers and traitors alike, and coaxed it from queens with nothing but shadow and a quiet smile. He had watched courts shatter like glass when he slipped the right word into the right ear.

It was disbelief in Thiago's gaze, curdling into something sourer: crushing recognition that he hadn't seen this coming. Father's suggestion that I remove the ember beads marking me out as one of the Circle of Emberlight had been a clever one. His rival stood, not in silence, but in stunned, wretched stillness, hands flexing as if uncertain whether to strike.

Elowen's voice slid into my head. *He has a habit of underestimating females, Ysadora. He caged me with pretty words and thought I'd forget the bars. He'll learn you weren't raised to be grateful for cruelty.*

I met Elowen's eyes across the wreckage, where she stood with Xaire to one side and Orin to the other, then I turned back to her father.

"Remove the mouth binding," I said, voice cold. "She's earned that much."

Thiago's nostrils flared. "And if I don't?"

589

Zephyr's shadows rose like a tide.

"Then I will," I said. "And what comes next will not be quick."

He relented with a flick of his wrist, a whisper of regret in his expression before it hardened again.

Elowen's first breath was ragged. Her second was a blade. "You always mistake silence for submission."

Satisfaction surged through the mate bond. The King of Silence's own court had turned to ruin beneath him.

And stars above, the dragons were a sight to behold.

They had descended like falling stars made flesh, shattering the atrium with a sound like worlds breaking. Moonlight caught on wings vast enough to eclipse the stars, and for a breathless moment, Thiago didn't move.

He simply stared as Caldoron, who had rescued Father from his captivity here, narrowed golden eyes on him, his bronze tail coiling around a cracked pillar. Smoke curled from his nostrils, and brimstone filled the court like the memory of old wars in the faerie tales Danaë had collected.

Then there was Ryvaris, with his indigo hide and its myriad of constellations, a creature fiercer still than Caldoron, with his ridged horns curved like the strokes of a master calligrapher and his wings outstretched like cathedral arches. His ridged horns curved back like the flourishes of a calligrapher's finest stroke, and the sleek muscle beneath his scales spoke of storms weathered, skies conquered. His long tail swept behind him like a whip of ink, carving furrows in the broken stone. His teeth—skies, teeth the colour of glacial bone—were bared in a silent snarl.

I did not blame him. We were ankle-deep in shadow

and blood, and the golden smears of ink on my
fingertips were telltale signs of how hard we had fought.
Neither had our kin escaped unscathed. Blood streaked
one side of Zephyr's face from a shallow cut across the
brow, yet he hardly noticed. His left shoulder favoured a
strain that I would scold him about later, and his storm-
cloud gaze was already raking over me, checking for
injuries.

Zephyr's fingers brushed against my ink-streaked
wrist, his voice rough from battle-smoke and shouting, as
he asked, "Are you hurt?" It was the first thing he needed
to know. It didn't matter to him if he was hurt. He could
still rage and wield shadow like a god, but only if he knew
I was whole.

I nodded. "Only a little blood. No broken bones."

And he let out a shuddering exhale. The mate bond
throbbed between us: tender, heavy, threaded with
exhaustion, and the quiet shock of surviving. He didn't
smile, not yet, but the look in his eyes said: *You were always
meant to survive this.*

My *Fatebreaker*. My heart. My refuge.

It turned out that Ferrith's duplicates could indeed
bleed, and he had sustained a lancing strike from a spear
on his shoulder. Loxley limped towards us, axe streaked
with blood and one eye swelling shut, but still upright, his
expression tight with pain and satisfaction. Sequoia's tunic
was torn, and one arm grazed, but she was already
angling for more bloodshed.

Siphoning ink from the earth had dulled and depleted
me again, but just standing near Ryvaris aligned my
body's rhythm with his cosmic being. My mind cleared, a
euphoric thrum filled me, and for a moment, I was

limitless, as if my cells remembered starlight and burned with purpose again.

His moon eyes found mine, and the bond between us flared, a whisper of stars and memory through my spine. *You took your sweet time summoning me. What was the plan, exactly? Die gloriously and hope I'd write the ballad?*

I stepped towards him without hesitation, ink rising in my quill, chaos curling at my fingertips. *You sound offended.*

He shook dust from his wings with a thunderous beat that sent rubble skittering. *You think dragons are only flame and flight? My wisdom, Ysadora, is my best quality. You should have called when strategy was still on the table, not after the atrium turned into a slaughterhouse. I expect you to make amends. Something shiny. Or clever.*

Father gave a low, knowing chuckle nearby, but wisely said nothing. He, too, went to Caldoron's side. He and Mother seemed to have watched the violence unfold from a safe distance, though for different reasons: Father had, for the most part, passed his mantle to me; Mother seemed intent on assessing whether my mate and I had been worth the trouble. In that she seemed quite satisfied.

Zephyr, at my side, murmured through the bond, *Remind me not to keep a dragon waiting.*

I arched a brow at Zephyr before saying to the dragon, *I'll garland you in flowers once this is over.*

Ryvaris's tail lashed, but I could sense his mirth. *Make it a crown. It seems there are some to spare. And make it silver. Starlight suits me.* He huffed, smoke steaming from his nostrils.

Very well.

Then the dragon turned his attention towards the throne.

Thiago's pale face had lost all semblance of command. The shadows that had obeyed him without question now trembled at the edges of obedience. His voice cracked like old ice, and he cast his words into the atrium like a curse, "You think this is over? A king of Faerie cannot be slain on his own soil without consequence. The land itself will not bear it. While the bloodheart still clings to its leaves, this court answers to me."

Maren came to my side, radiating quiet fury. "I hate to break it to you. But there is no court left to speak of."

It was true. There was no one there who would have accepted a command from him. Not one soul.

My eyes met hers, a silent acknowledgement of battles fought apart but won together.

"Just put him in a void and be done with it," panted Loxley, his energy clearly diminished by poor nutrition and lack of training during captivity.

Ryvaris's luminous eyes narrowed. *That would not be wise, Ysadora. Killing Liora Bramick was dragon justice, but Faerie chooses its monarchs, and we cannot kill the King of Silence in his own court without a rightful exchange of power.*

The dragons must have communicated this to one another, because Father said cheerfully, "The problem of the bloodheart tree is easily remedied. Caldoron, shall we?" He clambered up the bronzed dragon's scales in a spritely manner that had returned only after his reassembly in the bone pool. At the ridge, he turned, offering Tanuhja a rakish smile. "There's room for one more, if you're feeling bold."

"I'm not," said my mother tartly.

Father held fast, and Caldoron rose with a thunderous beat of wings, his bronze-scaled body glinting as he soared through the roof of the shattered atrium. His shadow passed over us like an omen, and the wind rippled through Father's sparse hair. They rose higher still, above the bloodheart tree, circling once like a storm gathering weight, before Caldoron lurched forward and loosed a roar that reverberated through me.

Father beamed, crouched low against the dragon's spine, his palms pressed to the gleaming bronze hide.

Then came the flame. A jet of golden fire burst from the dragon's jaws, arcing through the night towards the bloodheart. Heat kissed my face, even where we stood, my hand wrapped in Zephyr's.

The bloodheart ignited in an instant, its crimson leaves turning to falling embers, its twisted trunk cracking in protest. It curled and blackened like burned paper, bark blistering, black sap flowing, steaming on contact with the fire, and then the tree was gone. Ash snowed from the sky. When the smoke cleared, only a smouldering stump remained, seared deep into the ground.

Emotion bled through the mate bond, bittersweet. There was a tension to his brow, but a quiet serenity flickered there, like someone paying tribute at a holy site. *The tree was older than any crown. It listened long before it was used.*

Even scorched, it still stands, my love. Waiting for what comes next, I replied.

Above it all, the bronze dragon wheeled in the smoke-heavy air, my father triumphant.

For all the King of Silence had orchestrated that day, I wondered if the fleeing fae noted that the calligrapher and his dragon had returned, and if they whispered about the second dragon and the daughter who did not kneel.

Inside the atrium, Thiago's pale eyes darkened as the last echoes of his reign flickered in his mind. His last avenue for manoeuvre had closed, and the cold weight of inevitability settled on his shoulders. The noose had tightened.

No more shadows to hide behind. No more tricks.

"Do it," said the King of Silence.

Xaire turned to Elowen, and a conversation passed between them telepathically.

She nodded, eyes steady, and I held my breath.

Cyprian stood to my side, arms folded. "He'll be okay."

My chest wasn't tight. It was braced for joy. "I know."

Then Zephyr and Xaire walked forward to wield the magic they had learned as boys, magic that had never been strong enough to subdue a king. But now they were grown, war-tempered, and no longer under his shadow. Thiago bared his teeth and summoned a wall of darkness to thrust against them, but the shadows flickered as if the very land had abandoned him.

Thiago threw himself at them with the remnants of his strength, not as a king but as a father betrayed. His magic struck, uncontrolled and vast. Glyphs hidden in the floor ignited: etched spells flaring red-hot beneath the sigils of old courts. Spires of shadow speared upwards, ripping through the tiles, forcing the younger males back. I flinched as one hit Zephyr square in the chest, hurling him backwards. When Xaire countered, Thiago caught the shadow and turned it in his hand like a dagger, slicing the air between them.

"Do you even know who you are?" the faerie king hissed at his son, his voice cracked and wet.

Zephyr and Xaire exchanged a glance and began to move in tandem with one another, two dark-haired masters of shadow. Despite Thiago's efforts to cast them as rivals, they were united now by necessity, if not affection. Zephyr was taller, more muscular and gifted with his shadows, but I noticed how he held back, allowing his cousin to set the pace.

Their magic wove together like two halves of a broken whole.

There was anguish in the faerie king's face then, a surrendering of centuries-old control, and I thought maybe that Elowen and Orin had weakened him enough that this might just work. Thin nooses of shadow whipped out, coiling towards Zephyr and Xaire like serpents, and the younger males dodged them with fluid grace, but one caught Xaire's shoulder, tearing through fabric and flesh. Blood bloomed across his shirt as he hissed through gritted teeth.

Xaire retaliated immediately, sending shadows that were spiked and cruel, aiming for tendon and throat. Two of the strikes bit deep, opening gashes that painted Thiago's pale skin crimson, and bone gleamed white through one particularly vicious cut across his shin.

A mixture of hurt and pride flared across the Spymaster's face as he grunted and nearly buckled.

Thiago rallied, slashing at Zephyr with shadows sharp as razors, but my mate was ready, a shadow cloak rippling like a shield to absorb the blows. He countered with a wave of shadow from his palms, pushing his uncle backwards with a force like a black tidal wave that audibly cracked Thiago's ribs, doubling him over as he coughed up spatters of blood that steamed against the stone floor, black with corrupted magic.

Their combined assault—Xaire's controlled strikes with Zephyr's overwhelming force—methodically destroyed Thiago's faltering defences. They moved in tandem, magic threading like a rope between them.

Tendrils of shadow slipped from the faerie king's control, spooling away from shielding his chest like bandages unwrapping from a wound. Zephyr leaned into his mercenary self, punching through his uncle's shadows with breathtaking force, his knuckles sparking darkness. Blood sprayed across the marble. Thiago's breath rasped.

It was almost child's play, but I didn't pity him. Not after all he'd done.

Thiago paused, breath heaving and rattling in his damaged chest, muscles coiled for the next move. A trickle of sympathy flowed into the mate bond, even as I watched him bleed. I bit back my concern that Zephyr would choose mercy, loath to break his focus.

My mate's storm-cloud gaze flashed silver, sharp with command and cunning. "Now, Xaire. Use his own shadow against him."

I noticed it then: the shadow that Thiago had sacrificed so that the Wraithwoods would make Danaë fae. It had slinked away during Orin's earlier attempt to wield it against his brother. Zephyr had once told me that a shadow torn from its master remembered its origin and hated its exile.

It could grow its own hungers. Its own loyalties. It knew every weakness, every secret pathway through its former master's defences. Now, starved of its host for decades, it hungered to reclaim what had been torn away.

But a pair of skilful wielders might just be able to twist that hunger into particularly cruel punishment.

The darkness coiled with predatory intelligence, eager now to face the king who had abandoned it. Xaire's breath hitched, his hair damp across one eye, but his hands did not hesitate. It did not come gently.

At first, the shadow recoiled, reluctant to obey a new master. It tore across the stone like a beast uncaged, shrieking through the air. Xaire caught it—barely—his hands flaring with power, his mouth tightening as he forced it under his control. It strained and snarled, biting at his fingers, trying to return to its old master.

Zephyr stepped behind him, sweat streaking his brow, adding his strength, his control. The mate bond flared hot and bright with the intensity of his effort. They pulled the severed shadow towards them, and it came: skulking, vicious, intimate with every vulnerability Thiago possessed.

Where Xaire's control faltered, Zephyr's strength steadied him. Where Xaire held back, Zephyr pressed forward. The stolen magic writhed and resisted, but their will pressed like heated iron, bending it inch by inch. Xaire wrestled control of the cursed shadow, coaxing it with a fierce determination born of long-buried pain. While my mate was not exactly enjoying himself, the mate bond rippled with catharsis.

The severed shadow hissed, then obeyed as it made its new allegiance.

Thiago's lips twisted in disbelief as the very magic he had sacrificed to protect Danaë turned against him. The shadow hit Thiago like a scream, wrapping around his torso and sliding beneath his skin.

It struck with vicious hunger, gouging open his chest. It remembered what he had been and what he had done, and now it took him cell by cell. Thiago was no longer silent and stoic. He howled as it burrowed through muscle, crawling like worms beneath flesh. His eyes rolled back. His veins bulged black.

The shadow ravaged him, devoured him, inching up his throat, his own magic turned traitor. It knew exactly where to strike: sliding between ribs to constrict his lungs, coiling around his throat to crush his windpipe slowly, seeping into old scars to reopen them.

Zephyr watched, jaw clenched, his palm on Xaire's trembling shoulder. Elowen and Orin joined them.

"You made it this way," said Xaire to his father. "You taught it pain."

Elowen lifted her chin. "Now it returns the lesson."

The darkness coalesced around the broken king, and blood frothed at Thiago's lips as his shadow-self suffocated the life from him. Then his face went slack in terror as the shadow sealed his mouth, binding him in a sarcophagus, spurning their separation in a final, intimate embrace.

"Silence," Elowen said clearly for all to hear, cold and absolute.

"Begins with you," Xaire finished, his words sealing his father's end.

In my mind, Ryvaris's voice was a rumble of starlight and sky. *May I?*

Please do, I replied.

The dragon's vast wings unfurled like the pages of a celestial scripture, casting his own vast shadows over the court. His indigo hide shimmered, and heat rose up his throat before he opened his jaws in judgment. His breath ignited the sarcophagus not in a single burst, but in excruciating coils of fire, enveloping the King of Silence, turning his shadowy prison into a pyre. There were no screams: only the sound of cracking bone, as the flames danced higher.

We watched Ryvaris's flames consume the faerie king, and our kin closed ranks around Zephyr and his family.

Xaire turned to Zephyr. "I will not fight you for the throne, cousin. Not when you freed me of my father's chains."

My mate squeezed his kin's shoulder. "The throne belongs to you and Elowen."

"I have no wish to stay here," said Elowen quietly.

Her twin flinched, then composed himself as a just king would. "Do you think Mother will forgive me?"

Elowen bit her lip, and her mouth was sore where the binding had been. "No. But she'll be in thrall to your power now."

Xaire nodded, pensive. "I want you to stay, Elowen, but I give you permission to go."

"I would like to go too, if my son will have me," said Orin to Xaire.

Zephyr gave a curt nod, and the mate bond was a complex weave of feeling.

The King of Silence had ruled with fear.

But dragons had no fear. And now, neither did we.

I threaded my fingers through Elowen's, alarmed to find her hand not whole.

As we turned, the Court of Silence began to stitch itself together, at the bidding of its new king.

ZEPHYR

Frostbite Wyrm: icy scales, blue eyes, significant speed. Once Celyn Frostglade of the Court of Lore, mother of Jivan, gifted at preserving ancient stories and memories in ice.
– The Secrets of Faerie's Veiled Beasts by Zephyr Ashmoor

T he calligrapher and his daughter asked the dragons very nicely if they would mind carrying a small group of kin back to Ebonspire. In fact, the group wasn't small at all. It included his mercenary family, Cyprian, Loxley, Sequoia, and Wylda, of course. And his new family, Ysadora, Maren, and Ferrith.

But their circle had now widened to include Kazimir, and his own father and the tentative rebuilding of their relationship, and Elowen, who was quiet and withdrawn.

On top of it all, it seemed that thanks to his beloved,

two dragons were now in permanent residence at the gatehouse, and the Queen of Chaos had threatened to visit.

For a male who adored his kin but at times needed solitude that only his mate could happily breach, Zephyr didn't mind at all. His lips curved. If it all got too much, he'd simply whisk his mate to their bed chamber or ride Mythros hard along the salt-streaked cliffs, sea-mist clinging to the stallion's mane, both wild with freedom.

Until he missed his Inkheart.

Zephyr leaned forward over Ysa's shoulder as the spires came into view and the dragon landed. His joy was profound to be back at Ebonspire. The fallen Prince of Lore showed it not with words, but with the loosening of his shoulders as the wind tugged at his cloak and carried the scent of home. The tension that had gripped him like a vice through every trial, every vote, every battle, finally eased. They dismounted, and he took his mate's hand, lacing their fingers together.

This was a homecoming not just of body, but of spirit. Behind them, their kin laughed and bickered and limped, trailing dragon soot and healing magic in equal measure. Even Loxley and Ferrith seemed to have forged an unlikely rapport, stitched together by battle and bickering, wounds and wisecracks.

Zephyr drank in the sight of the training field and the stables, the towering spires, then the gatehouse that had once been his family home and now was again, in this new brood of kin. Soon, the chambers and dining halls would be full again, and even the solemn hush of the Room of Remembrance would lighten.

How obvious it seemed to him now that the unfinished face in Veda's portrait of Echohold was Xaire. Tomorrow, he would look at it again. His body had endured the past weeks, but his mind—steeped in strategy and history—was fraying at the edges.

For his sake, and for those who loved him, he knew it was time to heal. For now, he allowed himself the rare luxury of rest next to the female who had claimed his heart, knowing that he would not have been able to live in the bleakest version of events.

His Ysa was safe, and it hadn't been walls that had saved her; it had been kin, even those with darkness in them.

They had survived, because even apart, they had fought together.

"Let's go home, Inkheart," he said, his velvet voice low and certain.

Her violet gaze glimmered with warmth. "Only if there's toffee. And sleep."

Even in her fatigue, she was beautiful, with her heart-shaped face, soft curves and twilight eyes, her gaze darting to the dragon before settling on him with a small, tired smile. As soon as she was able, she wove the ember beads back into her hair. She was entirely his, and he was hers, and ancients, he was proud that was so.

His cheek dimpled. "Oh, I think I can manage that."

Hand in hand, they led their kin back into the gatehouse, towards the peace that waited inside it.

But Zephyr could not help thinking of the monsters that he had once fed and soothed in the belly of Ebonspire, and how they were scattered throughout Faerie, still cursed, still waiting for someone to save them.

YSADORA

The Circle of Emberlight is a female order of
dragon riders, established millennia after its male
counterpart. She who rides the mightiest dragon
leads. With the deadly Kindling rite thinning
recruits, its leadership seldom shifts.
– The Dragons and Riders of the Nebula Court

Only when the battle had ended did Ryvaris tell me that he had called for the other dragons, but none had answered. A courier moth arrived soon after, bearing a curt message from Araminta and Phaedran. They were not overjoyed that we had won, and it was clear that the manner of Liora's death had splintered the fragile bond of our sisterhood beyond repair.

But for now, we were home, our kin reunited, and that was all that mattered.

Stars, Zephyr's hands on me when we finally

disappeared to our chamber: it was like he was relearning every inch of me. The door had barely closed before his shadows unfurled, sealing us inside a cocoon of quiet and dusk, so he didn't have to share me, so I didn't have to bite down my moans.

He kissed the chaos from my skin, slowly, licking, nipping, sucking, until the world outside dissolved. His fingers brushed over bruises like he could smooth the ache from my muscles and the war from my bones.

Every button he undid, every inch of fabric removed, was a prayer to something older than the stars.

"Say it," I whispered against his lips.

"I love you," his voice rasped low, shadows moving with his breath, slicking across my bare spine as though they craved me too. "Every second I didn't touch you was a little death in itself."

His mouth followed the curve of my hip, my thigh, his sighs hot as the shadows climbed higher, stroking where his hands could not reach. Then, skies, his tongue lapping between my spread thighs, drinking in the scent of me, the petalled core of me. I shuddered with my release within seconds, and he laughed softly at the proof of my need for him.

He climbed over me as I still quivered from his touch, his body blanketing mine, the lines of his body, his cheekbones, his lashes so bewitching that I gasped when his calloused hands found my waist. He braced himself on his elbows as he lowered, our breath mingling, his gaze never leaving mine. Stars, there was heat in those eyes, yes, but also awe and relief.

You're still here, still mine, he said through the bond. His heart drummed a war rhythm only I could calm.

I nodded, guiding his thick manhood into me. *No walls between us.*

He just stared, memorising my face as if the world might rip me away again. Then he started to move. Skies, he started to move. Deep and slow, not rushing, but building in pace, until my nails clawed his back and my back arched.

Shadows coiled around us like a second skin, rippling in tune with his pulse. One hand framed my face, thumb brushing the corner of my lip, gifting me a feral grin as I bit it, before he dropped lower, to the column of my neck, slightly rougher there, possessive, before his palm tightened around my breast.

The air between us thrummed with every thrust: thick with magic, want, and the joy of what we'd achieved together. The bond roared like a tempest through our bones, tangled in a pulse that was no longer mine and his, but ours.

Zephyr's emotions filled me—his want, his awe, his hunger—braided through it was love so savage it nearly broke me. Through it, I sensed the echo of his restraint slipping, but he held back for one last gift.

With his lore magic, he gave me an image of us transported, as we were, in the throes of our lovemaking, to the creek in Larkspur. We lay on the banks there, amidst soft grasses, with the sounds of Bloomtide drifting our way, as he pushed into me, over and over. My fingers curled into his shoulders. The waves of coiled need in me built so that I couldn't hold on; I could only shatter against him, wild and helpless.

I came hard then, not because I missed Larkspur, but

because of him, how he loved me and how he knew me so wholly.

And still, it wasn't enough. I needed all of him. Every fractured, perfect piece.

I moaned his name, and the sound made something inside him snap. He moved with dark grace, pinning me with both body and power, his mouth at my throat like a vow, like a curse undone. There was no space between us, no breath that wasn't shared, no thought that didn't echo in both minds. Then he came, too, and we were back in our bed chamber, and he called my name into the shadows that I loved, because they were part of him.

"Look at me." Our eyes locked, and he lay his forehead against mine. "This is where I belong. Over you. With you. Always."

He kissed me then, as if to seal the truth into my bones. The bond was quiet now and vast, like the stretch of sky just before dawn. It pulsed soft and sure with the rhythm of trust and safety, enough to make me wonder how I'd ever lived without it.

Then, wretch that he was, he left me panting, lying languidly on our bed palette while he dispelled the curtain of shadows, washed, and pulled on his leathers.

I propped myself up, ensuring he could see the full glory of my breasts. "Where are you going?"

He growled low in his throat, and I thought he might come back to bed, but a shadow flickered in his stormlight eyes. "To hold the Queen of Bones to the promise she made to help with the cursed fae."

"Zeph. A mission, already?" I frowned, then flicked two fingers. A coil of chaos magic, shimmering like oil on water, slid from my palm and curled around his wrist, anchoring him to the bedpost.

He raised a brow, amused. "You know I can slip that in two heartbeats."

"Then take three. Just stay a little longer."

He laughed, torn between duty and the warmth of me. Then he sighed and slipped the coil of my magic. "I'll sleep better when this is done, Inkheart."

I bit my lip. "Then let me come."

There was hesitation in him I hadn't seen before, and the mate bond flickered like a guttering candle as if the monster stories left small marks in the corridors of his mind. I worried that, for all his determination to help the cursed fae, he was harming himself by holding on so tightly to their demons.

His eyes drifted to the blue shadows beneath my eyes. "I'd rather you rest. Besides, Thalindra was quite clear. Recent events mean that her courtiers have grown wary of dragon visitors. Cyprian and your father are accompanying me. If we turn up with two dragons, the Queen of Bones and her court will suspect an ambush." I scowled, but he leaned down and kissed the furrow between my brows. "Let me do this, Ysa. You've already carried more than your share."

"Father's coming with you?" Caldoron bore the burden of ferrying us across the realm with only an occasional huff.

Zephyr gave a curt nod as he tied his boots. "He knows how to cajole her."

I relented. My mate and Cyprian were a formidable force together, and no harm could come to them. "Don't let

Thalindra twist your passion to help the cursed fae to her advantage."

His mouth twitched into that frustrating, infuriating, reassuring smirk. "You have my word."

"Or charm her into a second alliance." I tugged the sheets up to my chin.

He cupped my jaw, pressed a kiss to my palm, eyes sparkling with wry amusement. "I've already got the only queen I need."

Then he sent a pulse of reassurance into the mate bond, then vanished into the noon light.

Later, I sat in the dining hall with our kin, sharing stories of our exploits and even Gabor seemed a distant memory. Time and toil had softened the rifts that had once yawned between us. Wylda and Maren had baked golden bread inspired by her mother's bakery in Larkspur. It was infused with healing herbs: honeybloom for strength, silverleaf for clarity, and a touch of sun mint to soothe frayed nerves.

To my surprise, the memory of the village now brought a quiet sweetness, not pain.

I tore off hunks of warm bread and sipped tea as I listened to Ferrith and Loxley, who were already on their third tankard of ale and argued merrily about whose near-death experience had been more dramatic.

"Sometimes I look at my reflection and I don't recognise myself," said Ferrith, clearly not as tolerant of fae ale as the mortal kind.

"You're still the same rosy-checked fool I love," replied Maren, pulling out a stool for Wylda.

I followed Wylda's gaze to where Elowen and Orin walked arm-in-arm through the grounds in the last of the evening sun. Since our return from the Court of Silence, Elowen lingered on the fringes of our hearth.

In quiet moments, I sent her small inked messages that flickered like fireflies, to remind her she belonged. I think she liked that, although she had not yet had the courage to answer. Her cellmates watched over her carefully, as though they feared one wrong move might send her fleeing again, as though they coaxed a wild creature to trust the light again.

Sequoia kicked up her feet. "It must be driving Zephyr crazy that you kept her telepathy a secret."

I scanned the horizon for Caldoron before turning back to the table. "He didn't like it, but he took it in his stride."

Loxley sloshed his ale. "I knew."

"I knew, too," said Ferrith.

Maren gave a long-suffering sigh. "I think I preferred it when they weren't friends."

I laughed. "This is them being civil. Friendship's still a few brawls away."

But then shadows trembled along the stone walls, shadows as familiar to me as my own breath. My chest tightened because I didn't know Zephyr was home. I hadn't sensed it. I looked up, over the moon to see him, though he had only been gone half a day at most. Outside, the ground quaked as Caldoron landed, his scales burnished gold in the evening light. The wind from his descent stirred the grasses in wild spirals and sent crows fleeing from the nearby trees.

Ryvaris turned his great head towards the bronze dragon and said through the bond, *Something is wrong with the shadow prince.*

The laughter died in my throat. I stood up abruptly from the table and ran to the window. *What do you mean? Is he hurt? Are they hurt? Do they need Wylda?*

Cyprian dismounted first, his braids plastered to his cheeks from the wind. Father followed, a hand bracing against Caldoron's scales as he stepped down. Zephyr didn't wait. He dropped like a stone, landed hard, and walked towards the gatehouse without turning back. Without even greeting Elowen and Orin.

Something inside me rang like a bell struck wrong.

It wasn't the way he walked, stiffer than usual, or that he didn't look back or greet our kin.

It was the absence. A sudden silence in my bones.

Maren's voice was tight with concern, and the mercenaries' attention focused to a point. "Ysa, what is it?"

A low rumble rippled through the dragon. *Not hurt. Not bleeding. But hollow. As if something precious has been scooped from his centre and buried somewhere I cannot reach. I do not like it. Tell the healer if you must. But it is you he needs.* Then, quieter, with a draconic solemnity that felt like thunder stalling behind a mountain. *He does not feel like your mate, Ysadora. Not entirely.*

I opened my mouth, but a sob caught behind my teeth. "It's Zephyr. Something's wrong. I didn't know he was home, Maren." And the look on her face was confused, as if she did not understand why I was so worried, and I didn't want to give voice to my worst fear: that he had put up walls between us again.

Then I was running, tumbling like I had once before,

away from a table at Ebonspire, back when I understood nothing of Faerie, nothing of magic or fate or love or him. But this time, I wasn't running away. I was running towards him, sending frantic pleas to the stars that he was still whole, still himself, still mine.

This time, I wasn't wearing a cloak of invisible ink. I needed him to see me, to really see me. To ground himself in my body and my love. I ran through the corridor, down the worn steps, past the flaring sconces of our beautiful home.

My magic responded to my panic, chaos crackling around me. A sconce spluttered out as I passed, plunging the hallway into darkness. I was going to tear Ebonspire apart if I couldn't get control of myself. Stars, the ache of that distance, the anguish in the not knowing.

It was in some ways kinder than the knowing.

Another wave of chaos magic rippled out of me when I reached the gatehouse entrance, causing the great doors to groan on their hinges. Cyprian was there, waiting, and he took one look at me before stepping back, ushering Father behind him.

"What happened?" My gaze darted between the two of them. "Where is Zephyr?"

Cyprian caught me by the shoulders, as if he were trying to ground a lightning strike. "Listen, okay?" He looked more haggard than I'd ever seen him. "We thought we were just going for discussions today, but Thalindra had gathered some of the cursed fae as a sort of *gift* for dealing with the problem of Thiago. Zephyr was so happy, Ysa. He thought if he could just do this, you'd be so proud."

Ink seeped from my quill to pool at our feet, turning

my tunic dark in the process. "Do what?" I demanded, breath ragged.

"He put them in the bone pool. Thirteen of them. And it worked. It worked, Ysa. They came out whole." The words were light, beautiful, but Cyprian's face was crumpling. "He fed them back their memories. Gently. Kindly. The bone pool sloughed off the curse, and Zephyr's lore magic restored their minds."

"You're scaring me, Cyp." But Zephyr was right. I was so proud of him.

"I told him to stop." Cyprian's voice was barely more than a breath. "He was tiring. You could see it. One of the fae he and Thalindra mended was Celyn from the Court of Lore. They embraced. And then—"

Night-blooming jasmine wound through the door, its sweetness sharp against the bitter tang of grief. "And then what?"

"He just pushed himself past his limits," Cyprian said hoarsely. "For the briefest moment, he was still him. He looked at Kazimir and said, *break the mate bond*. Like he knew that he wasn't himself anymore. I couldn't help him. I tried to rewind the clock, but the damage was done. It was too deep."

The world blurred. My magic exploded outwards in a shockwave that sent both men staggering back, ink and chaos magic painting the entrance hall in wild, destructive beauty. My knees buckled, but I didn't fall. Cyprian steadied me.

He wasn't himself anymore. Hearing those words was like being flung into the abyss.

"How could you?" My voice splintered with disbelief. "You had no right, Father."

"I hated that task when the Order of the Glyph required it of me, and I hated it tonight." Father reached for me, but I recoiled, my breath caught somewhere between my ribs and my throat. "He did it out of love, Ysa. Love makes cowards and heroes both."

I let his words pass through me like wind through ruins. "He hasn't even come to find me."

Zephyr was a fallen prince who had lost his family and still known how to love. A male who had rebuilt this gatehouse brick by brick and offered it as a sanctuary to those in need. Who had defied a cruel court, who had wielded shadow like silk and steel. Who had waited without demand and touched my ink-stained fingers like they held galaxies. Who had bled to protect my chosen kin. Who let me see the softness beneath his silence. Who laughed in rare, unguarded bursts that made the stars seem nearer. Who protected others, without ever expecting them to do the same for him. Who learned the names of every one of my fears, and faced them beside me.

But Zephyr was also the master of Ebonspire, and the gatehouse was where he came to heal.

Where is he? I asked the dragon.

The Forgotten Garden, replied Ryvaris.

My breath hitched because Zephyr had avoided the Forgotten Garden since his mother and Veda had died. Then I was running towards him, each step towards him was a small act of faith: that somewhere beneath whatever had taken hold of him, the Zephyr I loved was still there. The corridors grew quieter as I moved deeper into the gatehouse, away from the warmth of the dining room and towards the forgotten corners where grief lived.

By the time I reached the garden, my magic had stilled to a low hum beneath my skin. The small garden had grown wild in our absence, the rising moon catching on tangled vines and crumbling stone. Zephyr stood facing the sea, his back turned to his mother's statue, a shadow amongst shadows.

Only then, yards from my mate, did I dare to look inside myself. There was a terrible stillness there, as if something essential had gone quiet in the world. The mate bond had always pulsed like a star inside me, but now it had gone cold, extinguished, as if the sky itself had blinked and forgotten the story of us.

I kept reaching for its warmth, its light, its rhythm. Nothing answered. The universe had swallowed it whole. As if some cosmic silence had consumed it mid-hum, leaving me earthbound. I had never realised how much my soul had leaned towards that star until I spun without it.

A keening sound of anguish almost broke free, but Zephyr needed me. So I folded my wail down like parchment, sealed it and offered him every ounce of strength I had left.

His silhouette was cut from starlight and sorrow, the slope of his shoulders too familiar to mistake, yet too stiff to be home. I wanted to press my hand to his back and feel his breath, to find in it the rhythm that had once sung through my bones. Without that steadying rhythm, without Zephyr's calm to balance me, I was dangerous. Something that could tear Faerie apart with grief alone.

How often I had wanted to stand precisely here together, in this tender place where I had written to Elowen, with the sound of salt waves crashing against cliffs far below, flower beds of irises, marigolds, and roses, and the tufts of emerald moss.

When he turned to face me, there was recognition in those stormlight eyes, but no warmth, no love. Just an empty vessel wearing his face. In his hands was *The Secrets of Faerie's Veiled Beasts,* which we had written together.

My *Fatebreaker* had achieved what he set out to do.

"Zephyr," I reached out for him, hoping he would sweep me into his arms.

"Hello, Inkheart." Though he used his name for me, his voice was too formal, too distant. "I've been waiting for you."

Behind him, the stars were so bright that I thought perhaps the Binder listened as she worked. They lit the heavens, untouched by the wars of kings or the grief of queens. Perhaps, somewhere beyond our sight, Lunarys had not forsaken us, but was threading the pieces of our unravelled bond back together, one fragile, silver filament at a time. Perhaps, she still cared.

I walked towards him, heart pounding, cupped his face and kissed him as if it might wake him. Not out of desperation, but out of the aching belief that I might be able to bring him back, like after Tanuhja's dream.

I had known he'd been teetering on saturation, known that he was holding too many threads in that clever mind of his, and it gutted me that I hadn't been able to stop this. My lips pressed gently to his, soft as a promise, trembling like a question. But his mouth did not soften. His shadows did not curl around my spine. His hands did not reach; they held the manuscript still. When I opened my eyes, his were distant.

He looked at me like I was a stranger who had once mattered to someone else.

Once when he had kissed me, it was as if my name had written itself across the walls of his heart.

This time, nothing. And I wanted to cry out and tell him all the ways he had tasted me.

Ryvaris's voice rumbled through the bond. *Take heart, Ysadora. Despite the disappointment of that kiss, buried deep amongst the rubble of his mind, the shadow prince endures. This I can sense, even if you cannot.*

I stepped back, studying Zephyr's face in the moonlight. This was so like him: the ultimate act of love disguised as abandonment. He'd asked Father to break our bond not to hurt me, but to protect me from his reeling mind.

"You tried to save me again, didn't you? Even from yourself." His shadows flickered: not with malice, but with an inkling of recognition. Then, so subtly I almost missed it, they stretched towards me like fingers seeking warmth, before recoiling as if burned. Hope blazed in my chest. The gesture was so achingly familiar, I almost leaned into it.

"You should have taken me with you to the Court of Bones. We could have found another way."

"Are you always this stubborn?" asked Zephyr.

As the dragons curled into their quiet vigil guarding our kin, the shadow prince and I stood together on the moss-worn edge of the Forgotten Garden and looked out over the starry sea. The cliffs fell away in sheer drops of shadow and stone, and the sky was a blanket of constellations we'd once traced with hope.

The wind ruffled our hair, the salt of the sea brushing our cheeks, and still we didn't speak. We stood close enough that my shoulder brushed his arm, and Zephyr didn't seem to feel it. He stood so near I could feel the thrum of his magic. The moonlight cut a clean line along his profile: the proud set of his brow, the sharp slash of his cheekbones, the shadow of thought pressed deep between his brows.

He looked like a prince in a painting: solemn, remote, beautiful.

Mine, still, though he did not know it.

I stood beside him, patiently waiting for the stars to blink their blessing. I ached to reach for his hand, but I didn't. Not yet.

Though I was desperately afraid, I knew that our dream of building a fairer Faerie had well and truly begun.

In the pinpricks of light in the ink-dark sky and somewhere in between them, I felt the echo of what we had been and what we might become again. The mate bond might be severed, but love wasn't so easily broken.

I would find a way back to the Prince of Lore.

We all would.

ACKNOWLEDGEMENTS

This was a hard year for many reasons in our immediate and wider family, not least because we lost our cat Mogo. He inspired the big cat characters in my novels and is the reason I am equally a dog and cat person.

Through the ups and downs of this year, I kept diving back into the *Ink of the Fae* story world for solace and joy. It was a gift, and I hope you feel the same way.

Thank you first to the readers in my group, those who have followed me for years through my newsletter and who have come to me new. Creativity and reading are empathy in action, and you are my tribe.

To my beta readers Debbie and Sherry, true story harpists, thank you for your friendship and insights. Thanks also to my Reviewers Team for spreading the word and cheering me on.

Thank you, Fay, for the beautiful cover art. It always feels like play to work with you.

To Trish, my editor, who had the patience of a saint when this story kept needing more chapters. Thank you for the calm you brought. To Toni, who gives my words their final polish and lifts my self-belief at precisely the right moment, thank you.

To Nafu Aunty, who brims with empathy and her own words, you are a blessing to all those who know you.

To my parents, who continue to hold us like we are

little chicks, and who have been there for us in small and big ways, a thousand thanks.

To our children: H, R & N. Watching you grow and discover your individual passions is our greatest privilege.

To my Jan, always my safe harbour, my most cherished conversation partner, my reason to giggle and strive. I love you more than words.

SHARE YOUR READER LOVE

I hope you enjoyed *Tower of Bones and Dimmed Stars*. Please take a few moments to leave a review online. Reviews are so appreciated. They tell authors which stories resonate and help readers discover our work.

If you are a book blogger and would like to feature my books, please get in touch at www.NilluNasser.com.

N. Z. Nasser

xoxo

STAY IN TOUCH & GRAB YOUR SHORT STORY

Come and be part of my tribe and join my facebook reader group at <u>Nasser's Book Nymphs.</u>

To receive a free short story and keep up to date with my news, sign up for my fantasy newsletter at <u>www. nillunasser.com</u>.

Here's a coupon for the first time you make a purchase in my online store at <u>www.nillunasser.com</u>: NILLU15.

WILDS OF CHAOS AND INDIGO RAIN

INK OF THE FAE, BOOK 3

Dragons fall. Darkness rises. Stars weave their fates.

With the mate bond severed, Ysa's chaos magic spills turmoil into the mortal realm, deepening her rift with her fellow sisters from the Circle of Emberlight. Even her aunt now views her as a danger to contain.

Zephyr no longer cares for his kin or his beloved Ebonspire and is consumed by his mission to save the cursed fae. Ysa faces a choice: to assert leadership over the Circle of Emberlight or remain in Zephyr's shadow. She resolves to keep him in her bed, even if she can't win back his heart. But the Binder insists: only through the mate bond is a fairer Faerie possible.

As dark forces rise against the dragon riders once more, Elowen burns with secrets stolen from the Spymaster that could help, if her rage doesn't destroy them first. Outrunning her own darkening magic, Ysa must restore the broken mate bond and discover why the dragons of her father's order chose to plummet from the sky long ago.

If she fails in either task, not only are the dragons doomed, but Faerie itself—and with them, her own bruised heart.

ALSO BY N. Z. NASSER

INK OF THE FAE

Garden of Ink and Ancient Stone

Tower of Bones and Dimmed Stars

Wilds of Chaos and Indigo Rain

DRUID HEIR

Midlife Dawn, Book 1

Midlife Tremors, Book 2

Midlife News, Book 3

Midlife Drift, Book 4

Midlife Portals, Book 5

Midlife Eclipse, Book 6

Midlife Battle, Book 7

MAJESTIC MIDLIFE WITCH

To Save a Sister, Book 1

To Curse a Rival, Book 2

To Trick a Raja, Book 3

NEWSLETTER EXCLUSIVES

The Magical Grandmother, Druid Heir Short Story 0.5

A First Date in Paris, Druid Heir Short Story 1.5

Midlife Battle, Druid Heir 7 Bonus Epilogue

To Become a Witch, Majestic Midlife Short Story 0.5

ABOUT THE AUTHOR

 N. Z. Nasser is a writer of fantasy fiction. Her stories are about women who change the world, filled with magic and rooted in friendship.

A lover of barefoot walks along the beach, she is glad to have left behind her career in the civil service and to never wear heels again. Whether she is writing in her garden office or wrangling laundry, she is happiest with a cup of tea at her side.

She lives in London with her husband, three children, two cats and a fox-mad dog.